Sweet chillies

Omi, at twenty, is in danger of turning into a pukka badmash, a Number One Don Juan. So his family and father Khatri, ex-sweet-vendor who now runs Chandigarh's exclusive 'Pall Mall' restaurant, have decided that Omi must get married.

As the wedding bus lurches to a halt, horns honking, brass band playing, the whole of Chandigarh's Sector 23 is abuzz with sightings of the groom and his unexpectedly gorgeous new bride.

Omi had not been amused by the idea of an arranged marriage. But now he suddenly feels weak at the knees. Munni looks sweet, edible, impossibly desirable – like a miracle out of an Indian *Gone with the wind*. How to kiss her? How to smuggle her away for an immediate honeymoon in Simla? How to become a millionaire by the time he is twenty-five?

These and other pressing problems are the stuff of this gloriously happy bubble of a novel. Balraj Khanna's humour is wicked and charming, and he paints his hustling, bustling picture of the new capital of the Punjab in warm, bright primary colours.

Sweet chillies returns us to the beguiling world of his award-winning *Nation of fools* – and not since R. K. Narayan created Malgudi has a writer conjured up an Indian comic world of such spontaneous magic and delight.

Also by Balraj Khanna

Nation of fools (Michael Joseph, 1984)

SWEET CHILLIES

Balraj Khanna

CONSTABLE · LONDON

First published in Great Britain 1991
by Constable and Company Limited
3 The Lanchesters, 162 Fulham Palace Road
London W6 9ER
Copyright © 1991 Balraj Khanna
The right of Balraj Khanna to be
identified as the author of this work
has been asserted by him in accordance
with the Copyright, Designs and Patents Act 1988
ISBN 0 09 470550 X
Set in Linotron 11pt Baskerville
by CentraCet, Cambridge
Printed in Great Britain
by St Edmundsbury Press Limited
Bury St Edmunds, Suffolk

A CIP catalogue record for this book
is available from the British Library

FOR NATHALIE AND KAUSHALIYA

Author's note

Chandigarh is a real city, but its inhabitants in this
novel are all figments of my imagination and bear
no resemblance to any real person, living or dead.
The events described are equally fictitious.

B.K.

BOOK ONE

Twenty-odd men in red and gold regimental uniforms crowded the back street of the Pall Mall in Sector 23. The cut of their tunics was old-fashioned but it didn't matter. For those who wore them weren't aware of it, nor were those who watched. Cradling shiny brass musical instruments, they sat on their haunches in the shade of dusty mango, jamun and tahli trees that swayed leafily in the summer morning breeze. They chewed paan and pulled at beedis and looked around them anxiously. Away from them, on both sides of the street, people formed murmuring groups, as did neighbours in windows and on balconies of their Bauhaus-inspired houses. They were all waiting.

They waited and waited, but nobody moved away. The uniformed men were paid to be there. The others held on because they wouldn't miss for anything in the world that which they were about to see.

Then, suddenly, a cloud of dust rose at the street corner, and out of it blared the shrill horn of a Punjab Roadways bus. This sight and sound worked like electricity on the men in red and gold. They grabbed their instruments and sprang to attention, falling in twos, parade-ground style. Their leader, a portly little man with a fierce Rajput moustache, expelled a stream of orange-coloured paan spittle from the left corner of his mouth and waved his baton about briskly. His men and their brass came alive and the sultry summer air of Sector 23 of Chandigarh rang out with 'Here comes the bride'.

Down at the street corner, the bus cleared the dust. It advanced slowly, blowing its horn wildly. This was Omi's marriage bus. Bedecked with flowers, it was coming home with much dhoom-dhaam (pomp and show).

Everybody heard. Everybody saw. Everybody came. As the bus emptied, the groom's mother, Paro, whispered to her twenty-year-old son to stay on and supervise the unloading of its precious cargo, his bride's dowry. Paro didn't trust servants in such matters – there were six of them. She trusted well-wishers even less – suddenly there were scores of them. 'They rob with their eyes when they can't with their hands.'

And there was so much to be robbed. 'Ten thousand rupees worth. Minimum,' Paro hissed, pointing to the bus's roof which carried the dowry. 'Are you listening?'

Omi heard his mother. But he wasn't listening. His mind was lost in that mass of scarlet silk and gold and flowers a few yards away, his wife of a few hours, Munni. He was thinking of what lay underneath that silk. His hands were itching to get inside it. He had been allowed a glimpse of her face during the festivities last night, and that was all. But that one glimpse had done it – turned all the tables on him. Then had come the night-long wedding ceremony. The two of them had sat cross-legged around the holy fire, their knees touching. Three feet in front was the mantra-muttering pandit. Behind them were huddled their parents and a hundred half-asleep guests. It was an ordeal, an endless yawn. To survive, Omi had to do something – put a bit of spice in it. Whenever he could, he engineered little accidents which pressed his body into hers. Once he even managed to land his inquiring right elbow on her unprotesting left breast and kept it there during a whole mantra. The result had been electrifyingly shameful: a killer erection in the presence of the holy flame! Omi should have died. He didn't.

But the question now was how to get close to her? For guarding her was a thick wall of more red silk – tens of ladies fussing over the new bride.

Like the bloody wall of Delhi's Red Fort. Endless and unscaleable. Omi loathed those ladies. *Why don't they bugger off? – they've been fed and fêted.*

Omi's beautiful young aunt, Vidya, saw. Vidya knew her nephew. She could read him like an open book.

'Omi, you have to wait. Our rituals come first, other things *after*. We are not mallachaas, we are Hindus, the chosen ones, you know.'

'I know . . .' The Hindus were special, the original caste Aryans, pure of spirit and lofty of purpose, an altogether higher species. The mallachaas – everybody else in the world – were not. They were casteless, therefore impure, hence untouchable and so infinitely lowly. It was a God-made fact. 'But chosen by whom, Aunt Vidya? And, for bloody what? Nine-tenths of the country has always starved and the rest . . .?'

It was hot. Omi was the only one in the throng in a woollen suit. He had to wear it, being the groom, to look important. He mopped sweat off his brow with a finger and moved to obey his mother. But he was prevented. More people started arriving, hordes of them. Women added to the Red Fort wall. Men embraced Omi, men Omi had never seen before.

10

'Hell.' Omi was fed up with all the embracing. He felt like a stranger in his own back yard where it was all happening.

The back door wore a fringe of mango leaves and jasmine strung with mohli, the hand-woven sacred red thread with yellow dots. This thread came from India's distant past, bringing with it luck for the wearer, man or house. Lengths of it were also tied around two coconuts which hung on either side of the door, their hairy roundness smeared with a paste of flour and turmeric. The door-frame itself was decorated with red and yellow swastikas. Separating them was the most sacred of words – OM – in Sanskrit, the language of the gods. OM is not a word, it is a sound, the eternal sound of cosmos and its maker. To be repeated again and again.

Omi liked that, for *Om* was his first name. His middle name – Parkash – meant light. Now that he was reminded of it, he liked that too. Omi liked most things about himself.

Women packed the veranda and upstairs. Nameless children got in their way – leg, knee, elbow, nudge, push and runny noses. Men filled the back yard. More nameless children got in their way – nudge nudge nudge, push push push – in a shambles of bodies. Out in the street had materialized a few dozen ill-clad men, women and yet more children. Their faces were coated with dust, their clothes were in shreds. They were the bhangi (untouchables), who had turned up in the hope some crumbs would fall to them. But they kept their distance. The band now played Indian tunes – songs from the all-time box office hit, *Mughal-é-Azam*, India's *Gone with the Wind*.

Suddenly, the music stopped. Suddenly, everything stopped, and there appeared at the door of Omi's back yard a group of men who looked like women or women who looked like men. They were neither, even though they wore saris and lipstick. They were hijras, eunuchs who turn up at every wedding and sing and dance for a son for the couple and don't go away till their palms are crossed with silver.

The hijras sang and danced. They sang with heart and danced with love – they became intoxicated with it. The intoxication spread. 'Once more, once more,' clamoured every man, woman and child. The hijras obliged. Their performance over, they looked at the boy's father, Shadi Lal Khatri. Khatri counted the men who looked like women, then he dipped a hand in the side pocket of his raw silk kurta. From a thick wad of notes, he counted out twenty-four rupees, two per man or woman.

A bad move. It brought the monsoon floods prematurely. The noble-looking man in courtly silk and an elegant Peshawari turban

11

had insulted them. The rich owner of Chandigarh's top restaurant had kicked Chandigarh's top artistes in what they hadn't got. What would the world think of him now?

Khatri looked at the world. The world looked away – it had turned against him. Khatri was shamed. He dipped in his pocket again and increased the offending sum to thirty-six rupees. The artistes shook their heads. 'Rupees one hundred and one,' they chorused, shedding more tears.

'No, no, no.' Khatri threw his arms up.

'Yes, yes, yes,' the world chanted.

Khatri met the hijras and the world half-way. He shelled out fifty-one rupees. Tears evaporated and the band in the street broke into an English tune again – 'Prince Eugene', last heard there at the Republic Day Parade on 26 January.

Slowly, the mass of scarlet silk and gold and silver and flowers was advanced. At the fringed doorway stood the mistress of the house, Paro, one hand on the hip and the other holding a bottle of mustard oil. Laden with emotion, quite tearful in fact, she poured oil on both sides of the threshold as her new daughter-in-law stepped across it. It was a ritual as old as Hindusim itself, one of the several to follow. It said welcome, and more. 'Now you have become mine,' Paro said, waving a fistful of rupee coins around Munni's head three times. Then she scattered them into the yard. She repeated this several times. It caused a riot as the waiting street urchins and untouchables fought to gather them from the dust.

'Now you have become irrevocably mine,' Paro repeated.

'What about me, Ma? I married her last night,' Omi yelled.

'Go see to the unloading. What did I tell you about those eyes?' Paro yelled back over the general hubbub.

Omi didn't want to go anywhere. He wanted to be where all that silk was.

'You have all your life to be with her. Go see to the bus.'

'Seva Singh is looking after it, Ma.'

'Only fools and my men would leave such things to servants. But where is your father? Where are *they*?'

Like all Hindu women, Paro addressed her husband in the third person plural. It was a sign of respect.

Khatri stood in the shade of a papaya tree, the only green thing in his back yard, watching it all with detachment. He had done his bit. He had educated his son. He had married him off. He had set him

12

up in the world – the restaurant was doing fine and money was pouring in by itself. *Like rainwater in a bucket.* The rest was in the boy's own two hands. *From now on he'll have to dig with his own spade.* As Khatri had done all his life.

Now Khatri had other things to devote himself to, higher things – God. He had declared in the marriage bus that from now on he was giving up the high life of the Pall Mall to work in his 'little shop' in Sector 15, doing what he liked most in life – making sweets with his own hands. But now he didn't want to do even that. Now he wanted to withdraw completely from this worldly life, like a good Hindu, and sit at the feet of his guru, Baba Gokul Swami, in the jungle near Dhalli. So much the better if Paro came with him. If not . . . Khatri's head itched. It always itched after a journey.

Omi saw that withdrawn look on his father's face and came along to be near him. Without a word Khatri took off his turban and handed it to him. Omi was glad, for this gave him a legitimate reason to be where he was not permitted to be just yet – in the rang mahal (inner circle) of the Red Fort – to hang his father's turban on a wooden peg in his parents' room on the first floor.

'Out, out, out,' snapped Aunt Vidya sweetly upstairs. She took the turban from Omi and waved him away cruelly. 'Not time for you yet. Catch the door.'

'Aunt Vidya!' How could she be so heartless?

'Munni, did you see? This majnu (Romeo) of yours! Only last week he was crying he didn't want to get married. "I'll drown myself in the lake. Eat a pill of poison," he was saying. But look at the pot of glue now. Devouring eyes. Dribbling mouth. Shame on you, Om Parkash. Go catch the door. And wait.'

Omi had to wait. He heard the Red Fort sing a thousand silly songs – he hated each one of them with all his heart. He heard them chant a million meaningless mantras – oh, how he loathed those!

But this was not all. Custom demanded that the beaming Paro 'showed' her daughter-in-law's dowry. She turned the whole of upstairs into an Ali Baba's cave – so vast was Munni's dowry. Paro wanted all the world to come and see and be awestruck.

The world came and saw and was awestruck – such abundance, such splendour, such . . . The world was lost for words. It had never seen anything like it – a brand new sofa-set in lush green velvet, a dining-table complete with six chairs, a full-length-mirror dressing-table, twin palangs (beds) with sculptured legs and feet and lush green velvet quilts, a Murphy radio, a revolving electric fan, a Royal Albert dinner service, his 'n' her made-in-England Raleigh bicycles, a Singer sewing-machine, a Godrej steel almirah, two Romer wrist watches, two Parker pens, an Afghan carpet, more furniture and crockery and cutlery and brassware, two trunkloads of saris and silk and cotton cloth and woollen cloth and . . . People were truly lost for words.

There was a question, though, on every lip. How had the bride's father, a mere railway stationmaster of a tiny station like Dhulkote, managed to give so much?

The hot morning melted into a hotter afternoon. Omi fumed. When really fed up, he seized his old bike for a sprint around town, something he often did to kill boredom. Somehow, better sense prevailed. *Omi son, you'll look an idiot – cycling around in this arse-splitting heat on the first day of your married life. People will laugh their heads off.*

Hungry and angry, Omi sat down in his father's new chrome and leather swivel chair in the restaurant office, waiting. Waiting for – for the word to go into the rang mahal upstairs. Heroically, he held on. Finally, it came, the *word*. The round-faced Bawa, his trusted servant and contemporary, brought it.

'Omi bau,' Bawa said.

And that was all Bawa said. But Omi's heart, perfectly well-behaved till this moment, now began to pound against his chest like a dholuk (drum). He described a swift half circle in the chair and shot up. He gave Bawa a friendly slap on the head – it acknowledged delivery of the message. He pulled out a comb from his hip pocket and combed his hair six times in the Gents mirror. Still not happy with his Elvis puff, he made his way slowly where his pounding heart already was – upstairs.

Upstairs, Omi was told in no uncertain terms by the Red Fort management committee how to disport himself at his first meal with his wife.

'Get out of your shoes.'

'Sit down cross-legged on Munni's left side.' A wife must be on the husband's right side during meals and religious ceremonies.

'And don't ogle her too much.'

Omi hadn't once looked at Munni. He sat down next to her, making sure that their thighs touched, like last night. This in broad daylight was indiscreet. He stole a sidelong glance at his wife to see if there was any effect on her. Alas, Munni was completely veiled by her beautiful scarlet sari. Omi couldn't tell what she looked like, but from the whispering around he gathered that there was unanimity about her appearance: 'Delicate but out of this world.'

14

A hundred dishes were laid out before them. 'Feed her well. She is so thin, poor girl.'

'Bugger off! Get lost! Vamoose! I'll do what I want. My wife,' Omi yelped in English. He knew the Red Fort didn't understand a word of English.

'Om!' But Vidya understood, even though she too didn't know English.

'Aunt Vidya, I thought you loved your nephew,' Omi said in Punjabi.

'Well, a little. What do you want?'

'Can't see a thing. Not fair,' Omi complained, pointing to the translucent silken drapery that cascaded down Munni's hidden face.

'That's a ghund (modesty veil). Old customs demand . . .'

'To hell with old customs,' Omi said, and did something shocking. He pulled the veil off Munni's face.

'Haa hai!' wailed the Red Fort in consternation. How forward, how besharam (shameless) this boy was! Unbelievable!

Omi was stunned by what he saw. A child-woman of eighteen. A babe's face. A pre-adolescent body. And all that seductive make-up and alluring gold and silver!

'Aunt Vidya, it's a plot. The Gunpowder Plot,' he said in English.

'What?' Vidya asked in Punjabi.

'It's like putting a starving man in charge of the king's kitchen!' Omi couldn't believe it – that somebody so desperately beautiful could be so suddenly his, all his, only his. What had he done to deserve her? The answer came from his aunt.

'You must have done something really good in your past life, Om, like feeding Brahmins,' she said.

'I used to feed a whole villageful of the bastards. Daily.'

'But you are totally besharam, you know. Totally. Poor Munni.'

Poor Munni had gone the colour of her drapes. In ten seconds she died ten deaths of increasing embarrassment – he should have waited till they were alone, according to the custom and common sense.

'Now to some serious business, Aunt Vidya,' Omi said, rubbing his hands.

'Meaning what, Om?'

'Meaning this, that I am starving. Meaning this that if I don't eat *something* immediately, I'll have to eat *someone* immediately.'

'Then eat. Eat as much as you like. Eat shamelessly,' said neighbour Mrs Devan Chand, the homeopath's wife.

'Frankly, I am going to. Shamelessly,' Omi said, looking directly at his wife and licking his lips noisily.

15

'Haa hai!' shrieked the Red Fort, going six shades redder with consternation. No one in the present company had known such a brazen beast. 'Paro, your boy . . . haa hai!'

'Aunt Vidya,' Omi leaned over and whispered in his aunt's ear, 'do your favourite and only nephew an all-time favour – send these bitches away.'

'There are things an aunt can do and there are things she can't, even for her one and only nephew.' This was the bride's first day in her new home. These ladies, relatives and friends of the family, had to be there, around her. This was law.

'I'll take the law into my own hands if you don't, Aunt Vidya.'

Knowing that her nephew was perfectly capable of making a fool of himself and his family, Vidya conjured up an excuse for a mass exodus. The just-married couple were left alone. They wouldn't be for long, Omi knew. *Make the most of it, Omi son*, he said to himself. But how? His wife looked a dream. A small oval face. Large, perhaps too large for the face, almond-shaped eyes with enough kohl for four more. A fine nose. And her lips – her lips broke his heart – were full and red and very suckable. Omi's blood stirred and his heart began to perform somersaults like a runner who had struck gold in the hundred metres at the Olympics.

'I want to stand on my head.' Omi spoke fast. There wasn't much time.

'What?' Muni replied. She felt bewildered. Before she had been bewildered because all those women were there. Now she felt so because they were not.

'What's mightier than love?' Omi asked.

'What?' Suddenly, Muni couldn't hear well.

'Like *The pen is mightier than the sword* – there must be something bigger than love. Surely?'

'Pardon?'

'There must be. That which makes you want to stand on your head as I want to do at this moment in time.'

'Sorry?'

'Didn't they teach you anything other than sorry-pardon-what in Dhulkote?'

Munni choked.

'Indian Railways – not what they used to be,' Omi said.

Munni's lips parted in a smile at the mention of railways, and she thought of her home in Dhulkote. As she did so, a tear oozed out of her heavily kohl'd eyes and rolled down her child's cheeks. Omi's heart broke in two. A longing rose in him to reach out and fill his

16

arms with her and press his burning lips to her eyes. But those bitches could walk in any second. *India!* At times like these Omi hated his country.

His heart aching, Omi decided to dare it, if only for a moment. He put his arms around his bride, closed his feverish lips on hers and shut his eyes. Munni couldn't keep hers open either. It was a mistake to shut their eyes, for the kiss lingered.

It was an even greater mistake to re-open them. For when they did, there was that great Red Fort wall again, thick with hysteria.

'Haa hai!'

'Piss off!'

Omi's old room became the new bridal suite. The dowry palangs (beds) with sculptured legs and feet, the dressing-table and the rest replaced the old furniture. The room became crammed, sweetly crammed. And it had a new smell. It smelled of its new occupant. It was a mouth-watering smell.

This was upstairs.

Downstairs, it was business as usual in the Pall Mall restaurant. Though there was a little difference – Omi, who, till yesterday, couldn't be parted from it even for a minute, today didn't want to know the place existed. He was in a panic. He had heard what his father had to say in the marriage bus about giving it all up and reverting to the humble art of making sweets. *Only in this gandoo (queer) country do you renounce the world when it is lying at your feet, licking them.* Omi couldn't understand it, even less accept it.

So at six in the evening when he saw his father leave the Pall Mall to go to Sector 15, his heart sank. What if his father stuck to his word? What if he got involved with something unimaginably ridiculous like making jalebis or barfi or laddus or what-have-you, and forgot he had a son who'd got married only last night? He wouldn't be able to get back till . . . till God knew when – maybe ten, maybe eleven, maybe twelve. By then Munni would be fast alseep. Omi would have to wait till tomorrow.

His heart sank to new depths. His first night of married bliss! *How can Father do it to me, his only son?*

Omi was sick of it all. And there was no one around to open his heart to, not even his own wife. She was still surrounded by that wall. Didn't the witches have a home to go to? He hated Chandigarh, Punjab, India.

Six-thirty. Seven. Seven-thirty. Eight.

17

Soft lights. Soft piped music, *English* music. Softly spoken guests. Golden Eagle lager being sipped decorously, pappadoms crunched quietly, legs of red tandoori chicken pulled apart dextrously. Seva Singh, Bawa and the other waiters moving about noiselessly like mechanical toys.

This is Omi's hour. All Chandigarh is there. It has come in imported cars. It wears imported shirts and slacks. It gives out whiffs of imported smells. Among these people are, sometimes, Omi's old college friends, the Simla Pinks. They are so called because they have spent years in expensive English-style public schools in the Simla Hills nearby (which put the roses in their cheeks). And because they speak English so well that no one can understand what they say. Everybody present in the Pall Mall restaurant at this hour has a halo like Christian saints in paintings. This is Omi's hour, and usually he presides over it with a halo of his own behind his oft-combed, Brylcreemed head. He sends chota or burra pegs of Black Knight whisky or Bradshaw's brandy on the house to . . . he knows who. He sits with them. He knows what to say to them and how to make them laugh.

But this is not Omi's hour tonight. Tonight he is pacing up and down the Pall Mall like a caged animal. And he is sighing. *What if Father comes back at ten or eleven or twelve?*

But Khatri did not come back at twelve or eleven or even ten. He came back just then, on the dot of eight. He hadn't gone to the 'little shop' in Sector 15, after all, only to the temple next door.

'Phewee!' Omi began to like life again. Even India.

Khatri saw and heard the caged animal. 'All right, boy.' He pointed to the door with a jerk of his head.

'Sure, Father?' The restaurant was aflutter with life and abuzz with hushed glamour – would his father manage on his own?

'Yes, boy. Go have dinner with.'

His heart in his throat, Omi went up the stairs in two leaps. With the third he was at the bridal-suite door. There he suffered a setback. His heart stopped beating and courage flew out of him like a bird from an open cage. But in he went all the same, smiling foolishly.

The room smelled maddeningly good. Munni sat in front of the new revolving fan next to a table with their dinner. She was reading one of his books – *The Man-Eaters of Kumaon* by Jim Corbett, the legendary English tiger-hunter – Omi had had to read it for his FA a couple of years ago. She put the book down. She adjusted her sari on her breasts. The sari shimmered and trembled in the jet of air from

18

the electric fan. The bride and groom exchanged nervous glances. Neither of them knew what to say. Both of them knew one thing, though – Omi had to speak first. He was the man.

'How nice you look. Is there anything that you want? Is there anything I can do?' Omi chose English to speak in. This was a special moment; Punjabi seemed too vulgar for it. But wasn't it unfair on her – a girl from Dhulkote, a faceless little village buried in dust and anonymity? How on earth could she be expected to speak English? She might be able to read a bit of it, but to speak it . . .? *Omi son, aren't you putting her down? You should be ashamed of yourself.*

Omi son had a surprise.

'I am fine. I don't think I want anything, thank you very much,' Munni replied in English.

It was more than a surprise, it was a 440-volt shock. Munni spoke English just like an English girl. Unless, of course, it was a mere chance, a fluke? After all, she had spoken only a dozen words so far. Omi would wait before he allowed himself to be electrocuted.

'Just the book to read on one's bridal night – *The Man-Eaters of Kumaon*,' he said. Suddenly he felt like a man-eating tiger.

'Oh, I don't know. It was just lying around and I began to read bits of it while . . .'

While what? Waiting for him? Omi's heart started to somersault at the thought, but he resisted the temptation to ask. 'What do you think of our Chandigarh, then?' he said instead.

'I think it is frightfully cute.'

It was amazing. Omi had never heard anything like it, not from an Indian – not even from the Simla Pinks. Only in English films.

'Where did you learn to speak like that?'

'Oh, you have to ask Miss Doolittle.'

'And who is Miss Doolittle?'

Munni explained. Miss Doolittle was a very old English lady who lived in the Good Christians' Mission in Ambala City, a mile from Dhulkote. Munni didn't know much about her, but she was one of those English people who had stayed on after Independence in '47. She lived on a small pension and to supplement it, she coached young Indian girls from aspiring families. Years ago when Khatri in Chandigarh had hired a college professor, Bhatnagar, to teach his son to speak English, Munni's father, Kandhari in Dhulkote, had employed the services of the ageing Miss Doolittle to groom his girl. The English Munni spoke was more than four years of Miss Doolittle at thirty rupees per month – flawless.

'Well, well, well. Didn't you do well, Omi son?'

19

'Pardon?'

'I mean, it's pinker than Simla Pink English at its pinkest.'

'What's Simla Pink?'

'Tell you another time. But wait till they hear it . . .' Omi meant his fashionable friends – Arun, Harry, Duke, Lord and the girls – the North End trendies. 'It's going to be a right kick in their backside.'

'You have an extraordinary way of saying things.'

Had he? And he hadn't wanted to get married! But wait a minute . . . what, besides speaking like them, had she learnt about the English? Had she learnt . . . er . . . their fast, liberated ways? Suddenly Omi wished his wife didn't speak English like the English after all.

But he had other things on his mind – man-eating things – and he didn't know what to do about them. He begged God, his old favourite, the blue-bodied celestial cowherd, Krishna, to help. He saw Him looking at him. Krishna wore a gold crown with a peacock feather. He stood leisurely with one foot across the other, holding a flute to his beautiful face, eyes sparkling. A docile cow stood behind him, a young calf nestled into her rump.

'Please, God,' Omi begged.

But Krishna was not listening. Omi pleaded with Him. He pleaded and pleaded. Krishna remained unmoved. *What help? You haven't made yourself clear, Omi son. In such matters you have to be perfectly frank.* Desperate, Omi made himself perfectly frank: *I want her cunt my Lord,* adding, thoughtfully, *Promise to feed every Brahmin in Sector 23 tomorrow.*

A wonderful thing happened. The azure God was moved. He stopped playing the flute and smiled – He actually smiled – and said: 'I help those who . . . you know very well who, you 24-carat fool.'

I know, Sir, Omi answered and cleared his throat like his father did whenever he had made up his mind about something.

'Yes, you have,' Munni said.

'I have what?' Omi said. He had forgotten what he and his wife had been talking about.

'An extraordinary way of saying things.'

'Oh, I don't know. Nobody ever told me that before. The things men learn about themselves from their wives! What shall we do? Any ideas?'

'There are two or three things we can do.'

'What?'

'Have dinner . . .' Munni pointed to the dinner. 'Play Ludo . . .' There was a Ludo set nearby. 'Or . . .' Munni was going to say, 'Or just talk.' But Omi didn't give her a chance.

'I prefer that! Let's do "or".'

He took Munni's hennaed hand. It was soft and moist, like a child's. He pulled her to him. Munni came, all sighs and smiles. The next step was easier – filling his arms with his dreams. Then he did what he had been dying to do, let his itching hands *into* that silk. The moment that happened their lips found each other's and they shut their eyes on orders from Lord Krishna.

They forgot dinner and remained cemented like that till . . . till hours later when they were alarmed out of their embrace by a strange sound. It came from outside the house – someone calling out a familiar name in a shrill sing-song voice. Omi and Munni rushed to the balcony. It was cool and fresh, and still quite dark outside, but morning was peeping through. Wrapped around each other – there was this sudden and insatiable need to cling to each other – they looked and listened. Immediately before them was the barren Khatri back yard (Munni made a quick mental note that she had to do something about it if she was going to spend the rest of her life here). Beyond swayed darkly the great mango, jamun and tahli trees that lined the Public Nurseries. The noise was coming from their dark lushness. Two birds were singing there, loudly.

'Munni. Munni. Munni,' sang one.

'Love you. Love you,' crooned the other.

They sang so clearly – in English, too – that there was no mistaking what they said in their duet.

'Munni. Munni. Munni.'

'Love you. Love you.'

Munni stepped back. 'Well, I'm blowed,' she said.

Shadi Lal Khatri was a man of habit: *Good habits are a man's best friend.* His kept him in *fine walking-talking order.*

Khatri rose before the sun tipped the spine of the blue Kasauli mountain with gold. He folded his hands on his chest. He looked up at the sky. He said thank you for *all this* – the restaurant, the house above it and its still-asleep two inmates. Then he addressed himself to the morning's essentials – emptying the bowels, cleaning the teeth and bathing the body before he touched food.

The first of these he did behind bushes out in the open, exactly a mile from home. He detested what all Chandigarhias loved – their new porcelain bowls and 'train-stopping' chains. *How can they?* – how could anyone? – *sit in a concrete box full of his own body gases?* Khatri called the place 'Pakistan' and the practice of locking oneself in it

21

'ungodly'. He blamed the designer of Chandigarh, Le Corbusier, for infecting the mind of its good folk. For Khatri there was nothing like a good shit, but there was only one place for it – under God's blue umbrella.

Cleaning the teeth and bathing took place at home, under the 'Corbusier shower'. This Khatri liked.

After his bath, Khatri would wake Omi. Paro, already up, would give father and son ice-cold lassi, the summer drink made of yoghurt. The father took his with salt, the son preferred his sweet. The lassi drunk, the two were ready for the day's single main thing – shopping in the food market.

The market was in Bajwara, right behind Sector 23. Bajwara was a Harappan village. It was in Chandigarh, yet it was not Chandigarh. Chandigarh was concrete and steel and glass; it was buried sewers and spotless straight wide roads and lush green parks. Bajwara was made of the earth it stood on; it was wooden shacks and open drains and flies and cow-dung smoke and weightless wandering cows and mangy dogs and dusty lanes which became rivers of mud in the monsoon. No one knew how it had become the Punjab's new capital's Covent Garden or les Halles. The fact was, it had. Food came to it from all parts of the state. It came from as far afield as Kashmir, Himachal and UP. It came in lorries, trucks and bullock carts. It came on donkey, mule and horseback. It came on the human head.

The taste of the lassi still on their tongues, father and son would be in Bajwara – it was a short walk. Once there, Khatri selected every potato, lamb cutlet and chicken with equal care – *the best for the guest*. This took a while. By nine father and son were on their way back home with a rickshaw full of things that were *best for the guest*. The sun, well up now, would have begun to bite at the shoulders through the shirt. But the breeze would still be there, a gift the Kasauli mountain breathed on Punjab's new capital, so sitting in a moving rickshaw felt good. While the father planned his day, the son looked forward to arriving home for a long cool shower and his butter paratha breakfast.

This was Khatri's morning routine, part-shared by his son. But today it was gone twelve and the sun glared mercilessly and still there was no sign of Omi. On his way down to the restaurant, Khatri looked at the bridal suite door. He gave Paro a slap on her bottom and laughed. Although they slept on the roof, they had heard the girl scream each time she came last night, and feared that the neighbours had too.

'Whose son is he, then?' Paro said. She was drenched in delight.

22

Her only concern at the moment was – what if they started all over again on waking up?

'But tell him I'm retiring.'

'Tell him yourself. Anyway, retiring from what?'

'From work, woman. There are other things in life than making money. Higher things.'

'Not yet forty-five and thinking like an old man. What has taken over your brain? Look to your left. Look to your right. Look at Dr Devan Chand. Look at Satya's husband . . .' Their two neighbours were not on talking terms with each other, but they both talked to the Khatris. 'Ever seen how they look at their wives? They undress them with their eyes, even in company. And look at you. Ever look at *others*? Ever think of *others*?' The *others* was Paro herself. 'Higher things, indeed.'

'Paro, you will ever remain the peasant girl I wedded, fit only to live in your father's village. A buffalo happy in the muck of the village pond. Five years in our capital haven't broadened your mental horizons, nor given you an ounce of spiritual sophistication.'

'Mental horizons? Spiritual sophistication? Where did *they* learn these fancy words? They don't impress us. The few pennies God put in *their* pocket have hijacked *their* brain.'

'Talking to my wife is like playing the flute to the bull in the hope you can charm it . . .'

Omi's door opened. Avoiding the young couple's eyes, Khatri hurriedly moved on.

Omi and Munni bathed and got dressed. Paro first gave them breakfast, then, what Omi was fearing, a lecture.

'People as far as Bajwara could hear. Sound travels at night,' Paro's words were addressed to Omi, but their victim was Munni. She died on the spot. 'Moderation. Our elders said moderation is the key to the lock of married bliss. They knew what they were talking about, they were no fools. And another thing: your father. A kala keera (black worm) has slipped into *their* head. *They* are retiring. Moving on to "higher things". To God via the guru at Dhalli. So what do you think?'

Omi was not thinking. But his head was not empty, in fact it was full. Of just one word, an English word, which had entered there via Miss Doolittle under cover of darkness last night like an *agent provocateur* and taken up permanent residence. He blurted it out: 'Honeymoon, Ma. Honeymoon.'

'What's that?' Paro had never heard of it.

23

Omi explained. 'Civilized people go on honeymoon when they get married. Everybody in England and America does. Ask anybody.'

Paro slapped her forehead is disgust. 'Ram, Ram, Ram!' She pinched her earlobes in shock. 'Over my dead body. We are respectable Hindu people, not . . .'

Just then Paro's old friend from pre-Partition days, the Brahmin widow Chatkarni, turned up for her daily handa (alms of bread).

'Ram, Ram, Ram . . .' Chatkarni muttered, also pulling her earlobes in utter disgust at the suggestion that a newly married couple should go to another town and stay in a hotel for the sole purpose of . . . 'Ram, Ram, Ram . . .'

More ladies arrived for the daily natter. Vidya too. As things were quiet downstairs, Khatri also came up. Omi thought it wise to absent himself from the scene for a while and took Munni to the balcony to look at the world. The world, green and dusty, looked good, but their back yard was a disgrace. It was bald and barren.

'There ought to be garden here,' Munni said in Omi's ear.

'How? The damn thing is, not a blade of grass ever grows here. Not even weeds,' Omi said in her ear. They only talked in each other's ears now. It was so much nicer. Whatever they said linked their groins.

'Leave it to me. We'll borrow our gardener, old Mali. Mali is magic. I'll write to Mummy to send him here.'

Inside the house, speech returned to Chatkarni. The house and the balcony listened. 'Why, Paro, you must have done something heinous in your past life to beget a son like Omi. You must have killed a poor cow like me.'

'I must have killed ten cows like you. Minimum,' Paro said.

'Omi, a boy like you from a family like yours saying things like you are! You will blacken your mother's face,' said the new family friend, millionaire Lakhpati's wife, Lakhpatni. Lakhpatni usually travelled with all her seven children – six boys and a girl. Her boys – aged between six and thirteen – were awful. They caused havoc wherever they went. They were born enemies of china, glass and furniture. Everybody called them 'hell bastards' and hated them. Omi loved the 'hell bastards'. They listened to no one, only to Omi.

'Auntie Lakhpatni, where are the boys today?' Omi shouted.

Lakhpatni didn't answer. She turned to Dr Devan Chand's wife who had been rather quiet hitherto. 'He would be blackening his mother's face, no, Doctorani-ji?'

The Doctorani coloured. Her own face had been blackened not long ago in circumstances far more horrendous. But this was a subject

24

no one ever opened their mouths about in her presence. So everyone thought it tactless, even bitchy, of Lakhpatni to seek her opinion about 'blackening faces'. There was a moment of awkward silence.

Sensing the general disapproval, Lakhpatni tried to humour everybody. 'Omi, I'll cut my nose if even one of my boys turns out like you. I swear I will.'

'They all will, Auntie. They would want to. I am an excellent model. I represent new India. Times have changed,' Omi said.

'True, true. The zamana (times) have changed. We must march with the zamana. India must make progress. Free country now,' said Vidya. In her thirty-first year, she was the youngest of the ladies, with the exception of Munni.

'Call this progress, girl, living in sin in a hotel for *that*? Ram, Ram, Ram!' Chatkarni's fingers reached for her earlobes again.

'Chatkarni Auntie, this young man is married to this young woman over here. So where does sin come into it?'

'It does. Examine your purpose for living in hired rooms in distant towns and cities.'

Khatri was sitting on a charpoy outside the room in which this conversation was taking place. He was reading his newspaper. He was also listening.

'You heard?' Paro shouted at him. She knew he was listening.

'I heard.'

'Your son, too, has got a kala keera (black worm) in his head. Why don't you tell him something?'

'Silly woman, I have told you what I had to tell you – *I am retiring, going to our guru.* You come with me if you want to. But don't torture me. Let the boy take Munni on holiday.'

Omi couldn't believe what he heard. He dragged Munni into the room. 'Honeymoon, Father, not holiday.'

'Whatever you call it. I'll wait till you come back. After that you dig with your own spade with your own hands. But where do you want to go, oi?'

Omi hadn't really thought about it. But as usual, he had an answer. 'Kashmir, Father,' he said just like that. Every hero in Indian films went to Kashmir, the valley of lovers, for his honeymoon.

'Kashmir? Kashmir is too far off. Take her to Simla.'

'Simla?' Paro, Chatkarni and Lakhpatni said in one voice. It was the voice of shock – only wicked people went to Simla and stayed in expensive hotels and did all kinds of wicked things. Once it was the shameless Angrez, now it was any Lallu Panjoo Tom Dick and

25

Harry, whoever had lined his pocket with a bit of 'post-independence boom money'.

'Simla!' Omi said. Simla would do nicely. Thank you very much.

'Yes,' Khatri said. 'Simla's air and water are as good as Kashmir's. Nor is its scenery any worse. So go have fun, boy.' Khatri folded the *Milap* and stood up from the charpoy.

'Hai, hai, hai my mother. What's happened to my housewallah? Pushing his own son into the arms of debauchery.' Paro slapped her forehead in heart-rending agony.

'And stay at the best hotel there. How much do you want, oi? Madame Parvati, lady, give the boy five hundred,' Khatri said from the stairs.

'Five hundred?' Why, that was what her husband had earned in six whole months once. Paro knew the black worm had completely eaten up his brain.

'The zamana has changed. A parting gift from your father, boy. When you come back, *I retire*. Understood?'

The honeymoon: it was better than winning the Derby lottery. But *Father's black worm!* It was going to eat into Omi's new house of bliss, brick by brick. Turn it into a structure made of sand.

What is the matter with Father?

For weeks he had been behaving as if he was not quite *there*. Even so, *He can't be serious about this God business*.

Omi couldn't see his father chanting *God, God, God* at his guru's feet for the rest of his life, at the bottom of that blasted gorge by Dhalli. And for what, pray? For his precious peace of mind. If peace of mind came through mumbling *God, God, God* one could do it anywhere. What was so special about praying in jungles and gorges and on river banks? Those fucking gurus, they chose tiresome locations to make God hard to get.

Omi was furious – with God, the family guru, Baba Gokul Swami or whatever his name was, and with his own father. Time he told him how he felt about the whole thing.

It was easier said than done, standing up to his father. When Omi appeared before him, all that anger hissed out like air from a punctured balloon or a bicycle tube. He went dumb.

'Yes, boy?' Khatri said.

Omi couldn't utter the words he had rehearsed so well in his head – *Father, it is irresponsible of you to take up God full-time at this stage. You can't do this to me, your only son . . .*

26

'Father, one can be a man of God yet remain a man of the world. All a question of striking the right balance.'

'Oh, yes?'

'In my opinion you should give it a try. Kill two birds with the same stone. And why not, Father?'

'In my opinion you should mind your own business – your wife, her happiness and your work.'

How could Omi explain that that was where their HMS *Happiness* foundered – on the rock of work, before-dawn-to-after-midnight work. When would he have the time to make her happy. Happiness was going to bed with her at eight. Happiness was going to sleep in her arms when the Munni birds began their duet next morning. Happiness was waking up at noon. Happiness was a two-to-six siesta in the afternoon heat. *Newly married, dammit. What the hell? Obviously Father has forgotten all about it.*

It was hopeless. What to do? When all seemed lost, Omi had an idea – *Get help. Get all the people Father listened to.* This would be bound to change his mind about God and his guru.

The first to come were the immediate neighbours – Dr Devan Chand and Satya's husband, Ujjagar, the shoe-factory wallah. The homeopath had a Juliet for a daughter. The shoe-wallah's wife had a Romeo as a brother. This Romeo and Juliet did not commit suicide, they did something far worse. They had eloped a few months before and got married and disappeared, and cut the noses of the two families, who hadn't talked to each other since that day.

In a stage-managed move, Dr Devan Chand arrived first.

'Omi is right, Lala-ji. God-business *is* combinable with world-business. I know it. You know it. So?'

The shoe-wallah was not far behind. 'There's something to be said about a double-kill with one stone. Brings satisfaction of a rare kind. So pick up the stone.'

Others were equally succinct. For instance, Gulati, Khatri's old friend from Manimajra, who worked in the Government Secretariat. Gulati had pull. He had got Khatri his first big break. Khatri listened to him. 'Tuck in a rupee or two more while the going is good. A man with a deeper pocket is closer to the guru and God than one without. Fact of life.'

'Man's first priority is to build a decent house on this humble earth. Building one on higher ground comes later. Here time is on

27

your side. Lala-ji,' said Professor Bhatnagar, Omi's ex-tutor. Bhatnagar spoke such good English. Khatri had high regard for him.

'Wash your ears of this upper nonsense. No such thing as Higher Things, it's all *here*. I am not joking,' said jeweller Heeralal.

Nanda, the Hospitality Officer of Governor House, said something really important. Nanda was a VIP. Once he had helped Khatri in an important way, got him his first government contract – supplying to Governor House. Omi knew his father listened to him more than to anyone else. 'Can you leave the empire you took half a decade to build in the hands of a kid of twenty? Tell me the truth.'

'A house cannot stand without the right foundation, especially a spiritual one. And you haven't dug deep enough yet, Lala-ji,' said Bassi, the America-returned architect who had built the Pall Mall.

Khatri shook his head. It brought tears to his wife's eyes.

'All right, then, I'll wear white for the rest of my life. Happy?' Paro said, stuffing a handkerchief to her nose. White is the colour of widowhood in India.

'My mind is made,' Khatri said. 'I am a Khatri. Don't you know, woman?' Once a Khatri said something, he said something. That was it.

'Don't I know a Khatri when I see one? Don't I know a mule when I see one? Don't I know why it's difficult to tell the difference? Because God made them in the same short sitting,' Paro sobbed.

Postmaster K. P. Singh was so distressed he didn't know how to express his anguish. But he found words. 'I agree with Bassi sahib. Lala-ji, you are simply not ready. Sending you up would be sending a half-written letter without a postage stamp on it. You know what I mean?'

Khatri remained unmoved. Omi was shattered. His married life, hardly begun – and begun because his father had insisted on it – had already come to an end. What a tragedy.

Bent and broken, Omi rolled out his old bike. He didn't go for his new, dowry Raleigh. He didn't know why. He cared for nothing any more. The Pall Mall had been his life before, but now he couldn't stand the thought of it, the sight of it. He wished he could plant a few sticks of dynamite under the air-conditioning plant, and race away on his bike to blow up the whole damn thing from a distance. Good thing the place was handsomely insured.

The sky was thick with the first monsoon clouds. A brisk breeze blew from the clay hills crowning Chandigarh. Omi cycled aimlessly on the habitually empty roads of the capital. Without thinking about it, he took the direction of Panchkoola. Panchkoola was seven miles

28

away. It was a bus stop at a road junction in the middle of nowhere. Once upon a time his father had had an eat-house there.

Omi cycled on and on, going nowhere. But he arrived somewhere, at an important conclusion, as he passed by the Power House three miles from home. The conclusion was that he had to call off his honeymoon. *No point in it now.* Kheer pudding today, starvation tomorrow – that was how Omi saw life *after* the honeymoon. He saw no life *after*. *Oi, you fella with the blue umbrella. Why do you do it? – play salt 'n' pepper tricks on us, put a lump of sugar in the mouth and push a red chilli up the behind at the same time? Do you get a kick out of it? Pervert!*

The breeze had become a strong wind. It made cycling difficult. *You may be great, Old Boy. But sometimes I don't understand you.* Omi didn't care for life and God any more. He pedalled on. In the heart of the vast dry riverbed past the Power House he saw a sight which made his heart leap to his throat and him off his bike. *It can't be. It can't be!*

An old sadhu sat cross-legged in the sand dunes. He was bald and toothless. His face and bare body were smeared with white ash, making him seem part of the dry white riverbed. His *trishul* (trident) was stuck alongside in the sand waves. He faced the Kasauli mountain, now obliterated by the monsoon cloud, muttering, mumbling, *God, god, god.* This surely was Baba Gokul Swami, Omi's father's guru, the root cause of all Omi's misery! No, he was not – only someone who looked like him.

It was not a remarkable sight – the bloody country was full of such men; it was a sight as old as India itself. But Omi found it so. He saw the hand of God in it. A thought crossed his mind, a brilliant thought – get to Father's guru before Father! *Old Boy, I beg your pardon. You are great after all.*

There was a blinding flash overhead a few hundred yards away, followed by an ear-splitting roar of thunder; God was saying thank you for the compliment. Then rain, thick and heavy, pelted down. Omi clicked his fingers decisively and cycled home like a maniac.

'Ma, Ma,' he yelled, breathless and dripping, on reaching home. 'I have an idea. A brilliant idea.'

'What is it this time?' Paro knew about her son's ideas. They were always brilliant.

'In fact, it's more than an idea, it's a trump card against Father's black worm. A *coup d'état.*'

'Koo d'what?'

'Never mind. I'll bring it back from Simla, promise. Then you can have him around your little finger again.'

29

'I don't want him around my little finger. I only want him to be the man he always was.'

'That too, Ma. Wait and see. You'll have your man back. A new man, a spring chicken all over again.'

'It'll need a miracle.'

'That's what I'm going to bring back, Ma – our miracle.'

Omi and Munni had been gone an hour. Khatri sat restlessly in the office. It was the pre-lunch period and the place was empty. Khatri spotted something odd – a fiercely attractive young lady in a corner, all alone. Her face was wrapped up in her dupatta (scarf). A young maiden sitting by herself in a restaurant! *Toba, toba, toba!* Most unusual. What had the country come to? No self-respecting woman went to a restaurant alone – restaurants were man's world. Unless she was a slut.

Eyes met and Khatri recognized his son's ex-flame.

Well, well, well.

The last time their eyes had met was at . . . Khatri didn't want to think about it . . . in circumstances Khatri wanted to think about even less. She had been alaf nangi (stark naked) in the arms of – *shame, oh shame* – of a stark-naked man with a military bearing. In bushes dark and deep by the River Jhajjar at Pinjore, only a hundred yards from where his jilted son had sat abjectly, throwing pebbles in the river.

Well, well, well. *She has a nerve coming here. What does she want?*

Khatri sent his smart 'English-speaking' waiter, Bawa, to go and take her order. He hoped the bitch would talk. She did.

'Where is your boss?' The young woman spoke like a rani.

'Boss there, miss.' Bawa jerked his head in the direction of the office to which Khatri had beaten a tactful retreat.

'Not the old man. I mean Omi.'

'Gone on the honeymoon. Married now, you know, o yes. Married very very pretty.' Bawa also knew this lady. He had heard a hundred and one stories of Omi bau and her from sources local and foreign.

'Has he?'

'Any order, miss?'

'Yes. When he comes back tell him I came. Tell him to phone me. Tell him it's urgent.'

'By "order" I mean food-shood, miss.'

'Just a cold coffee, then. Be quick. And the bill.'

Bawa brought the coffee quickly. Then he brought the bill. It came

30

to a rupee and a half. She gave him three. She was surprised that he didn't seem grateful.

'Can I trust you?'

'Totally, miss. Your servant.'

'What's your name?'

'Only Bawa, miss.'

'Bawa, you understand what you have to do?'

'Totally, miss. Your servant for life.'

'Good. Omi sahib will also reward you. And remember – not a word . . .'

'I am sealing the lips, miss. Both of them.'

'Never to open them to anyone else.'

'Promise. Cross my heart and hope to live.'

'But not for long if you don't keep your word.'

'Miss, please. Promise is promise.'

Miss went out of the door and drove off in her MG, noisily. She hadn't gone a yard when Bawa unsealed his lips to the 'old man'.

Indians stare.

The great bus stand in Sector 17 stared. It stared at Munni.

Frenzy gripped the place. Dust-coated buses honked as they arrived from all corners of the world. Dust-coated buses honked more as they departed for those places. Hooded rickshaws hooted as they arrived or left. All were disgorging haste-eaten, 'hurry, hurry' passengers. It was wheels and bicycle frames and bare sweaty legs and shimmering heat and mirages. The bus stand was a place for fleeting moments of meeting or parting. But there resided in permanence *Divine Astrology – English and Vernacular, Miracle Massage, High-Class Dentistry, Enemy of Catarrh & Chest Complaints, Know-Your-Tomorrow Palmist* and . . .

And noise! *Hatt, hatt, hatt, bau-ji – out of the way . . . Save yourself, sardar-ji . . . Move, you unfortunate . . . Paradise Kulfi, Glacier Ice Cream . . . Guaranteed Cooler Water . . . Saharanpuri Banana, Dusheri Mango . . . Hatt, hatt, hatt . . .*

There was urgency in the air. Travellers rushed around. Bow-legged coolies with skyscrapers on their heads – trunks, bedrools, suitcases, baskets – hurried helter-skelter. Pedlars peddled. Hawkers hawked. Onlookers looked. All of them shouting, as if it was on the Punjab Roadways timetable. All of them staring, at the delicate teenage bride, making Munni want to hide. She did. She hid behind her groom. Still they stared.

Munni wore white cotton trousers and a sky-blue silk blouse. On

31

her arm she carried a red cardigan to be worn in the mountains. She had rouge on her cheeks, lipstick on her lips and plenty of kohl on her eyes. With an impressive amount of gold on her wrists, around her neck and attached to her ears, she looked what she was – a very newly married young lady. And everybody wants to see the bride.

'Why do they stare at me?'

'Because you look a box-office hit, Bublashoo.' Omi invented a name for her.

'What does it mean – Bublashoo?'

'It means you.'

The Simla bus was unlike any other in the bus stand. It was a *de luxe* bus, the pride of the Punjab Roadways. It was also tiny, a toy, a matchbox on wheels. It had to be tiny to climb 7,000 feet up and down valley and mountain to Simla in the Himalayas. Its engine was that of an average Tata Mercedes bus – strong – but its body was its own – toy-like.

While their two suitcases were being hoisted to the bus roof, a man approached Omi. He was dark – a Madrasi or a Bengali, thought Omi. Everything he wore was new. He wore a beige serge suit, a mauve silk shirt, a yellow striped tie, and black and white co-respondent's shoes. In that sweltering heat he was a sight, and sweated like a horse.

'Excuse me, you would be from these parts, correct?' The man spoke *phoren* English – Madrasi or Bengali, Omi wondered.

'Correct,' Omi said.

'You been to Simla, no doubt.'

'No doubt. Lots of times.' Omi had never set foot there before.

'My first time. I hear it is all razzle-dazzle and heavenly glamour, like United Kingdom. Am I correct?'

'Spot on.'

'I wouldn't know what to do there. Reason why I'm so nervy.'

'Why are you going there, then?'

'Won this competition with one-rupee ticket, would you believe? A week in the Queen of Hill Stations. Plus this boot-suit. Would have preferred cash, frankly – married by God's grace with five monkeys. Wife said go, enjoy, but not too much! No, she was only pulling. But is it really like UK up there, I mean glamour and all?'

'Actually it is better.'

'You been there too – UK, I mean?'

'We were both born there.'

'Heaven born and very tip-top. One look and I can tell. But tell me, what does one do up there? I really don't know. Any tips?'

32

'Make friends.'

'But how?'

'When you enter the bus, shake hands with all male passengers. Give them your address back home and ask theirs. A piece of cake from then on.'

'Sure?'

'Positive. We Punjabis are a friendly type. We like this sort of thing.'

'A coincidence. Thank you for the tip. By the way, name is Dampat, Mr G. R. Dampat. The address back is one-o-one oblique one-o-one Block . . .'

Till Kalka twenty miles up-country, the toy bus went roaring like a racing car. From then on things changed. The Kasauli mountain rose abruptly and the little bus began to groan. A few minutes after Kalka they crossed the Himachal border and came to a wayside stop, Dhalli. This was where Omi's father would come to seek his 'higher things'. He would get off the bus here and hire the local guide, Billa, a boy of Omi's age. Billa would lead him to the bottom of the gorge on the right, where his guru lived by the bank of the fast-flowing River Jhajjar.

But Father won't now. Will he? Omi had worked it all out.

Dhalli was only a couple of little shops, but it was famous for what it sold – duty-free liquor from Solan in Himachal. Omi knew the place well. He had shopped there once with Arun.

'Oh no!' Think of the devil! 'No! No! No!' Omi yelled in disbelief.

For there stood his old friend in the middle of the road, loading the boot of his new Fiat with bottles of beer and blocking the way. With him were Harry, Lord and Duke. Omi didn't want to be seen. He tried to duck, but it was too late.

Omi hadn't invited any of his friends to his wedding. He hadn't even told anyone about it. He had been too ashamed to be getting married so young. But the world being what it was, everybody knew by now.

Arun and the others saw. They guessed where Omi was going and for what. They went wild. They jumped in the Fiat, rode along beside the toy bus for a mile and simply went mad. They hurled practical advice at Omi. It was juicy. It was graphic. It made the bus heave from side to side with laughter. It made Munni cut her throat with shame.

'Bastards! Wait till I get back. I'll chop your balls off, I swear I will. By God I will,' Omi shouted at his friends.

*

33

The mountains became steep and rough and dangerous, but the bus raced on unconcerned along hair-raising khuds (ravines). Each time it swerved to left or right, Munni's heart jumped to her throat and she clung to Omi. 'Happy-go-lucky. Very happy-go-lucky,' Mr Dampat said about the driver, a Sikh.

'Mad's the word, if you ask me. Mad-dog mad,' someone else said.

Munni agreed with the second opinion. Omi neither agreed nor disagreed. He was grateful to the 'mad-dog mad' driver whose antics made his wife cling to him. Her breasts – they killed. They caused earthquakes and landslides and wildfires. And a killer . . . cock-a-doodle-doo!

The air had turned cool. Soon it became cooler and aromatic – all those pine-tipped peaks and pine-drenched depths. *Mountains, lovely mountains. Let me get to the top, inside a hotel room with her and . . .* Omi's heart did somersaults of delight, imagined and anticipated.

Munni had a problem. As the bus looped and swirled along craggy edges and steep jungle slopes, she feared she might be sick. This on her honeymoon didn't seem dignified. Miss Doolittle would not approve. But Omi had come prepared. He gave his wife a pill – he made her swallow two, to be on the safe side. The effect was immediate. Munni leaned over his shoulder and fell asleep. Omi, one arm around her under her blouse, held her right breast with the bra undone. He took her left hand and buried it inside his fly and put his jacket in his lap. '*The* way to travel,' he said in her ear.

In the seat in front two long-haired intellectual types talked in English. 'India can do it. It can cope.'

'Meaning what?'

'Meaning this, that it always has. Look back at our history. Makes me angry when I look back. But look back. We made allsort blunders, but we survived. Including them British. What did they give us? The railways and a habit to argue, usually with each other, and named it demo-cracy.'

'Balls. You are talking balls, Chopra sahib.'

'My dear chap old fellow and dear boy, you can be as rude as you like. But facts are facts. History. India and Pakistan, natural versus the un. Real versus the un. Can't last. A clash is inevitable. Inn-evitable.'

'You prophesying war?'

'You can say that. Ancestral voices whispering to me.'

'Mr Chopra sahib, it is my duty as a friend to inform you you need treatment – psychiatric treatment. Mrs Chopra too ought to be informed.'

'How does that Ayub – O how I hate the S.O.B. – keep that country down? I'll tell you: by spreading fear, by spreading Indophobia.'

'So?'

'So translate that phobia in the language of reality and what do you get? Just one word: war. But we won't perpare for it, we Indians are not the preparing kind. Trouble is we are too damn trusting and easy going. Even too good, you can say. And remember what Burr-naad Shah said when Gandhi was shot? He said it is dangerous to be too good.'

'Stop worrying, Chopra sahib. Take life as it comes, as Laard Byron said.'

The bus braked, half throwing everybody from their seats. The driver emptied a bucketful of obscenities at a man on the road whose cow he had almost run over. Munni stirred. Her hand in Omi's fly shrank as if it had touched a hot electric iron. But she pressed Omi's hand which fondled her inside her blouse and dozed off again. She did not wake up till Solan, Himachal's second city after Simla.

Solan was the poor man's Simla – small, sparse, drab. People here, Himachalis, looked different. Fair-skinned – cold mountain air pre-serving the original Aryan-ness Indians are so fiercely fond of – and small-boned, they were unlike the sturdy Punjabis down in the plains, also Aryan, but darker and bigger because of the sun, diet and hard work. Yet they were the same – they also stared. At Munni.

Solan jumped to attention as the *de luxe* bus pulled up at a dust patch on a bend in its main bazaar.Khokha (wooden) shops on one side; on the other a lush mountain face. In front of the *de luxe*, a single-storey complex of wood and corrugated iron spread itself above a rocky crevice. 'Taj Mahal Hotel', said a huge painted sign above its door. Underneath it said: *World Famous like its namesake. Seen by Viceroys, Lords and Ladies* in small letters. This duly reminded everyone, not that anyone had forgotten, of the bygone days when Rolls-Royces containing such personages drove past it to and from Simla, the Raj's summer capital. When the rest of India burned, the Viceroy moved his government to the cooler heaven of Simla.

Two more *de luxe* from Simla arrived there at the same time. The three buses emptied simultaneously and quickly. The weary passen-gers, eighty of them, rushed into the Taj Mahal which they knew was not a hotel, only a restaurant – Indians love to call their eating-joints hotels. The hotel, completely empty a minute before, suddenly became full.

35

Being the handsomest and the only just-married couple of three *de luxes*, Omi and Munni were given the *de luxe* table of the Taj. It was at the back with an electrifying view of Solan – a whole mountain sliced into terraces for cultivation.

Omi was tired. No, he was not tired, he was fed up. He wanted this journey to be over, now. He just wanted to be inside that hotel room with Bublashoo, and the stopover was costing him a full half-hour. He looked around at the seventy-eight mutts who seemed grateful for it, and his eyes fell on another very young and 'very tip-top' couple who had just walked in. This couple had nowhere to sit. All the tables were taken, and in India you don't share tables. You never know who you might be sitting next to – someone of a caste lower than yours, even a bhangi (untouchable) who had made good in the new India with its 'silly equality laws' which gave the untouchables 'ten per cent of every bloody thing – jobs, places in universities . . . even seats in parliament'. Eating with such persons is pollution, the real thing. Only a dip in the holy Ganges can cleanse you.

The new arrivals frowned and turned back. Omi didn't care about pollution and dips in the Ganges. He went up to them and invited them to join him and his wife. This proved to be of interest, for the newcomers too were newly married and were from Simla on *their* honeymoon.

'Ah, another honeymoon bunch. Well, well, well,' the man said.

'Well, well, well,' Omi said. He asked where they were going.

'We are doing the honeymoon triangle: Delhi-Agra-Jaipur.'

'What, in all that heat?'

'We'll be in the Ashoka in Delhi, Claridge's in Agra, and the Ram Bagh Palace in Jaipur. All air-conditioned. So is the Cadillac outside.'

The Ashoka of Delhi, the Claridge's of Agra and the Ram Bagh Palace of Jaipur – a one-time palace of the maharajah – were legendary names. And an air-conditioned Cadillac! The man was twenty-five, his wife three years younger. They were dressed like the Khatris, but they looked smarter, much smarter. They had that extra something Omi knew but could not name. *Simla wallahs*. The British Raj had long gone from India, but not from Simla. Simla still had the elegance and style of the good old days when it had glittered with the Viceroy's court.

'Khubchand, Sundarban Khubchand. But call me Bunny. Everybody does. And this is Bunty. We have rather conventional names, I'm afraid,' the man said with a little laugh which sounded friendly. He spoke an English which was music to Omi's ear. But wait till they heard his wife's!

36

'Munni and Aimie Khatri,' Omi said, recalling the Simla Pink name given to him by that rotter, Arun, in a moment of friendship ages ago.

'We'll call her Moni, like my little sister,' Bunny said.

'I like Munni,' Omi said.

'Of course you do. I'm sorry, I'll shut up,' Bunny said to Omi. Then he turned to Munni. 'You know something? You do look just like my little sister. Carbon copy. Utterly amazing. And it is her birthday today. May we call you Moni, just for today?'

'Darling, you can't go around giving people new names,' Bunty said. She too spoke like Bunny. More music.

'Only for today – Moni's birthday. Do you mind, Munni?'

'I don't mind. But where is your sister? In Simla?'

'At school in England. You look *so* like her. You even speak like her, *just* like her. Unbelievable. Did you also go to school in England?'

Munni was going to say no, but Omi didn't give her time. 'Yes, she did,' he answered for her.

'Where, Moni?'

What have you done, you fool? What if she doesn't know the name of a girls' school in England? What if she only knows Eton and Harrow and says she went to one or the other?

'St Paul's Girls' in London,' Munni said.

'Oh really? Daddy went to St Paul's Boys'. He couldn't have to the girls' St Paul's, could he? Ha ha . . .' Bunny laughed.

'I hope you folks are hungry. We are.' Omi tried to steer the talk to safer grounds. But Bunny pressed on.

'When were you there?'

'Till last year.'

'You know, it is quite amazing . . . I mean the likeness! Don't you think so, Bunts?'

'I am starving,' Bunty said.

'Me too. What will you both have, Aimie?'

'But you are our guests, dammit.'

'Nonsense, nonsense. What will you have, Moni? Remember you are my little sister and it is your birthday.'

Munni felt annoyed with herself – she had lied. And the journey hadn't done her any good, it was written all over her face.

'These mountains. Awfully pretty to look at, but dreadful to travel in,' she said.

'Simply dreadful in a bus driven by a sardar-ji. Tell you what, have some soup. And you, Aimie?'

'We have ordered. Besides you are our guests. So?'

37

So Munni had tea and toast and the other three had what Omi had ordered for himself, the local delicacy – mountain goat – which, the menu boasted, was 'shot this morning'.

The stopover lasted exactly half an hour.

'The girls are getting on like a house on fire, don't you think?' Bunny said to Omi. Omi knew why – Miss Doolittle and St Paul's Girls'.

Bunny and Omi talked as if they had known each other all their lives. The Khubchands were obviously very rich. The Khatris were not, but they looked rich and spoke rich. And so, as it happens among the rich, it was friendship at first sight.

'Where would you be staying in Simla, Aimie?'

'Don't know yet.'

'Ah, one of those we'll-find-out-when-we-get-there type chaps. I myself am like that.'

'But you have booked.'

'Bunts did all that.'

'We didn't.'

'Simla is tricky. You are not going to find a decent joint, you know, not at this time of the year. The Season is still roaring.'

'Didn't think about it. Decided on the spur of the moment.'

'Oh dear, oh dear, oh dear.' This looked bad.

The Khatris looked at each other. 'What shall we do, Munnishka? Turn back?' Omi invented another name for his wife – Munnishka. It came just like that.

'Nonsense. You must take Munnishka to Simla. City of delights, city of surprises. And I like that – Munnishka. We'll call our Moni Monishka when she returns. But seriously, what are you folks going to do?'

'Really don't know.'

'Listen. Do the following when you arrive. Take a taxi to the Ritz.'

'Wait a minute – isn't that the most expensive hotel in Simla?'

'And the best. Nothing but the best for my little sister. What do you mean, Aimie?'

'I mean . . .' Omi had been thinking of something middle of the road. But he didn't say it – the Khatris had made a good impression and he wanted to keep things that way.

'Now listen, go straight to the Ritz and ask for Major Mahesh. The chap runs the joint. Tell him I have sent you, and he'll look after you. I'll phone him from here before we leave. You'll like it there, I promise.'

'Awfully nice of you, Bunny.'

'Forget it. Go and have a ball.'

The *de luxes* outside blew their horns. The Taj Mahal began to empty. 'Blast. We were having such fun. Now don't forget what you have to do when you get up there – Major Mahesh, I mean. And lots of *it*, giddy honeymooners. Go destroy Simla with *it*. Promise? And let's meet again.'

'You go do the honeymoon triangle thrice. And wreck it each time with *it*. Promise? We'll meet again.'

Before making his way out, Omi went to the counter and settled the bill. Bunny saw him do that. 'You are rotten, you know!' Bunny shouted by way of farewell.

'Yes, you are,' Munni whispered at the door. 'And a liar to boot. Why did you say I went to school in England?'

'St Paul's, eh? Good thing you knew the name.'

'You got me into it, so I had to say something. But I could have died.'

The mountains after Solan became mightier and the driver madder. He revelled in the death loops he described. He made sure that the no more than six inches remained between his wheels and the chasms thousands of feet deep. And the bus cried *Ah ah!*

'Never. Never,' said a voice in English from behind Omi and Munni each time the bus didn't end where the happy-go-lucky driver wanted it to.

'Never what?' asked Omi, turning around.

'Never again will I sit in a Sikh driver's bus,' said the owner of the voice, an elderly Sikh gentleman. He was turning a rosary and praying.

'If you survive this journey, that is,' said his companion, another elderly Sikh gentleman.

'That is,' echoed Mr Dampat.

Omi laughed. Munni, half asleep on his shoulder, also laughed. Cock-a-doodle-doo! The 'giddy honeymooner' rearranged their hands – his around her on her right breast under her blouse and hers in his fly. Wild fires blazed – in him and her. *Him* put his tongue in *her* ear and whispered: 'Oi, Simla, city of delights, city of surprises. Here we come!'

Him couldn't wait another minute.

'If we survive this journey, that is.' *Her* couldn't either.

Simla was a fairy-tale writ large in white on a wooded mountain. It was a massive mountain of tranquillity. Buildings great and small clung nervously to high cliffs, or were perched precariously atop ledges and footholds in unbelievable greenery at dizzy heights. Below them – nothing for hundreds of feet. Shapely pines and deodars and shrubbery and mammoth boulders huddled along frightening slopes, ready to roll down at the gentlest push into bottomless ravines. The houses were made of wood, some standing on wooden legs, and had roofs of corrugated iron. They looked frail. Munni feared for those who lived in them.

'Will our hotel be like that – tin-roofed? What if there is a storm tonight while we sleep?' Their tin roof would fly away like a paper kite. The woden walls and floors would fall apart. They would slip down a gorge, feet first . . .

'But who is going to sleep tonight?' said the giddy honeymooner.

The bus stop was in Cart Road which circled Simla at its base like a belt around a pot belly. Motor traffic was forbidden beyond that point on this magic mountain, this pleasure city of burra sahibs and their mems of yester-years. Scores of matchbox buses and lorries spilled along the serpentine road. But for the towering heights and bottomless depths and a vast horizon dotted with mountain peaks, it would have looked just like any other bus stop: *Hatt, hatt, hatt* . . . *Garam Chaa haat tea* . . . *Hatt. Hatt. Hatt.* Even the same habits. Among them that of staring.

'Bloody Indians. Same everywhere.'

'Ignore them.'

Omi couldn't ignore those hungry wolves undressing his wife with their eyes. He wanted to get the hell out of there and get into a hotel, any hotel. 'We want a hotel.' He stopped a taxi.

'What kind, sir? Simla is full of them all kinds.' The taxi-driver spoke English.

'Not too expensive. Not too cheap.'

'So you are talking of second-class hotel, sir. All second-class hotel is full. It is groaning. The floorboard is sinking under second-class weight. Only second-class people come to Simla now, present company excluded. Is not like then.' The taxi-driver was obviously a talkative man.

'Not like when?'

'Like when he lived here. The Englishman.'

'Ah. I thought you were talking about God.'

'Sir, the Englishman was more than God. He might have treated us bad, but one thing is he knew how to live. Then Mall Road shone like a mirror – after five p.m. Indian was not allowed on it. Then everybody behaved. Not like now. Now everybody thinks he is God's personal gift to Simla. Where to?'

'Let's try a first-class hotel, then.'

They drove to the Clarke's. It was full. They tried the Grand. It was full. They went to the Cecil. That, too, was full. They inquired at another couple: they were all full. That left the Ritz.

'Ritz, sir, is costly tea-cup. Fifty-sixty rupees minimum. Maximum – who knows? High and higher class. Maharajah of hotels. Embassy ambassadors in ongoing residence.'

'My father, too, was an embassy ambassador once,' Omi joked. He liked this chatterbox.

'Which country, sir?'

'UK, of course.'

'His name was, please? I am well-read and well-written. See paper daily.'

'His name *is* Mr S. L. Khatri.'

'Mr S. L. Khatri. Famous name. I have read and seen photo in newspaper. With Pandit Nehru. And here is the Maharajah of . . .'

'No,' whispered the girl from Dhulkote, that faceless village buried in dust and anonymity, even before she came within breathing distance of the maharajah of hotels. Five storeys of grey stone rose imperially from a massive plinth. Carved wooden balconies jutted out confidently over a deep crack in the mountain face. And there were hundreds of lead-encased windows. The place looked too expensive. And intimidating. 'Please, no.' Munni pulled Omi by his sleeve in the marble arches and columns of the hotel porch.

Omi knew he should listen to his wife. But he couldn't. The moth had found its flame.

A number of turbanned men in white and gold uniforms leaned against the porch walls. They were waiting, just waiting – for someone to come or go. They jumped to attention and saluted the taxi smartly. Two of them held open its doors.

'Boy, luggage,' the driver shouted. Four 'boys' ran to take charge of the boot.

'We want to see Major Mahesh,' Omi said in Hindi to the 'boy' at his door.

'Major himself coming, sir,' replied the 'boy' in English. A man with a dashing military moustache was walking up a palatial corridor. By his side was a pleasantly plump lady in a red sari. 'Major Mahesh,

41

I presume?' Omi said, paying off the taxi. The driver grabbed Omi's hand and shook it enthusiastically.

'May I shake your hand for being the son of our ex-ambassador?'

'Ah, Mr Aimie Khatri, welcome to the Ritz. I was expecting you earlier. Bunny-ji phoned. Major Mahesh. Mrs Mahesh. Come in, come in.'

The Major led the way. They passed by many hotel guests, among them several old Englishmen and women. Their faces were tomato-red. They were beautiful faces. Omi had never seen such beautiful old people. They looked different from old Indian people – they radiated a special kind of glow. The Major and his wife had a word for each one of them.

'Good evening, Mrs Hardy . . . How wonderful you look, Mrs Simpson . . . Hasn't it been a lovely day, Colonel Saunders . . . Hot water okay now, Miss Toohey?' Out of earshot, the Major whispered to the Khatris, 'They came with the hotel. They stayed on because they really love India.'

The Major took them to his office. It was immense, its walls lined with stuffed heads of tigers and stags. Below them were fading photographs of Britishers in full Raj regalia and pictures of bejewelled maharajahs and nawabs. As he looked, Omi now began to sweat. Two voices spoke to him: one said, *Run, Omi son, there is still time*, and Omi nearly ran. The other said, *Keep your cool, you fool*. Omi listened to the second voice.

Munni couldn't keep her cool. She looked how she felt – terrified.

'Oh-ho. Is madame all right?' Major Mahesh said, looking truly worried about madame. He could look truly worried about the Ritz's guests at a moment's notice, or even without it.

'It's the journey. I adore mountains, but not travelling in them in a bus. No, I am fine, thank you,' Munni said.

Munni's English – the Maheshes noticed it. But they gave it no further thought – an ambassador's daughter-in-law, after all. A trifle too young to be married. Must be a love marriage. Rich spoilt brats.

'Would you like to powder your nose?' Mrs Mahesh said.

'No, no, I'm fine. Honestly. What a charming place.'

'You remind me of someone,' Major Mahesh said. 'That actress in that film we saw the other night. With that chap from *The Lady-Killers*.'

'Grace Kelly is *The Swan*,' Mrs Mahesh said. Munni coloured – she had never heard of Grace Kelly, she had never seen an English film. Omi also coloured, with pride. 'Same face, same brittle voice . . . Darling, do take Mrs Khatri to the Powder Room.'

Reluctantly, Munni went with Mrs Mahesh. The moth glanced around at the flame. *Look indifferent, Omi son. You've lived in such splendour all your life, haven't you? So?* So Omi pulled out his Parker and signed the Ritz register with an indifferent flourish. A brief chit-chat followed the ritual. Major Mahesh liked talking; everybody in Simla seemed to. He did most of it. He had worked here since it changed hands 'from white to brown' in '47, when had come Independence 'or whatever you call it'. He was not of the army at all, only the moustache was. Ha ha, what? He had two 'issues'. The boy was at the world-famous Bishop Cotton School and his daughter was at the world-famous Tara Hall.

All along, Omi desperately wanted to ask, *How much is the room?* But he couldn't bring himself to do so. People of class, of whom the Ritz was full, didn't talk about mundane things like money. Not on their honeymoon. They just paid.

The ladies came back, their noses powdered.

'How long would you be staying with us, sir?'

'A week.' At sixty rupees a night, Omi could just about manage, just about.

'Why not stay another week? By then Bunny-ji will be back. Wouldn't that be nice?'

'It would be. But.'

'I understand, sir. But the room is no problem, you understand?'

Omi nodded his head. He understood the Major. The Major nodded back. He understood Mr Khatri. Munni saw. She understood nothing. She remained terrified.

The four came out of the Major's office. It was a film-set all around – polished parquet floors, gilt-edged mirrors, shimmering chandeliers and guests gliding about complete with haloes behind their heads. This also was India, but here nobody stared – the only thing about the place Munni liked.

'*Bonsoir, madame. J'éspère que vous avez passé une bonne journée?*' the Major said to a fat European lady accompanied by another fat European lady. Both of them walked fast, like a pair of ducks in a hurry to get to the pond.

'*Oui, Capitaine. Merci. Merci beaucoup,*' she replied, without slowing down.

'*J'éspère que nous aurons le plaisir de vous voir* tomorow at our *petite soirée, oui?*'

'*Mais oui. Oui, oui, oui. C'est très gentil . . .*'

'The Bulgarian Ambassador's wife,' Major Mahesh said.

'Belgian Ambassador's wife, ji. You have an elephant's memory,' Mrs Mahesh said and left them to take another corridor.

A tip-top Indian couple passed. The man carried a tin of 555 State Express cigarettes. He was jet black. He was Omi's father's age. The woman was fair as Munni, and not a day older. She was smothered in make-up and jewellery. The two studied the Khatris with interest.

'Good evening, First Your Highness.'

'Good evening, Major.'

'I trust Second Your Highness is better.'

'Is and is not. You know these wretched migraines. At her age!'

'I know, sir.' The Major knew all about these wretched migraines. Probably he got them himself, Omi thought. 'I used to get them once.'

The royal couple gave the commoners another glance, as if they were trying to recall where they had met them before.

'H. H. of Kalan Pur. Also on honeymoon. His fifth,' the Major whispered.

They had to wait for the lift, a polished brass cage. It let out a handsome European woman and a handsome boy of Omi's age in red and gold livery.

'*Bonsoir, madame.* Everything to *votre* satisfaction?'

'Good evening, monsieur. My husband – gone horse-riding this afternoon with Bolivia, and is evening now.'

'Not to worry, madame. His Excellency is such a fine horseman.'

'Is not of the horse I worry.'

'Chillean Chargè d'Affaire's madame. They are not married. He went riding with some Bolivian embassy women,' the Major said in the lift.

The Khatris' room was on the fifth floor. It was a room and a half. It had a view for which alone Omi would have paid twice the going rate, even if he knew the going rate – a dream sprawl of a hundred mountain peaks holding up white, grey, black, purple, pink, orange, and flaming red tufts of cotton wool. Omi was grateful to the Major. Truly, truly grateful. 'If all hotel managers were half as charming as you, nobody would want to live at home,' Omi said after the inspection.

The Major acknowledged the compliment with a grin and a nod. He was leaving. 'Ah, I was forgetting. May I have the pleasure of inviting you to our little soirée tomorrow at six p.m.?' he said from the door.

'What's that?'

'A little get-together for a few like-minded guests in our rooms in

44

the annexe. Mrs Majesh and I would love you to come. Sorry for the short notice.' But then the Major had had no more notice, ha ha.

'I think we would like that – we are not doing anything tomorrow. Thank you very much, Captain Mahesh,' said the ambassador's son.

'Major.'

'I beg your pardon. Well, thank you very much, Major Mahesh.'

Major Mahesh grinned and left.

Pink wallpaper with blue and gold flowers. Pink sofa and chairs. Pink dressing-table with lines of gold and blue. Hymnal-red bedcover and pink sheets. Pink and red roses and overhead a thousand diamonds in a crystal chandelier. Dhulkote seemed a long way away.

'Gosh!' Munni said. She started crying. 'Why are you wasting so much money on me?'

'I am not wasting it, you fool. I am investing it.' Omi collected Munni in his arms. He was finally *in* the hotel room, on top of a mountain.

'In what?' Tears, big tears.

'In my future. You are my future . . .' More tears. Big, big tears. Omi's heart broke.

'What's mightier than . . .?' He lifted her up. He laid her down on the hymnal-red bed and removed every stitch of clothing from her in thirty-one seconds flat. He was on his mountain, in his hotel room. He kissed her wet eyes. He sucked her red lips. 'What's mightier than . . .?'

Munni told him. She tore off his clothes. She kissed him on the eyes. She sucked his lips.

'I'm hungry. I wanna eat you. All of you. Shamelessly!'

'Eat me. All of me. Shamelessly!'

Omi ate her. He ate her mouth. He ate her tongue. He ate her chin. He ate her ears. He ate her neck. He ate her nipples, her sides, her navel, her thighs and . . . and, and, and . . . he darted his tongue in what he had begged Lord Krishna for.

'Ohhhhh . . . Gosh!' Munni screamed. The valley resounded with her scream. Munni was finished, in that instant. She started crying again.

'What I done?' Omi stopped.

'You made mincemeat of me. You had the whole night . . .'

'We *have* the whole night.'

The 'old man' gazed at the Milky Way and tossed and turned.

'What worm is eating *them* now?' Paro said to the Milky Way. When her husband didn't sleep, she couldn't either.

Khatri heard but he didn't reply. He stared into the darkness and saw shadows which were not there. He had thought his life's work was completed. Was it? Forces were at work which could destroy it easily. He had seen the ugly head of the she-cobra nestling in the undergrowth at the edge of the garden of his happiness, ready to strike. Once she struck . . .

Khatri tossed and turned.

They had the whole night.

There was a storm. The wind howled outside like a pack of moon-crazed wolves. The tin of all Simla roofs orchestrated a music which echoed deep in the valley. But Munni heard nothing.

'I am tired,' she said at two.

'But we promised not to sleep tonight.' Omi, too, didn't hear a thing. He was too pleased with himself to hear anything.

'I didn't, you did. You threatened not to let me sleep.'

'And I meant it.'

'Good.'

'Then why do you complain?'

'I wasn't complaining. I only said I was tired.'

'That's one luxury you are not allowed. We are paying through the nose for this room. Might even have to sell your jewellery.'

'So?'

'So I want to get some decent mileage out of it.'

The storm outside became desperate. Nine more packs of moon-crazed wolves joined in and the tin orchestra went wild. Still Munni didn't hear a thing.

'I am tired. Aren't you satisfied?' she said at three.

'No. Are you?'

'No.'

At four Munni sat up. 'I am knackered.'

'Too bad.'

'No, it's too good.'

At five life drained out of Munni. 'I have had it. I am sore. I am finished. Kaput.'

'Me too. Total mincemeat.'

'You got your mileage?'

'For the moment.'

The wolves were going away. Omi and Munni fell asleep in a heap. Some time later there was a knock on the door. 'Bed tea, sahib,' came a voice from the door.

46

The heap didn't hear.

'Bed tea, sahib. You ordered.'

The heap stirred. It woke up. Omi went to the door and Munni to the window. She pulled the curtain. The wolves had gone home, and there was light outside. Munni couldn't believe what she saw – nothing. Absolutely nothing. Only a cloud wafting by. They were in the clouds, real tufts of cotton wool. She opened the window. The cloud just drifted in, as if it had been waiting to be let into their world. It made the room cold, very cold.

'Silly girl, you'll catch your death of cold. Shut that bitch window. It's the famous Simla mist,' Omi yelled, shivering.

'I don't care. I want to touch it.'

'Munnishka, my little fool, you'll catch pneumonia.'

'I don't care.' Minni had never seen mist before, not this kind – just like the muslin of the curtain. 'Simla mist, I love you,' she said and the Simla mist spoke back to her in clear-cut Queen's English which sounded just like Miss Doolittle's: '*Munnishka, I love you.*'

Munni heard it. She couldn't believe her ears – a talking cloud?

'What?' Munni said.

'Munnishka, you are a total fool. Do you know that?' Omi said.

'I know that. And I happen to like it.'

'Bed tea, sahib. Bed tea.'

Omi opened the door a few inches and took the tea-tray. 'Boy, bring us breakfast. Lots of it.'

'What, so early-early? Going somewhere, sahib?'

'Yes. On a long journey. Bring it fatta-fatt – at once!'

'Standard breakfast, sahib?'

'Extra standard. Eggs – fried, boiled, poached, scrambled. Six of each, you hear?'

'I hear, sahib. And I'm going and coming. One minute each way.'

'Mr Khatri, you are also a total . . .' Munni couldn't mention the word 'fool' to her husband. It wasn't done. She was a well-brought up Hindu girl. Her husband was her lord and master in this life and all those to come. This was something Miss Doolittle had never discussed with her.

The breakfast came immediately. They brushed their teeth and ate. They ate shamelessly – love-making makes a man ravenous; a woman too. And fell asleep again. Bearers came at eleven to do the room. Omi sent them away. They came an hour and a half later to ask for lunch. Omi said go away. They came back at tea-time and got the same answer. At five, when Omi and Munni finally woke up, they had been in that room for a full twenty-four hours.

'I am starving. I could easily eat something or someone.'

'What do you want to eat?'

'You.'

'What are you waiting for, then?'

Omi ate her again. He wanted to go back to sleep. But Munni said no. 'Think of the bearers and Major What's-his-name . . .' Omi thought of the bearers and Major What's-his-name. '. . . They must be laughing their heads off . . .'

Omi let them laugh their heads off.

'Haven't you forgotten something? You didn't telephone home. You should have last night. Mother must be worried.'

Omi booked a call to Chandigarh. He was told it would take two or three hours; there was 'a traffic jam on the line'.

Yet another knock on the door. This time the bearer had come with a message: 'Sahib, Major sahib reminds you not to forget his so-warri.'

Omi looked to his right. He looked to his left. He was used to smart parties, but this outclassed anything he had ever known. Chunks of Bombay and Hollywood were physically transported here. Every face radiated glamour, every head was set against a halo. *This is it, Omi son. The world you have to make a splash in. The pool of life you have to swim in. Henceforth. Forthwith.*

Munni looked to her right and left. She had read about these things in books Miss Doolittle had lent her. This was the brave new world. It looked beautiful, but it terrified her.

'Your father gives such parties every Saturday, doesn't he? So look natural,' Omi said without moving his lips.

'I can't. I am frightened.'

'Rule number one of life is never look frightened when you are frightened.'

'How?'

'Just look these beautiful people in the face and do what they do when they don't have anything bright to say – grin. Then look at me. It will strengthen you.'

In one clutter of shiny haloes one woman was doing all the talking. No one seemed to be able to get a single word in. She was buxom, bare-shouldered and looked striking in a yellow sari with black and red flowers. She was going on and on like a gramophone: 'Aré yaar this, nahin bhai that. But listen. Listen, listen, listen . . . Oh-ho, you don't understand, Musty . . .' Then her eyes fell on Munni. 'Oh hi! How's married life?'

Munni felt trapped like a rabit. Three-quarters dead, she looked at Omi. It did not strengthen her.

'I say, you do look stunning. Stun-ning. We stopped in Delhi for the day and heard all about it.'

'Who from?' Munni knew nobody in Delhi.

'From your Uncle Georgy. But he said you had gone to Ooty for your HM. Fancy finding you here. Ever such a fibber – Georgy Porgy. Anyway, how's your *innamorato* treating you. What's the name? – Jimmy, no?'

'Lothario,' Omi said.

'O yes? Funny, are we? Is he, darling? Sorry we missed the wedding. Simply couldn't get away. Bombay grabs you by them Bs. Had to stay on for Nargis and Rajji's mahurat. Big budget film, bhai. Big big. They would have killed me like goat-meat had we not. So how's the funny boy treating you? Hope he's not working you double-shift. I can see he is. Just look how he looks at you. Bad bad boy . . .'

'Excuse us,' Omi said and turned Munni around. They found themselves face to face with Major Mahesh. Munni was saved.

'And what did you do today, Aimie? May I call you Aimie? Have you met Major Musty?' Major Mahesh said, pointing to the man the gramophone had been lecturing till she spotted Georgy's niece. Musty was a dashing Sikh of thirty who stood erect like a ramrod, a real army major. 'Aimie and his "Grace Kelly."'

'How do you do?'

'How do you do?'

'But what did you do?'

'Oh, we had a memorable day,' said Omi. 'A hectic day. Went up and down the Mall. Did a spot of shopping. Had lunch at Tiger Tops and saw *The Swan*.'

'Best to be busy when young. Best.' Major Mahesh knew Omi was lying. He knew they hadn't set foot outside their room. So did Mrs Mahesh. She wore an expensive natural-coloured Kashmiri pashmina (shawl) over a black silk sari and red woollen socks under it. She held an ivory cigarette-holder in one hand and a glass of whisky and soda in the other. She inhaled, sipped and beamed a beatific smile at the Lothario. He knew she knew. *But so bloody what?* Omi smiled back, equally beatifically.

'Smile,' he whispered to his wife who was trying to hide behind him.

Haloes merged and mingled with each other. Everybody was

49

friendly. First His Highness was friendlier than the others. He clutched his tin of fifty 555s in one hand and a glass of whisky and soda in the other. He looked bored. But his eyes lit up each time he spoke to Omi, and Omi knew why: *My personal charm. I do have have this effect on people.*

'I say, what a splendid couple you make. Splendid. Splendid.'

'You too, Highness.'

'No, I really mean it. And your young lady. Speaks as if she was born in England. Was she?'

'She had an English nanny. Miss Doolittle.'

'So had I, but my Miss Simpson spent more time ensconsed with Highness my uncle. Hardly ever saw her in the nursery. What?' Highness laughed loudly. People hearing him also laughed and Omi thought it a good idea to do likewise. He stole a glance at Munni. Munni was talking to her contemporary, Second Her Highness. They were busy admiring each other. Munni discovered that the princess was as uncomfortable in that gathering as she was, that she was really from a poor family and had been married off in circumstances she wouldn't talk about. 'One day I left home and was seen. It was written. My karma.'

'You lovely in red.'

'Blue suits you.'

'Love your ear-drops.'

'I adore your necklace. It's cute.'

'I give. You take.'

'Of course not.'

'I have many in the Palace. Many many too too many.'

The four of them hit it off. Highness admired Omi's raw silk tie. Omi thought Highness's cufflinks were the most 'splendid' he had ever seen. At this point Highness put a royal arm around Omi's shoulder. Leaving his princess with Munni, he led him to the Ritz's gardens outside. Outside it was a manicured riot of colour and perfume – roses, dahlias, nasturtiums and sweetpeas, and sweeter this and sweeter that.

'Absolute first-class show, yaar.'

'What show, Highness?'

'What show? Suppose you tell me about it.'

'Tell you what, Highness?'

'Aré, badmash scoundrel, we are in the same boat. Aren't we? So we are related by soul. So no secret-shecret between us. Right?'

'Right. But Highness?'

'Aré, what bloody Highness? Twenty-four hours you remain

ensconsed, may I say, and you say, "But Highness what?" Not fair this, dammit. Not at all. Just tell us how many times?'

'How many times what, Highness?'

'How many times you did it? Eight, nine, ten? More? Fantastic. Atrociously fantastic! But how do you manage, damn you? Can't get the fellow up more than once. That, too, hardly these days. Not without a helping hand.'

Omi was flabbergasted. A king talking like a randy old schoolboy! Omi wanted to roll in the dahlias and laugh and laugh and just die laughing – he didn't mind leaving a young widow behind.

'I know you are young and all that. But ten times? There must be something – a lotion-potion, surely. Yes?'

Suddenly Omi had an idea. It was a fantastic idea, an atrociously fantastic idea. 'Actually, yes, Highness. Now that you've asked.'

'Tell us then, dear boy, and make a contribution to the quality of our life. I am bored. I want an uplift.' Highness laughed – he had cracked a joke.

'A royal uplift you shall have, Highness.'

'Give us a glass then, yaar. Even a thimbleful. I hope you've got lots of it. A friend in need . . .'

'Just enough for two doses.'

'One for us then, tonight. Has to be tonight – we are leaving first thing tomorrow. Back to my worldly duties. I have responsibilities, you know.'

'We are going out for a stroll. I'll bring it to you when we return.'

'That'll be atrociously good. Atrociously.'

'Which floor are you, Highness?'

'The suite next to your room, dammit. How I know of your multiples and your twenty-four-hour ensconsement? Plus what Major Moustachio told me. Watch out. That bugger is a snoop.'

The Khatris did what everybody does in Simla every evening in the Season. They meandered up its famous Mall Road where 'Indian was not allowed after five p.m.' once upon a time when 'everybody behaved'. A giant of a mountain towered on one side of it, on the other gaped a stupendous drop. Houses mushroomed along the drop all the way down to Cart Road. They had beautiful names – The Belvedere, Ganymede, Green Gables, The Glen . . . Lights shone from them, making the long-departed Englishman's fairground a mountain of glowing fireflies, a dream.

'Love you,' Munni said to the dream.

51

'What about me?' Omi said.

They walked to the heart of the city. Omi wanted to see Tiger Tops, *the* restaurant of the old Raj. He had heard all about it, as about other Simla landmarks. T.T. would open your eyes, he had been told. T.T. did. Tiger Tops was vast and packed with people and fun. It was garden green and a great glass wall with Munni's dream smack on it. And it had enormous mirrors and green-painted cane chairs and glass-topped tables and a glistening parquet dance-floor with couples in each other's arms dancing to English tunes played by a fourteen-piece Goan band. A half-naked, half-Indian and half-English beauty sang English songs into a hand-held microphone which looked like an ice-cream cone about to be licked. There was loud clapping when she finished. Then people sent chits of paper with requests, which waiters carried to her on silver trays. Some chits were accompanied by pink two-rupee notes. Others were wrapped in green five-rupee notes. The 'green' requests were sung straightaway with a smile in the direction of their origin.

'This is it,' Omi said every five minutes. 'Absolutely it. Our Pall Mall is going to look just like it.' He knew exactly what he had to do to make the Pall Mall *the* restaurant north of Delhi.

'Where will the money come from?' Munni dared ask.

'From the Old Boy.' Omi pointed at the starlit sky through the great glass wall.

'How?'

'We'll send him a chit wrapped up in a five-rupee note.'

They had the rest of Simla to see. Back at the Mall, expensive-looking shops and more restaurants lined one side. Swarms of people milled around, suited-booted and scented – well-dressed locals and tourists. They were out and about to see and be seen. The place had an air of unreality about it, an air of gay abandon. Simla, the Jewel of the Raj, was a place of pleasure. Its Mall was its main promenade, and this was the time for it. The Mall was drunk with joy. People heaved up and down its gentle slopes, ten thousand of them. Men walked hand in hand or arm in arm. They talked. They laughed. They ogled women.

Omi loved all that. Munni too. But she was uncomfortable – all that ogling. Tired, she stopped by the statue of the patriot Lajpat Rai at Scandal Point. Omi gallantly took the blame for it. 'Hard work, honeymoons,' he said with a honeymoon smile.

'Why is this place called Scandal Point? Extraordinary name.'

'Because a great scandal once took place here. Long ago in the heyday of the Raj, a local maharajah fell in love with the daughter of

52

the English Governor, and vice versa. But Dad wouldn't let her marry him.'

'I know why – because he was already married. These majarajah types!'

'It was not that. It was because he was a wog, an Indian.'

'So?'

'So he came to Simla to plead with the Governor. The Governor told him to get knotted and haul his arse back to his kingdom, or . . . The maharajah did just that. But on his way back he kidnapped the woman at this spot and fled with her to his palace.'

'Good for them. But what did the Governor do?'

'He confiscated the maharajah's palace and booted him out of his kingdom. Made him an outlaw in his own realm.'

'And the poor girl?'

'She was retrieved. But Dad sent her back to Blighty, in disgrace.'

'What a shame.'

'Not the end of the story, though. Six months later the lovers met up in the South of France where they lived in sin happily ever after.'

'That's better.'

'Atrociously better.'

'Are you sure you haven't cooked it all up?'

'Munnishka!'

They walked to the Ridge, a table-top hump above the Mall, where a band resplendent in colourful army uniforms played Raj tunes from a bandstand with a conical roof. More people milled around idly.

'Old Indian disease – idleness. Reason we remain backward.'

'What are you talking about, Mr Khatri junior?'

'I mean look at these buggers. Loafing around as if they have nothing else to do.'

'What about us?' What have we to do?'

'A lot, Mrs Khatri junior. A lot.'

The mammoth Jakhoo mountain shot up from the far end of the Ridge. A larger-than-life statue of Mahatma Gandhi stood at its foot. It was flood-lit. Fifty people ringed it, staring at it in awe. It seemed they expected the old man to speak to them, make a speech or something. Some bowed down to touch his feet. Omi felt embarrassed by the sight. He felt ashamed of being one of them, an Indian. 'Bloody fools!'

They walked on and came to Lakkar Bazaar, the bazaar of wood. Every shop here sold the same thing – locally crafted wooden walking-sticks. Omi bought one with an ivory handle for his father and heard him say, '*You think I'm an old fudd-dudd, then?*' He felt like a proper dandy as he strolled with it like English gentlemen in old movies.

Omi saw a big chemist's shop. He flashed his teeth and stopped. 'One minute,' he said. He left Munni outside and went in.

'A friend of mine is suffering from acute constipation.'

'No problem.'

'But it is a severe case. The fellow hasn't been for a month.'

'No problem at all.' The chemist, a dimunitive Sikh, pulled out a dimunitive bottle from a long row of shelves. 'Supalax, 100 cc. One spoon four times daily. And.'

'Can I have two bottles?'

'Unnecessary. Totally. Two spoons taken straight will make your friend the happiest of men. They will happify him within the hour. G'runtee given.'

'What will a whole bottle do taken in one go?'

'Keep him running for three days minimum.'

'Can I have two bottles, then?'

'You can have three or four or five, if you like. But waste of money.'

'What did you buy?' Munni asked outside.

'Something for a friend in need.'

They found their Highnesses in the Ritz Ballroom. Chandeliers glittered. Silk saris shimmered. Here, also, a Goan band played, and a half-naked, half-Indian half-Englidh woman sang English songs. Chits with pink and green notes were conveyed to her too on silver trays. People drank and smoked and talked and waltzed and fox-trotted and quick-stepped and rumba-ed and samba-ed. First His Highness only drank and smoked a 555; Second Her Highness did neither. She looked miserable. She was glad to see Munni.

As the two girls talked, Omi hissed in his royal friend's ear: 'In our room in ten minutes.'

Omi left Munni with their Highnesses. On his way up he ordered two whiskies, two Coca-Colas, tomato ketchup, salt and pepper, and some spicy titbits to be sent to his room immediately. These things arrived almost at once. Omi emptied the two little bottles into one whisky glass. He added some Coke to both, squirted in ketchup, and sprinkled salt and pepper in both glasses. He was ready. There was a royal knock on the door.

'Ah, Aimie, dear boy. You got it then?'

'It's here, First Your Highness.'

'Jolly good show. This is what I call friendship. Sure mine is as strong as yours?'

The telephone rang: Omi's call had come through. He told his mother all about the beauties of Simla, but his mother wasn't interested in any of that. All she wanted to know was if they were all right. Omi spent several minutes convincing her that they were. Still Paro was not satisfied.

'And what about what the elders said?'

'What did they say?'

'Moderation . . .'

'Oh, Ma!'

When Omi returned to his royal guest, he found the prince grinning mischievously like a schoolboy who had done something he shouldn't have done.

'Highness, pinch your nose with one hand and down the love-potion with the other in one go. *In one go.* Like medicine. Like this.'

They pinched their noses with the left thumb and forefinger and downed their drinks in one go. His bloody concoction did taste awful.

'Sure it'll work, Aimie?'

'As sure as my name is Aimie. Ghastly taste, though. But don't worry – bitterer the pill, sweeter the result.'

'Good lad. You know, only in places like the Ritz one meets people like ourselves. People of quality. People with a heart. Ever since the Congress-wallahs took over, the country has gone to the dogs. Life has lost its L. And what is life with the L removed? You tell me.'

'Highness, you have a point there.'

'So you reckon it is going to be, how should I put it – a night of poetry?'

'Quite a few nights of poetry, I would say. Guarantee provided.'

'Soul-mate and doctor. And so young, yaar.' The prince had that naughty look again as he said that. As if he wanted to say something else, make a confession or something.

In the lift he did.

'Aimie, dear boy, I have been rotten to you,' he whispered.

'How, Highness?'

'Fearing you had mixed a weaker dose for me and a stronger one for yourself, I drank yours.'

Omi's jaw fell. Something happened to the lift. Power failed and it fell *dhrrumm, dhrrumm, dhrrumm* . . . and it kept falling – *dhrrumm, dhrrumm, dhrrumm* . . .

'You mean I drank yours, Highness?'

'I switched the drinks while you were on the phone. A royal prerogative to cheat like that, you can say.'

*

55

The night was long. Two storms raged all through it – one outside the Ritz, the other, the more ferocious, in a Raj-time 'thunderbox' inside it. *This bitch night.* Omi was not amused, he was in agony. He hadn't slept a wink. *When will it end?*

The 'bitch night' showed a sign of ending only when there was a knock on the door – a bearer.

'Bed tea, sahib.'

'Tell him to get lost. But you have a cup,' Omi said to Munni. Munni hadn't slept a wink either. She could do with a cup of tea. She went and took the tray.

'I bring early breakfast, memsahib? Eggs?' the bearer said.

'Tell him to get lost or I'll make an omelette of him.'

The bearer got lost. But an hour later he was back.

'Tell him to piss off.'

Politely, Munni told the waiter to go away.

'But, memsahib, there is parcel and a letter for sahib.'

A parcel and a letter?

It was a one-line letter. Omi read it in one glance. Clutching his stomach, he rolled on the carpet and laughed and cried and cried, tears streaming down his haldi-yellow cheeks. '*It worked wonders, Poetry, poetry all the way. In eternal gratitude.*'

The parcel was not a parcel, only another envelop. In it – the princess's necklace and the prince's cufflinks.

'Well, well, well.' Simla, city of surprises.

But Simla had yet another surprise for Omi – the hotel bill. It came to twice what he had in his pocket.

'Oh-ho! You all right, sir? Your face, it's gone white like – what shall I say? Your stomach again? Shall I send for Dr Lyall?' Major Mahesh was all concern and worry, genuine concern and genuine worry.

'It's the heart this time.'

'My considered opinion is you should stay on another week and rest. By then Bunny-ji will be back and you can thank him personally.'

Thank him for bloody what? For all this humiliation which is spitting me in the eye? What the fuck am I going to do? Sell my wife's jewellery to pay for the honeymoon? I'd better jump off the Jakhoo mountain.

'You are definitely not well enough to travel, Aimie-ji. Suggest you stay on till Bunny-ji returns. Then you can a), get better without any hassle-shassle; b), say thank you to him personally. My humble suggestion.'

'Say thank you to him for what?'

'For this hospitality. You have been his guests. His birthday present to his sister Moni-ji. He wanted it to be a surprise.'

'That was rotten of Bunny.'

'That's our Bunny-ji. He owns this hotel. He owns this mountain, plus half of Simla.'

'But I must pay the bill, of course.' Omi reached for his half a wallet, suddenly looking very anxious to pay.

'Of course not. All you have to do is sign it for my records.'

Omi made a face (to which colour had returned). 'Well, all right.' He looked very reluctant saying that. 'I'll sort out the rotter when I see him.'

The honeymoon over, real life loomed large and largely miserably.

Father's black worm. Omi had to get it out. Otherwise? Otherwise life would lose its L. And what was life without the L?

'Chandigarh, here we come,' Omi said as they arrived at the bus stand. He had a thousand things to do there – Tiger Tops had opened his eyes. Everything depended on one little thing – a stop on the way. *Will it work?* There was nothing like trying. The suitcases posed a problem. But a five-rupee note pressed discreetly into the palm of the driver, another Sikh, with the instructions, 'Sardar-ji, have these looked after in Chandigarh and drop us at Dhalli,' did the trick.

'No problem, bau-ji,' said the driver and dropped them off at Dhalli.

He wondered though, what was the matter with the newly married, suited-booted fool getting off with his bride in the very heart of jungle which that place was. The bride, too, wondered. Left standing in the middle of the jungle, she looked around, wide-eyed, open-mouthed. On the right soared the Kasauli mountain, 'talking with the clouds'. On their left howled silently a bottomless gorge. She didn't know her husband's destination was the bottom of that gorge.

'Why have we got off here, may I ask?'

'I'll tell you later.'

'First it was your stomach. Then your heart. Now I think it is your head,' Munni said. Whom had they married her off to? Till now her view of her husband had been that he was a bright fellow, a whizzkid even, one could say. But now she was not sure. She had been brought up to be a servile, dutiful and obedient wife and never to ask questions. She no longer wanted to remain servile, dutiful and obedient.

'I am too young to be eaten by a tiger. And newly married, returning from my honeymoon. Some honeymoon,' Munni said.

Omi flashed his teeth. He went to the two little liquor shops he knew so well and asked for the local guide.

'Ao-ji, bau-ji. Ao-ji, ao-ji. Long time no see. Long long time.' The shopkeeper recognized the smart Chandigarh babu, an old customer. He snapped shut a Godrej padlock on his steel cashbox, came out of the shop and shouted, 'Billa!'

Billa, a sturdy young man of Omi's age, emerged from a little hut in the foliage. He also recognized Omi. He was taken aback, though, to see a young bride by his side.

'Memsahib, too?' Billa asked. This was jungle, man-eating jungle. Not a place for city dandies; certainly not one for a frail-looking memsahib dressed up for an English-type party. Billa drew exactly the same conclusion about his client as the bus driver had done. Omi saw. Omi knew what was going on in his mind.

'Billa, chal – move. Chal, chal, chal!' Omi said in a stern voice. He knew these rustic types. They had to be spoken to like this, sternly.

'Sure memsahib too?' Billa asked again, waving a hand at the death-gorge and man-eating jungle.

'You heard. Memsahib too,' Omi said.

'But where are we going?' the memsahib asked in memsahib English.

'Memsahib, you just follow the sahib and guide,' Omi said in English.

'What if a tiger ate us up?'

'Tigers don't eat people in love. Do you love me?'

'No.'

'Then prepare to meet your tiger.'

They made their way downhill. They went single file along a steep, serpentine footpath, an endless arcade of thorny bushes, twisted trees and boulders and rocks. After half an hour, they came clear of it. At the bottom of the valley the jumpy blue water of the Jhajjar smiled through the last of the foliage. Two mud huts stood in that awesome setting, humbly, meekly. It was the home of his father's guru, the toothless Baba Gokul Swami.

'I am touched,' Baba Gokul Swami said. He looked it. He blessed the young couple. 'But what brings you to this old man in this jungle, Om?'

'To seek your blessings, guru maharaj. To introduce my wife.'

The guru was touched more to hear that. He blessed them more. He called upon Lord Krishna and Lord Rama to shower non-stop happiness on them. 'Enjoy the spring of your life, flower by flower. Do. The garden of your life is green.'

'But things are not looking rosy, guru-ji. Not at all. Nettles threatening the garden. What is needed is some divine weedkiller.'

The guru gave them tulsi (holy water) and a patasa, a sweet wafer. 'Mother well? Father well?'

'As well as they can be under the circumstances.'

'You say that with a creased brow, Om Parkash. I see a cloud in your thoughts. Come sit at my feet and tell.'

Omi and Munni sat down at the guru's feet. In a language which would have melted a heart made of stone, Omi told him of his father's black worm. 'Not yet forty-five and . . . Mother is mortally sick. She can't sleep a wink, nor eat a morsel of food. She rightly feels living widowhood is being curelly thrust upon her. She is ordering white kurtas and white saris. This can't be allowed to happen. What do we do, guru maharaj?'

'Let us pray and the answer will come to us.'

Omi was not very good at praying – all his praying in the past had been done during exams and just before the results were published. But this was hardly the sort of thing one said to one's guru. He joined his hands on his chest like the guru and followed him. Baba Gokul plucked a handful of flowers from the bushes around the huts and ambled along to the river, Omi following his every move. One by one the old man dropped the flowers in the crystal-clear water and watched them spring along the swift stream. He rinsed his mouth and washed his face and muttered: 'Om . . . Om . . . Om . . .'

Omi threw flowers in the water one by one like the guru. He rinsed his mouth and washed his face and mumbled his own name: 'Om . . . Om . . . Om . . .'

Munni watched this 'men only' ritual, her hands folded on her chest.

'I am ready,' the guru said after what seemed a very long time, seven and a half minutes precisely.

'Ready for what, maharaj?'

'Why to come with you, Om Parkash.'

This was what Omi had come here for. But he had not dared hope it would be so easy *as all this*.

'Now you understand?' Omi said to Munni in English. He did not know that Baba Gokul Swami had a doctorate in philosophy from Oxford. Or was it Cambridge?

59

'Of course the poor girl does, Om Parkash. What on earth do you mean? Come to think of it, I think you are a jolly lucky man indeed,' the bald, aged gentleman with hardly a tooth in his mouth said in English which was as impeccable as Om Parkash's wife's.

'Ma, our miracle,' Omi shouted from the rickshaw a hundred yards from their house in the shopping centre of Sector 23.

Paro stood on the balcony. She had been standing there off and on for most of the day in spite of the sun, scanning the street. She had made her husband telephone Simla. Reluctantly – Khatri hated the telephone – Khatri had phoned the Ritz and had been told that Mr and Mrs Aimie Khatri had left Simla in the morning. They should have been home in the afternoon – it was a five-hour journey – and it was evening now. They had had an accident. Paro knew. She wept inside.

'Ma, Ma. I've brought our miracle,' Omi shouted again as their rickshaw came a little nearer.

'What miracle? Where is it?' Paro yelled back, now happy as ever.

The miracle was in another rickshaw twenty yards behind Omi and Munni's. It took Paro five whole seconds to understand. Then she jumped.

'I say, come and see,' she yelled to her husband.

Khatri sat inside the room on a charpoy in front of the revolving electric fan. He was reading the *Milap* and shaking his left leg. This shaking of the leg was a sign that he, too, was worried. He abandoned the paper – Paro was given to yelling, but this shout of hers had been special, meaning something either very bad or very good – and ran out. He craned and looked. He was overwhelmed by what he saw – your gurus didn't come to your brick house in towns on buses and rickshaws, you went on foot to their mud huts in man-eating jungles in distant valleys forlorn. His heart turned to pulp and his eyes became moist.

'Guru maharaj. Guru maharaj . . .' He said, folding his hands. He and his wife raced downstairs to greet the family guru.

Omi and Munni helped the old gentleman off the rickshaw. The old gentleman enjoyed being helped, especially by Munni. He put one arm around her shoulder and the other around Paro's – like Mahatma Gandhi who always walked flanked by two young ladies and called them his 'walking sticks' – and allowed himself to be led into the back yard. The back yard was dug up and another old man

60

limped about there with gardening tools. This was the new gardener, Mali, from Dhulkote.

'Welcome, guru maharaj. What an honour. This son of mine – springing such surprises on his old man,' Khatri said as he bent down to touch his guru's feet.

'Which old man? You, Shadi Lal? Pluck this sordid thought of being an old man from your mind as you would a thorn from your flesh,' the guru said.

Baba Gokul Swami stayed overnight. His evening was taken over by the people. As the word spread that the Baba was here, they came from all the 27 Sectors of the capital and sat at his feet. Khatri, the host, too. Eventually, the people left, but Khatri remained at his guru's feet. Together they talked till midnight. Next morning Khatri seemed a different man. He looked his old self again. The miracle had happened.

It was time for the morning business, the daily ablutions. Omi foolishly pointed a finger to the pride of the place, but the old man shook his head. Omi's father quickly filled up two brass gadvas with water. He handed one to his guru and led him to the open countryside behind Sector 23.

'One thing I never understood about England and the English – how could they do it like George V on his throne?' Baba Gokul said on the way.

A game of cricket was in progress in a field they passed. Baba Gokul stopped to watch. It was a contest between ill-matched teams, for the batsmen were flaying the bowlers mercilessly.

'Yet one of them is not bad. He's got a good line and length . . .' Baba Gokul said.

'What, guru maharaj?' Khatri said. He did not know a bat from a pad.

'But why is he bowling round the wicket? Let's watch a couple of overs, Shadi Lal.'

Gadva in hand, the two men watched the dust-faced teenagers and young men scamper about on a dusty white pitch.

'Give the ball a little air and try bowling over the wicket, young man,' Baba Gokul shouted at the bowler with the line and length when he came back to bowl again.

The 'young man' was sixteen years old and four times that number of inches in height. He didn't like being told by a rustic old man how to bowl. He knew where he was going with the gadva, and why. He looked over his shoulder sourly and nearly told him to mind his own business, shitting. He bowled as before – round the wicket – and was

61

lobbed over the unmarked boundary for a mighty six. He hung his head on his chest and walked back to his mark to wait for the ball.

'Take an old man's advice, young man,' Baba Gokul shouted again.

Ball in hand, the harassed-looking youngster paused. He was desperate for a wicket; his team was desperate for a wicket. *Try what the old man says. What can you lose?* He bowled over the wicket, giving the ball more air. The result was a mouthwatering delivery – slower and almost half volley. The butcher of a batsman sprang forward to make chutney of it. He swung his bat lustily. But he was deceived by the change in speed and flight of the ball: he missed, and was clean bowled. The fielders and their supporters, a score of dusty-faced schoolboys, erupted in an earth-shattering roar. They clapped and clapped – not for the bowler, but for the old man with the brass gadva on his way to answer nature's call. The old man grinned.

'So you've played cricket, guru maharaj?'

'Captained my university the year they sank the *Emden*.'

Back home after the bath and breakfast, the Khatris gathered around their guru. The guru blessed them all. He singled out his main disciple.

'Now your family is growing, so are your responsibilities.'

'How true,' said the disciple's wife.

'You have many things to do yet. A bigger house to build. Other buildings too . . .'

'How true. How true,' said the disciple's wife.

'You have much else to do beside,' the guru went on, looking from his disciple to the disciple's wife.

'*They* have,' said the disciple's wife to his guru.

'And look after Munni – she's frail. Now take me to the bus stop.'

Paro, drenched in delight, washed her hair with dehi (yoghurt). She had it oiled and combed by Munni. Then she did something which made her son whistle – she put Munni's lipstick on her lips and wore a star-spangled sari that showed four inches of her belly. Omi knew his father had had it.

'Ma, don't forget Father isn't a spring chicken any more.'

'Madam, why have you blackened your eyes like a bumble bee? Why have you reddened your cheeks like a Kashmiri apple? And that lipstick? Got a yaar-shaar coming?' Khatri said.

They were in their private little temple in the house. They sat cross-legged in front of a wooden statue of Lord Krishna and several colour prints of various other gods and goddesses. Paro threw her head back and gave him a sidelong glance with teasing eyelashes. Khatri thought she looked just like the girl he had married all those years ago. Something in his heart stirred. Something stirred somewhere else as well. This made his cheeks burn a little.

'Anari (novice). Pushing forty-five and still the anari of yesterday,' Paro whispered. They should be praying, not talking about *such* things.

'Don't forget that – me pushing forty-five.' Khatri slapped her on her round bottom. He let his hand remain on that delicious roundness.

'And your son says you are not a spring chicken any more. Ram! Ram! Ram! In God's temple no less,' Paro pinched her earlobes. 'What if he walked in with your daughter-in-law? I would be shamed to my grave.'

But Omi and Munni had gone with Mali to the nurseries to buy grass, seeds, saplings and flowers for their new garden, and wouldn't be back for a couple of hours. After that they were going to the lake for the newly-weds' tour of the capital's beauty spot. Paro knew it. She knew he knew she knew.

Electricity was in the temple's scented air. A current of it raced from where Khatri's hand was to the middle of his sutthan leggings, causing an uprising there. Khatri did what he used to do in his 'spring chicken' days: he took his wife's hand and guided it to the afflicted area.

'Hai, my mother. Badmash wicked man. Just look at it! Things droop with age, but this . . .! Look at the size of it! Put a mule to shame.'

'Well, well, well. God made us both in the same sitting, according to some.'

'Where are your "Higher Things" now?'

'Just where your hand is. My guru said I had a lot to do yet.'

'But not in God's house? Not in broad daylight?'

'I am not committing a robbery.' Khatri put his hand through her sari. 'Not looting anyone. Though I want to.'

'You do?'

Paro was ready to be looted. She turned and faced Khatri. She did something she hadn't done for a long time and took his breath away. She kissed him on the mouth. She kissed him like the Punjabi jatni (peasant) that she was – hard and long.

'Shameless hussy. What on earth has happened to you? What are

63

you doing?' Khatri had forgotten when last she had kissed him like that.

Paro stopped. 'What do you think?'

'Don't stop, woman. But who put this idea in your head?'

'Your guru.'

'*Our* guru.'

'So?'

So it was all right.

Munni made a friend, Asha. Asha was also newly married. She had a pleasant face but she was very dark of complexion – almost black, like Rano, the Khatris' untouchable girl. She had been married for six months and seventeen days. She lived a hundred yards away in a row of two-storey, low-salaried 'hundred two-hundred rupee' houses. These houses were made of red bricks. They were identical. On the first floor they had a white painted cement screen with holes which seemed to have been made by poking a finger.

Asha was twenty, her husband, Janak Bahal, much older – thirty-five. He was an Overseer in the PWD and was often away 'on tour', sometimes for weeks. Janak had four unmarried sisters – Banti, Manti, Santi and Bhagwanti. Their father was a swaragwasi (heaven-dweller). Their mother, Damyanti, was very much of this world. She had a loud voice which could be heard across any two Sectors. She didn't like anything or anyone, especially Sector 23 and the people who lived there. She led the house with 'cane and whip', it was said.

Asha spent a good deal of her time at the first-floor window, looking out. For this she was known in the neighbourhood as Kali Jharokhe Wallih – Black Lady of the Window. From a distance she looked like a bird in a cage – the pock-marked white screen around the window made it look uncannily like a cage. People said that all she needed was a couple of wings.

'And . . .'

People said other things about the Bahals as well. Why were the sisters still unmarried? Unmarried ageing females were a slur on a Hindu family. Why had Janak himself married so late? Why was his wife always hanging around the window? Did she have a secret lover she was waiting for? Why wasn't she ever allowed out of the house? And was she being beaten up? People could swear they often heard muffled cries of a night from the Bahal house. If so, by whom? By Janak? But Janak was away a lot on PWD business. Besides, he was so gentle and so meek that people called him 'his sisters' sister' behind his back.

Munni found herself sitting next to Asha one evening in the temple on what was her first visit there. During a lull in the priestly proceedings, the two girls got talking.

'How beautiful you are.'

'You too.'

'No, I am black. I am ugly.'

They told each other where they were from.

'Patiala?' Munni said. She was impressed. Patiala meant maharajahs. It meant palaces and princesses and jewels and matchless glamour.

'Dhulkote?' Asha said. Dhulkote meant nothing. Asha, like everybody else, had never heard of it.

Munni felt ashamed of herself. She wished she too came from somewhere with a name, with some claim to fame. But as the two girls conversed, Munni realized that she was doing most of the talking. Asha hardly opened her mouth, and whenever she did, she looked elsewhere, not at Munni. Even when she chose to look at Munni, Munni felt she wasn't looking at her at all. She was looking through her, as if Munni was like the perforated screen of her window. This was off-putting. But Munni decided to ignore it, for she felt drawn to Asha. There was something sad, even tragic about her which made Munni want to befriend her.

When the service finished and the congregation stood up to go home, Asha surprised Munni by speaking to her without prompting.

'You're going home? You want to?'

'Yes, I do. Don't you?'

Asha changed the subject. 'I am matric pass. And you?' she said. Matric was high school.

'I did FA,' Munni said. FA was two years of college after school.

'Do you have a radio?'

'Yes, we do. Don't you?'

'No.'

'Come home with me. We'll listen to Radio Ceylon.'

'Asha,' came a shout from the crowd, and Asha hurried away to join the Bahal women without saying another word to Munni.

'Strange girl, Asha,' Munni said to Omi at home.

'They all are, the Bahal bitches. Poor sod, "his sisters' sister".'

What nobody could understand was why a maharajah should have given Omi such valuable gifts – real jewels.

'Must be pagal (mad). They all are – crazy and round the bend.'

'Remember the old Maharajah of Patiala? Married 365 – one for each day of the year. Which man needs 365 wives? Can't manage the one. Drives me round the crazy bend, she does.'

'These maharajahs and mawabs!' There were a thousand and one stories about them.

'It can't be that this one liked our Omi so much. There must be more to it than is meeting the eye.'

'Nobody does nothing for nothing. Not even a pagal rajah.'

'Omi, you must have done something for him.'

'Yes, I did him a favour.'

'What favour?'

Omi thought for a moment. 'He had a deficiency, a serious lisp. I cured it.'

'My housewallah has one too,' said Subhadra. Her husband, Thatha, the ironmonger, had a terrible stammer. 'Cure him, and take anything you like from the shop.'

'I don't like being paid in iron, Auntie Subhadra. Only in jewels.'

'But how do you know your maharajah was a real one? Or these so-called jewels, for that matter?'

'He was as real as these jewels.'

'Or as fake. If only looks could speak.'

'Jeweller Heeralal should speak. Somebody, go fetch jeweller Heeralal.'

Somebody went and fetched jeweller Heeralal.

'Heeralal-ji, take a good professional look and give us their royal value,' people said, pointing to the royal jewels.

Heeralal was about Khatri's age. He had long protruding teeth which always had bits of his last meal stuck between them. Omi did not like people with long protruding teeth. He could tell what the jeweller had had for lunch today – black dhal. Reluctantly, he let him take the necklace and cufflinks in his hands, which were long with long fingernails.

'Hum,' Heeralal said, twisting the gems around professionally. His face turned sour as he did it. Omi didn't like that at all. *The sister fucker is jealous*. Omi detested people like that, the jealous types with sour faces.

'Well, then, Heeralal-ji?' the people said.

Heeralal was deciding what to say or what not to say. It made him scratch the middle of his spotless white muslin dhoti, his balls to be precise.

'Better be disappointed today than tomorrow, Om Parkash,' he said at last with a consoling grin.

'Meaning what, Heeralal-ji?' Omi said.

'Meaning this – you don't mind my being frank? – meaning that this is rubbish. Imitations. These rajahs and maharajahs, notorious for this sort of thing. They wear imitation and keep the real thing in cellars under the ground. Old royal trick. I am telling you – I am a jeweller.'

You are a bastard. A bastard with a sour face! Ma chod, mother-layer. Beti-chod, daughter-taker. You should be stood facing a brick wall and . . . and peed on!

Omi was heart-broken. He was heart-broken for Munni. He wished he had never set his eyes on the *other* bastard, the *other* mother-fucker, First His Highness of Kalan Pur or wherever it was that that Major What's-his-name had said he was from.

'Don't worry. It's nothing – I really don't care much for jewellery,' Munni whispered. 'Anyway, easy come easy go.'

Next morning – it was a hot lazy-hazy morning – the phone rang downstairs in the office. Bawa made a dash for it. Bawa was crazy about the telephone. He loved 'talking English' into it.

Omi's Simla Pink friend Arun wanted Omi. It was 'very import-ant'. Bawa worshipped Arun. Arun was handsome, 'Bombay actor'. What was more, he was generous with tips. Nothing about him was ever less than 'very important'.

'One minute, Arun bau,' Bawa said and cranked the 'Up-Down' phone which connected the house upstairs with the office downstairs. 'Up-Down' phone was a personal invention of the America-returned architect, Bassi, the designer of the Pall Mall.

It rang and rang. 'Not getting voice, Arun bau.'

'Run up and get him down, Bawa.'

'That . . .' That Bawa dared not do. Omi bau had a very short temper.

'Then let the thing ring. Flush the bugger out.'

Bawa let the thing ring. Barri bibi, Paro, wasn't at home. But Bawa knew Omi bau and choti bibi were. Five and a half minutes later, Bawa spoke to Arun on the real phone.

'All I am getting is un-get, sir,' Bawa said in the telephonists' English.

'What on earth is he doing?'

'Guess what, Arun bau. You have imagination even if not wife.'

'Yes, I have imagination. But what I can't understand is why he never told us he was getting married . . .'

67

Some time later another of Omi's friends, Kapoor, dropped by.

'Not available,' Bawa said.

'What is he up to?'

'Guess what, Kapoor bau?'

'What, at 11 a.m.?'

'A.m. p.m., same guess-what story now, Kapoor bau. Daily.'

An hour later Shambhu and Tully looked in on their way to the fashionable neighbouring Sector 22. They were going there for a look-and-see (girls) stroll. They wanted their newly and secretly married friend to come along for old times' sake. They also wanted to peel his skin off for getting married without inviting them, without telling them.

'Omi bau told no one. He invited no one,' Bawa said.

'But why not? Man doesn't get married daily.'

'He did not want to get married.'

'And now?'

'Now he is totally un-get doing guess what. What marriage does to man, Shambhu bau!'

Omi remained un-get to his old friends, doing guess what. For weeks.

Munni had never seen an English film. The prospect of going to one filled her with excitement. It showed in everything she did. She dropped things. She walked into things. 'My tummy is giggling, ji,' she said.

The Kiran in Sector 22 was showing 'an all-time great' – *Witness for the Prosecution*. It only showed 'all-time great' English movies, one every Sunday morning. This morning, like every Sunday morning, there would be an all-time rush to see it. Omi gave Bawa five rupees and fifty paisa for two tickets in the expensive upstairs gallery seats. The film started at eleven, and Omi sent him at nine to stand in the queue. The ticket office opened at half-past nine. By this time the queue was at least a furlong in length, winding its way around the belly and back of the cinema. By ten all the tickets were gone. Then they started changing hands on the black market, sometimes five, six, or more times their face value.

Bawa was one of the first in the queue. He was back with the tickets minutes after the ticket office opened.

'Crowded?' Omi said.

'Teeming. Could have bought twenty tickets and sold them on the black market and made myself a lumpsum. Not kidding, Omi bau.'

'Why didn't you?'

'Because I am think-after fool Indian. But honest. The place is teeming, teeming.'

'Good.' This meant *everybody* would be there, all the Simla Pinks. It was the first time Omi was taking his wife out in public. He wanted all his friends to see her. And hear her English. He wanted them all to get a kick in their backsides.

'Munnishka, dress to devastate,' Omi said.

'Devastate who?' Munni only dressed for Omi, no one else.

'Them Simla Pinks.'

Munni wore a blue and gold silk sari and a shocking-pink choli. She put rouge on her cheeks, surma on her eyes and Yardley lipstick on her lips. And she wore all her gold.

'How do I look?' she said.

They stood in front of the tall mirror of the dressing-table, Munni in front, Omi right behind her, both putting finishing touches to themselves.

'Not bad.'

'No, seriously. How do I look?'

'Box-office hit. Bumper crop. Cream top. Boompty-boom. Moon and star.'

'You lie.'

'And mouth-watering.'

'I don't believe you. Prove it.'

Omi proved it. He pulled her closer, right against him, pressing her into him. Munni felt the proof. Hard proof.

'QED?'

'Disgraceful.'

'I want a kiss.'

'No. We'll be late for *Witness for What?*'

'Forget the *Witness for What* and give us a little kiss.'

'No.' Munni was dressed to see that which she had never seen before – an English film. And she was going to see it.

A chase began. Omi, as he was – QED and leaping out of himself – jumped over the palang and went for Munni. Munni yelled and ran around, cutting corners. Then, just as suddenly, Omi stopped.

'Postpone. Postpone,' he said. He, too, was dying to go. He wanted to impart that kick to his friends and foes. He had worked it out carefully. They would arrive at half-past ten, and he would lord it over the place for the next half-hour till the film began.

'I am feeling funny,' Munni said at quarter past ten when Bawa announced their rickshaw was outside.

'Nonsense. You look fine to me.'

'But I feel funny.'

'You'll be all right once you are there. Believe me, why don't you?'

Munni believed him. But she was not feeling right. 'I don't think I should go,' she said as they took leave of their parents and their dog, Dabbu – Dabbu also wanted to go with them.

'Nonsense. You look perfectly okay to me.'

Khatri stepped in. 'She is not all right. She looks pale, can't you see?'

Omi felt annoyed. His wife – he would do with her whatever he wanted! Why was his father interfering?

'Honestly, I don't think I should go,' Munni said.

'Nonsense. You are coming.'

'I said no.' Khatri raised his voice. 'You are not to take her. Go yourself if you must. The girl is not well. Are you blind or something?'

'But, Father, I've got the tickets.'

'Go by yourself. Sell the other ticket or give it someone. Take Kapoor with you. The loafer is outside.' Khatri had seen Kapoor coming.

Omi was dashed – to pieces. He no longer wanted to go. But he had those bloody tickets, and Kapoor was yelling: 'Omiii . . . *Omiii!*'

The Kiran floated on a sea of cheerful, glad-to-be-here, Old Spice and Afghan Snow faces. People had come to see and to be seen – what life was about, no? Tidal waves of humanity heaved to and fro. The cinema had 750 seats. Today, like every Sunday, four times that number had turned up. Those who couldn't get in would go back home and no hard feelings – the next all-time great was only seven days away. They would get in then.

All Omi's Simla Pink friends were there, complete with their haloes which moved with them as they circulated. They had come in their imported cars, wearing imported jeans and shirts, issuing unobtainable foreign smells. None of them had seen their Aimie since the swine had 'done a bunk on them and got married'. First there were hugs; then came accusations – where was she? Why was the son of a bitch keeping her out of sight?

'Got married like a chor (thief).'

'Didn't invite even *me.*'

'Mean bastard.'

'Possessive bugger.'

'Uxorious shit.'

70

Omi tried to explain. But who would listen to him? A volley of laughter met his pleas and the bantering continued Punjabi-style, which is to say, relentlessly. Finally and mercifully, the bell went. A tidal wave pushed Omi towards the cinema's grand staircase. There he found himself crushed against someone. Even without turning to see who it was he knew. It was the perfume – only one person in all Chandigarh, perhaps in the whole world, wore it: Titli, his ex-flame. Omi's heart stopped beating.

'Didn't you get my message?'

'What message?'

'The message I gave to your waiter, Bawa.'

'You came to the Pall Mall? Why?'

'Why do you think? Think, bastard.'

'What?' Omi decided to go deaf temporarily.

'You walked out on me. What is she like?'

'What?'

'You gone deaf? What is she like?'

'Out of this world. Best in the world.' *This bitch of a crowd that pushed me into you. Or was it an ambush?*

'Bastard!'

The bitch of a crowd heaved and pushed and pulled. Omi was lucky – he was separated from Titli. *Phew!* His heart started to beat again. In the upstairs foyer, he looked around for Kapoor but Kapoor, too, had got separated from him. *Son of a dog. Never there when needed.* And Kapoor had never been needed more than today – to protect him.

How glad Omi felt that Munni hadn't come after all. What if Titli had said all that in front of her? Or something much worse – spilled some juicy titbits of their affair. Titli was capable of saying or doing anything. Horrendous thought.

The bitch. What does she want from me now? Beautiful? All right. And a general's daughter, and rich, and the rest. But what a cunt! How could he have fallen for her?

Omi had an answer: *It was in a different life. A pre-life.*

Usually, the Simla Pinks entered the hall after the others, the common folk, the 'ordinaries' as they called them. It was one way of proclaiming the difference between the two (and also of drawing attention to themselves). But today everybody was shoved in at the same time in that mad rush. Omi held back, waiting for that fool. He waited two, three, four, five . . . minutes and gave up. The hall was pitch dark when he went in, and the trailer of next Sunday's 'all-time

71

great' was nearly over. Omi was furious with Kapoor for making him miss it. *Son of an owl. Couldn't he wait? And who paid for the bloody tickets?*

Omi fumbled his way through the black ink of the cinema darkness, looking for his row. He waded to his seat across outstretched legs, stumbling every two yards. *Fucking Indians! First thing they do when they see a cinema seat is to stretch out like nawabs. Or reptiles.*

As he sat down in his seat finally, he turned to his left to tell Kapoor what he thought of him. His heart stopped beating again. Completely, this time. For lo and behold, who sat there? Titli. She had swapped tickets with the traitor! Omi shot up, as though stung by a wasp. But Titli took hold of his hand and pulled him down in the upholstered velvet. 'Sit,' she hissed.

'No,' Omi hissed back. He was getting out.

'Sit, sit, sit!'

'No!'

'I have missed you, you bastard! And you went ahead and got married.'

'Quiet,' people hissed from behind.

'Yes. I did.'

'You love her then?'

'Yes. To distraction.'

'You walked out on me.'

'I didn't! You ran off with that army prick, what's-his-name.'

'No one walks out on me, no one . . .'

'*Shut up!*' came a shout from behind.

They shut up. Titli kept his hand in hers. As the film proper got going, she did what she always used to do in the sweet darkness of a cinema – she put her hand on his thighs and began caressing them. It used to set him ablaze – if they had had a row, it would be instantly forgotten. It set him ablaze now. Only divine intervention could save him. Or the sudden apperance of Baba Gokul Swami. Or his father.

Minutes passed. The film rolled on.

'Let's go somewhere. I have the MG outside. We'll drive to the River Jhajjar at Pinjore and make love. Me on top.' Titli brushed her cheeks with his and whispered in his ear, touching it lustily with her tongue.

O divine intervention, intervene! Omi thought of Munni with a thousand jabs in his heart. He thought of their love-making – beautiful, pure, sacred. But how much more exciting it was with this experienced bitch who sat next to him, her hand where it was! Omi wanted to run, but he was transfixed.

72

Titli knew she had him where she wanted him. She took his hand and placed it inside her blouse. 'Like it? You love it.'

'I hate you.'

'Tell me something to surprise me.'

Omi surprised her. He stood up and started walking away.

'*Sit down, man. What the hell?*' shouted someone in English from the row behind. Just at that moment a torch was flashed in Omi's face. Behind it were two men – an usher and . . .

'Bawa!'

'Omi bau, you must come home fatta-fatt. Lala-ji . . .'

Omi didn't have to be told more. He knew. His father had had an accident. His father was dead. It was not divine intervention, it was divine retribution.

Total darkness. They hurried out.

'What, Bawa? What's happened to Father?'

'Nothing has happened to Lala-ji. He sent me to fetch you at once. It's choti bibi . . .'

Munnishka, if anything happens to you, I'll take a capsule of cyanide and be cremated with you.

Parked outside was a *phitt-phitti* auto-cycle Quickly. Omi knew who it belonged to – Doctoress Pritam Kaur, MBBS. Omi didn't know her personally, but he knew where her shop was – next to Corbusier Gem Palace in Sector 22.

Doctoress Pritam Kaur was with Munni and Paro in the bridal suite. With them were Mrs Devan Chand, Chatkarni and Panditani, the wife of Pandit Ram Narayan of the temple. Khatri was in the other room with Dr Devan Chand and Pandit Ram Narayan. Mali and Seva Singh sat on their haunches outside the door. Omi went and joined the men. He looked at his father who merely nodded his head, acknowledging his arrival – or was he accusing him for having gone in the first place?

'Don't worry too much, Om Parkash. These things happen in their condition,' Pandit Ram Narayan said.

'True. True,' muttered Dr Devan Chand, the homeopath.

'Most trying period in a woman's life,' the Pandit said.

'True. True,' Dr Devan Chand said.

What the hell are you talking about? Dumbfounded, Omi looked at his father again. Khatri said nothing. The bridal-suite door opened. Doctoress Pritam Kaur came and joined the men, wearing a stethoscope around her neck like a necklace. She selected Omi and spoke to him in English. 'Whatever it is, one thing is – she is not *that*.'

73

What the fuck?

Khatri, who didn't know a word of English, seemed to have understood. 'What? Isn't she . . .?'

'No, she is not. Was not and is not. Definitely not. Definitely.'

'I too thought the same,' the homeopath said.

'Then . . .?' Khatri said.

'She fell and fainted and is concussed, that's all.'

'Will she be all right now?' Khatri asked.

'Fit as a fiddle in one two hours. Young girl.'

'How much, Doctoress sahiba?'

'It's all right, Lala-ji. We are neighbours. But it is five rupees – Sunday home visit. Week day home visit is three.'

'Neighbours should keep their slates clean,' Khatri said and paid her. 'Any dwaii (medicine) etc?'

'No medicine needed, only vitamins and iron. Om-ji, you come with me.'

Om-ji went with Doctoress Pritam Kaur. Or rather twenty yards behind her *phitt-phitti* on his Raleigh. Fifteen minutes later he was back with the vitamins and iron.

'I am awfully sorry I spoiled your fun,' Munni said when they were finally alone.

'That stupid bitch of a film. I wish I had never got the tickets. But what happened?'

'I was feeling funny. I slipped on the bathroom floor. I don't know what happened then.'

'I know what. This bloody fool, this son of a whore, this son of a pimp went away from you . . .'

'Have you gone mad – talking like that of Mother and Father?'

Omi had gone mad. He punched the door so hard that his fist went through the wood. He kicked a chair so violently that its leg broke and he cried out in agony and hopped around on one foot.

'Bawa, go bring me a bicycle chain,' Omi yelled. He wanted to lash himself like he had seen Muslims do at Moharram as a little boy back in Peshawar. He punched and kicked whatever there was.

'What are you doing, fool boy? Breaking the house down?' Paro shouted.

'Yes!'

74

BOOK TWO

Easy come easy go. God, stuff, that. Allah talking. Krishna up to His old tricks – giving with the left hand and taking it back with the right. Fine. But why did that royal shit play the dirty on me? – he seemed friendly enough, atrociously friendly. Omi burned. Without telling Munni, he made a little parcel of the necklace and the links and put a note in: '*First Your Highness, what a third-rate thing to do. Stuff them.*'

Omi didn't sign the note but put his address outside the parcel boldly. He did not know where Kalan Pur was, but there couldn't be two princely states with the same name. He wrote:

First His Highness
The Maharajah of Kalan Pur
The Royal Palace
Kalan Pur

On his way to the post office, Omi ran into Heeralal, of all people. Heeralal's lips parted in what was a smile calculated to hurt. Those teeth! Heeralal had eaten yellow dhal for lunch today. Omi would like to smash the lot of them. He hoped never to see that son of a bitch again.

But he did.

Exactly two weeks later, he came face to face with him early one morning in Bajwara food market. Their eyes met and Heeralal produced that toothy grin again, this time to kill. For his age the man looked stupid, thought Omi. He decided to ignore him and just walk past.

'I say, Om Parkash, you don't talk to your neighbours any more? Twice I see you in two weeks and not one hello-shello. What is that, yaar? What have we done to you?' Heeralal said in English.

This made Omi think. *What has Heeralal done to you? Nothing really. Only given his professional opinion. Come on, Omi son, be fair. Not the bastard's fault if the jewels were fake.* He felt a little ashamed of himself, and smiled broadly to camouflage his shame.

'What are you doing here so early, Heeralal-ji? Never seen you in the market before,' he said in English.

77

'My birthday today . . .' Heeralal's 'birthday' sounded like 'burp-day'. 'Madam said, "Your burpday, ji. Let's celebrate – go buy a couple of chickens and invite somebody," she said. I said why incur unnecessary expense? But would she listen? "Go, go, go. A man is not forty-five twice. Go buy a chicken-shicken and other things. We are celebtating," she said. Women, they love celebtating.'

'Well, happy birthday, Heeralal-ji,' Omi said and turned. His father was somewhere in the crowded market. He wanted to go and find him.

'Anyway, don't despair, Omi Parkash. Nor be angry with me – think of me as your own father . . .' Heeralal said 'father' as 'farter'. 'I was only joking the other day, you know.'

Omi felt the earth slip from under his feet.

'Joking about what, Heeralal-ji?'

'About them royal jewels. They are *real*. Worth two thousand, minimum. So friends now? Don't say no – I'm like a farter to you.' Heeralal showed his teeth again in an utterly charming smile and offered his hand for a shake.

Quickly, Omi took Heeralal's hand in his. But instead of shaking it in the spirit in which it was offered, Omi did what he had learnt to do at school in Camp Baldev Nagar to people he wanted to kill. He pulled him forward, tripped him over his left foot in the same movement, and kicked his head.

'Happy burpday, dear farter. Eat the dust of Bajwara.'

Heeralal ate the dust of Bajwara. Omi kicked him right and left and centre. He kicked him where it would hurt him most, between his thighs. Heeralal howled.

The market came to a standstill and watched the contest with unabashed revelry. There was no contest. Heeralal howled in pain. Omi yelled, 'Happy burpday, dear farter . . . Happy burpday!' And the spectators formed an eight-deep circle around them to watch the tamasha (fun).

Finally, a few shopkeepers whose business was being ruined by this otherwise delectable diversion leapt into the circle and held Omi.

'What are you doing to the poor man?'

'Giving him birthday present.'

'Want to kill him?'

'Yes. Totally. The bastard cost me thousands.'

'How, Omi? What I did?'

Omi lashed out again. He wanted to finish the job *once and for all*. But his father appeared on the scene and he stopped.

'Khatri, your son is a mad dog. You should be ashamed of yourself,' Heeralal yelled, getting up slowly and dusting himself.

Khatri was ashamed. He dragged his son away.

'Khatri, I am going to have him thrown in jail for unprovoked assault and battery. I have one hundred and one witnesses. I am sitting on a mountain of gold. I am a lakhpati, a hundred-thousander. I can hire the best criminal lawyer. You should be very ashamed of yourself.'

Khatri was very ashamed. He would have kicked his son were he not a married man now – Omi had made him look a fool in the eyes of the world.

'Finished. The tamasha is finished,' Khatri shouted at the crowd of spectators, waving them away angrily. But Heeralal was not finished. In a belated surge of anger and strength, he pierced his way through the crowd, and instead of going for the son, he went for the father. 'Khatri, I am going to bust your gaand (backside).'

'Yes, bust his gaand,' said some spectators who didn't like the way Khatri had waved them away, as if they were dirt – they were only watching, for Godsake.

'Khatri, I am going to beat you into the shape of a peacock's arse!'

Heeralal took a lunge at Khatri. He missed. At the second go he knocked Khatri's elegant Peshawari turban off his head. This was unfortunate. A turban is a man's izzat (self-respect) – be he Hindu, Muslim or Sikh. Knocking it off his head is a serious matter; dangerous, too. You shouldn't expect to get away with it lightly.

Khatri's izzat in the dust, his nostrils flared and his mouth frothed. So did his son's. But a number of men grabbed hold of Omi to prevent him from going to his father's rescue.

Khatri needed no rescuing. Nor any help. Two respectable grown-up men, two pillars of the local society, rolling in the dust like two street urchins! Bajwara was electrified with joy. Bajwara went bonkers with delight. Bajwara wanted to see blood – the famous restaurateur's or the rich jeweller's, it didn't care. Bets were drawn. Most people went for the tall and long-boned sunara (gold-wallah). They had underestimated the small-limbed ex-halwai (sweet-vendor). The sunara was a vaishya (trader) by caste; Khatri was a kashatriya (warrior). His kashatriya temper ignited, roar after roar thundered from his throat. Bejwara watched. His son watched.

But before any blood was actually spilled, the warrior and the trader were separated.

'Khatri, I am going to sue you. Have you both thrown inside. I know every judge in the High Court . . .'

79

'Barking dog!'

'. . . I am a lakhpati, I can buy and sell ten of you. I am going to ruin you. I am going to smoke burn you . . .'

'Farting mouth!'

Khatri turned away. He had licked Heeralal the hundred-thousander, and licked him thoroughly.

Their clothes in shreds, father and son went home in smouldering silence. A certain feeling of pride throbbed in Khatri's limbs, but he was also full of shame. The son, however, experienced only one of these conflicting feelings. He was proud of his father. Very proud.

Omi's mother was less so. In fact she was mortified.

'Hai, hai, hai, my mother,' she wailed. 'Munni, our men! What did we do in our past life to deserve them in this one?'

'Ma, listen . . .' Omi pleaded.

'First it was the loafer son brawling in the streets of the Camp. Now it is the father too . . .'

'Ma, listen!'

'Listen to what? Listen to who? To shirtless, shameless street-fighters? Godless goondas who have buried my name in mud? O Munni, what face can I show the neighbourhood now?'

'Shut up, woman. What could I do? The man came at me just like that. The man is not man, he is a mad dog. We live in a neighbourhood of mad dogs,' Khatri said.

'Then change the neighbourhood.'

'How do you change the neighbourhood?'

Paro had been thinking about it ever since the miracle. She had been waiting for the right moment. The moment was here. 'Build another house, as the guru said. In the North End. By the lake near the High Court.'

'High Court? Heeralal says he knows every judge in it. He says he is going to sue me.'

'He is a barking dog. Now go and bath again and change your clothes, both of you. Do not humiliate me before my daughter-in-law. Vidya will be here soon, and what will she say?'

While Khatri went to change, Omi disappeared into the bathroom. Once there he did what he always did while bathing – he sang. Today he sang loudly a song from India's *Gone With The Wind*, *Mughal-é-Azam* – 'Vive, vive l'amour '. He did not hear Bawa come and say, 'Omi bau, the dakia (postman) brought this for you.'

80

It was a little packet. Bawa left it on the new dressing-table in the bridal suite.

Ten minutes later Omi emerged from the bath, a towel around his waist and still singing 'Vive, vive l'amour'. He sprinted to the bridal suite. Munni was already there, putting the clothes of his she had just ironed on the palang with sculptured legs and feet.

'You smell nice.'

'You smell nicer.'

'Nice bath? How do you feel?'

'Hungry. Like the tiger you didn't meet in the jungle. Now come to claim his lamb.' Omi roared and sprung on Munni. He wanted to eat her – gobble gobble – she looked so edible. Like a child with immense eyes and silken skin and silken cheeks and snow-white teeth and honey mouth.

'You are always hungry. Hungry after lunch. Hungry after dinner. Hungry at midnight.'

'But mornings are the best, especially after a nice bath. Especially after you have beaten a ma chod into the shape of a peacock's arse on his burpday.'

'Is that how you beat him?'

'Yep. I kicked his head in. I flattened his balls out. And I sang "Happy burpday dear farter" . . .'

'You are awful. But why did you? I don't understand.'

Omi almost told her what Heeralal had done but for once good sense prevailed. It stopped him just short of breaking her heart, too. Done was done. It couldn't be undone. Besides, if he told her she would think he was a fool, which Omi knew he was, in any case. *Best not to think about it, Omi son. Just change the subject. Do what you are dying to do.*

Omi changed the subject. He roared like a tiger and tore off Munni's clothes and began to eat bits of her. Munni liked being eaten up. She wanted to be eaten in chunks. She wanted to be eaten whole. Omi ate her whole. Spread under him, enveloped by him, she looked in to his eyes and for no reason at all she started crying. Huge tears – whenever she cried it was always quick huge tears, like a baby's – slid down the sides of her cheeks, wetting the corners of her ears.

'Munnishka! Why do you cry?'

'I don't know.'

'Stop it.'

'I can't.'

'If you don't the tiger will . . .'

The tiger roared again. Munni now laughed. The tiger roared and roared. Munni laughed and cried. They had forgotten that the door was made of thin pine wood only from the Kasauli mountain. Paro, passing by, heard. She yelled at her husband. 'Your son is going to kill her. Do you hear?'

'So what do you want me to do? Send him to a castration camp?'

'Your guru said we had to look after her. She is weak.'

'He didn't mean *that*, you village idiot. My God, what did *I* do in my past life to be surrounded by idiots?'

Omi heard his mother. Moderation: the word flashed across his mind like a major announcement on the Cinemascope screen of the Kiran cinema. He chose to ignore it and went on roaring and chasing the lamb around the room. It was then his eyes fell on the little packet on the dressing-table. The parcel he had sent to the royal joker had come back.

Return to Sender
Wrongly Addressed

The tiger went mad. He grabbed the parcel and lifted the lamb in his arms and ran to the door, yelling: 'Ma, Ma!'

'Shouldn't we get dressed first?'

'Good thing you thought of it. You think of everything. Reason I am so loco over you.'

'Omiii . . . Munniii . . .' Paro shouted from the balcony. She was watching Mali in the back yard. He had brought some new flowers to plant, and wanted Munni bibi and Omi bau to see them.' 'Omiii! Munniii!'

Omi and Munni didn't hear. There was a good reason for that. They were wrestling in their room, so they were deaf to all sounds except their own groans and grunts.

This wrestling was a new sport. The young couple had taken to it like monkeys to trees and played it every afternoon. As usual, they had joined up their two palangs to make a large square arena. On it they tugged and pulled each other by the limb in all sorts of locks and tackles and tangles, huffing and puffing and roaring. Overhead the ceiling fan whirred. They didn't need the fan now – the weather was turning – but they left it on to cool their bodies.

They both thought they were rather good at it. Secretly Omi thought he was better. But today was not his day. Today Munni had him in the classical bottle-neck: Omi was caught between her thighs, with only his head popped out. He had tried every trick in the book, but the daughter of the stationmaster of Dhulkote had her comely legs around his neck like unbendable steel rails. Omi huffed and puffed and begged for mercy. But this was serious business: no mercy-shercy here.

A knock on the closed door gave Omi a breather. Bawa. 'Omi bau, Arun on the phone. Says it's urgent.'

'Tell him I am un-get.'

'Omi bau says he's un-get,' Bawa went back and said to Arun.

'What is he doing?'

'Guess what, Arun bau?'

A minute later Bawa was back at the door. 'Omi bau, it's Kapoor this time. He's downstairs. Says if you don't go down he'll come up.'

'Tell him I'm not at home and that if he dares come up I'll shoot his arse off.'

These diversions were to prove detrimental to Munni. Her attention was distracted, her concentration lapsed. Omi, the opportunist, took advantage. Fortunes changed and Munni found herself where Omi had been just a moment ago – in the bottle-neck. Now she huffed and puffed and begged for mercy.

'Mercy? What mercy? No mercy-shercy here,' the opportunist said and beamed a smile of satisfaction at the whirring fan overhead. The fan whirred a smile back like a co-conspirator.

Just then Munni remembered something – she had to write to her mother. If she didn't write now she would miss the last post, and tomorrow was Saturday. Her mother wouldn't have heard from her for another week.

'What's the time?' Munni asked. She always took her wristwatch off before a wrestling bout; Omi kept his on.

'It's the same time it was yesterday at this time,' Omi said.

'If you don't tell me, I won't talk to you again.'

'If you won't talk to me again I'll put the lid on you.' The lid was the last word. Only a king's ransom or something more precious than that got one out of it.

'Will you talk to me or not? Yes or no? Quick quick.'

'No.'

'Right. You stay where you are then. Like this, forever.' Omi put the lid on.

On another day Munni wouldn't have minded. She would have fought, and sooner or later things would have changed as they often do in wrestling matches, and she would have got him in her favourite spread-eagle, another lethal hold. She loved having him spread-eagle – and, boy, she was good at it. But today Munni had to write to her mother.

83

'Ma, Ma . . .' She applied to her mother-in-law for help.

Paro heard. She came. She saw. 'What are you doing to her, fool boy?'

'She won't talk to me, Ma.'

'Let go of her neck. You'll break it,' Paro said and turned back, slamming the door behind her. She knew these newly weds' games – anything which kept their bodies glued to each other.

'Let me go.'

'Not unless you promise to talk to me twenty-four hours daily. Minimum. To love me twenty-four hours daily. Minimum.'

'All right, I will.'

'You will what?'

'I will talk to you.'

'And?'

'And love you.'

'Twenty-four hours daily minimum.'

'Twenty-four hours daily minimum. Awful English, that, for one with a BA.'

Omi relinquished his hold and let her go.

'It hurts, you know?'

'Where?'

'On my neck.'

Omi kissed her neck. 'Better?'

'No. It hurts on my shoulder too.'

Omi pulled her kamiz down and kissed her between her shoulders. 'Where else does it hurt?'

'Here.' Munni held her hand on her left breast.

Omi pulled her shirt down all the way. Now he would go bananas. He went bananas – cock-a-doodle-doo. He cupped her breasts in his hands and fondled them. Then he kissd them. Tenderly. He sucked her nipples, ready to leave this world.

'It's getting worse and worse. Now my lips hurt. They are burning.'

Omi extinguished the fire with a kiss. This proved fatal. They got bogged down. This was how their wrestling maches ended every day.

'Look what you made me do? Another week and I haven't written to Mother. I am not going to talk to you.'

'You want to be in the bottle-neck again?'

'Yes.' Munni moved fast and put him spread-eagle. 'Now what are you going to do?'

Omi did nothing. He was happy as a skunk.'

*

The thing Omi loved most in the world was a kiss. The thing Munni loved most in the world was a kiss. Depending on time and place, they could kiss for hours. And there lay the snag – there was never enough time and they were seldom left alone.

First it was Omi's work. Then there were the people.

But whenever there was time and they were alone, they fell into each others' arms. If they happened to be behind closed doors in their room, only a fire or an earthquake – or a shout from his father – could unglue their lips from each other's. Omi could ignore his mother's, 'Bass bass, enough enough,' but not his father's, 'Oi, where are you?'

They could talk and kiss at the same time. 'My favourite kiss is a long-distance one,' Omi delcared during one, without detaching his lips from Munni's. He loved the taste of her mouth.

'What will you give for it?' Munni said, without stopping kissing either.

'My shirt. My trousers. My everything.'

'Is it love or is it lust?'

'Lust,' Omi said and received a jab in the ribs for saying it. 'I love my wife lustily.'

'For how long will you love me like this.'

'Before during and after forever.'

'Time will tell.'

Time only worsened matters. Khatri had to develop a new habit he was not particularly fond of – of coughing loudly while coming up the stairs when he knew Paro was not in the house and they were. He didn't know where he would find them wrapped around each other so shamelessly – on the landing, in the doorway, on the floor: 'Oblivious! He feared that his son and his daughter-in-law would disgrace themselves, and him, publicly one day by being 'too oblivious' of the world and what it stood for.

Days passed. They were happy days. Then one Sunday morning Omi's BA exam results were published in *The Tribune*. Omi was dreading this day, the day he would be humiliated before his wife whom he loved lustily and would before during and after forever. He knew he was going to fail.

But Omi passed – if only just. He needed 180 marks to pass. He got 184. Khatri was over the moon; Paro was over the moon and beyond it – their son was a *BA Pass* now. Omi was not quite where his parents were. He was visibly worried.

'The newspaper made a mistake,' he stuck his tongue in Munni's ear and whispered. 'Instead of 148, *The Tribune* has printed 184.'

'Smile, yaar. BA proper and all that now,' Dr Devan Chand said. He came over with the Doctorani and their five kid-kiddies to congratulate the Khatris. 'Best wedding present university giving you. So smile. Say cheese.'

'You have luck, Paro. Much luck,' the Doctorani said. Inside her breast she lamanted her own lack of it – her daughter eloping and disappearing from the face of this earth. She, too, should have sat the BA exam, and who knew?

'Laddus, I want to send laddus. Five hundred and one laddus,' Paro said. On auspicious occasions one sent laddus to friends and acquaintances. The laddu was a popular sweet, the size of a golf-ball.

'Send a thousand and one, if you want,' Khatri said, slapping her on her bottom.

The laddus being dispatched and delivered, the Lakhpatis turned up to say mubarak (congratulations), the whole tribe of them, all dressed up as if they were going to a wedding or coming from one. Of their seven children, the only girl, Billi, aged fifteen, was the eldest. The youngest son was Puppie, aged six. In between were Truman, Attlee, Churchill, Bandar and Langur.

'Mother-laying hell,' Omi yelled when he saw two rickshaws pull up at their back door and spill out the Lakhpati litter, pushing, shoving and tripping each other. Omi loved the Lakhpati boys' names. He loved the boys, too. 'They are so bloody awful that they are lovable,' he said to Munni.

Munni didn't mind the boys, it was their sister. She didn't know what to make of her. Billi had blue, wild-cat eyes – which was why she was called Billi – and they were always on Omi. She had a pretty but sullen face and she never stopped pouting when they came to the Khatris', more so since Munni's arrival there. She was in the First Year of Omi's ex-college, the *world-famous* Chandigarh College.

'She fancies you,' Munni had said to Omi the first time she had met her. She fancies you,' Munni said again that Sunday morning when Omi became a proper BA Pass. The Lakhpati invasion was well under way – doors slammed noisily, Munni's dowry furniture creaked threateningly, and things from shelves fell and broke as Truman, Attlee, Churchill, Bundar, Langur, etc. hid and fought under beds and up and down the stairs and in and out of cupboards. And Lakhpatni said not a thing, not a world of apology to Paro nor one of warning to her 'monkey brigade' (Munni's name for them).

Omi had never noticed Billi. He had always thought she was ten or twelve and still at school, which she had been till three months ago. He loved playing with her brothers – the common hide-and-seek or the kingly *hathi ghora palki, jai jai Hanuman ki* – games the boys loved, games which kept them away from crockery and other breakables. He jerked his head from left to right at his wife's observation, saying, 'Balls,' and decided to join the boys in *hathi ghora palki*.

'Hathi or ghora?' Omi shouted at the boys, meaning elephant or horse?

'Hathi, hathi,' yelled the boys with one voice.

Omi instantly became an elephant, and Puppie, Langur, Bandar and Churchill came and sat on the howdah, Omi's back, urging him on by kicking his sides.

'*Hathi ghora palki* . . .' they screamed.

'*Jai jai Hanuman ki* . . .' yelled Truman and Attlee, Attlee scampering about the place like Hanuman, the monkey god, whose victory was being celebrated by this kingly procession.

'I can't believe it!' Munni said and went away to join the others.

'Come, come, Munni beta,' Lakhpati said.

Lakphati, the millionaire, was a 'gem of a man' as the world called him. He had a schoolboy's face. He wore a Gandhi cap and the Congress khadi (homespun) – being very rich he had to look poor – and could easily pass as a Congress leader. He owned cars but avoided being seen in them, hence the rickshaws. They got him noticed more.

'I have a suggestion, Lala-ji,' Lakhpati said to Khatri. 'Our Omi is full BA today, so let's celebrate. Let's go for a picnic. Let's go to Pinjore Gardens, and why not?'

'Valuable suggestion. Valuable,' said Dr Devan Chand. Whenever Dr Devan Chand liked a suggestion he pronounced it 'valuable'.

'Why not?' Lakhpatni said, looking at Paro.

'Why not?' Paro said.

Just then Vidya and her husband, Bhajjan, arrived.

'Why not?' Vidya said. She was also over the moon that her one and only nephew had made it.

'Munni, get ready, then, girl. And tell that fool boy to stop playing the donkey,' Paro said.

'Ma, can I ask Asha to come as well? Poor girl is all alone. Her husband is away on a PWD tour,' Munni said.

'Asha Bahal?' Paro and the Doctorani said. 'Damyanti won't let her go.'

'Why not?'

'Go ask if you have the time to waste. And see.'

87

Munni stood up to go. Billi stood up with her. The two went.

'Nice to be married, no?' Billi said in the street, in English.

'Yes, it is,' Munni said.

'I don't want to get married young. I want to live.'

'So do I. I live.'

'No, I mean really live.'

'I assure you I do really live. And I love it.'

'You don't understand, with all your English and all. You are from Dhulkote. This is Chandigarh. You don't understand.'

Asha's mother-in-law, Damyanti, opened the door to the girls. 'She is ill. And asleep,' she said, shutting the door.

'But there Asha is,' the Doctorani said when the girls came back, pointing to the Bahal house a hundred yards away. Kali Jharokhe Wallih, the Black Lady of the Window, stood there like a bird in a cage, looking out. 'All she needs is a couple of wings. And.'

It happened to be the day of Goddess Chandi, after whom the Punjab's new capital was named.

Chandi had been Goddess in residence since the twelfth century at her temple just before Pinjore. Chandi had legendary medicinal attributes. She healed disorders for which there was no known remedy. Her speciality was 'mad' women, those who had inexplicable fits during 'duty to husband' or after miscarriage. But that was not all about her: she had an open fist as well – she 'gave'. She granted all kinds of wishes if they were 'reasonable'.

It being Goddess Chandi's day, thousands of people from near and far with thousands of wishes flocked to her temple. Hordes of them decided to combine divine business with a bit of worldly fun. After all it was a glory of a day – a high cloud, a whispering breeze, the River Jhajjar calling . . . and those wooded hills! All too good to be true. After acquainting Goddess with what troubled their hearts, they turned up at the Pinjore Gardens just up the road.

The ex-royal gardens had been spruced up for the occasion. All the fountains were turned on full blast, sprouting sky-high jets of multi-coloured water. The lawns were trimmed to perfection. Every flower bloomed. Elephants, camels, horses and peacocks sculpted out of dense green bushes looked on. Pinjore smiled, breathing out an air of festivity. Thousands of people walked up and down the seven terraces of the famous gardens, each terrace celebrating a stage of the human life as it strove to achieve union with the Maker of all things great and small. To go with the mood of the day and the place, people wore a lot of colour. There were brightly coloured saris and scarves and turbans as far as the eye could see.

'Just like the Baisakhi fair,' Munni said. Baisakhi was an ancient fertility event which took place around waters annually – riversides, lakes, canals – when everybody wore loud colours.

Omi loved fairs and festive crowds. But not this one. He detested it – firstly, because it stared, and secondly because he wanted to be alone with his wife. He could hear the river at the bottom of the valley calling the two of them by name. He could swear he heard it over and above the cocktail of the fair noises, shouting: 'Omiii, Munniii . . . Omiii, Munniiii!'

The picnic goodies eaten, Omi couldn't take it any more. 'Let's go somewhere,' he whispered in Munni's ear.

'I like it here.'

'This shitty place? We are lovers, dammit. This is no place for lovers. Come, let's go.'

'Where?'

'Down the Lovers' Valley, to the river.'

'What for?'

'Guess what?'

'Oh, that.' Munni blushed. 'Mother won't let us go.'

'Leave Mother to me,' Omi said and turned to his mother. 'Ma, I'm taking Munnishka for a walk by the river.'

'Don't go too far in the jungle. It is infested with tigers like a headful of lice.

'Huh,' Omi said with a laugh – tiger hadn't been seen in these parts for decades. The burra sahib on his way to his summer capital, Simla, had dealt with him summarily and turned him into rugs and wall hangings and his memsahibs' coats and handbags. 'Huh,' Omi said again, and brought his wife to the yellow-painted gates through which once royalty had passed – first the Moguls and subsequently the Patialas. Before they stepped across to the common ground outside, a voice from behind stopped them: 'I am coming too.'

Billi.

'Billi, there are big big tigers where we are going. They will eat you up, *ghrrumm ghrrumm ghrrumm*,' Omi said.

'What about Munni? Won't they eat her too?'

'Maybe they will.'

'Then I don't mind.'

'But I do, Billi. I hate to see little girls being eaten alive by silly tigers with teeth this long.'

'I am not a little girl, okay?' Billi said, petulantly. She stamped her

89

feet on the red Mogul stone of the pavement and stormed away. She went and stood under an elegant palm tree, watching them. Omi and Munni chose to ignore her behaviour. They walked on.

Out on the highway, the Simla Road, they came face to face with a khud (ravine). It was not a ferocious khud, like those Munni had almost landed at the bottom of from her honeymoon bus, but it was a khud all right. Omi took her hand and led her down a narrow path, custom-made for this sort of excursion – there was the thorny bush, the twisted tree, the scarred rock, the hunchback boulder, the wound-inflicted mountain-face . . . the lot.

'Place for lovers indeed . . .' Munni said, casting a sweeping glance at the lonely grandeur. The khud, not very deep, was still majestic, and the river at its base, mostly dry, was vast. Threaded by slim lines of mercury and heaped with boulder, rock and pebble, it stretched to the hills on the other side of the valley. And it was silent.

'Where are they, then?'

'Today the place is reserved.'

'Do we have another guru down there?'

Munni had said 'we' instead of 'you'. It meant more than she had said. Omi liked it. He flashed his teeth in answer.

'Anywhere particular we are going to?'

'Somewhere very particular.'

They were going to a beauty spot on the river – an historic spot for Omi. It had changed his life. How? Omi had been seen there by his father (he never found out how) throwing stones in the water abjectly while his Simla Pink friends lay in each others arms in the tall grass, and Elvis Presley was '*all shook up*' on a His Master's Voice gramophone. Being seen there like that by his old man had resulted in something Omi was then wildly opposed to – his marriage.

'I am dressed for a walk in the Mogul Gardens of Pinjore, not for a mountaineering expedition,' Munni said. Her shoes were thin-soled chappals.

'A full-blooded Punjabi wench of eighteen – what is a little mountain for her? And by the way, did I tell you how you look?'

'How do I look?' Munni said, glancing back as if they were being followed by a wild animal, startled, wide-eyed. Even frightened.

'Box-office!'

'You've brought me here to tell me that?'

'Yes. But why do you keep looking back? Don't fear, Mr O. P. Khatri junior is here. He will beat the shit out of the tiger. He'll do a Heeralal on him.'

They were exactly half-way down the wild path. Not far below in the valley the river made a lapping sound – a thirsty dog drinking. Around them the trees swayed noisily in the breeze, and unseen birds chirped somewhere. They walked another hundred yards and stopped. The next ten minutes they spent doing what they liked most in the world. A hundred yards from the river they stopped again, glued to each other. They would have spent the rest of the day there in that state if a silly mountain goat hadn't rammed into them as if it were being chased by a tiger. They pulled themselves together and walked on downhill. Suddenly, the foliage ended, and it was all river and the tall green grass.

Their previous kissing record was one hour and forty-one minutes non-stop, by Omi's Romer (Munni's dowry) watch. Omi was determined to break it. This was the place, this the day. The river water leapt naughtily. The breeze rustled through the foliage musically. And there arrived, only God knew how and where from, the Munni birds. 'Munni. Munni. Munni . . .' sang one. 'Love you. Love you . . .' sang the other.

'Well, I'm blowed,' Munni said and rolled with Omi in the tall grass. Their lips relocated upon each other, their two bodies became one. Their hearts began to beat with one beat and they breathed with one breath. Nearby, in the tall grass, a pair of wild eyes watched them hungrily. Nearby, the trees went on swaying with a leafy rhythm, the Munni birds went on singing and the Jhajjar went on flowing.

It grew cool. The Munni birds went away. The sun dipped over the far hills. It became dark.

Still Omi and Munni remained where they were, as they were, now fast asleep.

Then there was a mighty roar. The bushes at the edge of the grassy clearing parted abruptly and there appeared a huge presence. Instinctively, Munni knew!

She screamed: 'Tiger . . . tiger!'

'Tiger . . . tiger!' screamed someone else simultaneously.

Billi!

Billi, hiding in the tall grass twenty feet away, leapt in the air.

The warden had shut the Pinjore Gardens. People had gone home. Only the picnic party from Chandigarh hung on there in uneasy silence – even Truman, Churchill, Attlee, Bandar and Langur had shut up. They sat on a low stone wall by the roadside, waiting. They held their breath and scanned the khud in to which Omi and Munni

91

had disappeared. They were all thinking the same thing. Billi: where was she? Had she gone with them, after them? Why?

The question scalded the entrails of Lakhpati and his wife. It tied up the Lakhpati 'family honour' in knots.

Time ticked by painfully but surely. Half an hour became an hour, then two and three . . . Darkness fell. There lingered no longer any doubt in anybody's mind that something dreadful had happened. The Lakhpatis were ominously quiet. Khatri fumed, sighing audibly every other minute. Paro swore time and again that she had heard cries from the bottom of the gorge. She started weeping.

'Tiger,' she sobbed and looked sideways at Lakhpatni.

Lakhpatni said nothing. Nor did she sob like Paro. Thoughts far worse than her daughter's being eaten alive by a tiger haunted her. They were unthinkable thoughts that made her want to throw herself into a deep well. She preferred the tiger to any one of them.

Khatri spat on the roadside. He wished he could lay his hands on his son. In the old days, in his son's pre-marriage days, Khatri would have pulled all the hair from his scalp before asking any questions and let his Peshawari sandal do the talking. But the boy had a wife now. And the son of a bitch was a BA Pass today. Khatri had a fairly good idea where Omi had taken his wife – where once he had seen him throwing pebbles in the river. But why the Lakhpati girl, too? And why were they taking so long to get back? Khatri scratched the middle of his sutthan and spat on the road again.

When more waiting became unbearable, Khatri and Lakhpati rose from the stone wall, and Dr Devan Chand and Bhajjan rose with them. They walked up to Pinjore's scruffy little bazaar nearby. The shops were shut. But people were helpful.

'Tiger? Only comes when very very hungry. Sometimes he takes a goat, sometimes a calf. But humans? No. Not till tonight.'

They hired half a dozen local hands. They armed themselves with knives and lathis and dandas, and made their way down the ravine now looking quite dangerous. The local men had brought dholuks (drums) and empty tin canisters to make a noise.

'Courage and caution,' they said to the smart city-wallahs. They beat the canisters to frighten the tiger away.

'Omiii . . . Omiii!' shouted all ten of them in one voice. Back came the echo from the dark valley: 'Omiii . . . Omiii!'

The search party advanced with courage and caution. As it advanced, the foliage thickened. Near the bottom of the valley it was like midnight. Then the foliage ended and they saw clear light of the evening as they emerged on to the grass clearing by the river.

Something moved. They beat the drums and shouted and saw a horrendous sight – two bodies heaped on each other haplessly. In a split second Khatri knew the tiger had done its job. A shrill, heart-rending cry of anguish escaped from his throat, piercing the still of the valley. It coincided with the girls' screams.

Everybody had expected the worst for Billi – at least a shoe-beating by her mother on the roadside. Billi, having followed the couple all the way down, had remained hidden from them in the grass even when it had become too late to do anything about it. She could neither make her presence known, for the fear of being laughed at and ridiculed, nor could she risk making her way back on her own, for anything could happen to a young girl in a jungle. She simply had to wait till they called it a day, to follow them back to safety.

'Silly Billi,' they all said, feeling sorry for her for the shoe-beating she was deservedly going to receive in a matter of minutes.

The shoe-beating did not come. Lakhpatni was too relieved to see her girl unharmed and untouched. But it would come later, at home in Chandigarh, if they ever got back there. Billi was in no hurry to get back.

Up on the roadside, reunited with their daughter, the Lakhpatis herded all their children. Without saying a word to anyone they moved away towards the shops, marking the end of their friendship with the Khatris whose son, that dog-faced BA Pass loafer, was responsible for all their misery and, more than that, their shame. They got a lift straight away. A car coming from Simla side, its headlights flooding the road, stopped. One of its four passengers had recognized the Congress leader look-alike millionaire.

'Lakhpati-ji? What are you doing here in this jungle at this time?'

'Waiting for a bus, to tell you the truth.'

'Get in. Get in.'

'What, all of us?'

'Plenty of room. Plenty.' There is always 'plenty of room' every-where for a millionaire.

'We are nine, bhai. No joke.'

'We will manage. We are Indian, don't forget. We can squeeze-squeeze.'

The Lakhpatis departed.

*

93

It was the most embarrassing day of the Khatris' life.

Omi: *Call yourself a man falling asleep like that, dog-turd?*

Munni: *I'll never go anywhere with him again. Never ever!*

Khatri: *I should have known it was coming.*

Paro: *Ram, Ram, Ram! – what a son! Paro, what did you do in your past life?*

Only Aunt Vidya thought differently. She laughed. Then, suddenly, everybody laughed, Khatri too. Suddenly, he felt happy. He made a little bow southwards, to where Goddess Chandi's temple was, and said, 'Thank you,' in his throat. He made a little bow towards Dhalli a few miles upstream as well.

But the laughter and Khatri's happiness was short-lived. Two Chandigarh-bound buses refused to take them on – they were already overloaded. The third didn't even stop on seeing the size of their party. The next bus was due only in half an hour's time. It was the last for the night.

'What if it also doesn't stop?' Khatri said.

'Don't worry, Father. It will,' Omi said.

Khatri admired his son's optimism. 'How will you stop it if it doesn't want to?'

'Piece of cake, Father. Leave it in my good hands.'

Three-quarters of an hour later they saw a firefly sliding towards them a mile up the slope of the road. Soon it became two fireflies. A minute later they heard the bus tearing downhill. Omi asked everybody – man, woman and child – to join hands and make a human chain across the road. Blinding them with its headlights, the bus blew its horn hysterically, saying *Get out of the way or I'll mow you down, the lot of you*! It stopped short of doing just that. The driver, a Sikh, went mad.

'I can see you people are tired of life, but why choose my bus to commit suicide? Spare me, will you? I've a wife and kid-kiddies,' he yelled.

As they had feared, the bus was full up. They pleaded.

'Room not even for a fly, Lala-ji,' the driver and his conductor said.

Khatri waved two five-rupee notes. 'What did you say, sardar-ji?'

'I said maybe we could take two-three people at most, Lala-ji.'

Khatri waved two more five-rupee notes. 'Think again.'

The driver and the conductor thought again. 'Perhaps another two-three maximum. Not a fly more. Not even a mosquito. Government bus, Lalal-ji.'

'You can't strand the others in this jungle. Mr Datta sahib won't like it when he hears about it,' Omi said.

Mr Datta was Secretary of Transport, Punjab, a pukka burra sahib with a government villa by the Lake and a government Chevrolet. Omi had never met him.

'You threatening me, bau-ji?'

'You said you had a family and all, didn't you? You want to keep your job, don't you?'

The driver didn't like that at all. 'These threats won't get you a seat on my bus, bau-ji.'

'Who is threatening you? I was talking about life. And what is life? It is you scratch my back I scratch yours, no? I know Mr Datta personally. Eats once every week at our famous restaurant Pall Mall. Heard of Pall Mall?'

'No.'

'You wouldn't have. It's high class. Anyway, all I was saying was I'd drop a word in his ear for your promotion. Plus you get ten rupees each. Plus our goodwill. What more do you want from people stranded in the jungle?'

The boy was too cocky. The driver did not like people like him. He wanted to make a batti (roll) of the fivers and stick it up his . . . He was also afraid – the son of a bitch was well dressed and obviously well connected. Still, the driver wanted to teach him a lesson.

'All in. All in,' the driver said.

Relieved, everybody hurriedly clambered into the already over-crowded bus, afraid the mercurial driver might change his mind. Omi supervised the operation outside. But when it was his turn to get in, the driver shut the door on him. 'Not taking you.'

'You can't do that,' Khatri said, coming to the door and producing another fiver.

'You can't do that,' Omi shouted from the road.

'He makes his own way back or all of you out. *Out*.'

'But,' screamed the ladies.

'No but-shut, sisters – I am not taking that phooky (air-filled) young man in my bus. If he's lucky he can hitch a hike home on a lorry. If not . . . it's only fifteen miles. Or he waits till the morning.'

It was either that or all out.

'It's all right, Father. I'll manage,' Omi yelled. Hundreds of lorries and trucks kept coming all night. He would get a ride on one, no problem. Why should he grovel to this brainless fool who hadn't even heard of his Pall Mall? (That bit hurt.)

Omi got a ride, all right. But not till ten. That, too, on a lorry

95

going straight to Delhi in the south, which meant he had to get off at Panchkoola road junction and wait there for something going to Chandigarh. Panchkoola was fast asleep. An odd laltan (kerosene lantern) burned here and there, but otherwise it was quite dead. All its dhaba (eatshops) were firmly shut and there was not a living soul in sight.

Omi sat under a tree and waited. The roads remained uncooperative. Fed up, he decided to walk the rest of the way home. *Only seven miles. What is seven miles for a full-bloodied Punjabi nut like your good self, Om Parkash?* But he wouldn't have to walk all the seven miles. If he was lucky, which he knew he was, he would catch a rickshaw at the Power House – that would cut a good three miles off.

Omi looked at his watch. Half-past ten. In Munnishka's silk-satin arms and against her honey breasts at the stroke of midnight. *She's up and waiting.*

In half an hour Omi was at Manimajra, a little town two miles on. Manimajra, too, was fast asleep. Dogs barked in distant streets and cats fought nearby in a dilapidated, disused mosque. An owl hooted in an imli tree overhead and a bat kept whizzing past his ear. Owls mean bad luck. Bats circling you like that mean much worse. They are a clear sign to a traveller to select a suitable tree and settle down under it for the night. *No way. She is waiting.*

Omi marched on, singing 'Vive, vive l'amour'.

Half a mile out of Manimajra he met up with company, a bunch of thugs. They stripped him of his watch, emptied his pockets and took away even his sleeveless sweater. As a farewell gesture, their leader thumped Omi on the head and kicked him up his backside.

'Be thankful we've left your shirt on.'

Thankful, Omi hurried on. No cars or lorries passed till he got to the great dry river before the Power House, then suddenly there was a convoy of four vehicles coming up from behind him. Omi stood in the middle of the road and threw up both his arms, determined to stop one of them. This stopped the entire convoy, two jeeps and two cars. Four men leapt out of the jeep in front and Omi heard someone say from a car: 'Well dressed and all, he looks of a good family. Bring him here. Step forward, son.'

He stopped forward.

'Be you from Chandigarh, young man? What in God's name are you doing here by yourself at this time?'

It was a familiar voice. But Omi was too confused, and afraid, to be able to place it. 'Sir . . .' he tried to explain.

'Get in. Sit next to me and tell me all.'

Omi had the shock of his life as he entered the car, a limousine. He was sitting next to the Punjab's Chief Minister, the tiny Sikh, Har Raisingh himself.

Well, well well. What a day? A BA Pass, tigers, highway robbers and now the Chief Minister! What next?

'Sir, I am honoured . . .'

'Never mind that, just tell me why are you eating the jungle air at this hour? Myself I am returning from a long conference with Pandit Nehru in Simla.'

Omi explained.

'Thank God they took only your money and not your life. Pandit-ji worries about mine. There have been threats, you know. And guess who from? From my own Sikhs, would you believe? They want their own Punjabi-speaking state. I won't have it. We are Indians first, Hindus and Sikhs after. Bengalis and Madrasis after . . .'

Thereupon, the great man broke into a lecture good and proper. Omi had heard all that before, on the radio and elsewhere. But he loved to hear it again. Each word Raisingh uttered reduced by a few yards the distance to her who was waiting.

'Wed evenings' were *it*.

Every Wednesday evening the clearing in front of Sector 23's busy shopping centre became a bustling street market, selling anything and everything worth the name. Pedlars flocked to it from all the four known corners of the world. Proudly they set up their pitches, fighting tooth and claw for an extra square foot of space. Rehri stalls-on-wheels jammed the square and naked incandescent lights lit up the place like Diwali. Sabzi-wallahs sprinkled water on their vegetables to make them fresher; the flower fellows did the same to their mountains of marigold. Almost everyone sprayed water on and around their 'earth'. It killed the dust, and it made a walk in the weekly market a thing of joy.

All this happened right in front of the Pall Mall. Paro often watched the tamasha (fun) from upstairs. On the 'Wed evening' after Omi became a BA Pass, she saw a heaped stall of secondhand clothes under their window. She spotted Omi's sweater, *the* sleeveless sweater, on top of the heap.

'Munniii,' Paro yelled. 'Stop whatever you are doing and come.'

It was not Omi's sweater. Nonetheless, they turned the heap upside down.

Disappointed, they moved back. But Munni stopped. She had seen someone – Asha. Asha was with the Bahal sisters at a shoe-stall nearby. The sisters were loudly denouncing the boot-wallah as public enemy number one for overcharging them.

'Daylight robbery this – one rupee and twenty-five paisa for a Number Five slipper,' said Banti, the eldest.

'We'll pay rupee one, and not a paisa more,' said Santi.

'Bibis, you've already made me halve my price to one twenty-five. And one twenty-five it is.' The boot-wallah was firm.

'You are a pukka chor (thief) if you want to know; worse than the bandit Sultana. One rupee maximum.'

'One twenty-five minimum. I have mother-father, kid-kiddies plus a wife to feed. They eat every day, you know.'

'And you think we don't? And you think we own a mint or something? One rupee, take it or leave it.'

'Bibi-ji, you'll make me go bankrupt . . .'

'Take it or leave it. Come on, Santi, let's go.'

'All right, then, bibi. Let my ruin be on your head.'

Asha stood behind her sisters-in-law, contemplating her feet, waiting patiently for the ritual of bargaining to be over. In fact she was fed up with it. She looked up and saw Munni. Their eyes met. They smiled.

'Asha, how are you? . . .'

'I am as I always am.'

'How's life?'

'Life is long. Very.'

'Oh!' Strange answers, thought Munni. 'Why don't you come up with me for a little while? We'll listen to Binaca Geet Mala, Top Ten. It's just started.'

Asha's face lit up at the prospect of listening to radio's most famous, most riveting weekly song programme. But she shook her head.

'Why not?'

'Because my mother-in-law won't let me. Nor them,' Asha whispered.

'I'll ask them.'

'Pointless.'

Munni asked the eldest Bahal sister, Banti, who looked just like the Brahmin widow, Chatkarni.

'Girls from good families don't listen to film songs,' Banti said, curtly.

'I do,' Munni said.

'But girls from good families don't.' Banti screwed up her nose as

98

if there was a bad smell about, and pulled Asha away, hissing, 'Film songs today, films tomorrow, and God knows what the day after. You must not mix with girls like her.'

'Nothing wrong with her. Anyway, you don't let me mix with anyone,' Asha said.

'How dare you speak back to your house wallah's elder sister? I'll see to you when we get home.'

'Home? It is a jailkhana (prison).'

'Ma, what did Asha mean by life is very long?' Munni asked Paro as the crowd swallowed up the Bahals.

'When you are lonely life is long. When you are very lonely it is very long,' Paro said.

Early one morning a loud shrill voice made Bawa prick up his ears like the family dog, Dabbu. Bawa knew every voice around. Every voice around was loud and shrill, but there was something about this voice. It made Bawa, who was always curious, 'double curious'. He ran out to see its owner.

'Letter for Mr Esquire,' shouted the new dakia, a boy of Bawa's age.

'No Mr Esquire-Shwire here,' Bawa said.

Omi stood idly in a window upstairs, listening. As the postman turned to move away with the letter, he ran downstairs. 'Wait, you fool,' he yelled.

Downstairs, he snatched from the boy the letter which said: *Mr O. P. Khatri, Esquire*. He whacked him on the head and ran back upstairs. The letter was from Kurukshetra.

'Kurukshetra?' Paro's forehead creased. Kurukshetra was famous and holy, as famous and holy as Mecca. Mahabharata, the world's first Great War, had been fought there thousands of years ago. Lord Krishna had spoken the Gita there on the eve of the conflict, making it one of the most sacred spots on earth. Paro had been there once when Vidya lived in Pipli near it. But she knew no one in the divine city who would write them a letter and put a postage stamp on it.

However, Munni did. 'It's from my cousin, Kukoo.'

Kukoo was a university professor. He and his wife Kaddu were inviting the young lovers to the city of Lord Krishna, 'the God who is in love with love'. The ten-yearly eclipse of the moon was approaching. Being there that night guaranteed all kinds of mouth-watering benefits. There were 'extras' for those married within the lunar year. '*Accept invitation heartily,*' the letter ended.

99

'Accept, boy. Accept,' Khatri said. It was a chance of a lifetime.

Omi looked at his mother. She said nothing. Omi wrote back: '*We accept invitation heartily . . .*'

'You are going to regret it, ji,' Munni said in a little whisper.

'How? Why?'

'Because my cousins don't live alone.'

'Let's go see the eclipse and claim our 'Extras'."

Kurukshetra lay fifty miles south off the Grand Trunk Road. Over-turned trucks punctuated the long highway, one every five miles. Their spillage – jute sacks bursting with grain from the Punjab and melons from Afghanistan on their way to Delhi – decorated the roadside. Buses from Chandigarh didn't go directly to the God's city; God-bound people got off at a road junction at Pipli. From there they took the local bus, or hired a tonga – it was a two-mile ride only.

Munni's cousins met their bus at Pipli.

'Nice to have ready-made relatives who already love you, isn't it?' Professor Kukoo said, hugging Omi. Kukoo was short, pot-bellied like Lord Ganesha, God of prosperity with an elephant's trunk, but otherwise good-looking. He was twenty-eight. He looked not a day older than Omi.

'Isn't it?' Omi said, hugging Kukoo and inspecting she-cousin Kaddu, also short and round of figure and happy-looking. She was twenty-six and looked it.

The Professor and his wife had come in their old blue Morris Minor.

'What a delicious looking car,' Omi said. It was.

'Vintage stuff, baba. Made in England too. Circa 1939. Journey okes? You okes, Munni?'

Munni didn't know much about the journey. She had slept through it with her silk scarf wrapped around her head. Buses had that effect on her – they put her to sleep. But she said it had been fine. 'And so am I,' she added.

'You know, Omi, this girl from Dhulkote – speaks better English than Princess Margaret of UK. Must take her to the Campus and let everybody hear her. Send my reputation sky-high if not higher. Now, gentlemen in front and ladies in comfy-comfy back. In, in, in.' Kukoo put the luggage in the boot and waved everyone in. 'How long did the journey take? Two hours? Take us that long to get home, at least.'

'What? But it's only two miles, no?' Omi yelped.

'Other guests also in town, baba. The eclipse in sixty-one hours.'

100

Kurukshetra, normally a town of 50,000, was playing host to forty times that number. For the last few days Hindus from all over the country had been flocking to it to ensure they got a ringside seat, as it were, on the night of the eclipse. There were no traffic jams as such, but roads and streets had become stagnant rivers of humanity. Bullock carts and tongas and lorries and cars moved only when the crowds did. Yet there was no panic, no hysteria. All was calm. Krishna, the Divine Traffic Controller, was fully in charge.

'Mother-laying hell,' Omi quipped.

'Language, Om Parkash. Krishna watching. Krishna listening. We'll get home all right. What's the hurry?'

They got home all right, but it took three hours.

Home was a very old three-storey haveli of thin red bricks, with a square courtyard in the middle and rooms all around. It stood in its own grounds a long way from other houses, past the far end of the city. A fruit-tree garden sprawled around it, enclosed by a bushy jantar mantar hedge. It boasted thirty-six rooms and seventy-two windows and secret stairways and tunnels. Kukoo and his wife lived here with his parents and grandparents and uncles and aunts and brothers and sisters and counsins and nephews and nieces and servants.

Tea came immediately. With it came half the inmates of the haveli.

'Mother-laying hell. This what you meant?' Omi hissed in Munni's ear.

'Sshhh . . .' Munni hissed back.

The tea was only for the guests and their two hosts; the others were mere spectators. After the second cup Kukoo took his cousins on a conducted tour of the house and its grounds. The children of the house, about fifty between the ages of four and fourteen, followed. They had fallen in love with the confection in colourful silk from Chandigarh whom they called Aunti Munni; some wanted to marry her when they grew up.

'Bhago bhago – run run,' Kukoo ordered them.

The children giggled.

Kukoo roared at them. The children roared back. Kukoo gave up and let them come. The tour ended face to face with another haveli sixty yards away, one much bigger and with large compounds. A fifteen-foot wall circled it, cutting it off from the rest of the world, with broken glass and bits of glass bottles stuck on top. Because of the wall, the house was called Old Fort, and Omi and Munni were informed that it now served as the ashram of a maharishi.

'A groovy ashram. Very. Very selective, too,' Kukoo said.

'How?' Omi asked.

101

In answer, Kukoo raised his right eyebrow and jerked his head meaningfully. His guests wanted to see Kurukshetra's famous temples and its great holy tank where two million Hindus would take a dip on *the* night. But sightseeing was out of the question because of the 'guests' on the roads. At the last eclipse the Divine Traffic Controller had goofed a little. It had resulted in a stampede, and 1500 of His devotees had been trampled to death.

'So what do we do, Munnishka?' Omi would rather be trampled to death in a stampede than die of boredom cooped up in that haveli with seventy-two windows for whole days and nights.

Professor Kukoo was visibly hurt by this remark.

'You mean you don't love Professor Kukoo then? How can you resist?'

It was difficult to resist loving the pot-bellied talk-machine.

'God's city, baba. Things here change from day to day. Tomorrow is another day. So give in, and wait for tomorrow.'

Omi gave in. He waited for tomorrow.

Kukoo woke up Omi at the crack of dawn for a 'men only' walk in the forest.

'Chlorophyll green and menthol-fresh, like Binaca toothpaste. Let's go out for an Ess Hetch Eye Tea in the healthy open countryside.'

Thousands upon thousands of Kurukshetra's 'guests' had the same idea. They sat on their haunches within a few feet of each other, revealing their all. The forest stank. The dandy from Chandigarh couldn't take it. He held his nose with a hand and made his cousin turn back. As the sun gleamed over the trees, they found themselves by the wall of the Old Fort. For a maharishi's ashram it appeared profoundly unwelcoming, even forbidding.

'Looks more like a prison,' Omi said.

'This wall is here not to keep people in, but to keep the world out.'

'Meaning what, Professor sahib?'

'This is an ashram with a difference, baba. Not where skeletons wearing the loincloth sit cross-legged and pray for nirvana. It is a lotus flower floating on the sea of bliss, the Sixth Inn of Happiness.'

'Not fair this, Professor sahib. What are you talking about now?'

'Maharishi Kishi Mishi who runs it drives three Cadillacs, four Chevvies, five Ambassadors and six Willy's jeeps. That's what.'

'Something about professors. Always beyond me.'

'Come, come, yaar. Don't you get it? This is how he comes and goes. Accompanied by his *phoren* only disciples – the blue-eyed Miss

Kennedys, Miss Fullbrights, Miss Salingers, Miss Dulles from New York, Boston, and Los Angeles with their Johnnies. The lost children of the West, come East to find themselves. And they do – at the feet of Maharishi Kishi Mishi. And one more thing: Kishi Mishi don't take no Indians on. No, sir. Only a selected few, very rich and very dumb. The rest all European or American with stinking rich daddies and neurotic mummies. Those who are disillusioned with riches. Boy, I would love to be disillusioned like that – with money. Wouldn't you?'

'I wouldn't mind.'

'So the poor rich kids turn up here to find *hope* and *peace* at Kishi Mishi's feet in the city of Bhagavadgita. They become his servants – ever seen or heard of white servants for an Indian? Our holy neighbour has – scores of them. They've been coming singly, in twos and fours, for days.

'They have come for the eclipse. Naturally.'

'And for something else. Something is going to happen.'

'What, Professor sahib?'

'Don't know. But I have this feeling something is. My gut tells me. My nose tells me. Can't wait for tomorrow night. O when will it come?'

Tomorrow night came punctually and not a minute later, steel-blue and deep. The moon, the size of a HMV 16 rpm record, began to rise sweetly over the ancient battlefield, shedding a sweeter translucence. Distant chanting and sounds of music wafted through, filling the liquid darkness with ripples of joy. Such sounds of mirth were common in this timeless city of priests and praying. Tonight they became special. They came from every corner of the night, leapt from every huddle of whitewashed buildings with conical domes aspiring towards the heavens. They jostled away all other sounds.

Now and then, for reasons of its own, the breeze picked up. It brought a whiff of jasmine and roses and motia from the Old Fort, laced with another, a hardly noticeable smell. No one detected it but Kukoo. The man had a nose.

'I knew it,' Kukoo whispered to Omi, jerking his head from left to right at an angle of forty-five degrees.

'You did what?'

'Sshhh . . .'

There was a demographic division in the haveli tonight. The older generation – the doddering grannies and uncles and aunts – was

103

spread out on charpoys on the roof. The next two generations, that of the Khatris' hosts and their offspring, were in the jantar mantar-hedged haveli gardens. The entire clan watched the gold disco in the sky from roof and garden, waiting for the ten-yearly miracle – its complete obliteration by the earth's shadow. Many had seen it happen before; others had not yet been born when it had last taken place. The long-awaited event was to commence at the stroke of midnight.

'Right, let's go,' Kukoo whispered again at the stroke of midnight. He needn't have whispered. Everybody was moonstruck. Everybody was talking, nobody listening.

'Where?'

'No questions. Just come unseen.'

'What about cousin Kaddu and Munni?'

'Forget them, just follow the leader. You're going to see what is for your eyes only. And mine.'

Leaving the garden unseen posed a problem or two – all those kid-kiddies who roamed about unclaimed, shouting, crying and quarrel-ling, 'even at this bloody hour'. 'Uncle Omi, I want to sit on your shoulder!' 'Uncle, will there be an eclipse in Chandigarh too?' . . .

The house itself was deserted. Kukoo armed himself with an Ever Ready torch and took Omi to a room in a remote part of the vast, rumbling house. The room was crammed with old, disued furniture, steel trunks and wooden chests, cobwebs and rat-droppings and kirli (wall lizards), and dust and and dust and dust. In the 40-watt electric light it looked as if it had not been entered for at least as many years. What was the matter with the Professor? Did his university know it employed a loony?

Kukoo bolted the door behind them. Then he opened a cupboard and flashed the torch. A flight of hidden steps, leading down! Kukoo stepped into the cupboard. 'Come on, follow the leader.'

Omi obeyed – nothing else he could do. The steps led to a well. Omi could tell there was water somewhere down that deep cavity because it was damp and cool. Next to the well there stood a brick wall, in it another door.

'Cousin sahib . . .' Everyone loves a mystery, but this!

Kukoo opened the door. More stairs. Now this was getting frightening. The hairs on Omi's nape began to stand.

'Nobody knows about these stairs,' Kukoo said, shutting the door behind them. The stairs were narrow, hardly a millimetre wider than eighteen inches. Kukoo, the tubby Lord Ganesha, had difficulties.

A few short flights and the stairs joined an equally narrow passage. Where it ended, they faced another brick wall. The medieval bricks here looked unhealthy. Red powder clung to them. They were crumbling. They had been crumbling for two centuries.

'Professor-ji!' What if this bitch of a wall caved in? Omi would be entombed alive. This would become his fucking Taj Mahal. Munnishka would never know what happened to her handsome hubby. She would cry her eyes out – Omi could actually see streams of tears racing down those baby cheeks, big tears. And wear white saris for the rest of her life.

'Look,' Kukoo said. He pulled out two loose bricks from a hole in the wall. Inches away, only inches away, was the great luminous circle of the golden disc, only that celestial body and nothing else. Nothing except that music and singing. 'Look, look, look!'

'Mother-laying hell.' Omi couldn't believe his eyes.

'Hell of hells. Fucking hell.' Even the Professor couldn't believe what he saw. It far surpassed anything he was capable of imagining.

In the grounds of the high-walled Old Fort, a couple of hundred men and women were chanting and dancing. They were stark naked. They were white. Their bodies glowed in the moonlight like incandescent ivory, some of them smeared with ash. Men danced with men, men danced with women, women danced with women, all swaying from side to side, all chanting and ringing little brass bells.

'Mother-laying hell. Are we still in India, Professor Kukoo sahib?'

'No, Mr O. P. Khatri, Esquire, we are in the Sixth Inn of Happiness. Or very near it.'

The dancers gravitated around a central figure which sat lotus-position on a throne of flowers. It was black.

'His Holiness, Maharishi Kishi Mishi,' Kukoo said.

In the Maharishi's lap sat a shapely female, wrapped around him like a goodess around the God himself, as Omi had seen in reproductions of Tibetan tankhas. After a while she stood up and a sister of hers took her place. She clasped the God like her predecessor and sat in the God's lap till it was the turn of another comely form.

'Om Parkash, what do you think?'

Om Parkash had stopped thinking.

The moon now shone directly above the Fort, as if by arrangement. There was a ripple of movement along the almost static dancers. The dark figure disengaged itself from the current goddess, and Omi saw something which was not to be believed. It was the most amazing sight ever seen – his Holiness had an erection which defied all belief. It was immense. Gigantic. Inhuman.

One by one the women came. They knelt and held the God-penis in their hands and pressed it to their bosom and kissed it and held it to their faces.

'How's your chap doing, Omi?'

'Which chap?'

'Your junior, you fool.'

'Oh.'

'Mine's gone cock-a-doodle-doo and ninety degrees. Totally berserk. Wish we could join in.'

'Mouthing-watering thought. But we can't.'

'If we *could*, would you come with me.'

'But how?' Omi playing along because he knew Kukoo was joking.

'Come, follow the leader.'

Secret stairs and more secret stairs and finally a low subterranean tunnel. In spite of its age, it looked surprisingly sturdy and clean. It led out and away from the house.

'Leads to a pit in the Fort grounds. Used to be a well, once upon a time. Now sometimes snakes are found in it.'

'Thank you for telling me, cousin-ji.'

'Not tonight, though. On full-moon eclipse night snakes go dancing in the forest. One night they don't bite humans.'

'I am grateful to you for this information. Can't wait to pass it on to all my friends back in Chandigarh.'

'We'll leave our clothes in the pit . . .'

Omi had thought all along that Kukoo had been joking. Suddenly he realized he was not. A snake-pit of his own developed in his stomach. As they stepped into the 'pit' by the Fort wall, his knees began to wobble, his mouth went dry and he felt a taste of bitter almonds on his tongue. 'I am not going.'

'Don't give me that shit, Om Parkash. Having come thus far you can't want to piddle back. Not on, this. The eclipse comes once only in ten years, yaar. What do you mean?'

'I appreciate that, Professor sahib. Fact is I don't want to be caught and beaten into the shape of peacock's arse. Second, what about our ladies? Aren't we deceiving them?'

'Don't be a damfool, yaar. First, these people won't know a thing. They are all doped. Bhang, opium, can't you smell it? Where's your nose? So don't worry, we *cannot* be discovered. My personal guarantee. Okay?'

'But . . .?'

'And second, we are about to partake of an ancient ritual – moon's total eclipse and the primeval dance of the flesh. Fundamental stuff, spiritual stuf *et hoc genus omne* – Latin that, meaning and all that kind of thing. So you can say what you are about to do is in the service of God. Hurry now. My chap is going down, already half-mast. Get naked.' Next instant the cousins stood naked.

'And another thing! No snakes-shnakes. Was only joking.'

Omi was not reassured.

There was a burnt-out fire in the pit and they rubbed ash all over their bodies. Satisfied, Kukoo put an arm around Omi and rolled him into the gently swaying mass of naked moon worshippers. Once there, he abandoned Omi. Omi saw him accept a glass of milk-white liquid from an outstretched hand and slip into a pair of silken arms.

The eclipse was well on its way. Everybody gazed at the heavens. Omi felt bewildered and terrified. Bewildered and terrified as he was, he made two discoveries – he was cock-a-doodle-doo and full ninety degrees, and most other men were not. A girl with pointed tits reached out and stroked his chap. Omi liked that. Next minute she bent down and kissed it as if it were a child. Omi loved that. Overhead, the celestial bodies were engaged in their divine love-making, going in and out of each other. The fair moon was gradually being consumed by the earth's shadow. Omi was an atom of it. He was now walking on the moon.

On the earth in front of him, people were calmly moving around. They were going up to the Maharishi to do homage to the God-penis. The woman with the pointed breasts took Omi by his hand and brought him to where it was all happening. Maharishi Kishi Mishi lay flat on his back on the flower throne, his eyes shut and his giant phallus reaching up to the blackening moon and its increasing corona. Women came and kissed it, some possessively – they had to be gently pulled away. Men, too, came. Omi was pushed forward. When he got to the exaggerated, unbelievable thing, he felt revolted, but he had to do something, pay his homage. Otherwise he might be found out, caught and beaten into the shape of a peacock's backside. Even killed – anything could happen at a time like this, in a place like this. Humbly, he bent down. Instead of kissing the magic totem of flesh, he artfully spat at it and, humbly, withdrew. A bearded man took his place. He bent over the God-man, licked the God-penis and hungrily closed his mouth over it.

Towards the end of the heavenly happening, God-man stirred. He lifted a light, lithe figure with burning blond hair and closed his body with hers, himself still face upwards. The blonde, united with the God, became a Goddess. She made a dream-like moan which became

107

a continuous drone as she heaved up and down, as if ocean waves carried her. And the earth around the throne became a sea of bodies writhing in the manner of the God and the Goddess.

Omi, at the edge of that sea, was in a daze. He gazed at the sky in wonder. The moon was there no more, only a black circle and an area of luminosity around it. Someone else with pointed breasts took Omi's cock-a-doodle-doo chap in her hands and knelt down and kissed it. Next she pulled him down. As they came in contact with the holy earth where once Lord Krishna had walked, a sliver of the hidden moon slid into view. The woman let go of Omi, rolled over, raised her chin to the cold fire in the heavens and started to stare at it. Omi was free. He felt foolish for no reason. He smiled to the enlarging crescent of gold. Not knowing what to do, he stood up. There didn't seem to be any further interest in him or his chap. Slowly, he walked back to the 'snake pit' and waited. Before long he saw a phantom shadow glide towards him. It was not the Professor, it couldn't be – Omi had seen him writhing with a body in that sea of writhing bodies. His heart stopped beating. He was found out. Now what?

Where are my clothes?

He panicked and looked at the foe for the last time before making a run for it. Run? In which direction? It was then he saw those white flashing teeth.

Kukoo had seen Omi walk back to the pit from where he was involved with that white young body. When finished, he rose and moved away ghost-like, flags down, his teeth gleaming proudly in the light of the growing moon being freed from earthly bondage for the next ten years.

'Piece of cake, wasn't it? Lovely cake. American lily-white body,' Kukoo whispered, pulling out their clothes from under a stone.

'Phew!' Omi began to breathe again. 'How could you tell she was American?'

'She said: "*Oh gee, it was cosmic*." That's how. How about you?'

'How about me what?'

Kukoo knew. He slapped his forehead in disbelief and disgust. 'Bloody fool number one. That's what you are, if you ask me. There it was, like Napoleon said about the French crown lying in the gutter circa 1804. And you did nothing to help yourself. I can't believe it. Anyway, not a word of it to the ladies if you want your Bs to remain attached to you.'

'You mean your Bs.'

'You think anyone is going to believe you didn't . . .?'

108

'Tell me, how was it? How does it compare?'

Kukoo had to think. He thought with a smile and a jerk of the eyebrows. 'Different. Good and different. But home-cooking is still best.'

Omi only had to alight from their rickshaw to know something was wrong. His mother wasn't standing on the balcony, waiting. No servant rushed out to take charge of their suitcases. Only Dabbu, Omi's old dog, showed up at the door to greet them.

'Bawa! Seva!' Omi yelled as Dabbu jumped at him, wagging his tail furiously as he always did whenever Omi came from anywhere. Bawa heard him and came running out. 'You dead, Bawa? Somebody dead?'

'Worse than dead, Omi bau.'

'What bakwas (nonsense) are you talking, Bawa?' Omi suddenly felt his hand shake – what did the fool mean? 'Mother all right? Father well?'

'They fine, Omi bau.'

'Then what is it? Speak, idiot.'

'That Heeralal.'

'Somebody shot him?'

'No, but he wants to shoot us. Ma-ji will tell.'

Omi and Munni raced upstairs. They found Paro and Vidya sitting opposite each other on a charpoy, looking glum. They had been crying.

'Ma!' Omi threw himself at his mother, hugging her, wiping her tears.

'That Heeralal. Wants to put you and your father in jail . . .'

'What?'

'All your doing . . .'

Heeralal stuck to his word. He took the Khatris to court. But the case was not tried in Le Corbusier's High Court where he knew every judge 'personally', it was tried in a makeshift court-house six miles west of Bajwara in Kharar, a little rustic town. The hearing took place in its Raj-time PWD Guesthouse with a long pillared veranda. Painted white, this British-built building was a court-house by day and a guesthouse by night.

'In the good old days only the burra sahib stopped here with his mem. Now it is any Laloo Panju Tom Dick Harry wearing his solar

109

hat. Independence!' said an old man to Khatri. He was the Guest-house peon and punkah-wallah. He wore a stiff khaki uniform and sat on a stool by the door of the court, a very long room with a high ceiling and the punkah in the middle. A wooden slab by the door said:

Mr B. K. Gangoli
PCS
Magistrate 2nd Class

Heeralal was already on the veranda with his friends, supporters and witnesses when the Khatris arrived with their friends, supporters and witnesses. The adversaries measured each other with their eyes. Heeralal spat from the corner of his mouth. Omi called him son of a ten-dog bitch in his throat. Khatri ground his jaw.

'Not quite your High Court, this. Or is it, Heeralal?' Khatri said.

'Is or is not, so what?'

'Nor is he one of your High Court judge friends. Or is he?'

'Is or is not, justice is justice. He will do justice. You will see, Khatri old cock.'

'A judge doesn't suffer fools easily, not even a Magistrate Second Class.'

'Who you calling fool?'

'You.'

'I'll have it added to the charges.'

'With my blessings.'

'Shove your blessings up your gaand.'

Everybody the Khatris knew was there – from the VVIP, Nanda of the Governor House, to Professor Bhatnagar, Omi's ex-English tutor – to boost the Khatri morale. Bhatnagar had had to bunk two lectures to get here. Besides, his brother, Pleader Dandeshwar Bhatnagar, was defending the Khatris.

'Smacks of E. M. Forster. It does. All this,' Professor Bhatnagar said in English, turning his boyish head around and pointing to the punkah-wallah and the punkah string which stuck out of a hole over a pulley above the court-room door.

Heeralal heard what the college professor said. 'Faster or slower, justice is justice. The Magistrate may be Second Class, but his justice will be first class, you will see,' Heeralal barked at Professor Bhatnagar in English.

'For that reason alone I am already sorry for you. By God I am.'

Heeralal didn't like that. Already angry, he became angrier. 'Who what are you? Your brother may be a Pleader, but who what are you? I'll tell you – a two-pie professor. I can buy and sell ten of you.' Heeralal was always buying and selling people, usually in their tens.

Everybody was talking about the judge. By every account he was zabbardast – tough, heartless.

'He was brought up on a diet of nails and rivets.'

'Has a tongue coated with caustic soda.'

Omi shivered. He had never met anyone who had been brought up on nails and rivets and had a caustic-soda tongue.

'Heeralal has gold. What have the Khatris? Not half a leg.'

'Fool Khatri boy. Why did he do it?'

'Do you think they'll put father and son in the same jail?'

Omi shivered again, for his father this time. Nanda stood next to Omi. He put an arm around him and led him aside.

'You have nothing to worry, Om Parkash. Not a thing,' Nanda whispered.

'How come, Uncle Nanda?'

'How come? Like this – I have had a word with Gangoli.'

'So?'

'So the case is as good as won.'

'How, Uncle?'

'This is India, bhai. Country of give and take. Gangoli wants to be Magistrate First Class and we want . . . Speak the truth when it is your turn to speak. Well, as much of the truth as is necessary, follow? Now let's go in.'

Half of Bajwara and half of Sector 23 had turned up. A quarter of Kharar, too. Suspense hung in the air. People talked inaudibly, leaning towards each other's ears, nodding. The court was to open at ten. On the dot in walked Mr B. K. Gangoli. He was hardly a year or two older than Omi.

Heeralal's counsel spoke. Heeralal's witnesses gave evidence. The boy judge listened. Then he lost his temper. Its first victim, or casualty, was *Mr Om Parkash Khatri, son of Mr Shadi Lal Khatri of the Pall Mall of Sector 23, Chandigarh.*

'What I fail to understand is why you took exception, so violently might I add, to Mr Heeralal's disclosure that he had only joked about the merits or demerits of those so-called jewels. You even declared your intention of taking his life, didn't you? Now if you are one of those men who kill because someone has cracked a joke with them, you are a walking hazard to a civilized society. There is only one place I can think of for such a person – a lunatic asylum . . .'

'There is another place for such a lunatic, your honour – the jailhouse,' Heeralal butted in, scratching the middle of his dhoti.

'Mr Heeralal, I am conducting this case . . .'

111

'I gave him my hand to shake as a friend on my burpday. What he gave me, Lordship?'

'*Mr Heeralal* . . .'

'Ask anybody what he gave me, Lordship.'

'*Mr Heeralal*! You are advised to curb your tendency to give free vent to your tongue. Speak only when asked to. Yes, Mr Khatri junior, what do you have to say?'

'Just a word about those jewels, Your Honour. They were no ordinary jewels,' Omi began in his best Simla-Pink-Munnishka English.

'Jewels are jewels, set in gold or silver or what have you. What was extraordinary about them?'

'They were royal jewels . . .'

Royalty! Nowhere in the world is royalty loved more than in India – you worship your maharajah, you weigh him in gold on his birthdays, you lick his arse and you kiss the ground he walks on. The court was spellbound. Omi could hear his own heart beat. He went on. His speech surprised everybody, his friends and foes. It surprised him more than them.

'Your Honour, a friend of mine, a prince of royal blood, in a moment of friendship, insisted that I accept his humble but royal gifts. In the same spirit of friendship I accepted them. Then a professional jeweller, a neighbour I held in great esteem, came along and pronounced them fake. He destroyed everything, reduced that royal hand's generous gesture to an act of cheap deception. Above all, he destroyed that friendship.'

There Omi paused.

'Broken in two, what did I do? I sent the jewels back by post and forgot all about the sordid business. Then, during a chance meeting a fortnight later, my worthy neighbour casually revealed the truth of the matter. He said, and I beg your permission to quote him, he said: "I was only joking. The jewels are real." By doing what he had done, he had broken not only my heart and my wife's, he had also made me insult my royal friend by returning his gifts as fakes. What I did thereafter that fateful morning in Bajwara was what any self-respecting man present, in this distinguished gathering, who loved a friend would have done.'

The hush deepened. When people realized that Omi had finished, they muttered, 'Wah wah . . . Wah wah.' Clapping broke out, first gently, then loudly. The young magistrate waited for it to die down. When it did, he cleared his throat noisily and fixed Heeralal with his eyes.

'Mr Heeralal, you knowingly misled this young man?'

'It was only a joke, my lord. Only.'

'A half-rupee joke. A sick joke, and don't call me my lord. You deceived him. You shouldn't have been surprised if his temper got the better of him.'

'How did I know he would be so stupid as to post the jewels back? And he very nearly killed me, ask anybody.'

'*Do not interrupt when I am speaking! Understood*? Do not speak unless you are required to, by me. This is a court of justice, dammit.'

'And that's just what I want, justice, Your Honour. Justice! I was beaten into the shape of a peacock's arse by father and son. Cheap people of yesterday and the day before. Ask anybody.'

'Constable, remove this person from my court.'

The court constable took Heeralal by the arm and dragged him outside. The two Pleaders did their pleading. The witnesses gave their evidence. Heeralal was readmitted.

'Speak,' Mr Gangoli said.

Heeralal scratched the middle of his dhoti. He scratched his balding head. He looked at the boy magistrate and spoke. 'I shouldn't have joked. Mistake I made.'

'I am glad you admit you made a mistake. We will give you an opportunity to make amends for it. What would you say, as a professional jeweller, was the value of those royal jewels?'

Heeralal shuddered. Things had taken an unexpected turn, a nasty turn. And there he was, thinking all along he had the case all sewn up and in his pocket with the Khatris inside for unprovoked assault and battery and compensation and what not.

'How much would you say they were worth, Mr Heeralal?'

'Two.'

'Two what? Two cows, two goats, two carrots, two rupees or two what?'

'Two thousand rupees, my lord.'

'Your Honour,' said Pleader Dandeshwar Bhatnagar, 'my client begs to make an interjection here.'

'Allowed. Mr Khatri junior, stand up and speak.'

Omi stood up. He wished Munnishka could see him. She would have been proud.

'Your Honour, the plaintiff gave me an entirely different estimate on the morning of that unhappy incident in Bajwara. He gave me the figure of five thousand, adding, "minimum".'

'Fabrication, my lord. A tissue of total lies.'

'Mr Heeralal, would you say Mr Khatri was a poor man?'

113

'No, I would not. It would be most untrue.'

'And would you say you are a poor man?'

Heeralal didn't answer. He scratched upstairs and downstairs again. It helped him to think. Or to stop thinking.

'I have got my answer,' Mr Gangoli said. 'Tell this court how would you like your neighbour, Mr Khatri, to treat you? Give us a good answer.'

Heeralal gave a good answer. 'As a good and kind-hearted neighbour treats his neighbour.'

'Wah wah, wah wah,' the court said in applause.

'You do the same then, Mr Heeralal. I suggest you make amends to him as a good and kind-hearted neighbour.'

'Meaning what, my lord?'

'Meaning you meet him half-way. You say the jewels were worth two thousand, he insists you told him they were worth at least five. Pay him half and the costs. The case is closed.'

'Wah wah, wah wah.' The court applauded the boy judge's judgement.

The court case was over but the drama continued outside the court.

'Every dog has his day,' Heeralal said to Khatri out on the veranda, spitting from the front of his mouth, landing the spit halfway between Khatri and himself.

'Maybe you'll have yours one day,' Khatri replied.

'Not finished yet, you and I. Only just begun. I am going to get you by them balls if you got any . . .'

'You tried once. You tried twice. Look where it got you.'

'I am going to buy you out. I am going to boot you out of Sector 23. Smoke burn you down.'

'Barking dog. Go read the *Kama Sutra* with your mother in bed.'

Something happened to Heeralal. A belated surge of anger overpowered him – anger always came to him belatedly. He pushed everybody aside and went for Khatri. A wall of his supporters held him back. 'I am going to smoke burn you down . . . I am . . . I am . . .' Heeralal's friends jammed his arms and led him down the dusty driveway.

'What oratory, yaar,' Professor Bhatnagar said, embracing his ex-pupil. 'But then who trained you, eh?'

There was much hugging and embracing in the Khatri camp.

'Calls for celebration,' Professor Bhatnagar said.

'In style. In pukka style,' Kapoor, Shambhu and Tulley said.

114

'Yes, yes, yes,' everybody else said.

Khatri knew what that meant. His head, already itching under the turban, began to itch more furiously as he counted his supporters and friends.

'Boy, do something to get us out of it,' he whispered to Omi.

But Omi didn't want to get out of it. He loved parties. 'Father, what's a few hundred rupees? We've just scored an historic victory.'

Back in Sector 23 – it was lunch-time – the Khatri supporters celebrated in pukka style. They and their friends – how *they* got there nobody knew – filled up the Pall Mall and began to eat themselves sick, making Khatri sicker. He slapped his forehead again and again.

'Father!' Omi said. He put an arm around the VVIP and led him to a corner. 'Uncle Nanda, how can I thank you?'

'Aré yaar, what sort of talk this? We are friends. So?'

'Still I want to thank you. I mean proper proper.'

'No need of that. I did something for you today, vice versa tomorrow. No?'

'Goes without saying, Uncle Nanda.'

Just then Paro came downstairs, looking for her husband. 'Laddus. I want to send laddus, five hundred and one of them.'

So laddus were sent, a parcel of them, to Lakhpatni, with a note in Paro's hand: *Children err, parents forgive. A laddu to sweeten your mouth from a friend's hand.*

Khatri looked back. From a hand-to-mouth dhaba-wallah to a successful halwai to a famous restaurateur: in spite of the holocaust of '47, in spite of losing everything once – nearly their lives as well – life hadn't treated him badly. God had been kind. In every way.

Khatri made a little bow in the direction of the temple. *Four times eleven plus one. Where do you go from here, Khatri, old cock*? His guru had said he had yet a lot to do, and gurus knew that sort of thing. They had eyes which saw far. They had senses which grasped all. *So get off your backside and . . .*

Paro looked back. Her conclusion coincided with her husband's – God had been kind. But she did not want to count the ways in which He had been kind: counting brought bad luck. She was grateful, though, very grateful. She left it at that.

Omi looked back. The past didn't interest him – the dhaba and halwai days filled him with shame. The present was fine but the future was the thing. Twenty-one next birthday with a BA to his name. Married, although against his wishes at so ludicrously tender

115

an age as his. Doing well in the world, as far as it went. But what next? What more did he want?

Everything.

'Ma, I want us to be very rich.'

'One should be content with what one's got.'

'Indian disease, that, Ma, being content with what you got. I am not. I want to be a millionaire. Before I am twenty-five.'

'How?'

Omi didn't know. All he knew was he would be, somehow.

The same dakia again but this time the letter was for Munni. It had come from Dhulkote. The sight of it brought tears to her eyes – a letter from home always did that. She saw her mother's lovely face and her frail figure and she started crying those big tears.

'Beta!' Paro said.

Beta in India means 'son'. Indian parents often call their daughters 'son'. Sons there are preferred. Sons grow into men. Men go to work. Men bring in the money. Men look after the parents when old. Men protect the women folk. Daughters, on the other hand, have to be looked after, provided for, and married off at crippling expense. No wonder sons are preferred. So when parents call a daughter 'son', they are saying they love her nearly as much as a son – in other words, more than she deserves. For they never call a son 'daughter'.

'Beta!' Paro said again. She dropped everything she was doing and hurried to Munni's side. 'Good news?'

The news was not good. Munni's father, the stationmaster of Dhulkote, had had an accident. He had tripped over the railway line near the station go-down warehouse and lain unconscious on the track for half an hour. He had been discovered only minutes before the Kalka Mail, when he was missed at the station. '*Balam, the signalman, went looking for him and found him where he found him. Otherwise . . . God was in heaven this day.*'

'Hai hai hai!' Munni's life flew out of her at the word 'otherwise'. She cried and cried. She wanted to go home, that very instant.

'Go.' Khatri gave his permission.

'Go.' Paro gave hers.

'Come, I'll take you,' Omi said.

'But you cannot go,' Munni said.

That was true. Omi couldn't leave the house that day or any other that week. Bhagwat and Sethi of Excise and Income Tax were supposed to be coming. Like previous years, the accounts had been

116

submitted to the tax office. But still the two of them were coming, like previous years. It was a costly annual ritual and the Khatris couldn't breathe till it was over.

'Bloody vultures,' Omi growled.

Bhagwat and Sethi were like that. Every year they said vague things such as 'visitation one day during next week or the next'. Then they turned up one morning, their backsides puffed up, looking menacing. They took over the Pall Mall. With a toothcomb they raked through perfectly well kept books – well, as perfectly well kept as they could be – and found everything wrong. The bastards! Then they spoke to Omi in fast tax-office English:

'Mr Khatri sahib junior, we have looked and we have seen. And you know what we have seen – bonked books and fiddled figures. So it is X thousand in real tax plus Y thousand in fine. But if Mr Khatri sahib senior . . .'

But if Mr Khatri sahib senior co-operated and did the done thing, the tax could be so many thousand less, and the fine could be waived. 'Old friends after all . . .'

Mr Khatri sahib senior co-operated. He did the done thing – some expensive tailoring to their pockets – but not before a long tug-of-war. Staggering sums were coolly mentioned. They were hotly thrown out of the window. Negotiations broke down. Negotiations got restarted. A settlement was somehow reached – a sum of money which was 'vastly less' than had been demanded but 'immensely more' than Mr Khatri sahib senior was happy to part with.

Ma chod (bastards). The real shits of India. It's people like them who held India back for centuries, sold it first to Islam, then to the British and now they are selling it to a future much worse – to people like themselves. And these two were interfering with Omi's personal life now – he couldn't escort his wife home.

'Mali,' Omi called the gardener. 'Take Munni bibi home by the next bus.' A young lady from a decent family didn't travel alone. A trusted family servant, usually of advancing years, went with her. Omi would join her after the 'visitation' and bring her back.

Munni went. Life lost its L. Days became long, nights endless. Omi couldn't sleep. He tossed and turned. And the Munni birds cried: 'Munni. Munni. Munni . . .'

Omi wished she lay by his side, snuggled up to him. Cock-a-doodle-doo all night, he longed for her. It was torture. A week passed: no 'vultures'. *Come, you shit-arses. Where are you?*

Omi wrote Munni a letter. 'I am going mad . . . can't live without you. Repeat – can't.'

Back came the reply on the third day: 'Nor can I . . .'

Khatri saw the pain in his son's face, but what could he do? Tax and Excise business frightened him – it had nearly landed him in jail once. He was terrified of the 'vultures'. He simply didn't know how to handle them. He needed his boy around to talk to them in English. Omi's English had an effect on people and he knew when and which names to drop.

Another week and still there was no news. And no news in this respect meant only one thing – bad news.

The son was going mad visibly and invisibly – he was always seeing something other than what he was looking at; he cut you dead with a knife in mid-sentence; he even forgot meals now, which was most unlike him. Early one evening, at 5.31 precisely – too early for business – the phone rang. Omi had gone to hear a lecture at his old college with Arun. Bawa, the phone-lover-and-snatcher, was out on an errand. So Khatri waved to Seva Singh to answer.

'Pall Mall speaking . . . No, you can't because . . . Because he's not here . . . Gone where? Gone swimming . . . Yes. In Sector 23 pool. Who shall I say called? Hello hello . . . Hello hello?'

'Who was it?' Khatri asked.

'A young lady. Wanted Omi bau.'

A young lady? Khatri's heart missed a beat.

'Why did you say Omi's gone swimming?'

'Because I know the lady, Lala-ji. Phoning fourth-fifth time. Don't know how she found out.'

'Found out what, Seva?'

'That choti bibi is not here. Had I told her Omi bau has gone to hear a lecture, she would turn up there.'

Loyal servant. One thing good India still has – loyal servants, Khatri said to himself. He looked at his watch: 5.33.

'Seva Singh, go to the pool in ten-fifteen minutes and see what you can see,' Khatri said.

The pool was in the Public Nurseries right behind the Pall Mall, a mere two-minute walk. Seva went. He was back at five to six.

'Yes, Lala-ji, lady came in car. Went in pool and is swimming almost naked, you can say. Thin green cloth bits hardly covering this and that.'

That night Khatri didn't sleep again. Again he tossed and turned. As usual, Paro couldn't sleep either.

118

'Why go on torturing yourself about the "vultures" and the books? Whatever will be will be. God is.'

'Haven't you begun to miss the girl, Paro?'

'From the day she left.'

'Om, you better go and spend a few days with your in-laws and bring Munni back. Your mother misses her,' Khatri said on their way to Bajwara Market early next morning.

'But, Father, the "vultures"?'

'To hell with them. I can handle them.'

'Father, you can't.'

'What do you think I am – a budda (old fool) whose brain has slipped into his shoes? You don't know me, boy.'

'I know you, Father, and that's why.'

'I know what I am doing.'

Khatri didn't know what he was doing. But he had to get his son out of the way, whatever the cost. Otherwise? Khatri didn't want to think about 'otherwise'. The boy was lonely, wilting, pent up and probably, no, more than probably – Khatri didn't want to use the word – very horny. Just the ripe moment for the she-serpent to strike. Anything could happen if she did. Khatri knew his son was not a saint.

'Yes, boy, yes. You go.'

Reluctantly, Omi went.

And as it turned out, the 'vultures' didn't come at all. Instead came a letter in a brown envelope *On Indian Government Service*. It was in English. Khatri went to Professor Bhatnagar to have it translated.

'Well, well, well. Calls for another celebration, Lala-ji.'

The accounts Mr S. L. Khatri had submitted had been accepted. The 'visitation' was now unnecessary. Khatri was delighted. He was also puzzled. 'But . . .'

'Forget but-shut, Lala-ji. Written in black and white.'

'But most unusual. Most.' It was unlike the 'vultures' to let him off the hook like that. What had happened?

His friend Gulati of the Secretariat came and told him. 'Bhagwat has been suspended without pay awaiting enquiry. And guess what's happened to Sethi? I am tickling all over.'

'He drowned in the lake?'

'Better than that. He's vanished. In thin air as a jinn bhoot.'

'But why?'

'Why do tax inspectors get suspended awaiting enquiries? Why do they vanish in thin air? Why does CID go looking for them? You tell me, Lala-ji. You are a man of the world.'

Khatri sent word to Omi. 'Take your time.'

Omi took his time.

Dhulkote was a litte station hut and a flower garden. The hut was nondescript, but the flower garden was famous. Mali's handiwork was so famous that the Railway had lengthened the stop-over of certain passenger trains owing to public demand. Train-loads of people got off to feast their weary eyes on beauty created by a cripple, which Mali was.

Behind the station hut and flowers stood five little railway houses. That was all there was to the place. The rest was fields and dust and yawns and boredom. But Omi had his loaf of bread, etc., and *her* beside him. Overnight the wilderness changed: it echoed with the sound of their laughter. The stationmaster and the stationmasterani watched from the corners of their eyes.

'What do you say, Mrs Kandhari?'

'What do you say, Mr Kandhari?'

'What more do you want?'

'Nothing. Only a little Munna.'

'He will come. At the double, at this rate.'

Every afternoon Omi and Munni took a train to Ambala Cantt five miles south. Ambala Cantt was another world. It was *big city*, a city of commerce and a sprawling army and air force base. Crowded cinemas, classy clubs, smart restaurants and strings of bustling bazaars with glittering shops made it the Delhi of those parts. Every afternoon they walked in those bazaars – the weather had turned two shades cooler, making the bazaars twice as attractive – shopped in those shops, ate somewhere smart and saw a matinée show. They took the 6.46 Kalka Mail back and were home just before seven. They saw a different film every afternoon of the week Omi was there, every afternoon except one, when they were invited to tea by Miss Doolittle.

Munni usually took minutes to get ready for any occasion, but that afternoon she took ages.

'Do I look all right?' she said, looking at Omi in the rectangular mirror. The mirror was propped up against the iron bars of the window.

'Sort of,' Omi said. He stood behind her, combing and recombing his Elvis puff.

120

'Only sort of?'

'You know how you look.'

'No, I don't.' Munni didn't today. Today she was too nervous – she was going to see Miss Doolittle.

'Then move back a bit if you want to feel how you look.'

Munni moved back, into Omi, and *felt* how she looked – hard proofs came easily in the Khatri family.

'Oh, no. I can't believe anyone can be so . . . what shall I say . . .?'

'Whatever you like.'

'So lecherous. We have done it twice today already, and here it goes again.'

'Nature of the beast.'

'Disgraceful. Utterly. Let's make a move or we'll be late,' Munni said. But she didn't move. A flush had crept into her cheeks and a certain languor set into her limbs.

'All right. But give us a little kiss first.'

'No.'

'Yes. My mouth is watering for you.'

'We will get bogged down.'

'Let's get bogged down.'

They got bogged down. The rickshaw driver waiting for them outside honked and honked. In the room next door Mrs Kandhari said to Mr Kandhari, 'Tell the fool man to be quiet, ji.'

Munni had to do her makeup all over again. In minutes this time.

Miss Doolittle lived only a few minutes away by rickshaw. She had a neat little one-storey yellow-painted bungalow in the Good Christians' Mission by the G.T. road. She was old, small, bird-like and wrinkled. All her visible skin – face, neck, shoulders and arms – was heavily wrinkled, just like an old Indian beggar's. But she had an air of some sort about her.

'Dignity. Which only the English have,' Omi said to himself, though he had never known anybody English.

Miss Doolittle was pleased to see her ex-pupil. 'Gosh, you have changed. But how wonderful you look, my dear,' she said to Munni. Then she had a good look at Omi. 'I had heard so much about you, young man.'

'From who?'

'From your young lady, of course.'

'But she didn't know a thing about me before we got married.'

'She did. Everything. You mustn't underestimate us girls.'

'I swear I don't.'

Miss Doolittle examined the couple collectively. 'Umm,' she said.

121

It was an un-Indian sound. Omi liked un-Indian things, including sounds, especially if they were English. In this he was very Indian. 'A trifle young to get married. But you both look fine. You are a lucky man, Omi.'

'My parents have very good taste. Hers too, Miss Doolittle.'

Miss Doolittle laughed. The wrinkles of her narrowed eyes laughed with her. Omi laughed. He knew he had hit it off with her, and he was pleased. Munni was pleased, too.

'Oh, look,' Miss Doolittle said.

They were on the arched veranda of the yellow bungalow, sitting in moora, straw chairs made in the local Widows' Ashram, a colony of women whose husbands had been put to death by Muslims during Partition. A neat little garden spread out from the arch, and a brick wall circled the garden. Suddenly on the wall there appeared twenty or thirty scruffy little children with dusty faces. They were some of the Mission children, orphans the Good Christians' Mission looked after.

'They have come to see you, Munni. They have been waiting for you all day. They could have washed before they came, though,' Miss Doolittle said. Then she spoke to a boy of twelve who sat on the wall as if the wall was a horse. 'Ramu, you are a bad, bad boy. You should have washed your face before you came to see Munni,' she said in perfect Hindi.

One by one the children jumped off the wall. Five minutes later they were all back, their faces washed and their hair plastered down with water. Miss Doolittle and Omi laughed. The children, too. Munni coloured.

'What fun,' Miss Doolittle said.

'What fun,' she said again after hearing all about Chandigarh, the new capital of the Punjab. 'You know something, Munni, I've never been there! And it is only twenty-five miles from here. Gosh!'

'We are going to do something about that,' Omi said. When their big house was finished, she would be their first house guest.

'Ah, so you are building a house?'

'Yes. Just started,' Omi said and received an I'll-never-talk-to-you-again look from his wife – they hadn't even bought a plot of land for it, yet. There wasn't any serious mention of it either.

'How long will it take to finish?'

'Another few months. You know how our builders and contractors are, Miss Doolittle. And how reliable.'

'I know. But somehow things do get done. Things take their time in India, but they do get done.'

'You must promise to come and stay with us when the house is ready.'

'I cannot promise. But we will see. Thank you anyway . . .'

The tea was a success. Miss Doolittle didn't have many people around these days, nor did she go out much. Only to the church in the Cantt on Sundays. Anyhow, everybody had gone back to England – or they had simply *gone*.

The young couple were pleased – it was an honour to be invited by a real English person. So what if she was old and birdlike and wrinkled like an Indian beggar? And wasn't it amazing, and flattering, too, how well she spoke Hindi? Just like them.

The Khatris spent a whole hour there. All the while something was nagging Omi, but he didn't know what it was. Then, just like that it came to him: *Miss Havisham. Miss Havisham without her bridal dress*! It made him want to ask her why was she still a Miss? Hadn't she ever got married? It was a delicate question, a personal question. Omi knew he was a fool, but he also knew that he was not so much of a fool as to ask such a question.

At the end of the hour, the young couple rose to leave.

'Miss Doolittle . . .' Omi *was* that much of a fool. He asked.

'Oh, dear.' Miss Doolittle looked at the murky autumn sky and became pensive. Her long forehead became even more creased as distant thoughts and memories screen-rolled across her mind like a Cinemascope film. She smiled girlishly, but underlining that smile as both Omi and Munni could see, was a long-distance pain. Or something like it. 'Oh, dear. Oh, dear, oh dear. It's been ever so long since I talked about myself. I don't know if I should.'

'Please don't if you don't want to, Miss Doolittle. But we would really like to know,' Munni said. Even she didn't know why Miss Doolittle was still a Miss. Nor had it ever crossed her mind to ask.

Miss Doolittle was in two minds. She smiled again that smile.

'Why not? Maybe I'll never live to tell anyone else, anyway. So why not?' she said and stood up from the moora and went inside the house. Two minutes later she was back, in her hands an ancient Peek Frean biscuit tin.

The biscuit tin was full of yellowing photographs of a bygone age. They were pictures of Englishmen and women doing what they were famous for and best at – being the burra sahibs. They drove in roofless cars with long engines strapped with leather belts. They rode on sleek horses attended by liveried syces. They trekked in elephant howdahs in jungles, shooting tigers. They played polo, croquet and cricket. They picnicked in the shadows of snowy Himalayan peaks. They danced in each others' arms in chandelier-lit ballrooms. The Indians in the photographs did what they were meant to do – serve.

In almost all of the pictures there was a young and vivacious little thing, a petite beauty with a familiar smile.

'But that's you, Miss Doolittle!'

'I'm afraid it is.'

'How beautiful you look!'

'Oh, that was a long time ago. Half a century. Gosh.'

Miss Doolittle handed Omi a photograph of a dashing young army officer. Omi guessed. 'Captain Robert Slade. Robert and I were engaged to be married. Then along came this young man – Sansi . . .'

Miss Doolittle showed them a photograph of a bejewelled young Indian – obviously a nawab or a maharajah. The story began to take shape in the minds of her audience.

'We met at the Lieutenant-Governor's ball in Simla – everything happened in Simla those days . . .'

'Still does, Miss Doolittle,' Omi interrupted with a smile.

But Miss Doolittle wasn't listening. She was in a different world, thinking. Thinking, thinking, thinking as only an old person does when crushed by memories of a painful past which is so distant and yet so near. Omi guessed there had been a tragedy somewhere; he erased his smile and became doubly attentive.

'Oh, yes, everything happened in Simla those days. The Great War was on in Europe, but it was too far from Simla. Simla still had its gymkhanas and flower-shows and dog-shows and races at Anandale. Simla still had its socials and balls and fancy-dress parties. As before, one had a choice of three or four every night. As before, there was this ball too, the ball of the season. 'Natives', as Indians were then called, were not seen on such occassions – they were simply not allowed. Only Indian royalty sometimes was – that too depended on who was giving the ball. Mrs O'Dwyer was fond of India and Indians, the royalty, that is, you understand. And so *he* was invited . . .'

Miss Doolittle looked at the sky again, then at the door – Omi noticed her colourless eyelashes flickered like the wings of a tiny butterfly – as if she expected someone to walk in. *Captain What's-his-name*, wondered Omi, *or the other fellow?*

'Oh, dear. Do you really want to know?'

'Yes, Miss Doolittle. Very much.'

'All right. Don't be shocked then . . .'

Omi wanted to be shocked: he couldn't wait. He cracked his knuckles.

'Well, it was love at first sight if ever there was such a thing.'

'With whom?' Omi asked, colouring instantly. *Omi son, you are a fucking idiot. Just shut up.*

Miss Doolittle ignored him and went on with her story. 'I didn't know who he was, all I knew was that he was a prince. And he was – Maharajah Sansar Chand of Kangra, a descendant of *the* Sansar Chand. Charming and rich, immensely rich. Your princes were different then. Everything was different then – you'll never know how different. The old queen had been dead for years, but she still ruled India. You know what I mean? No, you don't. How can you? Anyway, India was very different then. Indians were invisible.'

'What do you mean, "they were invisible", Miss Doolittle?'

'I mean one didn't *see* them. They were there all around – the ayah, the khansamah, the syce, the chaprasi, the dhobi, the babu, the dukandar, the coolie – millions of them, but one didn't see them. One gave them orders, but one didn't talk to them. And Englishwomen didn't fall for them, not even for the royalty. But foolish me, I fell madly in love with this Indian. What was I to do? I broke off my engagement with Robert. That was the right thing to do, but it shocked and enraged all Simla – nobody had heard of such a thing. Sansi was ordered to leave Simla.'

'Ordered by whom?' Munni and Omi said, looking at each other. They were thinking of the same thing, of the story of Simla's Scandal Point.

'By the Lieutenant-Governor, of course.'

'Did he leave?'

'He didn't. Trust him! He went into hiding. I became an outcast. I had disgraced the Raj. I had disgraced England in the year of its greatest misfortune – England, where I had never been.'

'You had never been to England? But?'

'Never. I was born here, in Meerut. My father was a major in the army Pay Corps. He, too, was born in Meerut in the year of the Mutiny. Gosh, that must date me. My grandfather was the first Englishman they killed. They hacked him to pieces – it's in all history books. It was Captain Doolittle's unit which was the first to mutiny. All to do with the new rifle cartridge parchment soldiers had to bite off before firing. The Hindus thought it was made of cow's fat, the Muslims were told it was made of pig's. It was made of both. Well, surely you know the rest. On the morning of Sunday, 10th May, 1857,

125

the men of the Captain Doolittle's unit stole arms from the garrison and stormed the church and . . . do you really want to know?'

'Yes.'

'My young grandmother and my infant father were the sole survivors of that gory morning. Every other European was cut down. An old family servant saved them. He blackened their faces and hid them in his village till . . . the awful thing went on for months . . . Oh, dear, what am I talking about? I was talking about Simla.'

Miss Doolittle looked at the door again. Her eyelashes trembled again.

'Well, I was a fallen woman. I had disgraced myself, the Raj, and King and country by falling for a nigger.'

'What's a nigger?'

'You children are very ignorant of your history. A nigger is a blackie. A negro.'

'But we are not black. We are not negroes.'

'Of course you are not. But in those days you were, as you were so many other things. Otherwise how else could they rule you? They had to make you feel all that, you see? Anyway, I had caused such a scandal. Poor Robert, the Governor-General's ADC, can you imagine? I had to be punished. While they were thinking of what to do with me, Sansi and I decided to put an end to it all and just disappear. We decided to run away to Europe and get married and live in France or Italy. One night we left Simla in a car belonging to the Maharajah of Patiala, Sansi dressed up as the chauffeur. You can imagine what happened next.'

'No, we can't. What happened next?'

'The big search began.'

'By whom?'

'By Robert, his friends, everybody. They looked for us all over. But once we were in Princely India we were all right. We spent a few days with one rajah here and another few with another somewhere else – Sansi knew everybody, you see. At last, we made it to Bombay which was in British India. Little did we know Robert was already there, waiting. We stayed with the Maharajah of Bharwal at his grand house on the Marine Drive. Tipped off by our charming host who wanted a favour from the British, Robert turned up a night before the steamer's departure and challenged Sansi to a duel, would you believe? They met at four next morning on Juhu Beach. They shot each other. I never went to Europe. There was nowhere for me to go.'

It was a very sad story. The young couple were shattered. Miss

Doolittle could see how shattered, and felt sorry – for them, for herself? She just felt sorry and her transparent eyelashes flickered. She was sorry she had spoken about herself. She also felt glad she had.

Once Khatri's back yard had been a bald patch of dust where nothing ever grew. That was before Munni came into his house and brought Mali. Now it was a lush green carpet of silk-soft Japanese grass that Mali had laid before the rains. Now it smiled with a hundred flowers in neatly dug lanes, and in rows and rows of red gamla (clay pots).

Chin in hand, Khatri watched Mali at work from his office. Mali was very old, nobody knew how old. He had 'only half a body' – he was mangled and deformed. But he had a handsome face and he was always smiling. He sat on his haunches and went from flowerbed to flowerbed with his khurpa, breathing life into soil, seed and sapling. In his youth he had worked for a rajah in the Punjab Hills. Then something had happened – 'an accident' – and he had come back to live in his ancestral village, Lalru, near Dhulkote, a cripple for life. Uninvited and unpaid, he transformed his village. Weed and wild bush vanished from the streets of Lalru, which became fragrant avenues of marigold, motia, chameli, blushing bulbul and raat ki rani. Years passed, yet there was no paid employment for Mali. Word of his magic travelled.

The gardener of Dhulkote station till the year of Indian holocaust was a Muslim called Abdul. Abdul was a good gardener, but he wanted to become better. He went to Lalru and made a deal with Mali. 'O Mali, tell me how you do it and I'll get you a job.'

'Flowers beget flowers. You should know, Abdul.'

'Tell me how, and I'll have you fixed on the line even as you are – with only half a body. Promise!'

Abdul did not live to fulfil his promise. Come the year '47 and the world went mad. India became a pagalkhana (mental hospital) whose patients were their own doctors. Overnight, friends became enemies and neighbours began to knife each other. From the middle day of that August the country was divided. Dhulkote, Lalru and that part of the Punjab went to India. The stationmaster of Dhulkote, who was a Hindu, told Abdul to take his family by train to Pakistan and save themselves.

'Chi chi chi!' Abdul pooh-poohed the idea. He was an Indian; he was going nowhere.

127

'Go, Abdul, go. Why don't you listen?' the stationmaster and Abdul's other friends begged.

But Abdul wouldn't listen. 'Chi chi chi!' Hindus and Muslims were one people, always had been. So what were they talking about?

Before Abdul could be made to see the reality, there decended on Dhulkote one night a jatha (gang) of Sikh murderers. One of them beheaded him with one sweep of the sword, others did worse things to his wife and four daughters before putting them all inside a train to Pakistan, headless.

Dhulkote no longer had a gardener. Soon that which was jungle once – Dhulkote's garden – returned to jungle. Not a trace of Abdul's efforts remained.

It took seven and a half years exactly for Dhulkote's fortunes to change. One day its new stationmaster, Kandhari, stopped the patwari, the headman, of Lalru as he got off a train to go to Ambala City. Kandhari congratulated the patwari on what he had only heard about – his famed garden village.

'What congratulations, sahib? Your own station wasn't too bad once, I am telling you.'

'And I hear your man can hardly walk?'

'A cripple, sahib, a cripple. And unpaid.'

'This I find hard to believe. Very hard.'

'Believe it or not, sahib . . .'

The result of this chance meeting was that Lalru lost its unpaid gardener and Dhulkote gained a magician at the cost of fifty-five rupees per month to the Indian Railways. The rest is history.

Now Kandhari loaned the magician to his daughter at weekends. The magician loved the girl as much as he loved his flowers. He loved to work for her. Every Friday afternoon he caught the express, and early every Monday he was back at Dhulkote by the morning freight. Sometimes he went back later in the week. While in Chandigarh he worked for Munni bibi and Munni worked with him, sometimes Omi too. Omi hated gardening, but he grew to love Mali, the beautiful, quiet and sad old man who said little but smiled a lot. That smile hid something – a secret?

'Tell us the story of your life, Mali-ji,' Omi often asked. Mali smiled in answer.

Khatri got up from the chair and walked out to 'Munni's Mogul Garden' as he called his back yard now. 'Mali, how do you do it?'

'Flowers beget flowers, Lala-ji. Man is only an instrument of nature.'

'How much does Railway pay you?'

'Sixty exactly per month, now. Increasing by rupee one per year.'

'Pay you a hundred. Work here from now on?'

Mali stopped jabbing the earth with his khurpa.

'What about Kandhari sahib?'

'Kandhari sahib is no problem. Kandhari sahib is my problem.'

That might be so. But there was another problem. 'My flowers, Lala-ji.'

'These are your flowers, too. And Munni bibi's.'

True. But the flowers at Dhulkote did not belong to any one person, nor even to the Indian Railways. They belonged to the world, and Mali was the instrument to bring them about. How could he, poor man, explain this to Munni bibi's father-in-law?

'What will happen when Kandhari sahib is transferred to another station? You won't be able to come here – the new man at Dhulkote won't let you. Or he might want to sack you because he has someone of his own.'

Mali nodded or shook his head, Khatri didn't know which. 'In that case, Lala-ji.' In that case, it was clear, Mali didn't care what happened to him.

'Doesn't money mean anything to you, Mali?'

'Frankly, no, Lala-ji. My flowers are my flowers even if hundred rupees is hundred rupees.'

Khatri understood: Mali was an artist – his art came first and last. *I am also an artist. What's happened to my art?*

Khatri became angry with himself when it dawned on him that he couldn't go back to his 'art' of making sweets with his hands as he used to before the restaurant – he had come a long way into the world of the Pall Mall. It was a humble activity, his 'art'. But it brought satisfaction – *making* those sweets. It did him good to have his hands deep in dough, with the syrup squirting out of his fist and fingers as he shapped his ingredients into things which people loved and which made them cry, 'Wah wah, wah wah,' as they ate them. Now he did nothing with his hands. Now he gave orders.

Humbled, Khatri walked back to his office.

A visitor awaited him – Nanda, the Hospitality Officer of the Governor House. With him was Omi. The two had come in together. 'Well, well, well!' The VVIP didn't come to you: you went to him. Khatri was visibly flattered. 'Calls for a drop of something.'

'No, no, no.' Nanda said what was expected of him.

'Yes, yes, yes.' Khatri did what he was expected to do – produce a

bottle. He produced Dimple Scotch which he never drank himself –
too expensive – but kept for VVIPs.

'Aah, an intoxicating bottle! One temptation one mustn't succumb
to.'

'One must from time to time. Otherwise life would become
unlivable, what with all that goes on around us. The Akalis demand-
ing Punjabi Suba and Salazar shooting down our jawans in Goa and
Pakistan inciting Kashmir again and the prices soaring.'

'Too true, too true. But a bit early, no? Only five p.m.'

'Dimple Scotch, Nanda sahib. Liquid gold. Just look at the bottle.
Made in England. Never too early for it. Succumb.'

Nanda succumbed.

'Just a drop, then. A chota peg.'

Again Khatri did what was expected of him: he ignored Nanda's
plea and poured him a proper Patiala peg, full three inches of the
expensive stuff. Nanda had done him favours, given him his first
break in the capital, and made him win the case against Heeralal.

'What what what are you doing, Lala-ji?' Nanda protested, accept-
ing the glass. 'What about your good self?'

'Never touch the stuff at work.'

'Make an exception, Lala-ji. Exceptional friends.'

Reluctantly, Khatri made an exception. He poured himself a chota
peg, a mere half inch. 'To good times,' he said.

'To better times,' Nanda replied.

'What are you two doing together?'

'Met Uncle Nanda at the door outside,' Omi lied. He had been
with Governor House's HO for most of the afternoon.

'This Mr N. K. P. D. Kesai,' Nanda said, taking a sip loudly and
wiping his mouth with his sleeve. Mr N. K. P. D. Kesai was the new
incumbent at Governor's House.

'I hear he is very saintly and all that,' Khatri said. The newspapers
had been full of the new Governor. He was a famous Gandhian. Like
his mentor, he had shunned high office all his life, and it had taken
the country by surprise when now, in his seventy-third year, he had
accepted a job. He was renowned for his simple ways.

'Neither eats nor drinks, if that is saintly. Totally unlike his
predecessor, the eating-drinking Babbar Singh. Totally.'

Has he come to tell me about the new Governor's gastronomic
habits, Khatri asked himself, and looked at his son. Omi looked
away.

'And one more thing,' Nanda went on. He leaned over and
whispered, 'He drinks his own pee, would you believe?'

130

'I don't believe!' Khatri had heard rumours to that effect. But he feigned ignorance and pretended to be shocked.

'Half a cup of it first thing every morning. Says it is better than the royal jelly. Like that Morar-ji Bhai fellow. You with me?'

'Our leaders, these Bhais and Kesais. I can see what you are up against. I can see your problem crystal-clear, Nanda sahib.'

'No, you don't. The problem is . . .'

'How to make him stop drinking his own pee?'

'No, no, no.'

'How to make him an eating-drinking man?'

'The problem is nothing of the kind. The problem is because of the way he is – non-eating-drinking and the rest – all hospitality is out.'

'Meaning what? You talk in riddles. Don't torture me.'

'Meaning this, that all hospitality in Governor House is banned. No party-sharties. No receptions. No this, no that. I am not joking.'

This was serious. Khatri could imagine the effect it had on Nanda's income. No parties, no receptions meant no contracts; no contracts meant no percentage for Nanda, poor man. 'I see your problem, Nanda sahib.'

'No, no, no, you don't and that's what I am saying: the problem is, yours sincerely is also out. Clean bowled. L.B.W. Over the wall and six and out.'

'Please, Nanda sahib, don't torture me. I'm a friend.'

'True. One zero one per cent! He is throwing me out, your Mr N. K. P. D. Kesai, or whatever his name is.'

'But you are a gazetted officer first class!'

'So I am and so I remain – even a State Governor can't minus that. This cadre was created by the Englishman. He knew what was what and what was not. He rewarded a man for the work he did, not punished him for doing it.'

'True. Too true.'

'Did we know our leaders would turn out like this when we were fighting for Independence and went to jail with them?'

'I didn't know you went to jail, Nanda sahib?'

'I didn't, personally. But others did, didn't they?'

'So?'

'So this man is kicking me out. He is transferring me to Corbusier's concrete jungle and appointing me Caretaker to the Secretariat. Can you beat that? Me, N. N. Nanda, a catering man all my life, looking after that shitty grey cement skyscraper?' Nanda looked a broken man when he said that.

Khatri was worried for his old friend and benefactor. What worried

131

him equally was that he didn't know what he was expected to say. 'Tut, tut, tut . . .' he muttered, as one does on seeing a tragedy – a roadside accident or something like that.' Our leaders . . .' he added, hoping it said more than what it said.

'Makes one wonder how we won Independence. We won it through the Englishman's magnanimity, if you ask me. No denying Mahatma Gandhi was a great man, a mountain of a man. And so is Pandit Nehru. But had it been the bloody Germans or those blasted Japs . . .? But that is not the point.'

Khatri wished Nanda would come to it. The longer he took the stronger Khatri felt that 'the point' had something to do with him, Khatri. Nanda had come to him for something. But what? To borrow money? Khatri hoped not – lending of money is a tricky thing, especially among friends. At the same time he felt for Nanda.

'The point is to be free from it all. Fly one's own kite. Pedal one's own bike. Captain one's own HMS *Kismet*. Like you, Lala-ji.'

If that was the point, Khatri had not seen it yet.

'What is your point, Nanda sahib?' He was direct.

'I have more than a point, I have a proposition, Lala-ji.'

'Oh! What is it?' Khatri didn't care what it was as long as he was not asked to shell out a thousand or two.

'A hotel.'

Omi, who had been mysteriously quiet hitherto, cleared his throat. 'Father, Chandigarh is expanding right, left and centre. Seventy thousand last year, ninety this. Before we count up to twenty, this place is going to be half a million minimum,' he said.

'And world-class tourists pouring in to see Corbusier's buildings. Therefore the city needs a decent hotel. You with me?' Nanda said.

'So the two of you have been talking?' Khatri said. Now he understood how they had happened to come in together.

'You can say. I had to clear it with junior boss before I came to the karta-dharta, senior boss,' Nanda laughed.

'But Chandigarh has many hotels. There is the Mountview, the Blue Skies, the . . .' Now Khatri wished it had been money, a couple of thousand.

'They are neither here nor there, if you see what I mean, Lala-ji. Ditto for Plaza. Others are all Indian gobar (dungheaps), fit only for Indians.'

'So?'

'So let's put our boots and hats on and come up with a knocker. A Taj Mahal on a moonlit night. A fifty-room air-conditioned heaven. With a pool-shool and first-class drinking bar . . .'

132

'But with what?'

'Where there is a will there is a way, Father,' Omi said.

'You keep your tail out of it. Dog!' Khatri said.

'Don't say that of him. Gem of a boy, Om Parkash is. Gem of a boy,' Nanda said, putting an arm around Omi and hugging him.

'Nanda sahib, fact of the matter is I don't want to go in the hotel line,' Khatri said, shaking both his hands in the air and meaning thereby the end of this conversation.

'But why not, why not?'

'Because I don't know half a thing about it.'

'Did you know about restaurant business before you started it?'

'He dragged me into it. *Him* you are hugging.'

'Look where it got you, Lala-ji. Made you king.'

'True, Father.'

'You keep out of it, oi.'

'Om has to be in. Our best Derby horse. He's going to do it again – run the hotel.'

'Truth is, Nanda sahib, I am not going to jump in the sea to see if I can swim.'

'Best thing, Lala-ji. Plunge in the waves and ride them.'

'Or they ride you. Drown you, more like.'

'Come, come, Lala-ji, this is defeatist talk. We are Indian. We may have been losers in the past, but we were never defeatists. Never.'

'But why me, Nanda sahib? I am a simple God-fearing man.' Khatri was puzzled. As someone close to the Governor, Nanda knew everybody who mattered, people with money and influence. Then why had he come to him?

'Because you have everything. Integrity. Heart. Judgement. And you have Om Parkash. I could have gone to ten others with twenty times more money, but I didn't. No, Nanda, I said to myself, go to Khatri. He is your man. And here I am, with a watertight plan. Your glass is empty, Lala-ji.'

Both their glasses were empty. Khatri filled them, giving himself a burra peg this time – he needed it. Omi briskly flicked open a bottle of soda-water and filled up the glasses.

'What is the plan?'

'The plan is . . .' From now on Nanda talked in whispers. A large plot of land was going for 'next door to nothing, you can say' by the lake. It was meant for a nursery or a children's park, but Nanda had Saxena, the Town Planning Officer, 'in the pocket'. It was all 'hush and hush', but it was 'all right, one zero one per cent'.

'I have done Saxena twenty-one favours in the past – got his

133

wheeling-dealing son out of the clutches of Anti-Corruption because Superintendent Bakwasi was licking my boots then because I had the Governor's ear. Plus this, plus that. And moreover, his sister's daughter is betrothed to my nephew who has neither a mother nor a father, poor boy – so the *when* of the marriage is in my hands. So Saxena is no problem. So planning permission for the hotel is one hurdle we have already leapt and crossed . . .'

'I like the word "we".'

Nanda wasn't listening. He had another sip, smacked his lips, wiped them on his forearm and carried on with his whisper. '. . . And America-Returned Bassi has come up with this.'

It was then that Khatri knew. Nanda carried a portfolio of some sort. Nanda pulled out a few sketches – blue lines on parchment-like paper. Khatri couldn't make head or tail of them. 'Hum . . .' he said.

'You follow?' Nanda said. He knew the fish was biting – Khatri looked interested. He took another sip, a longer one, of the Dimple Scotch, wiped his lips again and began to relax a little.

'Hum,' Khatri repeated. He had remembered something – passing by Bassi in Sector 22 the other day. Bassi had had a funny smile.

'Our Lake View Hotel. Fifty rooms. Part of the lake as our swimming-pool. Bar-shaar. Boating-shoating. Mountains there. Water here. Why, this is heaven on earth as Shah Jahan had it written in marble in the Red Fort.'

'Cost of plot?' Khatri said. *Why am I asking when I don't want to know it?*

Nanda whispered the cost of plot in Khatri's ear. Khatri's jaw fell to the floor.

'Peanuts, Lala-ji!'

'Cost of construction and furbishing?'

'Goes by the room. About four thousand per room.'

'So with the unseens you are talking of two point five.'

'I am talking.'

It was a staggering amount. It was laughable. Nanda had gone mad. Did he expect Khatri to be mad too? Khatri knew he did – *that's the thing about mad people. They expect you to go mad with them.* But Khatri also knew what he was going to do – nothing. Absolutely nothing. Only listen. *I may be a fool, but I am not mad.*

'Two point five minimum, eh, HO sahib? Where is it coming from?'

'We buy the plot cash down, now. It has to be now or we miss it. One of those now-or-never things. Om Parkash knows.'

'What about the rest?'

'The rest we borrow.'

'From who? The Queen of England?'

'From Punjab Himachal Bank. Manager Ahuja is in the pocket as well. His daughter is married to my brother's wife's cousin's niece. He will take his usual one and quarter per cent. And look who we have here.'

As Nanda said that, the front door opened and in walked Ahuja himself – tall, lanky and slightly bent with a twitching eye. He had never before set foot in the Pall Mall. The coincidence made Khatri scratch the middle of his sutthan.

Paro lay spread out on a charpoy on the screened balcony overlooking Munni's Mogul Garden. Munni sat by her on the same charpoy, massaging her legs. Or rather, pressing them – Paro always got a pain in her legs at this time of the year when a cold wind suddenly began to blow on a sunny afternoon. Winter was coming, and Chandigarh winters could be severe. A massage helped. At any rate Paro liked a massage, having given many a one to her own mother-in-law when she was eighteen.

They had been talking of this and that, mainly of the court case and Heeralal's threat to 'smoke burn' them. 'Dog,' Paro said and shut her eyes. Still she could see the pink-orange glow of the warm afternoon through her closed eyelids. This massage had become routine. Often Paro fell asleep during it. Today she made an effort to remain awake – she was waiting for her sister. She had a sari for her and cloth for a shirt for Bhajjan, and she wanted to talk to her about something important – a trip to Goddess Durga's famous temple near Jammu. She wanted to take Munni there and beg the Goddess for a grandson. She wanted Vidya to come with them and do some begging for herself as well.

'Vidya, you are thirty. If not now, when? When when when, old hag?'

Goddess Durga was renowned for this sort of thing – granting sons and heirs. Princes and paupers alike had been among millions of her satisfied supplicants.

Paro felt she was going to doze off. As Vidya seemed to be taking her time, she decided to do just that.

'Ma, don't,' said Munni.

'Don't what?' mumbled Paro, half asleep.

'Such a lovely afternoon. An afternoon for strawberries and cream.'

'What's stro'bry?'

'A little fruit which grows on little bushes in the fields.'

135

'Fruit grows on trees. Only vegetables grow in fields.'

'But strawberries are special. In England they eat them at Ascot and Wimbledon with cream, on a day like this. Their summers are like our winters, Ma.' Munni told Paro all about Ascot and Wimbledon.

'How do you know about these things, girl?' Girls shouldn't know such things, not girls from a good family.

'Miss Doolittle told me. And I have read about them in books.'

'Well, girl, you should not read such books. And another thing – you can't have your stro'bry, or whatever you Angrez log (English people) call it. It doesn't grow here.'

'Such an afternoon, Ma. Even cherries will do.'

'Even they don't grow here, so don't ask me. Ask God, maker of men and cherries. He might listen to you if He has nothing else to do.'

'Please God, maker of men and cherries . . .'

God had nothing else to do. He listened to Munni. Just then a tokri (basket) of fruit was delivered. Lakhpatni had sent it as a *yes-let-us-make-up* reciprocal gesture. A few years back her husband, who had an eye on the future, had planted an orchard of cherries on the slopes of Kasauli where the weather was just right, saying to Lakhpatni, 'Wife, India is independent now. Soon some of us will be rich like them gone English. The new rich will want to eat English fruit – things like cherries. So no harm in digging an orchard. What harm?' This was the first crop. Lakhpatni had thought of splitting it with a selected few, among them Paro. The fact of the matter was that she missed her natter with her. And Paro had made the first approach – those victory laddus!

The cherries woke up Paro. 'I knew,' Paro said. But she didn't say what she knew.

The cherries were jewel-like translucent pink. They glowed in the sun like Miss Doolittle's cheeks sometimes used to do on a certain afternoon. They tasted just as Munni liked fruit to taste – sweet but sharp. Her favourite mango was one which was as sweet as it was sour, if not a little more sour than sweet. She ate cherry after cherry, and thought of Asha for some reason. 'Ma, can I take a few cherries to Asha?' she asked.

'Why do you ask? Do what you like, beta,' Paro said.

Munni made a little pannier and said from the door, 'Ma, I'll be back in an hour. Is that all right?' She was back inside five minutes – with the cherries.

'What happened?' Paro said.

136

'Her mother-in-law said she wasn't at home, and she wouldn't take the cherries for Asha because she said they don't eat foreign food or fruit.'

'But Asha is at home, in her window. There!'

And there she was, too, in her window, looking towards the Khatri balcony and making signs with her hands – she was saying something. Then suddenly she vanished as if she had been pulled away by the tug of a string like a puppet.

Next day Munni saw Asha again in her window. Asha waved to her. Munni waved back. It was an afternoon like yesterday's – sharp, with a nippy breeze from the Kasauli mountain. Munni wrapped a shawl around her shoulders and walked up to Asha's house.

'Asha is not at home,' said Asha's sass (mother-in-law) from the door.

'But I just saw her in the window!'

'She is not in, I said.'

'Well, I'm blowed,' Munni mumbled to herself in English. She hurried back home and sat down with a book, feeling low and angry. Some time later she heard someone coming up the stairs.

'Asha!' Munni knew. She put the book down and stood up.

'Quick, let me in,' Asha said.

Munni took her to the bedroom. 'What's the matter?'

'Nothing.'

'Then? Are you all right?'

There was tea going. Munni handed Asha a cup. Asha's hand shook as she took it, and Munni saw that her usually dark face was a sickly pale grey.

'You don't look well.'

'I am all right.'

'Then what's the matter? Drink your tea and tell me.'

'I can't.'

'Why not?'

Asha put the cup down and stood up. First she shut the door, then she pulled her shirt down to her waist. Her shoulders and back and sides had ugly marks. She had been badly beaten.

'Haré Ram! Haré Krishan!' Munni was aghast. 'Who did this to you? Him?'

'No, them. His sisters and his mother.'

'Haré Ram! Haré Krishan! But why?'

'Because I am black – they call me bhangi (untouchable). Because

137

my father is poor and can't send them any money. Because I didn't
bring much dowry like you. Munni, you don't know how lucky you
are . . .'

Munni didn't know what to say. She felt sorry, helpless, even
guilty.

'Now I must go.'

'Don't go yet. Drink your tea. Talk to me.'

'I can't stay, I just slipped out. His sisters are not at home and his
mother is sleeping. If she wakes up and finds me missing they'll skin
me alive.'

'Does he know?'

'Yes. Of course.'

'Does he also?'

'Sometimes, but not badly. Only when they taunt him and call him
bad things.'

'What bad things?'

'Jhuddu (impotent). Unperformer. Minus-wallah. Zero man.'

'Is he?'

Asha didn't answer. She bit the end of her dupatta (scarf) and
covered her head with it bashfully.

'But why beat you?'

'I have told you. Now lend me fifteen paisa for a post-office
envelope. I want to write home. They won't let me write home unless
it is to ask my poor father to send money. They won't give me even
fifteen paisa for a stamp.'

'How will you go to the post office to buy a stamp?'

'I'll send Kaka, the little boy next door.'

Munni gave Asha a rupee, saying she didn't have any loose change
– it would buy her many postage stamps.

'Promise to pay you back one day soon.'

'Not to worry. You go and write your letter.'

As the two girls came out on the balcony, they saw Asha's sass at
the Bahal window. Damyanti was shouting: 'Asha, Asha! I know
where you are. Come right back, you churrail (witch), or I'll burn
your hair . . .'

Asha looked at her friend – *I have had it* – she trembled and ran
home. That evening Janak came back from his PWD tour. Next
morning the neighbourhood talked.

'I heard muffled screams from the Bahal house last night.'

'Me too. As if they had stuffed a pillow in her face.'

'It is that churrail, Damyanti.'

'And those bitches, the sisters.'

138

'Why doesn't Janak do something about it?'

'Janak? Janak hasn't got half a ball to him. He is still stuck in his mother's crotch, not fully delivered.'

'Can't *we* do something for Asha?' Munni said.

'Yes, find her another man and let her run away,' Omi said.

'You keep your long nose out of it, you hear?' Paro said to her son. She knew he was perfectly capable of interfering in other people's affairs.

'Hear what, Ma? You know me. I never put my oar in another man's boat.'

'Yes, I know you. That's why I am saying – keep your big long nose out of it.'

Another thing Omi loved in life was an early evening walk with Munni by the lake when there was no one around.

Munni too.

But it was not always easy. As usual, it was *work work work*. It was difficult to get away from it. Only on Sundays – and on Sundays every fourth Chandigarhia had the same idea. Omi discovered that Tuesdays weren't bad. Tuesday was Lord Hanuman's day. Most people fasted and went to the temple, or they stayed at home to pray to the mighty monkey god. On a good Tuesday the lake was often completely deserted in the evening. Omi regarded this as a personal gift from Lord Hanuman. He said goodbye to the world, disappeared with Munni on the far side of the lake and did 'guess what'. In the bushes. Spread under early evening stars. Waves whispering by. And Kasauli's lights twinling like cluster of celestial pinpricks so close that they could catch them with a hand.

Going by rickshaw was a nuisance – it was slow and boring. Besides, Omi had a stronger objection to it: *I have reached a point in life when I don't want to be seen around in stupid rickshaws.* Rickshaws were for ordinary people. Omi had put in for a car, but the queue for it was at least a mile long. With the help of the dealer, S. S. Majithia, Omi had jumped the queue. But, alas, only half a mile of it.

Now and then Omi borrowed Arun's new Fiat while Arun sat in the Pall Mall eating-drinking with mutual friends. For this, depending on how long Omi had been out, Arun's bill was halved. Or not presented at all (if Khatri wasn't around).

That Tuesday, as Omi had arranged with Arun, when the sun went down and the Munni birds began their duet Arun turned up with Duke, Lord and Harry. Exactly half-past six. Grey, misty, chilly:

139

ideal. *Please Hanuman-ji maharaj, rather cold today. Don't you think the good people of Chandigarh would be better off praying at home?*

The generous Lord Hanuman obliged. He kept the good folk of Chandigarh at home and cleared the lake for Omi and Munni. As there was no one around, they held hands. They even put their arms around each other – something only men did in public or public places, not men and women, not even those married to each other. Their hands in Munni's shawl and Omi's shirt and jacket respectively, they had gone a few hundred delicious yards when Omi had this odd feeling that they were being followed. It was an odd feeling indeed, for there was no visible evidence for it.

The lake was man-made. Rainwater pouring down an old seasonal river from the clay hills that rose beyond the northern city limits was dammed there by a high mud bandh curving gracefully for more than half a mile. It sloped sweetly into the biscuit-coloured water, the slope lined with local grey sandstone. On the other side was a sheer drop of about fifty feet. The top of the bandh was as wide as two cricket pitches, forming a delightful promenade.

Omi looked around them. Flower-bushes and decorative trees adorned the long walk. There were mazes of neatly trimmed hedges and little parks with swings and slides for kid-kiddies. Today there were no kid-kiddies around, thanks to Lord Hanuman. While walking past one such park, contained by a manicured hedge, Omi realized they were not being followed, they were being watched. Two men were hiding there. Unconcerned – why should anyone watch them? – Omi walked on. He didn't tell Munni. But Munni guessed something was wrong – Omi had suddenly become less feverish.

'Anything the matter?'

'Nothing. Nothing at all.'

'Then why have you taken your hand away?' Munni was just beginning to feel the waves of the lovely lake rise and rise inside her.

'I think we ought to turn back.'

'Why? We've only just come.'

'I know. But Arun said not to take long.'

'Don't worry. We won't be long.' Munni took his hand and placed it where it had been a moment ago.

Omi worried. Should they turn back? Would it not seem strange to the men hiding in the bushes if the newly married couple out for a lovers' walk turned back so suddenly? And if it was really them they were watching – Omi still couldn't figure out why, but he began to admit that they might be, *India, dammit, full of shit-arses, cheap thugs* – the bastards might get up to some mischief.

140

Mischief! The word hit Omi hard. It hit him even harder when he realized that he had seen something sinister in the men's hands. Not rifles, but something like that. Something smaller.

It didn't make sense. But it terrified Omi, making him break into cold sweat. They were in danger. What was he to do? In front lay the bald, flat, entirely deserted curve of the bandh shrouded in heavy mist, half a mile of it, with the lake itself on one side and only jungle on the other, fifty feet below. Then Omi saw another odd sight – a jeep at the bottom of the bandh where the jungle began. *Mother-laying hell!* Those men were going to shoot them, take Munni's jewellery – and there was a good amount of it on her – and make their getaway in that jeep. Or kidnap her. What would Omi do then? *Fight the bastards till the last drop of blood in my body. At least get one of them. Tear out his eyes. Rip open his guts with my bare hands.*

'What's wrong? Let's turn back if you want to,' Munni said.

Omi realized another thing – if they turned back they would put their lives, her life, at a greater risk. Nor could they carry on walking further, for that would cut off any chance of a retreat. They were trapped.

'Yes, I want to turn back,' Omi said. At least there was an outside chance that somebody might be coming along from the lake gates. Maybe a host of people who had finished with praying and had hit upon the idea of a stroll by the lake after all. *Not that bloody cold, is it? What's the matter with us Indians? Afraid of freezing when it gets below 100°F!*

As they were about to turn back Omi saw a group of smudges walking out of the mist towards them from the far side, where Omi's bushes were. People! He sighed in relief. They would join those people and walk back to the gates with them. The gunmen wouldn't attack them with others around. By now Munni was convinced that something was very wrong. Omi took her hand and they hurried towards the smudges in the mist. The smudges became five men – all wearing turbans: Sikhs. Two walked in front, two behind, and in between them, at a distance of fifteen or twenty feet from either group of two, walked a little figure. His hands were clasped behind his back. He was in deep thought.

As they drew nearer, Omi saw yet another strange thing – the men in front and behind the little man were armed. They had revolvers in holsters slung from their shoulders.

Revolvers? Now Omi knew what those two men hiding in the bushes had had – Sten guns. He shuddered. More cold sweat. Then in a flash it came to him. He recognized the dwarfish figure with his

141

hands behind his back – a certain little man who had given him a lift the night he had nearly lost his shirt to robbers – Har Raisingh, the Chief Minster of the Punjab. Raisingh, who lived half a mile down the Lake Road, had come here for a stroll and a think. Those four men were his bodyguard. But who were the other two, then? Part of his bodyguard? Obviously – Omi registered only now that they had also been Sikhs. *Twenty-two-carat fool, deserving a donkey kick up your backside! And you frightened her.*

Life returned to Omi. 'Phewee!' he breathed loudly, and chuckled as he folded his hands on his chest in greeting to the Chief Minister, hoping he had been recognized.

'What's the matter? You are behaving in a most peculiar way,' Munni whispered as she too folded her hands on her bosom to the Chief Minister.

'Everything is all right. We are all right now. No, we are not!' Something told him they were not. It was sheer instinct. Now Omi panicked.

'Sardar-ji, sir!' Omi stopped the Chief Minister as he returned their greeting.

'What do you want, young man?' said one of the two front-line bodyguards, reaching for his gun and placing himself between his leader and Omi.

'Sir, don't go a step further!'

'What do you mean, son?' asked Raisingh. He had recognized Omi.

'My wife and I just saw two men hiding in those bushes, with Sten guns. They couldn't be your bodyguard, sir?'

'I have no more bodyguard with me here. Only . . .' Raisingh couldn't even finish. There was a burst of gun-fire from the bushes.

'Down! Down . . .' Omi screamed as the Chief Minister's men returned the fire. He pushed the frail-looking leader and his own equally frail wife on to tarmac and covered their bodies with his own. The two men with Sten guns came running towards them, guns blazing. The Chief Minister's bodyguards, two crouching, one standing, the fourth lying – hit – fired back.

'Sir, roll down into the lake with Munni. Somebody is after you,' Omi said, sitting up and crouching over them.

'Does look like it, doesn't it? And you lie down flat, son.'

Omi didn't lie down. He crouched over them and rolled them over – first Munni and then the Chief Minister – like rolling out a carpet. He kept rolling them. He didn't know what he was doing. As guns roared and bullets hit the stone of the low wall of the bandh, Omi

142

gave them both a last push and then rolled with them down the stony slope into the ice-cold water. Within seconds it was all over. There was one last shot, then a chilling silence, broken by the exhaust of the getaway jeep at the bottom of the other side of the dam.

'You all right, Lehna?' the Chief Minister shouted from the lake. There was no answer. 'Looks bad, son. You all right, daughter?'

'We are all right, how about you, sir?' Munni said, shivering.

Two more shots tore open the evening. Then there was the sound of running feet and more shots, a barrage of them.

'Looks very bad. I don't understand why they are after me. I've given my whole life to them. Spent eleven years in British jails fighting for freedom for our country . . .'

'We got them, Sardar-ji,' shouted one of the guards, coming to the edge of the embankment. He and another man came running down the stones and helped the Chief Minister out of the water. 'We got them both. Everything is all right now, Sardar-ji.'

Everything was far from being all right.

'Where is Lehna?'

'They got him, sir.'

'Oh, no. My poor Lehna. Been with me since '49. Got married only four years ago. What are we going to tell his wife?'

'Sir, let's get you back home quickly. You never know.'

'Sir, I did say we should take a jeep or a car, but you wouldn't listen.'

'Sir, take off your wet wet achkan and wear my wasscut. We have some way to walk.'

Omi realized that the Chief Minister had walked all the way from home. *What a Sikh thing to do*! 'Sir, our car is at your disposal,' he said.

'Run, run, run, young man, and fetch your car,' a guard said.

Omi ran to get Arun's car as the Chief Minister, now in the waistcoat of one of his protectors, first inspected the body of his loyal Lehna and then those of the two assassins. The former was in his early thirties, the latter barely out of their teens. The Chief Minister, his eyes tearful, shook his head gravely and said: 'Tut, tut, tut.'

Omi was back with the car.

'You saved my life, son. You are a brave man, a true son of the Punjab.'

'I did what any Punjabi would have done. We love you, sir.'

'They were also Punjabi – these boys who tried to kill me. They wanted their own Punjabi-speaking Sikh state. But I won't have it and I am also a Sikh, a pukka Sikh, a son of the Guru. We are Indian before we are Punjabi or Gujarati. We may speak fifteen different

143

languages, we may have ten different religions, but we are Indian before anything. Why don't we understand?'

'Sir, your order?' interrupted a guard, the boss of bodyguard.

'Mahan Singh, telephone I. G. Sheshwani when we get home. Tell him to report on the double. Also General Dhillon. Get the Home Secretary and the PTI crew for any photo-shoto. And put a call to Delhi – I suppose I'll have to speak to Pandit Nehru myself. I hate to bother him with this local fool nonsense. He has so much on his plate – the Chinese massing troops in Leh and NEFA and every where. I can see the headlines tomorrow in every paper – *Hairaisingh Escape*. Haha . . . how do you like that, Om Parkash? It is Om Parkash, isn't it? Sad about Lehna. Tragic. My heart is broken like a china vase with flowers in it. But for you son, it would have been us too, I am telling you. Son, you are driving too fast. I am more fearful of mad drivers than mad gunmen. Have you not seen those overturned trucks on the G.T. Road?'

Omi, numb, was driving like a maniac. Munni, also numb and wet and cold and shivering, sat next to him, and next to her sat a bodyguard of the Chief Minister. Behind them the little man was sandwiched between two of his remaining men, agitated and quite unable to stop talking. 'We are Indian first, Hindu and Sikh after, Punjabi and Gujarati after . . .'

They were nearly there.

'You saved my life, son. What's your father's name?'

Omi told him.

'And your wife's?'

'Munnishka.'

'Munnishka sounds Russian, no? I know some Russians, namely Krushchev and Bulganin. Good men. Good friends. Listen, Omi and Munnishka, my children. I will send for you another day to say thank you proper. Today . . .'

They had arrived at the Chief Minister's Residence. Suddenly, they were surrounded by a large number of heavily armed personnel, as if by some unknown means the news of the assassination attempt on the life of the Punjab's leader had preceded them. Among them stood a tiny woman of fifty or so. She had puffed up cheeks, and she wore a loose set of salvar kamiz, both in the same light brown woollen material. She held her hands on her hips and stared blankly at the Chief Minister.

'Sardarni-ji, your sardar is all right, by the grace of the guru. Look, not a scratch. Not one. But Lehna got a bad hole in his head. I would have had one too, if not ten. But for this . . .'

144

The Sardarni glared. 'Resign. Resign tomorrow! Write the letter to Pandit-ji tonight. If you won't, I will with my own hands, even if I can't write . . .'

'Indians first, Hindu, Muslim, Sikh, Isai after. Punjabi, Gujarati, Bengali, Bombay-wallah after . . . Mahan Singh, give Omi and Munnishka an escort. And remember, Omi, not a word of your bravery to anyone except your parents. Now go, and come another day.'

Omi and Munni had an escort – a jeep with four policemen armed to the teeth clearing the way for Arun's Fiat down Chandigarh's empty roads.

BOOK THREE

First you wanted a red-brick shop 'n' house. Then a pukka restaurant, and now a hotel with pool-school, eh? Where is it going to end, Khatri, old cock?

Did Khatri really want a hotel?

Khatri had to do some hard thinking. Hard thinking meant sleepless nights. For four nights running Khatri tossed and turned in bed. Dogs barked from the 'Corbusier area', the build-up part of Sector 23 in front of his shop-and-house. From the 'God area' – the wilderness behind the Public Nurseries – howled jackals and hyenas. The noise they made was familiar to Khatri's ear, but these nights, when he couldn't sleep, it seemed different, like a collective wail. The city dogs and their wilder cousins sounded as if they were weeping in the hollow of the black well of night, echoing what Khatri felt. What had he done – agreed to gamble away with one throw of the dice all that which had taken him a lifetime to build?

Paro tossed and turned with him. He hadn't told her anything. He hadn't dared to. Paro would have torn her hair, beaten her breast and sent down the relentless monsoon and endless rivers of rain – the Ganges, Jamuna, Brahmaputra *et al*.

Why am I doing this? Khatri had everything going for him. He had his family's love and the world's respect and enough money. He didn't need more money. He didn't even want more money. Unlike his son, he didn't want to be a millionaire – he was happy as things were. *Then why am I bringing down the axe on my own feet with my own hands?*

He knew why. He had become too big for his boots, and God was about to teach him a thing or two, as was His way. Whenever God wanted to teach someone a thing or two, He first let them grow too big for their boots, sent them up dizzy heights in a hot-air balloon. When they were right up *there*, where Khatri now was, God pushed a needle into the balloon and watched the result from a distance.

Khatri knew God well.

There had been a heavy snowfall in Simla in the far hills earlier that day, which had made the air in Chandigarh very cold. In spite

149

of the quilt, Khatri shivered. He got out of his bed and quietly spread his quilt over Paro's and slipped in with her. Paro, awake, stirred and curved into him as he put an arm around her. In the distance dogs barked in 'Corbusier area', and their jungli (wild) cousins in the 'God area' answered back, but now they sounded only like dogs and jackals. Lying next to Paro, feeling her warmth, strengthened him. Khatri sighed. He had done his thinking. He did not want a hotel. He would tell that man Nanda tomorrow, first thing. He would pick up the phone and say *No, no, Nanda sahib, I don't want to own half a hotel. Not even a whole hotel. By God, I don't. So.* Khatri was sure this was what Baba Gokul would have advised him to do.

Baba Gokul! 'Shadi Lal, you have a lot to do yet. Build . . .' Baba Gokul's words flashed across his mind.

'*Build . . .!*'

In that instant it became clear to Khatri what his guru had meant, and all his worry vanished – just like that. Suddenly, he felt his path clear. He understood the meaning of life and its purpose – *build, make.* His chest became light, his head too. Sleep, sweet sleep, followed.

'Om, I have been thinking,' Khatri said to his son on the way to Bajwara Market four hours later. For the last four days Omi had watched his father think, from the corners of his eyes. For once he hadn't pestered him. But he knew whenever his father said *Om, I have been thinking*, it meant he had *stopped* thinking. It meant he had decided. Omi knew what he had decided. He wanted to stop there and then and stand on his head.

'Father, great minds think alike!'

'Am I included in that list?'

'You are tops, Father. Number One. Plus plus.'

'Aren't you forgetting the real great mind among us all?'

'Who? Mother?'

'What is she going to say – or, more frighteningly, do?'

'Mother is no problem, Father. Mother is my problem.'

'Only if you knew her as well as I do, boy.'

'I do, Father. Her habit to complain about everything – she wouldn't be hapy if she couldn't. Anyway, we don't have to tell her. Not just yet.'

But one look at her husband and son, and Paro knew.

'What are you two up to now?'

'Mother, is this the way to speak to men who love you as madly as we do?'

'Yes. What are you hiding from Munni and me?'

'Silly woman, what can I have to hide from you?' Khatri slapped his wife on her round bottom.

'Munni, they are cooking something, and whenever they cook something together it is lethal poison. Change my name if I am proven wrong. Shave my hair off if I am not found right,' Paro said.

'Ma, your love of cinema entitles you to a role in *Mughal-é-Azam II* even without an audition,' Omi said.

Convinced she knew who was behind this secret cooking exercise, Paro waved a finger at her husband. It was a warning. 'Don't let him wring out the last ounce of the remaining sense in your head. Sons bring laurels to those who beget them. Ours brings . . .'

'Ma, what are you talking about? You you know me,' Omi said.

'That's why I am saying what I am saying,' Paro said.

'Paro, woman, what are you saying?' Khatri said.

'I am saying you haven't slept in four nights. I am saying you have hardly touched food for four days. I am saying I saw that ganda (dirty) Nanda drinking with you the other day.'

'He came, I gave him a chota peg – so what?'

'When a man starts drinking at work at five with Governor House it only means one thing – hanky-panky stirred by this soda-pouring son of ours.'

'Ma, you should join Scotland Yard.'

'What's that?'

'World's best jasoos (detectives). I think they will decorate you. Give you a bronze medal at least. Ask your daughter-in-law – she knows more about England than I do. She went to school there – St Paul's Girls' in London proper.'

'Yes, joke with me, make fun of me. Sons bring some laurels; mine heaps insults on me. Munni, what did I do in my past life?'

'Paro, we are not up to anything. Nothing that Baba Gokul wouldn't approve of. Honest.'

'Ah, so you are up to something. Admit it!'

Father and son admitted nothing. After some more ball-scratching, Khatri went ahead and put down his fifty per cent for the plot. Khatri didn't like doing things behind his wife's back but this time he had to.

'Boy, I don't like it.'

'Father, it is statesmanship on our part. How Mahatma Gandhi and Nehru won us Independence? Through statesmanship.'

151

'Good thing they were dealing with Mountbatten, not your mother.'

'She'll be all right.'

'How? How are we going to tell her? It's going to be 1857 all over again. And Ganga and Jamuna and Brahmaputra in full spate, flooding the Bengal of my heart.'

'Just leave it to me, Father.'

Now Khatri left most things to him anyway. Father and son planned the next move carefully, in whispers behind Paro's back. The day for it was the coming Sunday, when they would 'tell' her. 'What will you do, boy?'

'I'll hire a Mysore elephant, Father.'

'What can a Mysore elephant do pitted against a Punjabi buffalo?'

Omi did not hire an elephant, he did the next best thing. On Sunday afternoon he hired a taxi.

'Ma, we are going for a picnic.'

'Not on my life. I returned from the last one with my head buried in the dust of shame. And minus my friend Lakhpatni.'

'This one is different. It is special.'

'How?'

'Questions, questions, questions. But today is not for questions.'

'What is special about today?'

'Ma, it is your birthday.'

Good heavens! Paro had forgotten. Khatri had forgotten. Vidya too. 'So what?' Paro said. They never celebrated birthdays anyway. What was so different about this one?

'So what? Your fortieth birthday and so what? Just get dressed quickly – the taxi is waiting downstairs. And dress to kill.'

Paro dressed to kill. She wore the peacock-blue sari her men liked, showing inches of her belly. She borrowed Munni's lipstick and wrapped a white Kashmiri shawl around her. They went, first to Sector I5 to pick up Aunt Vidya. 'Uncle Bhajjan, shut the shop for the day,' Omi said.

'But,' Bhajjan said. Their 'little shop' was open seven days a week.

'No but-shut today, Uncle Bhajjan. Just shut the damn-fool shop. And Aunt Vidya, dress to kill. We are going to kill the world today.'

Vidya, too, got dressed to kill.

'Where are we going?' the sisters asked.

They got no reply. The taxi was racing down Madhya Marg, through the heart of the city. At the red stone and glass Government Printing Press, the taxi turned north, and they knew.

'The lake, eh? So what is so special about it?' they said.

Again they received no reply. Near the lake, instead of joining the great festive Sunday crowd, Omi told the driver to drive along a mud track that disappeared in the jungle. Away to their left, Le Corbusier's High Court raised its grey contrete hood like a football stadium. Further along the same side, Nanda's 'shitty skyscraper', the Secretariat with hundreds of windows, towered above the flat and dusty countryside. The two famous buildings presented a bizarre sight, uninteresting and unIndian. The clay hills rising in front a mile away made them even more so.

But where the Khatri taxi was it was all jungle – the thorny kikar tree with the tiny yellow flower which becomes powder when you touch it, the akk cactus that sheds drops of white milk when you break a stem, the beri bush, the lasoora, imli, neem and bill pathar trees hugging each other, crushing each other, strangling each other, but looking the better for it.

Bemused, Paro issued a loud sigh and looked from her sister to her men, then at her daughter-in-law. 'Munni, sometimes you must wonder what sort of species are these Khatris. I have lived with them for twenty plus two years by the calendar and I am still wondering.'

Munni smiled. 'Look, Mother,' she said, pointing to a little clearing in the jungle by the left side of the lake. A shamiana (marquee) was erected there. The ground under it was covered by a blue dhurry carpet with a red and white margin. On the carpet was spread everything the Pall Mall was famous for, and whatever else Sectors 22 and 23 and Bajwara had to offer by way of food, fruit, sweetmeats and drinks. In attendance were headwaiter Seva Singh and Bawa, smart in blinding white uniforms with razor-sharp creases.

'Seva Singh getting married or going to a wedding? Which? Right spot for both, I think. Don't you?' Paro said.

'No ordinary spot this, Ma,' Omi said.

'I can see that. Taxi and shamiana and all this unnecessary food. Who is going to eat it? How much did it cost? Does money grow on trees?'

'Yes, Ma, it is going to. Right here, on the very earth you are standing on. On the very spot.'

'What, boy, what are you talking?'

'It is yours, Ma.'

Paro understood. As she understood, she slapped her forehead in despair, shock and dismay. 'Your guru said you had to build a house, but did he say it had to be in the man-eating jungle?' she said to Khatri.

'Our hotel, Ma. Our hotel. We are going to erect a Taj Mahal here.'

'Or our shamshanghat (graveyard). Sons bring laurels. Mine builds family graveyards.'

The bushes of the man-eating jungle stirred.

'Don't say that about your Omi, Paro. Best boy . . .'

The bushes opened up and out stepped Chatkarni and the Doctorani and Lakhpatni and her litter and all Paro's friends.

'Best boy, indeed. O Chatkarni, what did I do . . .?'

Omi couldn't keep his big long nose out of it. One Wednesday morning he bumped into Janak Bahal in the Public Nurseries. Before going back to Dhulkote that Monday, Mali had given Omi a list of things he wanted for Munni bibi's 'Mogul Garden'. Omi had gone there to order them. He saw Janak pacing up and down among the flowers, holding an open book to his face, muttering to himself. He was mugging up for a departmental exam. Omi hadn't known that sometimes grown-up men, too, had to sit examinations. He was glad he was his own burra sahib, in which capacity he would never have to take another exam. He put on a smile and slipped an arm into Janak's.

'Bahal sahib, let's take a short walk together.'

'Why, Khatri sahib?' Janak was slightly taken aback by this sudden show of friendship. He knew the Khatris well, but not that well.

'I must tell you what the world is saying behind your back.'

'I am not interested in the world. But what is it saying?'

'It is laughing its head off.'

'Why?'

'Stop for a minute and think, Bahal sahib.'

Janak stopped for a minute and thought. Then a strange thing happened – he broke down. Huge tears began to roll down his cheeks. *Mother-laying hell*: it was a shattering sight. Omi had not expected anything like it. *I should have kept my big long nose out of it, not put my oar in another man's boat.*

'What can I do, Omi? It is my mother. We can't fight our mothers. We are God-fearing Hindus, not . . .'

'We must, if our mothers are wrong. It won't turn us into mallachaas.'

'So what are you saying, Omi?'

'Next time you go on tour take our bharjai-ji with you.' Bharjai is brother's wife.

154

'You don't know what you are talking, Omi.'

'I do.'

'There are things a man can do and things a man cannot do.'

'This is something the man has to do.'

'And who will look after my mother?'

'Bahal sahib, you have four sisters.'

'Obviously you don't understand the custom. It says that the son's wife must serve them and look after them.'

'Just try it out once and see what happens. Your own wife, after all. When and where are you going on tour again?'

'To Ropar for four weeks, first thing tomorrow. By the seven a.m. bus. Anyway, they won't let me take her. They won't.'

'Don't tell them till tomorrow morning. Announce it at the last minute – at quarter to seven. Don't give them time to react.'

Janak pulled out a handkerchief from a pocket. He blew his nose in it loudly and shook his head. 'Won't work, guaranteed to fail. Then what?'

'Change my name if it doesn't work. I know what I'm talking about.'

Omi did not know what he was talking about. Come the evening, Sector 23 was ablaze with the Wednesday hustle-bustle. The market was going great guns with lights and sights and smells plus the noise. Arm in arm and hand in hand, young men roamed around, eyeing young women. Children yelled and pushed and kicked and cursed each other. Shoppers haggled. Dogs snarled and stray cattle, the giant black bull (sarkari saandh) prominent among them, poked their mouths into heaps of garbage. And beggars begged – *you my mai bap. Baby hungry. Baby sick.*

This was outside the Pall Mall, right in front of it.

Inside the Pall Mall it was a different story. Inside were people from a different planet. They had haloes behind their heads which outshone its soft lights and they talked in hushed voices as they sampled the Pall Mall specialities. Kharti was with the books in the office; Omi was seated on a tall stool at the bar, writing out bills. All was well with the world.

All was particularly well with Omi's world because he had done his good deed for the day – he had talked Janak into doing something about his life and his wife's. On his return from the Nurseries he had broadcast the fact to Munni and Paro, with the words, 'Ma, keep it to yourself.' But Paro had seen no harm in sharing this exciting bit of news with the Doctorani and Satya, her two neighbours, adding the words, 'Keep it to yourself, won't you?' The Doctorani and Satya hadn't been able to keep that unbelievable piece of info to themselves. They had felt a compulsive need to pass it on to their neighbours. Their neighbours in turn had thought it only normal that those around them should know that Janak had at last decided to do something about *it*.

At about ten, when the shoppers and walkers and hawkers in the market had drifted away, Omi's old friend Kapoor walked in, chewing paan and smoking a Gold Flake. He parked himself next to Omi on another tall stool and put an arm around him, smiling broadly, showing orange, paan-stained gums.

'Shabas (bravo), Omi son. Brilliant work, that,' Kapoor said.

'What are you on about, Dad?' Omi said. Owing to a long-standing custom which dated back to their college days, Omi called Kapoor 'Dad'.

'Dad is on about the fact that you have a brain and he deserves a drink on the house for being the first to spot it.'

'Stop shitting about the place. Explain.'

Before Kapoor could explain, the front door of the Pall Mall fell open angrily and in marched an angrier woman. She was slovenly – Omi hated slovenly people, especially women. She might be a cheap stallholder, selling second- or third-hand clothes – not the type ever likely to be admitted to the Pall Mall. Heads straightened, necks stiffened and eyebrows were raised. Bawa and two other waiters ran to stop her but the woman was determined. She pushed Bawa aside and marched heavily forward. 'Where is he? Where?' she boomed.

'Out, woman, out!' barked Bawa. Her presence there was an affront to his Pall Mall's honoured guests. It was bad for business.

Omi shot up. He had an uncanny feeling that it had something to do with him. He looked. Damyanti, the bitch!

'Where is the Khatri boy, the son of that cheap halwai?' Damyanti roared, and marched right up to Omi. 'I have come to sell you some sense free – *get off our backs, you hear?*'

'What?'

'*How dare you* poison my son against me? *How dare you* incite him to run away with his wife from my house?'

Pin-drop silence. Omi looked at his friend for support.

'I'm afraid I spoke too soon, as usual. It wasn't brilliant work after all,' Kapoor said in English.

'Stuff your wisecracks, Dad. I have a madwoman on my hands – what the fuck am I going to do?'

Hands on hips, the madwoman turned and addressed the elegant diners, jabbing the air with the forefinger of her right hand like a

Congress leader at a mass rally. 'He is pouring poison in my son's ear, turning him against me, telling him to elope with his wife.'

The word 'elope' brought a few hardly audible sniggers, but they died out quickly. The people with haloes from another planet returned to their food and drink, ignoring the woman completely. The front door opened again. Two of the Bahal sisters pushed their way in, rushed up to their mother and dragged her away. Life returned to normal just as swiftly as it had turned abnormal. The drama had lasted a mere sixty seconds, if not less.

'Phewee!' Omi breathed out. 'India! We call it the world's best country. Why, it is no more than a nation of fools if you ask me, Dad.'

'What was all that rolla-bolla about, boy?' Khatri popped his head out of the office.

'Nothing, Uncle. A silly woman came to sell my friend some sense – free. Believe it or not.'

'Kapoor, I thought you were intelligent. Unlike your friend.' Khatri slapped his forehead and withdrew.

'Bet you a bottle of Golden Eagle that the elopement is off,' Kapoor said to his friend.

Kapoor won the bet.

Munni knew that from now on Asha's every move would be closely watched, and that she wouldn't see her again for quite some time. Maybe never. To make matters worse, Asha's window was always shut now. This was strange.

'They have put four nails in it, that's why,' the eight-year-old Kaka, Asha's ally, confidant and courier, came one day and explained. He had a permanent line of mayonnaise between his nose and the upper lip which jerked upwards each time he sniffled. He sniffled every half minute.

'How is she? All right?' Munni asked.

'Auntie Asha cries all the time. She wants to die, she says, and Mother says it is Auntie Damyanti . . .'

Horrible. But what could Munni do?

'Auntie Asha says she must see you, Auntie Munni.'

'How? And where?'

'She says she will bolt the roof door and jump her wall and meet you on our roof. She says you must talk it over with Uncle Omi.'

Munni talked with Omi. Omi said go. Munni went. She met Asha on Kaka's roof, since his family allowed the two girls to meet there.

157

Munni had expected Asha to cry bitterly but Asha amazed her. She shed not a tear. She had something on her mind.

'Munni, they body-searched me and found your rupee and called me a randi (whore) and beat me blue. Every day since he left they beat me. Look with your own two eyes . . .'

There were newer and uglier marks on Asha's body. One of her breasts was almost entirely blue, a pitiable sight.

'If I open my mouth they hit me. If I keep shut they beat me. If I do anything wrong they beat me. And, Munni, I never seem to do anything right in that house.'

'What are you going to do? Why don't you go home to Patiala?'

'I want to but I can't. It will disgrace my family – a married daughter returning home like that! Tongues will wag in every street.'

'Go for a couple of weeks and see.'

'His mother won't give me the bus fare.'

'Do your parents know what's going on here?'

'No.'

'Shall I write to them?'

'No, no, no, Munni. She'll find out and . . .'

'But how?'

'She has a nose this long. She will find out and that will be the end, then. Every time I wrote home they took my letter and burned it.'

'I wish I could do something for you, Asha.'

Asha had been waiting for this moment. 'You can, Munni. Lend me two rupees.'

'I will, but what for?'

'I want to take a bus and run away.'

'Where to?'

'Home.'

'But you said it would disgrace your family.'

'Yes, I did. But what else can I do?'

'Surely the bus fare is more than two rupees?'

'Then lend me five. That'll make it six altogether. Promise to pay back the lot one day soon soon.'

Munni was about to give her the money, but something stopped her. 'How come you don't know the exact fare to Patiala, Asha? You come from there, don't you?'

'I forgot.'

Munni knew Asha was lying. She looked around the roof uneasily. A few old charpoys were stacked against a wall, and next to them was a heap of string that had come off them. By this heap stood an empty can of kerosene. Munni's eyes rested on the can and an ugly thought hit her. She shuddered. She wanted to leave there immediately.

'Okay, Asha, I'll send you the money with little Kaka.'

'Don't you have it on you? Not even two . . . I mean five . . . rupees? You Khatris are so rich.'

'No, I don't,' Munni lied. She wanted to run from Kaka's roof. Asha was up to something. This something was no good, and Munni didn't want to be the instrument of her realizing it.

'Asha, you'd better go back. Otherwise . . .' Munni helped Asha climb the six-foot wall that separated the two roofs and then hurried home. She thought the street stank of kerosene.

'What did she want?' Omi asked.

'Five rupees.'

'Told you! She has a secret lover and she wants to run away to him.'

It was either that or . . . Munni couldn't bring herself to think about it. Next minute Kaka turned up, and put his hand out.

'Tell Asha I'll give it to you tomorrow.'

Kaka came again the next day, and again Munni said, 'Tomorrow.' He came every day for three days. Then he stopped coming and Munni sighed in relief. On the fourth day there was a big scene at the back entrance of the Khatri house. Damyanti again.

'Paro, where are you?' Damyanti shouted from the street. The passers-by stopped and neighbours craned from balconies and windows. 'Paro, where are you? Show your face!'

Paro showed her face at the balcony.

'Paro, your daughter-in-law is a nose-poking troublemaker. Your son is a nose-poking troublemaker. You are a tribe of nose-poking troublemakers . . .'

'What are you barking about, Damyanti?'

'You are destroying my son's life. You are smoke-burning my home and hearth.'

'What's happened, woman?'

'Ask your daughter-in-law.'

'Munni, what's happened, beta?' Paro asked Munni who had joined her on the balcony.

'I don't know, Ma.'

'You don't know? You plotted it all and you don't know? You blackened my face and put a garland of shoes around my neck and you don't know?'

'In the name of your heaven-dwelling man, tell me, what has happened?' Paro shouted.

159

'Asha has run away. Your girl gave her the money to take the bus and she has gone.'

'Where?'

'To her secret lover, where else? She was a randi. Your girl is a randi – she plotted it at all.'

'Shut up, woman. How dare you talk like that of my Munni?'

'I dare! She has disgraced my name. She has ruined my son's life. She has made his wife run away.'

'She ran away because you are cruel and heartless. You beat her.'

'Ma, Asha wanted money to go home, but I didn't give it to her,' Munni said to Paro.

'You heard, silly woman? Your daughter-in-law has gone home. It has nothing to do with us.'

'I am going to call the police and have your girl put inside. Have you all put inside for interfering. Have locks put on your shop.'

'Barking bitch, go fetch the Dipty Commissioner if you want. Just go away from my sight . . .'

The spectators grew in numbers – in the street, on balconies and in windows. They loved what they saw and heard. Then they saw the Bahal sisters come half-running towards their mother, Kaka and a dozen other little boys behind them. They took Damyanti by the arms and led her back to their house, followed by Kaka and his friends. Passers-by passed on. People withdrew from their balconies and windows. Paro hung on at hers. She had been chewing the walnut bark, her favourite tooth-cleaner, and she let out a long arc of red spittle in the direction of the Bahals' house. The walnut-bark juice landed gracefully four and a half yards away by a bed of sweetpeas which Mali was tending to with his khurpa.

'Poor Asha. What did she do in her past life to deserve a mother-in-law like that bitch?' Paro said to Mali. 'Must have starved a whole village of Brahmins to death.'

'I know what *your* daughter-in-law did, Ma. She fattened them on rice-pudding and butter parathas,' Omi said, coming up with Khatri after hearing the rumpus in the street.

'What was all that about?' Khatri asked.

'That low-caste woman! I am sick of this neighbourhood. Build us a house in a respectable area,' Paro answered.

'Best thing Asha did. Should have done it ages ago, I think. What does my mother's daughter-in-law think?' Omi said.

Munni didn't know what to think. She was baffled. How had Asha managed – she didn't have a sou? In Dhulkote her mother had told her to be careful of the people in the new city – they had such superior

160

airs. But there was nothing superior about this behaviour: it was downright shameful.

'Shoot the Bahal bitches with five bullets and give us a cup of tea, Munni. Shouting makes me thirsty,' Paro said.

Munni made tea. As they sat down to drink it, little Kaka raced up the stairs, his cheeks puffed up, bursting with information.

'Auntie Damyanti and Santi have gone to Patiala to fetch Auntie Asha,' announced the budding news-spreader. Patiala was one hour away by bus. Omi looked at his watch. One hour going, one hour coming back, one hour of 'cinema' there . . . 'And one of to-ing and fro-ing to bus stops in rickshaws. They'll be back at eight, sadly. Kaka, come back at eight and tell us,' he said.

Kaka came back at eight, red in the face. He had come running, his favourite mode of travel. With him was an older boy from the 'hundred two-hundred quarters' – Babbu, a matric-sitter, also red in the face. Omi was downstairs. Munni rang the upstairs-downstairs phone. He came up at once.

'What did I tell you?' Omi said to Munni, looking at his watch. 'I said sadly they would be back at eight, and eight it is now.'

'Auntie Damyanti and Santi are back, but not Auntie Asha. And that is the thing,' Kaka said.

'Best thing,' Omi said.

'Not really. She is not in Patiala. She never took a Patiala bus. No one saw her at the bus stop in Patiala,' Babbu said.

'And that is the thing,' Kaka said.

'Still the best thing,' Omi said. He didn't care where Asha had gone as long as she had gone from the clutches of the Bahals.

'Then where did she go?' Paro said.

'To her secret lover, never to come back – everybody is saying,' Kaka said.

'This is a scandal number one. The best in the history of Sector 23. People are delirious with delight,' Babbu said.

'They should be drowned in shame,' Munni said.

'They are that too,' Babbu said.

Delirious with delight and drowned in shame at the same time, Sector 23 was also mystified – what had happened to Asha? Then rumours began to float around.

One was that Asha was beaten, dead and buried. That verbal attack on the Khatis had been play-acting, the trip to Patiala undertaken to pull wool over the world's eyes. People now recalled what they had heard the previous night – muffled cries and the thud,

161

thud of the kulhari (spade) hitting the earth in the dead of night. 'As if someone was digging for treasure or digging to bury someone.'

Here there was some disagreement over the direction from which the 'thud thud' noise had come. Godamal of Godamal General Stores thought the noise had come from the Public Nurseries; Thatha, the ironmonger, was convinced it came from the barren land behind the shops; Brothers Panwari and Panghatia, the textile wholesalers, had no doubt whatsoever that its source was closer to home. 'The hundred two-hundred quarters.' 'The Bahal back yard.'

A second rumour said Asha had been picked up by a black car with a Delhi registration number, while according to a third she had been seen going to the lake.

'Silly people, Indians,' Omi said. He stood at their bedroom window, looking at the starlit heavens – a blue-black sheet covered with glowing pinpoints. Munni stood by him, leaning into him. He addressed the heavens. 'Oi, You up there. Understandably You have to make some people thick. But why do You locate them all in India, and why always around where we live?'

'I don't think Damyanti was acting,' Munni said, 'I can tell when a woman is acting.'

'I can't,' Omi said. He did what was natural under the circumstances. He pulled her into him. The effect of this simple gesture on him was instantaneous.

Munni turned her face towards him for what they loved most in the world.

'What are you thinking?' Omi said.

'I was wondering what one does about such matters.'

'One takes such matters in one's hands.'

Munni wasn't sure if she had understood him, but her cheeks began to burn nonetheless. She took matters in her hands. 'Is that all you ever think of?'

'Yes.'

'I hate Chandigarh.'

'I hate India. Let us also run away. To England.'

Early in the morning two policemen turned up at the Bahal house. Damyanti screamed at them, but shut up when one pulled a pair of handcuffs from a bag. The policemen inspected the Bahal back yard. Not one square inch of the ground had been dug up there. Followed by a number of little boys, older boys and the unemployed men of the area, they went to the Public Nurseries. Nothing there either. The policemen and fifteen others went to the lake on bicycles. Two hours later they were back, shaking their heads with disappointment.

'We want a photo of the girl,' one policeman said to Damyanti.

'What for?' Damyanti said.

'To send to Delhi Police.'

'We don't have a photu of her. This is a resepctable family. Our girls don't get their photus taken.'

'But they run away all right.'

'She was not of this family. Sure you searched the lake properly? You don't look very intelligent to me. Third-rate country, this, full of stupid policemen and heartless neighbours.'

'Don't speak of the law like this, woman, or we take you in. Why don't you send word to your son that his wife has run away?'

'I have sent him a telegram to come home. He'll be here tonight, or tomorrow at the latest. Now get off our backs.'

Janak did not come back that night nor the next day.

'I think you should go and see him,' Munni said.

'What on earth for?' Omi said.

'We owe it him to let him know what happened. For Asha's sake.'

'I am not going anywhere. You must be joking, girl.'

'Please.'

When Munni said *please* – those eyes, those lips and that tilt of her head – there was nothing Omi could do. 'All right. But on one condition: you come with me.'

'What have I to do there?'

'To be with me.'

They took the bus to Ropar twenty-seven miles away. Janak's work was at the River Sujtlej, repairing a bridge. From the bus stop in Ropar they took a rickshaw to the river a mile away.

'Sahib's gone for lunch,' a labourer told them.

'Where?'

'Where he's staying. At the PWD Rest House.'

The PWD Rest House was in the city itself, right next door to the bus stop. It was identical to the one in Kharar – complete with a long veranda with pillars and arches and the punkah-wallah peon.

'Sahib in?' Omi said curtly. He was annoyed – all that to-ing and fro-ing and for what? *For a bloody impo who doesn't know how to look after his wife.*

'Sahib's out but bibi-ji is in,' said the peon, standing to attention and saluting like a soldier.

'Bibi-ji?' Omi and Munni said in consternation. Had the jhuddu (son of a bitch) taken in another woman?

163

Just then the door of the long room opened and 'bibi-ji' stepped out.

'Asha!' Munni could have killed her.

Asha, looking happy, laughed and looked happier. 'Munni!'

It was Vidya's doing.

One morning she came and saw Munni with her hands in a bucket of water, washing Omi's shirts. The morning was very cold. The water was freezing. Even though Munni wore a sweater, she was shivering. Her soft young cheeks were like petals of a white rose.

'Paro, have you seen?' Vidya yelled at her sister from the bathroom.

'Seen what?' Paro yelled back from the kitchen.

'Our girl's face. At her age she should have two red roses in her cheeks! Why do you make her work like this? God is giving you. So?'

Khatri, reading his paper on the balcony, heard. He was stung by shame. Within the hour he had hired the seventh family servant – a maid, a girl of Munni's age. Her name was Banwli, which means dumb. Banwli was busty and vivacious-looking and she had large eyes. She couldn't talk much but she spoke volumes with her eyes. She was painfully slow. She ate for two and was still always hungry – she could eat another meal at any time of the day or night.

'And she has hungry eyes. *And* they are always on him,' Paro told Khatri one day.

'On who?' Khatri said.

'On the boy.'

'Which boy?'

'How many boys do you have?'

Khatri fired Banwli on the spot and hired Maaii. Maaii was forty but looked fifty. She didn't eat much nor did she look at anyone or anything, especially at what she was doing. As a result she broke a plate or glass every day and earned herself the nickname of 'Plate-lover'. One day she broke Paro's heart – she dropped a quarter plate of the Royal Albert service – and was promptly dismissed. Khatri took another woman. She was also called Maaii.

Maaii II was thirty-five and looked it. She didn't eat a lot herself, either, yet the food disappeared. She took it home hidden over her person, under her clothes. She was always after Munni: 'Don't, Munni bibi, don't . . . I'll do it . . . Let me . . . You go be with Omi bau . . .' As she seemed devoted to Munni, Khatri told Paro to ignore her pilfering.

Maaii II was a know-all know-everything. Her speech was lined with masala spice. Every morning she gave Munni and Omi tea sweetened with some local, sometimes even national, gossip. 'Our bhola bhala (innocent) Jawaharlal Nehru. Always falling in love with other men's wives. First it was Mountbatten's, now it is that of the President of America, believe it or not.'

'That Heeralal, Omi bau,' Maaii II said to Omi one morning as Omi raced out of the bath towards his room, a towel around his waist.

Omi stopped in his tracks. 'Don't mention that dog's name in this house if you want to remain in service here, Maaii,' Paro said. Heeralal's name was not mentioned in the house unless Paro chose to mention it herself.

'But I must, Ma-ji.' Maaii called Paro Ma-ji even though there were only five years between them.

'Then come back tomorrow to get your wages. You are fired.'

'Mother, perhaps it is important. Otherwise Maaii wouldn't risk her job. Bolo bolo, Maaii – speak.'

Maaii looked at the mistress of the house for permission to speak.

'All right, Maaii, what about that gandoo? Tell quick-quick,' Paro said and shocked her daughter-in-law by using the word gandoo which means a man who enjoys being sodomized.

'Omi bau, he is plotting your downfall.'

'That pig-arse? How? Hasn't he learnt his lesson, the fool?'

'He is waiting to buy your restaurant and all.'

'He is not only a fool, but also mad.'

'How do you know, Maaii? Who told you?' Paro asked.

'My friend Dhanno works in his kitchen. She overheard talk.'

'He's a barking dog,' Paro said, spitting out the juice of the walnut bark she was chewing.

'And Dhanno says he prays to the Goddess for your destruction every morning at five punctual. He has promised to erect Her a temple in return.'

'Which Goddess?' Omi asked.

'Lakshmi, Goddess of Wealth – his Goddess.'

'Huh. Lakshmi has plenty of temples. Besides, men much bigger than him, multi-bloody-millionaires up and down the country and even abroad, are bribing Her. She is busy, un-get.'

'Omi bau, I've told you what I had to tell you.'

'Mad dog. Mad dogs end up fucking up their own mothers and daughters. Well-known fact,' Omi said in English so that his language didn't offend his mother. Old Mali, sitting on his haunches nearby and listening, smiled, as if he had understood even though

165

he knew not a word of English. 'Mali, why have you got that lighthouse grin?'

Mali smiled again – he had a soft spot for Munni bibi's housewallah – and hauled himself downstairs.

Mali never talked about himself. This for a Punjabi was not normal. What was he hiding? A secret, surely. The ever-present long-distance look on his beautiful face made that plain. Omi couldn't stomach it – someone close to him keeping secrets from him. But all his efforts to prise open his mouth had only resulted in that enigmatic smile, as if Mali was looking through the long tunnel of time. Early one morning in Munni's Mogul Garden, as Mali sat there like a sultan on a green carpet, Omi turned up and placed himself before him like a disciple or a devotee. This made a shocking spectacle – the master making obeisance to the servant.

'Mali-ji, tell me the story of your life or I shan't budge from here. I swear I shan't,' Omi said.

Mali smiled that smile of his.

'Mali-ji, open your heart to a friend,' Omi pleaded.

'My heart, Omi bau, is a museum of wounds. Its front door firmly shut,' Mali said.

'Open the side door then. Just a little.'

It was difficult to resist this boy. Mali weakened.

'But first a promise, Omi bau.'

'Anything you say, Mali-ji.'

'Not a word of this to anyone, not even Munni bibi. Especially Munni bibi.'

'Promise. May snakes bite me and may dogs pee on my corpse if I open my mouth to anyone.'

'All right then. Listen. Happened a long time ago – in another life, you can say. Father was from these parts, Mother from the hills in Kulu Manali where the women are fair and beauteous. From her side all were gardeners, so flowers were in my blood to start. My father, like his father, was a tiller. I came into this world the year the great Queen Victoria left it. I was in my fifth year when cholera struck our village, taking my father and most of the village. Goddess Durga spared me and my mother. After the cholera came drought and famine, the usual story. My mother took me to her father's village in the far far hills. In time I went to work with my Uncle Mama. Mama was the Rajah's gardener, in charge of all royal gardens. He worked inside the Palace. I was apprenticed outside the Palace.

166

'The Rajah's country was mountains high and mighty, well-known for tiger and bear. It was beautiful country. I grew there, amid those mountains and Mama's flowers. Time passed. I was my uncle's newphew. In course I made a name for myself as *The One Flowers Speak To*. And they did – day and night, even when I slept. Mama was happy with me. Mother was proud. Joy reigned in our hearts.

'It didn't last long. One night when Mama and I were returning home we had to cross a river. As we entered the fast-running water, the bushes behind us opened up and a tiger roared at us. "Run, boy, run,"' Mama said. As I tried to run, the current carried me along and I was saved, but the tiger caught hold of Mama and ate him. I was asked to work inside the Palace. The royal garden was a drama for the eye, filling half a valley. With my hands I made it paradise. The Rajah gave me a saropa (shawl of honour) and also a small wooden house all my own at the back of the garden, away from all other servants' huts.

'The Rajah had seven sons but only one daughter, Raj Kumari, the fairest in the land. She was a few years younger than me. Every day she came out to play in the garden with her sahelis. She always gazed at me. I never gazed back – she was a princess. The princess loved my flowers, that I knew. But that there was more to her frolicking in them I didn't know till one day the Rajah went away with his sons and his durbar to hunt the tiger.

'The Rajah lived for two things – the princess, and to hunt the tiger. There were many in his jungles, and one had become man-eating. He went to shoot him.

'Time was early evening. The sky had a few bright early stars. Bulbuls sang in the trees. The valley hummed with the scent of my flowers which I was tending to as usual. Two friends of the princess came running and said she had a fall and was hurt and that I must run to her. I did and saw her lying flat on the grass, looking at the stars. One by one her friends went and hid behind bushes. "My ankle, Mali," the princess said, looking into my eyes. "I've sprained it. Maybe broken it, even. Take it in your hands and look at it." I did what I was told and saw nothing wrong with the foot. "Press it, Mali. Comfort me." I pressed the princess's foot gently. "Now lift me up and carry me back to the palace, Mali."

'As I lifted her in my arms she clung to my neck. Halfway to the Palace she jumped to the ground and ran away, followed by her giggling friends. Omi bau, you can guess the state I was in after that. All evening I sat with my head in my hand, wondering what to do, what what what. When the night came she came again. Alone. She crept up to my hut and called out my name and swore her love under the mountain, moon and stars. And then – listen, Omi bau, listen – and then Raj Kumari took my hand and placed it . . . O Omi bau, do I have to go on?'

'Yes.'

'It was at that moment I decided. Bhago, I said to myself, quit! Run and save yourself. Go to British India – they love flowers as any Rajah.

'I told the princess of my intent. She kept my hand on her bosom and cried and gazed at me and came back same time next night and pulled out a pill from a little box. She said if I went . . . I threw away the pill and begged her to go back and to let me think. She obliged.

'The Rajah came back without having shot the man-eater. Days passed. When the tiger ate his nineteenth victim, the Rajah took his guns and his sons and went after him a-hunting – *thaa thaa boom boom*. That night again . . . O Omi bau, why do I have to go on?'

'You have to. Go on, Mali-ji. Go on.'

'That night again the princess came. She crept into my house and simply, and simply, I say, slipped into my bed. Another man could have taken advantage; I shrank away. She gave me a big diamond ring and said, "Go sell it to a jeweller and with the money you get we'll run away and hide and get married and live happily ever after somewhere in British India." I did not take the ring. There was some noise in the palace, voices calling her name, men and women. She ran out in the darkness. I made a bundle of all my things and sat down under the sky, waiting for the morning to come so that I could run, quit, go. The morning never came.

'As I dozed off there came some of the Rajah's men. First they broke both my legs with dandas, then they tied my hands and shoved me in a sack and sewed it up. They carried me down a deep ravine and left me there. Both legs broken and hands tied up and groaning with pain in a sewn-up sack in the jungle, I knew I was gone – the love of a princess is often a deadly thing. I hadn't asked for it. It was fate. I was finished.

'But man is never finished. He never gives up. There was nothing I could do physically, so I did something with my mind – I prayed. I prayed for a miracle. The mircale came – in the shape of the man-eating tiger. Why he didn't eat me all up? – you won't believe it, Omi bau, but you have to because I am still here.

'The Rajah's guns blazed – *thaa thaa boom boom*!

168

'So now you know why I am how I am. But not a word of it to anyone, Omi bau, especially Munni bibi. Promise?'

'Promise.'

Shattered, Omi broke his promise the moment Munni woke up.

'Pity he didn't take the diamond ring,' said Munni, also shattered. She told the whole story to her mother-in-law.

'Pity he didn't let her swallow the pill,' Paro, unshattered, said.

It had rained cats and dogs all night. It was still raining cats and dogs when the morning came, making a mother-father noise. In that noise there was another: the upstairs-downstairs telephone. Omi heard it in his room, his left hand where it always was at this time of the morning – between Munni's thighs – and he was cock-a-doodle-doo. He decided to ignore it. Khatri heard it where he lay, fully awake and asking himself what he was going to do about his morning excursion to the 'God area'. He looked at his watch: not yet seven. What could the matter be? He sat up and dangled his feet above the floor in search of his slippers. Before his feet found the slippers, Omi, still c-a-d-d and ninety degrees, ran out of his room to where the house phone was, by the stairs.

'Omi bau, it's Nanda sahib on the real phone.' Bawa spoke from the office downstairs. 'Wants Lala-ji quick.'

By now Khatri had joined his son. The two of them ran downstairs. Paro wrapped herself in a shawl and followed. She knew something was wrong. She had a nose for disaster.

'You all right, Nanda sahib? Wife well? Kid-kiddies well?' Khatri said into the phone.

'Heard last thing last night. Am coming first thing this morning,' Nanda said.

'What have you heard?'

'I am coming right away.'

'What, in this weather? But what is it?'

'Shhh. We are on phone, don't forget,' Nanda said and hung up.

Khatri ground his jaw. He looked at his son, then at his own feet. He did not look at his wife – he did not have the courage.

'I told you,' Paro said and started crying.

'Told me what, Paro woman?'

'Told you never to trust him. Never to buy that jungle. Now the sarkar has found out it was dhoka (fraud) – turning nursery plot into hotel because everybody was in his pocket. Now it is not giving

169

permission to build. So what are you going to do there now – grow turnips?'

'Silly woman, it can't be that. We already have the permission. It's here in the safe, signed by that Saxena himself.'

But Paro was not listening. Her hand went to her hair. 'I told you . . .'

'Ma, you jump to conclusions faster than a Derby horse. Just wait till Nanda gets here.'

They waited. Munni, half-awake and shrouded in a shawl like Paro, joined the family and stood behind Omi. Half an hour later Nanda arrived, his hair dripping, his face soaked and swollen, his arms long, very long.

'That Ahuja,' Nanda said.

'Dead?' Khatri said.

'The son of a ten-dog bitch is as hale and hearty as you and me, Lala-ji. It is his Head Office. You with me?'

'No.' But Khatri was – he knew these things.

'The Head Office has said no to our loan.'

'There,' Paro said. 'There goes your Taj Mahal. Now you are left with a piece of thorny jungle where even dogs won't cock their legs. Where even crows won't drop their dropping.'

'Ma!' Omi begged his mother to be quiet. This was an emergency.

'You have sunk fifty thousand in that dogshit plot. What are you going to do with it – have a picnic there every Sunday?' Paro went on.

'Ma!'

'Beta, take your mother upstairs,' Khatri said to Munni. Munni put an arm around her weeping mother-in-law and led her upstairs.

Father and son looked at each other. Then they looked at Nanda, both thinking the same thing in the same words – *Dog, you got us into it, you get us out of it.*

'I am in it as much as you, Lala-ji,' Nanda said.

'But the loan and all was sorted out, Uncle Nanda.'

'Was. Ahuja had wined them and dined them . . .'

'At my expense,' Khatri said.

'Ahuja thought he had them where he wanted them. That was was. Now is is. And what *is* is different.'

'How and why?'

'There is a new man at the Head Office. He wants Ahuja's job in the capital for his sister's husband. So he says no to everything Ahuja says yes to, to make his life so difficult that he will ask for a transfer.'

'Then what are we going to do, Nanda sahib?'

'Do the only thing left to do – sell the damn-fool place.'

'Who is going to buy that wasteland?'

'Somebody might if we lower the price.'

Khatri's nostrils flared. 'I am not lowering the price, not a penny, Nanda sahib. You got me in this soup. You get me out of it.'

'Question is how?'

'Your connections, all those people with pull – where are they now?'

'Lala-ji, I have tried everybody. From the Home Minister's PA down to who-have-you, including Ambala Deputy Commissioner, R. Vedi.'

'Why Ambala's DC?'

'Because that's where the Head Office of the bank is – in Ambala Cantt. I told them to tell the man . . . by the way he is also a Khatri I am sorry to say, one Mr B. K. Khatri . . . I told them to tell the man to take whatever he wants to sanction the loan. But R. Vedi bit my foot off for suggesting under-the-table payment. He's one of those young IAS officers who live in the cuckoo-land of ideals, who want to build a *new* India. They know as much about running a business as camels know about aviation.'

'No one else?'

'Spoke to Supt Police of Ambala, Bansi Lal. But he is busy with the Prime Minister's visit. Election year and Nehru is touring and Bansi Lal says he is up to his neck.'

'Why not try other banks?'

'Only if we had an Ahuja in one of them. But let's try. What harm? O this bloody rain.'

They waited for the rain to stop and the banks to open. The rain didn't stop, but the banks opened on the dot of ten. The banks were next door in Sector 22. Khatri and Nanda first went to the State Bank of India. Its manager, Mathur, shook his head.

'Let me be frank with you. Hotel in jungle? Won't touch it with the longest bargepole.'

They went to the Punjab National. Manager Nanak Singh said exactly the same thing, adding: 'Had it been a factory-shactory, we would have lent at least an ear. But.'

The Bank of Baroda was just as sympathetic. The man there gave them a cup of hot tea and shook Khatri's hand warmly. 'Take my adivce, Lala-ji – sell even if it is at a loss,' he said.

The manager of Tata, Birla and Dalmia Amalgamate was 'too busy' to see them. But he stole a moment for the ex-VIP of Governor

171

House. 'Jungle hotel? It was a mistake to start with. A grave error of judgement, you can say. Happens to the best of us. I would put it on the market tomorrow. No, today: now. I would consider myself lucky if offered half of what I paid, and accept it like a shot.'

Half of what Khatri had paid for the land amounted to a whole year's earnings: all twenty-five thousand of it. All gone down the drain. Just like that. Khatri would rather lose a leg or an arm (and make sure that Nanda lost both his).

Back home, he sat down on a charpoy and took the *Milap* in his hands. But he couldn't read a word. *Twenty-five thousand rupees, goodbye, adieu, alvida. Twelve long months of sweat and blood. Of dawn to midnight toil.* There was no justice in this world.

And the rain pelted down.

Paro came and placed a thali of food before him. Khatri covered his face with the newspaper he wasn't reading, couldn't read. He didn't even want to look at food. The very sight of it made him want to run to 'Pakistan' and . . . He ground his jaw and waved her away. He was thinking. All the banks had said the same thing – a capital *No* and *sell*. Perhaps the whole thing had been a bad idea to start with, *a serious error of judgement* as the Amalgamate had said. But Ahuja's bank had thought differently, at least at the beginning. What sort of man was this other Khatri?

Khatri had an idea. 'Om,' he called his son.

Omi was standing by the charpoy anyway. He knew how his father felt, so he had to be right near where he was, no more than a few feet away. It made him feel better. He knew it made his father feel better, too.

'Yes, Father?'

'Om, take the next bus to Dhulkote. Have a word with the stationmaster sahib. He is well-connected. Maybe . . .'

'But, Father . . .' Wasn't the stationmaster of a place like Dhulkote too small a fry really? This was a big loan – three times what he would earn from the Indian Railways in all his life.

'No harm trying. What harm? Kandhari sahib knows everyone. He might know this namesake of ours as well. Who knows?'

Omi went, in the pelting rain.

'Mother-father well? Munni well? How come, Om Parkash, in this weather of the pigs?' Kandhari said.

Omi explained.

Kandhari's eyes widened. His jaw fell. 'Big thing this, Om Parkash.

172

Big, big, big. But let's go to the Cantt. I am not unknown there,'
Kandhari said. Surely there was someone there who knew this Mr B.
K. Khatri?

They took the 1.20 Mail that Omi used to take with Munni on
their joyrides to the Cantt. The person Kandhari first talked to at the
other end was a man called J. R. Lomba. *Assistant Stationmaster,
Ambala Cantt Jn.*, a brass plate outside his office said.

'B. K. Khatri?' Lomba shook his head. 'Don't know him.'

'Anyone you know who might, A. S. M. sahib?'

'My sala (brother-in-law) is famous advocate. Everybody knows
him and vice versa. Let's go to the Law Courts and try him. This
bloody rain.'

They went to the Law Courts, a vast huddle of single-storey yellow-
painted buildings standing miserably in a foot-deep lake. Scores of
people criss-crossed the lake in hurry on foot or on bicycles with black
umbrellas.

'Balram Krishan Khatri?' The famous sala of the A. S. M. also
shook his head. 'Don't know him, but Shankar Das might. He works
for the *Tribune*.'

Shankar Das was the A. S. M.'s brother-in-law's brother-in-law.
He, too, didn't know B. K. Khatri. 'But let's go see my friend Dwarka
Nath. He owns the Rivoli and is a chalta purza (man about town).
Knows it brick by brick and face by face.'

They all went to the Rivoli cinema which Omi knew so well. They
were playing an oldie-goldie, *Nagin*, a film Omi loved. The matinée
was going full swing. Dwarka Nath had just gone into a box to see a
sexy dance number, and didn't seem amused to be draged out.

'B. K. Khatri? No. Sorry . . . But do stay and watch the dance.'

They found no one who knew Mr B. K. Khatri. Omi's father-in-
law was apologetic. Omi was heart-broken. What now? *Back to the
pavilion?* He hung his head down in despair.

Then an idea came to him. It was a brilliant idea. It was also bold.
And mad. *Omi, son, why not try the man himself? – Khatri versus Khatri.
What can you lose?*

'What can you lose, Om Parkash?' Kandhari agreed.

Omi bowed down to touch his father-in-law's feet in farewell – he
hated this 'Indian shit' of touching elders' feet, and he hated himself
for doing it. He hailed a passing rickshaw to go to the bank. It had
stopped raining and the day was nearly done. Omi found the bank
shut for business, but otherwise it was still open. A chawkidar
(watchman) in a khaki uniform guarded it with a double-barrelled
gun. He wore a ferocious-looking belt of twelve-bore cartridges, some

red, others green. He sat on a chair on the porch by the bank's door, pulling at a beedi. A dozen men sat around him on their haunches, also pulling at beedis.

'Bank is shut. God gave you eyes, can't you see?'

'My name is Khatri, Mr O. P. Khatri. I have come from Chandigarh to see your boss, Mr B. K. Khatri.' Omi was stern, imperious. He knew how to speak to these people, the chawkidars and such like.

'O, a relation of the burra sahib! Why didn't you say, sahib?'

'Couldn't you tell?' All Khatris came from the same family banyan tree with roots deep and far. 'A very close relation.'

'Now I am seeing the family resemblance.'

'He is also very handsome.'

'Very, sahib, very. I'll go and tell him you are here. But there he is, coming out.' The chawkidar sprang to attention, stamping out his beedi and saluting. The men around him also sprang to attention, hiding their beedis behind their backs. 'Sir, this chota Khatri sahib is here to see you.'

The two Khatris looked at each other, searching for any family resemblances. Omi saw a tall well-built man of fifty or thereabouts with a head full of white hair and an attractive open face – *will I look like him in thirty years time?* The older Khatri saw a very good-looking young man, well fed, well turned out and, no doubt, well parented. A thought crossed the mind of the white-haired gent – *did I not look like him when I was twenty or twenty-one? But who is? What does he want?*

'Sir, I take it you have finished for the day?' the young Khatri said in his best Simla Pink English.

'You are right, young man.'

'If it wasn't so important I wouldn't have bothered you, sir. But it is, and therefore may I have your permission to speak to you for a moment?'

Ah! He's well spoken, and well mannered, too. 'I am going home. Can't it wait till tomorrow?'

'I don't live in Ambala, sir. I've come all the way from Chandigarh just to see you.'

'If it is a job you are after, I have none going.' But the bank manager was sure the young man was not after the sort of clerical job the bank had. *Officer material, as they used to say. He is after something else.* The bank manager wanted to know what – he liked the young fellow.

'I am not after a job, sir.'

'I thought not. What is it, then? Walk with me and tell me – I always walk home in the evenings. Good thing the rain has stopped.'

'I won't waste your time, sir, I'll come straight to the point. I want to talk to you about a loan.'

'Young man, you must be mad.' The banker laughed.

'Completely round the bend, sir, sources close to me inform me daily.'

He even has a sense of humour. And he is self-assured. I wasn't like that at twenty! The older Khatri's interest was aroused.

'I have never discussed money on the roadside, not even with people I have known all my life, and I know not the first thing about you. But I'll make an exception. Tell me what's it all about.'

'Aimie Khatri at your service, sir,' Omi said with a bow, remembering how Gene Kelly had introduced himself to Athos, Porthos and Aramis in *The Three Musketeers* in last Sunday's all-time great at the Kiran. Then he told Mr B. K. Khatri all about it.

A puzzled look replaced the open expression on the bank manager's face – *what is the boy talking about? Should I indulge in a conversation about something my bank might be linked with? Wouldn't it be unethical?* But his bank's name wasn't linked with it, as far as he knew. Therefore ethics didn't come into it. 'I do not know what you are talking about, young man. No application for such a loan was ever made to me.'

What what! A thunderbolt hit Omi from the clear blue sky. In a flash he knew.

'The word is flabbergasted, sir: I am flabbergasted. You mean you don't know a thing about our loan for which Mr Ahuja said he had wined and dined the whole of the head office?'

'I know Ahuja, but I haven't seen him for months. Nor have I ever heard of this Nanda man . . .'

'Oh . . .'

'It seems you are being done in by him.'

'What can he be playing at?' Omi gave an account of the morning's events. 'Mr Nanda took my father to the four leading banks in the capital, and all four of them said exactly the same thing . . .'

'Can't understand why they said that. Nanda must have fixed it with the managers. You'd better watch out.'

'It's clear what he's after.'

'Crystal clear.'

'And we trusted him blindly.'

'You are learning.'

'I am also going to teach him a lesson, though.'

175

They were walking by a large body of dirty rainwater. A slight slope in the road had turned it into a canal about a hundred yards long. It was only five or six inches deep, and most ordinary people simply walked through it, taking off their shoes if they wore any, hitching up their dhotis and other forms of leg gear. The well-dressed bank manager and his companion from Chandigarh were no ordinary men. They shied past the canal, tiptoeing gingerly along a slim line of dry earth by the side of the road. They were nearly there when a rustic tempoo (motorcycle rickshaw) appeared from nowhere. It was supposed to have only four passengers. It carried eight. Its legal town speed was twenty m.p.h. It was doing forty. Its driver, a Sikh, didn't see the smart city babus shying past the filthy canal till he had all but drowned them in a fearsome spray of muddy water.

'Oh-ho,' said the tempoo driver with regret. Then he laughed. His passengers guffawed, heaving from side to side with mirth.

'Bloody fool!'

'India, sir.' Omi bent down, picked up a stone the size of a cricket ball and threw it with all his strength at the flying boat. The stone fell half a mile short of it.

'I am sorry, sir. Your suit.'

'Not your fault. Your suit, too. You were saying?'

'Crystal clear what Mr Nanda is doing – taking us for a ride on an aquatic tempoo, mud and all.'

'Don't be very surprised if you have a buyer tomorrow, offering you a quarter of half what the land is worth.'

May I ask what if *we* owned the entire plot – my father, that is? What would our chances be of getting a loan from you?'

'I would say the same as anybody else's in your position. You have an established business, by what you tell me. That is credibility. What a bank asks for.'

'Do you have a brother-in-law, sir?'

'No, I do not have a brother-in-law. Why do you ask?'

'Just like that, sir. Talking of Mr N. N. Nanda sahib, do I have your permission to teach that ex-Governor House mouse a little lesson?'

'Be careful. Keep your cards close to your chest – only way you can beat him.'

'Thank you, sir. If all Indian bank managers were like you, this country would be the envy of the world.'

'You are a flatterer. But I like you, and I don't mind telling you that I do. Now don't let that go to your head. And you have made me break all the rules by talking to you.'

They came to the Cantt's great maidan. Half of it was taken over by a shanty-town with a five-foot-high skyline. It was a colony of hutments of flattened tin canisters and sewn-up jute sacks held upright by bamboo sticks which somehow defied weather and gravity. Some were more substantial, with walls of mud coated with a paste of cowdung and earth. This shanty-town had started life in August 1947. A thousand families now lived there in a thousand rooms of mud, tin, wood and sackcloth, the smallest measuring four foot by four and the largest perhaps ten by ten. In the former there wasn't room for more than one human being, but in the latter a whole family of six could easily sleep and cook and eat and grow up.

The maidan began past a ditch lining the road. From a long row of hutments fifteen feet beyond the bank manager and the boy from Chandigarh there came the sound of laughter. It was a loud and gleeful sound, a happy sound.

'They may have nothing to eat, yet they can laugh. A lesson in there for us all, young man, don't you think?'

Omi was thinking of something else. 'Thank you for talking to me, sir. Just one more thing: do you know Prithvi Raj Kapoor, Raj Kapoor's father?'

'Not personally, if that's what you mean, but I have seen him in films. A handsome man and a good actor.'

'You look like him, sir. In fact better than him. And so you know a man called Spencer Tracy?'

'At this note I will say goodbye.' The bank manager laughed.

'You've made my day, sir. I feel I could run all the way back to Chandigarh, and get there quicker than by bus.'

As Omi raised a hand to hail a passing rickshaw to take him to the bus stop, a car turned a corner and came to a halt in front of them.

'I don't believe it,' Mr B. K. Khatri mumbled to himself.

'What a nice-looking car, sir. Morris Minor vintage circa 1939.'

'Omiii!'

'Cousin Kukoo! Cousin Kaddu!'

'Uncle B. K!' Kaddu yelled.

Doors of the Morris Minor were flung open and out came Kukoo and Kaddu. Embraces and embraces.

'You two know each other, then? I didn't know,' Kaddu said to her cousin and his namesake.

'What are you doing here, Omi?' Kukoo asked.

'Discussing a bank loan,' Omi said.

'Uncle B. K., don't lend him a penny. Not a penny. He's a pukka

177

chor (thief). Absolute Number One. He'll spend it all on his beautiful wife,' Kukoo said and embraced Omi another five times.

'Our uncle is your uncle, Omi,' Kaddu said. 'Money no problem.'

Omi ran back all the way. In fact, he sprinted – faster than Indian champ, Milkha Singh, the Olympic 400 metres Number Four. By the time he got home, he had worked everything out. Now the question was, would his father agree? His father agreed. Nanda had made a chutia (fool) of him and Khatri would do anything to get at his balls. He was fearful, though – one wrong move and all would be lost.

'Father, nothing risked nothing gained.' Omi was not after Nanda's balls, he was after his half of the plot. 'Leave everything to me, the thinking and the planning.'

Khatri was one of those people who preferred 'gaining' without 'risking'. But he let his son do the thinking and the planning.

'Father, we will play his game. We will suspect nothing. We will look and act dumb,' Omi said.

'That won't be difficult. You've been that all your life, father and son,' Paro said.

'Ma,' Omi pleaded, 'you keep out of it for once. For once let your men take the helm of the Khatri ship in their hands.'

'And sink it fast and final,' Paro said.

'Munnishka, you mind the home front. We'll look after the enemy front, barbed wire and all,' Omi said.

Omi's plan was to admit 'a grave error of judgement' had been made. His strategy was to agree to sell the land as soon as possible at half or quarter price (the latter, preferably) than make an offer for Nanda's half of the plot. Caught in his own trap, the bastard would be obliged to sell or be exposed. The Khatris would then have the entire plot, Uncle B. K. would give them the loan and they would have their Taj Mahal after all. All fifty rooms of it. All to themselves.

'One last thing, Father.'

'What?'

'Not to lose your frontier temper in the middle of the negotiations. Please, Father.'

That was difficult. That nobody could be sure of, least of all Shadi Lal Khatri of Peshawar himself.

'In the mean time what do we do, boy?'

'Nothing. We wait like the bagla bhagat (crane) – one foot raised over the water, waiting to pounce on the fish with beak and claw.'

Exactly two weeks later to the day, Nanda made his move. He phoned. Again it was raining cats and dogs. This time he got Omi.

'Am phoning to exchange views and news,' Nanda said in English, sweetly.

'Good thing you are, Uncle Nanda. Father is not well,' Omi replied in English, sweetly, sweetly.

'Oh-ho. Nothing serious, I hope. Looked strong and sturdy the other day,' Nanda said, getting sweeter still.

'We don't know. All this worry. So much money going down the dirty drain – all his life's savings. We had put total faith in you, Uncle Nanda!' – *and I'm going to give you 'the treatment', you just wait, you daughter-fucking beti chod.*

'What can I do, Om Parkash? All my money is tied up here, too. I am having heart attacks daily, a.m. and p.m. But I am coming. I have something for his ear. Can't tell on the phone. These days you never know who is listening. O this bloody rain.'

'Lala-ji, sorry to say this, but our property deal has become an arse-splitting joke in town. The market is laughing loud and louder,' Nanda said as soon as he arrived. Tea arrived at the same time – it was pre-planned, to soften what otherwise might be a tricky moment.

One look at Nanda's face and Khatri knew he couldn't go through with his son's plan – all he wanted to do was to spit at the face he was looking at. 'I haven't heard anything,' he said.

'Who is going to say it to your face?' Nanda said, taking a cup from Omi.

'Whose idea was it to buy it in the first place?' Khatri said. He knew this was not what he should have said, but he couldn't help it.

'I know, I know. And I am the picture of apology. Can't you see? But you can say your worry is over – at least half of it.'

'How? Meaning?'

'Lala-ji, someone is interested in that shitty plot. He'll pay half. So if we, if you, want to sell, we can get fifty per cent back. The rest you can put down to bad luck, an error of judgement as the Amalgamate son of a bitch said. Remember?'

'Who is the buyer?' Another wrong thing Khatri said – he should have played along sweet-sweet and baited Nanda. This time he received a little kick from his son under the table. But his frontier temper was beginning to get the better of him. 'Who is the buyer?' he said again, a little more haughtily this time.

'Approach has been made to me indirectly. Man wants to remain anonymous as per his request . . .'

'Interesting.'

'He'll pay half half, which is a quarter better than a quarter. He'll pay tomorrow. Today if we want. But he wants to remain faceless.'

'I never do business with anyone without a face.' Khatri received another kick from his son. *Think, Father. Think.*

'Think, Lala-ji. Why should we worry about the face? If the man is putting his money where his mouth is, what do we care about his face? Anyway, his right to remain anonymous if he wishes to. No law against it.'

'Would he be one Mr M. M. Nanda by any chance, your brother? Or A. K. Nanda, your son? Or both?'

Caught, Nanda's face became ugly. His jaw fell – to the floor. He put the cup down and stood up.

'Lala-ji, are you accusing?'

'Yes, I am accusing.'

'Careful, Lala-ji.'

'I am accusing you of deceiving me, swindling me, cheating me, defrauding me . . .'

'Father, careful,' Omi said. He knew his father had blown it – his frontier temper had lost them their Taj Mahal.

'Yes, Om Parkash, tell your father to be careful. I can sue him for it,' Nanda said.

'Go sue me for it. Get out of my house and go. I don't want to sell, neither now nor ever. I will sit on my land till . . .'

'Till when? Till you get boils on your arse?'

'Yes, till I get boils on my arse.'

'So it is a stalemate now – no talk, eh? So it is cold war?'

'It is a hot hot war. Between you and me. You fixed it with those bank managers to put me off. Well, I am not put off. And you get out.'

'Om Parkash, you were right – he is sick. In the head.'

'Get out or I'll have you chewed up by my dog.'

The man on the phone wouldn't say who he was, nor leave a message for Mr Om Parkash Khatri.

'When precisely would he back?' the man said. He was officious and stern, a government man, Bawa could tell.

'Precisely? The word not made for Mr Omi bau, sir,' Bawa said.

'In that case I will phone again later.'

'Can I at least tell him who called.'

'That won't be necessary.'

'He gets mad when I take no name.'

'Tell him not to, today.'

'Omi bau, nameless man called without message. Will call again later,' Bawa said when Omi came home.

'Couldn't you recognize his voice? What's the matter with you?' Omi gave him a slap on the head.

'Had voice like radio news-reader Devki Nandan Pandey. Words coming like a wall – brick by brick, smooth and hard.'

'Wasn't Father here to talk to him?'

'Lala-ji gone visiting VIPs to "break" Nanda. Ma-ji gone with him.'

Mother and Father both out! *Well, well, well.* This meant upstairs was all his for a few hours. A man-eating tiger began to roar in him. The starving man had been re-appointed master of the king's kitchen.

Now, now, now, Omi son. Slow and easy. Take your time. Make it last. Make it laaassst . . .

Omi had developed a system for making it last longer. First he studied the white ceiling and the furniture in the room. When the going got too good and reached an explosive moment, he began to sing film songs in his throat. It helped. But not for very long, for often he forgot the song he was singing. Then he took to counting up to a hundred. Or spelling difficult and long words – i.n.e.x.p.u.g.n.a.b.l.e.

His arms ablaze with the fire of yearning, Omi raced upstairs. Munni stood at the top of the stairs, waiting – she had seen him in the street from the window. She was done up – lipstick, rouge, kohl and all. She smelled as if she had just had a bath – she always smelled like that. There were two flights of the stairs, each consisting of seven steps. By the time he set foot on the fourteenth, Omi was half gone, and still going cock-a-doodle-doo. *Now, now, now. . .*

Munnishka was wrapped up in a black kashmiri shawl, its border embroidered in gold. Omi liked her in a shawl. He liked his hands inside it.

'Munnishka!'

Munnishka smiled. Boy, those eyes, those lips! She hugged her shoulders in the shawl and quivered, waiting to be touched, to be taken in his arms. Omi did just that and she shut her eyes. From then on it was what they liked doing most in the world.

'Nothing can separate me from you now. Not even London Blitz air-raid sirens,' Omi said without detaching his lips from hers.

An hour later, in their room, Omi had taken to singing in his throat.

'Omi bau! Omi bau . . .' came a shout from the stairs. Bawa – sending an advance warning that he was coming up. Bawa knew –

the upstairs-downstairs phone was off the hook upstairs. Anyway, he always knew.

Omi didn't stop. He didn't answer. He went on singing and hoped Bawa would get the message and bugger off. But Bawa didn't bugger off.

'Omi bau,' shouted Bawa urgently from the door. 'The man on the telephone again.'

'Tell him I am un-get.'

'I told him you are double un-get. But he insists I tell you he is from the Residence.'

'Whose residence?'

'The Chief Minister's Residence, Omi bau!'

The Chief Minister's Residence telephoning him! Omi leapt off Munni and looked for his clothes and shoes.

'But you said that not even an air-raid siren could separate you from me.' Munni was disappointed – she was almost there, almost.

'I know, but this is different. Stay where you are as you are. Back in a sec with all batteries charged, I swear.'

'Apology, Omi bau. Looks something big big, otherwise I wouldn't have. You know me.'

Omi gave Bawa another slap on the head. It meant it was all right.
'Hello.'

'Mr O. P. Khatri himself speaking this time?'

'Mr. O. P. Khatri himself speaking.'

'I am Mr S. S. Mann speaking from the C. M.'s Residence. I have his order to invite you and Mrs Khatri to his At Home . . .'

Omi's heart missed a beat. It missed several beats.

'He trusts she is well and happy . . .'

'As well and as happy as she can be under the circumstances.'

'He hopes you'll be able to come. He is looking forward to meeting you again.'

'We are honoured, Mr Mann. We would be delighted to come.'

'Good. I'll be sending you the invitation card. So we'll see you at the At Home, then. Yes?'

Mr Mann was going, but Omi had something to say. 'Just one little thing, Mr Mann.'

'Namely what, Mr Khatri?'

'Namely that my parents are great admirers of the Chief Minister. Do you think it would be all right if . . .?'

'Perfectly, Mr Khatri. Perfectly.'

The conversation over, Omi kissed the phone loudly and ran out of the office to return to the king's kitchen. Dabbu, true dog, sensing the importance of the occasion, wagged his tail furiously and barked madly and ran with his jubilant master. 'Munnishka. Munnishka!' the tiger roared as he flew up the stairs.

Upstairs, however, the situation had changed. Paro was back. She hadn't gone with Khatri, only to Sector I5 to see Vidya, and had come back with her. With them were Lakhpatni (her first visit here since *that* picnic), the Doctorani, Mrs K. P. Singh, another couple of neighbours and, of course, the Brahmin widow, Chatkarni. Maaii was also there, mopping the floor with a rag and a bucket of phenyl water.

'Oh, hell.' Omi knew life was cruel, but this was too much. About turn.

'Omi!' came a shout from Aunt Vidya as he pirouetted back from the thirteenth step. She had seen Omi was bursting with news. She wanted to know.

Omi loved his aunt. It was the other women who killed him with their yap yap tittle tattle mouth mouth. And hello hello hello. What was Lakhpatni doing there?

'Omiii!'

Caught, Omi turned again. He failed to see Maaii and her bucket. As a result, his foot hit the bucket, sending its contents flying in all directions, mostly on to his mother's honoured guest – Lakhpatni – drenching her exquisite thousand-rupee sari in filthy phenyl water.

'This stupid dog has his eyes in his tail!' Omi blamed Dabbu, but the dog had nothing to do with it and everybody knew it. Poor Dabbu, good dog, realizing his master was in trouble, out of instinctive sympathy began to lick Omi's foot and started to climb him as if he was a tree.

'But where are *your* eyes, Om Parkash?' Lakhpatni said. Ever since *that* picnic – *shame, o shame* – the very thought of this brash young man had revolted her. The laddus and the cherries had introduced a new era of friendship with Paro – they had agreed that bygones were bygones. But who could take stinking water thrown in the face by the very cause of all her shame? And look at this sari which she had bought just the other day from Connaught Place in Delhi and was wearing only for the second time today! This was the last straw. The camel's back broken in two, Lakhpatni stood up. End of friendship again.

'Sit, sit, sit, Lakhpatni. Sit you down,' Paro pushed her back where she sat and ran and brought her one of her own saris to wear. If her friend was drenched in dirty water, Paro was drowned in disgust with her son. She wouldn't have cared that much had it been the

183

Doctorani, the Postmasterani or anyone else. But Lakhpatni, the wife of the owner of seven petrol pumps and car, tractor, lorry and scooter showrooms – but, above all, her new old friend! Paro slapped her forehead. 'O Lakhpatni, this son of mine!'

'Omi!' Chatkarni said.

'The young of today. Only He knows where He put their brain,' the Doctorani said, pointing a finger to the window, as if God stood outside it.

Crushed with guilt and shame, Omi smiled foolishly. He was angry with himself. He was also angry with Lakhpatni – *so what, I knocked the bloody bucket. So bloody what if a few drops of water fell on her. She isn't made of sugar.*

'Beg huge apology, Auntie Lakhpatni. Promise to look out for buckets next time. Promise . . . Forgiven?' Omi said. He looked around for Munni. Munni was in the same shawl under which he had been making that body search not long before. Their eyes met and Omi realized his wife had a problem – how not to laugh. This had a certain influence on his guilt, shame and anger. As the crisis subsided and as the tittle tattle restarted, Omi tried to change the situation to his advantage.

'Guess what, Ma? We've been invited.'

'To what? By whom?'

'Who would you say was the greatest man in the Punjab?'

'Punjabis are dunces – the whole world knows. We never produced a great man. Great men are born far, far away from here.'

'What about Har Raisingh, Ma?'

'What about him?'

'We are invited to tea at his Residence, Ma. True.'

First it was royalty, royal jewels and the Ritz of Simla. Now tea at the Chief Minister's Residence. Lakhpatni was struck by lightning. She quickly changed her sari and sat down to hear more.

'Ma, dress to do what the assasins failed to,' Omi said on the big day, putting his arms around his mother.

'Huhh,' Paro said. Vidya had come to help her dress and to look after the house in their absence. And to hear all about it when they came back.

'Aunt Vidya, you too. Dress to kill.' Omi didn't want to leave his beloved aunt behind.

'No.' Vidya turned purple and hid her face in her hands. 'We'll look silly – the whole tribe turning up.'

'No, we won't. Maybe there will be a hundred guests, maybe more. No one is going to count how many we are. Even if they do, I'll tell them to go to hell. So come.'

Reluctantly, but not very reluctantly, Vidya agreed to come. She wore one of her sister's saris and, for the first time in her thirty years, wore 'English-style' make-up, Munni's. It made her look ten years younger.

'I say, Aunt Vidya, I hope there won't be any Bombay-wallah film-producer chaps at the party.'

'Why not?'

'I don't want to lose my aunt.'

Vidya looked out of this world – she couldn't tear herself away from Munni's full-length mirror. Paro looked out of this world – she, too, couldn't tear herself away from the same mirror, which the three ladies addressed. But the real beauty was, naturally . . .

'How do I look? No, no, no . . . Don't tell me how I look, go and see how Father looks.'

Khatri, in a raw silk shirt and a raw silk waistcoat with twenty-one buttons, shone like the rajah of a small kingdom on the North-West Frontier. But as he considered his reflection in the mirror his stomach was a well full of butterflies. The reason was he didn't know what he would say to Har Raisingh, a man he looked up to. He knew the moment he opened his mouth before the great man, something unbelievably silly would come out.

'Leave all the talking to me, Father.'

'Besides, I won't know a soul there.' Now that was lame and untrue.

'Father, you will. All our important customers will be there.'

'You go, boy, you go,' Khatri said. He had decided. He wasn't going. He took off his impressive Peshawari turban and hung it on its peg in the wall. Another day, he would have given it to Omi to hang it there.

'I won't go either-neither,' Paro said, half broken-hearted.

'Nor me,' said Vidya.

'Let's all stay home then, little people that we really are. Let's do the things that become little people – kill flies with our hands,' Omi said. He was disgusted with his parents, especially with his father. He took off his suit jacket and tie and smacked them on a palang. Munni, unable to understand any of it, looked from face to face. The mood of the house had changed. From the very festive, it had become one of mourning. She recalled her mother-in-law's words – *Munni, you sometimes must wonder what sort of species are these Khatris.*

185

Then Paro perked up again. 'You'll be insulting the host person-ally. That's bad bad manners. And one thing the Khatris cannot be accused of is bad manners,' Paro said.

This seemed to stir a chord in Khatri. He cleared his throat and pulled his turban off the wooden peg and put it back on his head again, clearing his throat for a second time.

'Your tie, boy, your tie,' he said.

'All that fuss for what?' Paro said. 'My housewallah – a specialist in making molehills of mountains.'

Sector 23 held its breath – the Khatris going 'a-tea-drinking with the Chief Minister'! Necks leaned out of balconies. Faces leapt out of windows when the the Khatris went. But when the Khatris arrived at the Residence they went unnoticed – so many heavenly faces and golden haloes, dazzling uniforms and loud turbans.

Khatri, the elder, was relieved. Khatri, the younger, was annoyed. But he waited for things to change. They did. Soon a man Omi recognized as one of the C.M.'s guards approached.

'Ao ji, ao ji, Khatri sahib. This way, this way.'

The Khatris were led through the high and mighty. There were ministers in white khadi (homespun) and white Gandhi topis. There were impeccably turned-out generals, colonels and air commodores. There were suited-booted 'civil' gentlemen flanked by fleshy wives in shimmering saris. There were tall and elegant Sikh zamindars, as there were portly banias (tycoons) and toothpick Congress-wallahs and other wallahs. All with glowing faces and that halo. All looking pleased with themselves.

The Khatris, Omi in the lead, were brought to the middle of the Residence's rolling lawns. Sofas and cane chairs and tables were tastefully dispersed around on grass and Persian carpets. Amidst a group of sofas on a vast carpet was the dimunitive figure of the Punjab's Chief Minister, Sardar Har Raisingh. A score of men, women and a few children surrounded him. He was saying something, jabbing the air with a finger repeatedly, Congress leader-style. Everybody was listening raptly. He stopped when his eyes fell on Omi, smiled, and threw his arms towards him as one does to hug a child. 'Ah, here is someone it soothes my eyes to see,' the C.M. said.

'Sat sri akal, sir.' Omi uttered the Sikh greeting. 'May I present some of your most ardent admirers – my parents, and my aunt, and of course you-know-who – Munnishka.'

'Munnishka, beta. I like the name. Lala-ji, you have a brave boy, a true son of the Punjab. You must be very proud.' The C.M. hugged Omi like a son.

People formed a circle around the C.M. and the new arrivals. Everybody was in awe of their leader, the strong little man of the Punjab, nicknamed Napoleon Singh. Khatri was more in awe of him than the others. Seldom short of words, today he didn't know how to respond to it all, especially to Raisingh who was talking to him as an equal, as if they had both been to the same primary school. He decided to keep his hands folded on his chest, keep smiling and let his son do the talking for him. Raisingh, realizing he was not going to get anything out of the boy's father – he knew of the hypnotic effect he had on common people – turned to the mother.

'Sister, you are a woman of great karma to beget a son like our Omi.'

'Sardar-ji, he is all right to look at. Trouble is he doesn't listen. Whatever one says to him goes into one ear and out of the other at the same time. He has a very short wind tunnel between his ears,' Paro said. She was also awed by Har Raisingh, but she was not hypnotized.

'Mother!' Omi said.

People laughed, Raisingh too. He recalled what his mother – the Great Guru, bless her soul – used to say about him when he was twenty. 'Boys will be boys, sister.'

'But this boy is special. A toofaan – a hurricane. Had I not given him birth myself I would have sworn he was born in a cabbage field. And . . .'

'Mother!' Omi groaned.

'And another thing. Ever since he got a wife, he has forgotten that his mother exists. True, hundred per cent.'

Everybody laughed, loudly this time.

'That I can understand,' the C.M. said, looking at Munni. Munni wanted to run and hide in the flowers or simply keep running till she had reached home in Sector 23 or Dhulkote twenty-five miles down the same road.

The C.M. turned to his saviour. 'Tell us, Omi, what is your ambition in life.'

This was not fair. Omi hadn't expected to be asked such a question in public. He knew one had to be ambitious; he also knew that one must never appear to be so. It was bad taste, vulgar. He searched for something else by way of an answer. When nothing came, he improvised one. 'To serve India,' he mumbled modestly.

'Wah wah, wah wah,' said the onlookers.

187

'Serving one's country is one's duty. By ambition I mean what do you want to be? Mr ABC wants to be a minister, Mr LMN wants to be a general, Mr XYZ wants to be a millionaire. What do you want to be, Mr OPK?'

'Well, sir, I prefer looking at uniforms to wearing them. The minister and the general both wear uniforms. The third invidual doesn't.'

'So you want to be a millionaire? Wah wah, wah wah,' the C.M. said and hugged Omi again. Photographers' bulbs flashed. Cameras clicked. People clapped. 'Now I want you to meet Sardarni-ji. Come, sister,' the C.M. said to Paro.

An ear-splitting screech tore open the sky. Omi, fearing it was an aerial attack on the C.M.'s life – Pakistan sending its air force? – nearly threw his mother down on the lawn. But no one else seemed concerned. Heads and haloes tilted. Everybody looked up, as if everybody knew what it was all about. Next second, a formation of low-flying Russian-built MIGs screamed past the Residence, showering its lawns with roses. Live music broke out from somewhere and people began to sing with one voice: '*Happy birthday . . . Happy birthday, dear Napoleon Singh . . .*'

There was clapping. The cake was cut. There was more clapping and the party really got going.

The Sardarni was just as tiny as her sardar. She had been married to Har Raisingh for thirty-eight years and yet she looked only a couple of years older than Paro who was sitting next to him on the same sofa. 'I was twelve on the day of my marriage, he nineteen,' the Sardarni told Paro. Like Paro, she knew not a word of English. As they talked, they discovered they both came from the same district, Gujranwala; even the same *tehsil*, Patti, in the old Punjab before the holocaust. All that, and the fact that the son of one of them had saved the life of the husband of the other, proved just the recipe for instant friendship. They talked. People with cups of tea and plates heaped with triangles of the birthday cake, conical samosas, and this and that, milled around, all talking 'happy happy'. Khatri began to relax when the C.M. moved away to greet the Governor, who had just arrived. Coolly, he surveyed the scene and spotted many an acquaintance, his filthy rich customers. He received many a good-to-see-you nod and many an isn't-it-nice-to-be-here? smile. This put him quite at his ease. *Not bad, eh, Khatri old cock? Not bad for a halwai from Panchkoola walking on Raisingh's grass. Rubbing shoulders.*

Khatri desperately wanted to do something private – scratch the middle of his sutthan. Elsewhere he would have done it in public, but not here.Here he would look a jat dhoosh jungli scratching his balls. But the temptation was killing him. *Resist, Khatri, old cock. Don't make a fool of yourself. Don't let your boy down.* Khatri resisted. He looked at his boy.

His boy, totally relaxed, was in his element. This was where he belonged. This. Here. Now. *This is it, Omi son. Your world. Henceforth. Forthwith.* He had no doubt about it. He belonged here, in this perfumed garden smelling of power and money and . . . well, just smelling good. Smells get into you. In due course, they become your body smells, your own smells.

The smells of the perfumed garden had got into Omi.

'I say, Aimie, old chap, what on earth are you doing here?'

Bunny!

'I don't believe it. I don't believe it.' Omi and Bunny hugged each other like long-lost brothers.

'Didn't you get my letter?' Omi said.

'I did, of course I did. It was very handsome of you to write.'

'Then why didn't you write back?'

'I am simply dreadful at writing letters. Loathe the act of putting pen to paper. Otherwise I might have ended up a novelist, with all I know and have seen. What?'

Bunny laughed. Omi laughed. It was time to take notice of their ladies who stood right behind them.

'Ah, Moni, my little sister, how are you? How is this son of a gun treating you?'

'You look wonderful, Munni,' Bunty said.

'You look gorgeous, Bunty,' Munni said.

'When did you arrive?' Omi asked.

'Just this minute.'

'Dinner with us tonight?'

'Afraid not, old boy. Going right back after the reception. Now, now, now don't you say it's rotten of us . . .'

'It is rotten of you. Why don't you stop for the night? Stay with us.' What had the fool said? *Stay with us* – where would he put them up? What would they say when they saw the Khatris lived above a

189

shop converted into a restaurant in Sector 23! *Nobody* lived in Sector 23. Omi hoped Bunny would say no. Bunny said no.

'Another time, promise. Will spend a whole week with you . . .'

Bunny took it for granted that the Khatris knew the Punjab's first minister personally. This had an effect on his regard for Aimie – it deepened it. He hugged him again.

'So good to see you, old chap.'

'But you are rotten, you know. Really rotten – playing that trick on us.'

'Thank you for Moni's birthday present. We loved it,' Munni said.

'I wanted it to be a surprise.'

'It was. But how do you make any money that way.'

'Next time you come we'll charge double! Ha ha, what? Quite a turn-out here.'

Everybody was there. Arun was there with his parents. Duke and Lord were there. So and so was there, and lo and behold (Omi didn't want to behold) so was Titli with her Mummy and General (retired) Daddy. A group of the Simla Pinks formed by itself, and Omi, not a true Simla Pink, found himself in its midst. Omi's stock, already high because he had been seen embracing the C.M., soared on being seen being hugged again and again by Simla Ritz's Bunny, who called Aimie's wife his little sister.

'I had heard so much about you,' Titli said.

'From whom?' Munni said.

'From everybody. I was told you were out of this world, and you are.'

While Munni blushed, Omi snatched a .303 rifle from a soldier on duty and shot Titli dead – he didn't like the bitch talking like that to his wife. In fact he didn't want her to talk to her at all. But there was nothing he could do about it. This was society, high society. He had to behave impeccably. It was difficult. He burned inside.

Titli stole a glance at her ex-lover. She knew how he felt. Delighted, she took complete charge of Munni. Munni was also delighted to be the centre of attention of so glamorous a person as Titli. The two girls talked and smiled and laughed. When the opportuniy arose, Titli whisked Munni off on a little tour of the C.M.'s garden.

'Munnishka – what a lovely name. We must become close friends. Would you like that?'

'Yes, why not?'

'I have a confession to make to you.'

'A confession?'

'Yes. It's called love at first sight. From now on we shall become inseparable, like sisters. Do you think he'll mind?'

'Who?'

'Your hubby.'

Munni's hubby was only a few yards away, talking to Bunny. 'Incidently, who was "His Highness" whom we met at your Ritz?'

'His Highness who? Which?'

Omi explained. Bunny shook his head.

'Kalan Pur? No such place. Wait a sec – it was H.H. of Shamshan Pur, that coal-black chap.'

'But Major Mahesh said Kalan Pur. Definitely.'

'Our Major has the memory of an elephant. Never forgets a face, only their names and where they come from. Sent a Russian delegation's bill to the American Chancellery, and they paid up, would you believe? Oh, our Major Mahesh has a brain. Where is my little sister?'

Munni and Titli were contemplating a wall of sweetpeas guarded by two eight-foot tall soldiers who stood erect like pillars, with lances twice their height. They were glancing at each other and smiling sweetly. Omi's heart burned to cinders.

'Moni, come over here,' Bunny shouted, even though Munni was only twenty feet away. Munni hurried back. It was more the look on her husband's face – strange, pained, angry – that brought her back. He had been all right a minute ago, on top of the world, she could swear.

'You don't have to shout at the poor girl,' Bunty said.

'Who is shouting? Come here, come here. What are you two talking about?' Bunny said to Titli.

'You know what – I wasn't coming. I said to Mummy, "Mummy, I can't stand these garden parties." But Mummy said Uncle Napoleon would be cross if I didn't . . .' Titli had a mesmerizing way of talking – no one could get a word in. Once, in an other life, Omi had been happily mesmerized by her. Now she had become a red chilli stuck in his arse. '. . . But I am so glad I came, wouldn't have missed it for the world,' Titli said, looking sideways at Omi.

'Why not?' Omi said. His day was in ruins. *This* no longer was his world. He wanted to get the hell out of it – Derby-horse time.

Titli didn't bother to reply. She had spotted someone – Captain Bubbles and his attractive wife, with a film-starry look. The couple were a few yards away in a group of army officers and their memsahibs. 'Rude woman, that, Bubbles's wife. You know Bubbles, Bunny?'

'Who doesn't?' Bubbles was a well-known stud. He was the son of a small hill rajah who had married well – to the daughter of a bigger hill rajah.

'Rude and arrogant woman, that, Bunny. Here I was talking to her about the Flood Relief Fund at the club the other night and you know what she did? The bitch yawned in my face . . .'

'Must have opened her mouth to say something,' Omi said and marched Munni away. 'Let's go and see how Mother is doing.'

Paro was doing well. She had struck up a friendship.

'First they wanted my man to become their leader. He fought. Went to jail. And now that he is their leader they want to kill him,' Paro's new friend the Sardarni said. 'Anyway, I am grateful to you, Paro. Your boy saved his life. Anything we can do for you – all you have to do is to ask.'

'What do you mean, Sardarni-ji?'

'I mean anything – a permit-shermit. Licence for import-export. Don't tell Sardar-ji – he is above this sort of thing. Just tell me. I want to do something for you.'

'By God's grace we are all right.'

'Surely there is something?'

'Now that you insist, Sardarni-ji – you see that man over there, the one in a black suit with lines?'

'Who, Nanda of Governor House?'

'Yes, him. He can do something for us he is not doing.'

The Sardarni raised a finger. A servant in a long white coat, with a red and gold turban and red and gold sash across him, appeared before her. She told him to go and fetch 'Nanda sahib of Governor House'. Seconds later, Nanda arrived, trembling, his hands folded on his chest. He knew. He had been watching the two women conversing for the last forty minutes and wondering how the Khatris had got there.

'Sat sri akal, Sardarni-ji,' Nanda said, sweetly.

'Nanda sahib, you know why I have given you the trouble to come? You should. You are an intelligent man.'

'I do, Sardarni-ji,' Nanda said, looking at Paro and calling her 'bitch' in his throat.

'Well, then?'

'It will be done.'

'When?'

192

'Soon.'

'Not soon. Today.'

'Impossible, Sardarni-ji. Sunday today. Lawyers are closed.'

'No such thing as impossible. Who is your lawyer?'

'Chuha Mal Kamina.'

'There he is. Go ask him here for a second.'

Trembling, Nanda went and brought lawyer Kamina. Kamina also trembled.

'Kamina-ji . . .'

'Will be done, Sardarni-ji. Sunday no problem. Sunday fine. As good as Monday.'

'Very kind of you. Now go and enjoy the party, Kamina-ji. You've done me a favour and I will remember it. Go, go. But you stay, Nanda sahib.' As the relieved lawyer turned his back, the Sardarni called Nanda closer to her with a finger. 'Nanda sahib, you want anything in return?'

Nanda hesitated. He felt like doing what his arch dushman (enemy) had been itching to do a short while ago at that very spot – scratch the middle of his trousers. Instead he scratched his head. 'I was Hospitality Officer at Governor House.'

'We all know that.'

'Now I have been transferred to caretake the concrete jungle of the Secretariat. Mrs Nanda doesn't like it. My children don't like it.'

'Do you like it?'

'Now, how can you ask me such a question, Sardarni-ji?'

'So you want a transfer back? You are transferred back. From tomorrow.'

'But there is zero hospitality at Governor House now. Mr N. K. P. D. Kesai is, as you well know . . .'

'The Punjabis are a hospitable people. Their Governor has to be hospitable too. So hospitality will restart at Governor House.'

'Sure, Sardarni-ji?'

'You arguing with me?'

'Much obliged,' Nanda said, and went away, still trembling.

'Anything else, sister Paro? Your son saved my man's life.'

'Just one more thing, sister Sardarni.'

'Name it.'

'I want you to come to drink tea at my house.'

This was a master-stroke.

'Ma, you are a genius,' Omi said on their way back home, hugging his over-the-moon mother.

BOOK FOUR

The speaker for that year's Sri Aurobindo Memorial Lecture at Omi's old college was the philosopher, Sri Rama Krishnan, or Sri R. K., as he was fondly called. Sri R. K. was spell-binding – 'A One'. People packed halls and maidans to hear him. He had an 'over-packed' speaking schedule, including 'foreign'. It was quite a coup that Principal Varma had managed to hook him for that year's Memorial Lecture.

Kapoor insisted Omi went with him 'for old times' sake'. He himself was going because all the girls were going. In the past Omi would have been among the first to arrive in the hall, but now the story was different. Besides, he didn't care for the spiritual stuff. But his father said go, boy, go: 'Can't do you any harm to listen to some sense sometimes.'

Sri R. K. was tall, thin, wiry and jet-black, with fire in his eyes. He had the voice of an angry woman – shrill, high-pitched and torrential. He spoke non-stop for an hour and fifty-one minutes according to the timepiece on his table, without once touching the glass of water next to it. Kapoor had a field day ogling ladies in the other half of the 'capacity' hall. Omi, for once, listened. Like most people in both halves, he didn't understand a word of what the famous philosopher said, but for some reason, Sri R.K.'s last words stuck in a corner of his busy mind: 'Man must, from time to time, pause and look before and after and not pine for what is not, but consider what is what.' It sounded like a line from a poem. Omi liked it.

On his way back from the lecture, Omi paused. *Pushing twenty-one. BA. We-love-you-parents. Turns-me-on-wife. House and garden; successful too. Happy as a pig in a pool of mud.* But what next? Where was he to go from there? What more did he want from life?

Everything. The earth's sputnik.

It occurred to Omi that he might be missing Sri R.K.'s point. But he had done what the enlightened gentleman had suggested: he had looked before and after and, frankly, liked what he saw.

'Ma, four more years and you will see,' Omi announced on reaching home.

Khatri and Munni first looked at Omi, then they looked at each other – baffled, embarrassed, even pained. But Paro knew. She slapped her forehead. She saw a field full of Brahmin corpses which she had slaughtered with her own hands in her previous incarnation.

Unrelated to his son's 'pausing', Khatri had been doing some of his own for his own reasons. *Time is passing.* Khatri had suddenly become aware of it as he had never been before. Before, today had walked into tomorrow and tomorrow into the day after, and that was that. Not now, though: now today still walked into tomorrow and the rest, but it made Khatri look back, all the way back . . . and think. It also made him look ahead – far, far ahead. Far, far ahead there was nothing, not even Paro. And that was painful.

Time is passing. Time is. Time had to pass. Unlike anything else, it was unstoppable – and that, too, was painful. For there were moments, like now, which Khatri would have liked to catch and hold, but couldn't. Many such 'nows' had slipped out of his grasp like water from a closed fist. Gone.

Khatri glanced at the newspaper. He ground his jaw, shook his left leg and thought of taking the little mountain bus to see his guru.

Paro saw. 'God is coming into *them* again,' she worried. When she saw that look on his face, her bosom heaved uncomfortably. '*They* are thinking of "higher things" again.' She dreaded her husband's 'higher things', which she equated with a kala keera. Worms, black or white, were no good for anyone, and her man's worm was eating her as well.

Omi saw. 'Ma, why do you worry? Father will be perfectly all right. At his age a man has the right to look at life and ask questions to which he knows there are no answers.'

'Then why ask them?'

'That's the thing, Ma – one has to. You don't understand.'

Paro didn't understand. She suppressed a rising wave of turbulence in her chest and caressed Omi's right cheek with her left hand. Then she gave it a tiny little slap. The mother and the son knew what it meant. Perhaps Khatri too – he had heard, he had seen. But he pretended otherwise. He went on shaking his leg and reading the *Milap*.

'I think I'll go to Dhalli coming Sunday,' he said to the *Milap*.

'Now when a man begins to talk to his newspaper . . .!' Paro said, shaking her head.

198

'Oh, Ma,' Omi said and put his arms around Paro to shut her up.

'Munni, our men – real specimens. Sometimes you must wonder . . .' Paro didn't finish. She reached out and touched Munni's cheek. It was a little gesture which did good to all four of them.

Scandal hit Sector 23 again – harder this time. Mr and Mrs Bahal's elopement was over, and now so was that of two other local lights – Romesh and Sarla. Romesh was Satya's brother; Sarla was Dr Devan Chand's daughter. They had run away last year and got married in secret and vanished into thin air. It had taken the combined secret intelligence services of the entire neighbourhood to track them down in the far-off Bhopal in central India, where, according to the intelligence report, they were living it up. The truth was somewhat different: Romesh, an MA, was unemployed; Sarla, 'a three-quarters BA' (she had never taken the exam because they had run away), was working three days a week as a stenographer in a new gas plant. They were bringing up a baby girl of three months on her salary in a tin-roofed hut in a slum by the plant. Their families in Chandigarh had not been on speaking terms since the elopment, though they lived almost next door to each other with only the Khatris in between. But the day the 'intelligence' came, they talked. The homeopath, being the girl's father, made the first approach. He did so through a middleman, Omi, who lived in the middle.

'Think of my izzat (honour), Omi. Speak to Satya with diplomacy. With dip-lo-macy. The woman is a drum of caustic soda.'

Omi used diplomacy. He didn't speak to Satya at all, he spoke to her husband, Ujjagar, 'a man worth his weight in sugar'. He arranged a meeting of the two on his roof. The meeting had to be secret, for Devan Chand didn't want the world to know he was talking to the family which had brought such shame on him. In such matters, fathers killed – they didn't talk.

That evening Dr Devan Chand and Ujjagar 'talked' on the Khatri roof. Next morning they took the train. On the third day they brought the runaway couple and the baby back with the words – *done is done*.

The elopers, all four of them, arrived back the same day, one couple by train and the other by bus, causing 'scandal number one'.

The Bahals dealt with it sensibly: they shut the door on the world and made themselves invisible. Romesh and Sarla remained very visible – they had nowhere to live. Neither the girl's parents nor the

199

boy's sister really wanted them in their houses, nor could they afford to set up the penniless couple somewhere else for the time being. What to do, what to do? The question gave everybody heartaches and headaches. But 'daughter is daughter', so the very visible couple went to live with her parents.

The same night four anonymous letters were slipped under the front door of the girl's father's shop. The first he opened offered medical advice: '*Why don't you empty a little bottle of poison in the teacup of . . .?*' '*Pack up bag and baggage and them and . . .*' said letter number two. Letters three and four said things Dr Devan Chand didn't show to anyone, not even the Doctorani.

Next night there were two more letters. Both said the same thing, as if the neighbourhood had formed a syndicate: '*If you don't do something about it, we will. We will break his face. And that is a promise.*'

The harassed homeopath folded the letters back neatly and hid them at the bottom of his cash box. He had been tempted to tear them up, but a morbid thought – that he might need them in a court or something one day – stopped him. He said nothing to anyone – who was there, anyway? When your daughter elopes and returns, you are the loneliest of men.

On the third night two more letters were pushed under Sarla's father's shop door: '*If you don't do something about it . . .*'

On the fourth morning, when Romesh was out in the 'God area', nature calling, four faceless local louts jumped him. They dipped his head in his shit and broke his face.

'What to do, Omi, what? You understand life.' The father-in-law of the broken-faced son-in-law consulted Omi yet again.

'Hum,' Omi said. He didn't know what else to say.

Omi had never liked Romesh, the 'superior son of a bitch' who, in the past, had made him feel he was no bigger than an average toad in a ganda nullah (sewer) – just because he had been a few years senior to him at College and attracted degrees like flies, FA, BA, MA. But that was in the past, when Omi was very young. Now he was not very young any more. Now he 'understood life'. And he was being sought for advice – for help. 'Hum,' Omi said. He cupped his chin and became serious. 'Straightforward matter, Doctor sahib. They should live somewhere else and on their own.'

'Where how where how?'

The son of a ten-dog bitch must work to support his family. The turd must take up a job. Any kind of job – clerical, teaching . . . even labouring if he has to, to bring up the child.

'Romesh-ji should teach. He has an MA.'

200

'A good one, at that. Second division. The question is who is going to give him a post in a school or college in this city?'

Quite.

'I know!' Omi clicked his fingers. He had an idea, a kill-two-birds-with-one-stone idea. 'He should go to the God's city.'

'What what?'

Dr Devan Chand didn't like that – God's city! Did the young man mean his son-in-law whom he loathed and whom, if he could, he would disown, but who was a son-in-law nonetheless, should die? The doctor had never really liked Omi and thought of him as an upstart. Anger flushed his face and he regretted his decision to talk to him at all.

'No, no, no, Doctor sahib.' Omi guessed what was going on in his neighbour's mind. 'I mean Romesh-ji should go to Kurukshetra, Lord Krishna's city. Munni's cousin teaches at the university there. Maybe he can help. I'll give Romesh-ji a letter of introduction.

Omi wrote:

Maharishi Kukoo-ji Maharaj,
The bearer of this letter is somebody very close to us. In fact too close for our peace of mind – the son of a bitch lives next door and is a red chilli in the backside. We want to get rid of him. It can happen only if he gets a job far from here. You are our only hope – the ma chod has a good MA. So if you love your cousins even a thimbleful, please help . . .

Mr O. P. Khatri Esq

PS When is the next moon eclipse? Can we bring it forward? XXX
PPS How's the home cooking going? XXXX

Romesh went off with the letter. He never came back. A week later Sarla and the product of their union joined him.

Peace.

'People's problem-solver, why don't you solve your own?' Paro said, pointing to the problem – Khatri, with the God-come-in-him look on his face.

Omi slapped the air with his left hand.

'Ma, don't worry. Uncle B.K. is there. Once money starts coming in, God will start going out. Pukka promise.'

*

201

Mali's face was lit like a 100-watt lamp. He had just come back from Dhulkote with news.

Munni saw from the balcony. She knew. Paro, standing next to her also saw. She also knew.

'Munni bibi, sahib's got it.' Munni dared not translate Mali's words into her own. Wide-eyed, she waited for Mali to do so. 'Sahib's got the transfer. He's got Chandigarh!'

One tear. Two tears. Many tears. Tears of happiness. Munni's father had been working on the transfer for months, ever since before her marriage. After greasing countless palms – the whole world was after Chandigarh – he had got it.

Paro pulled out a rupee note from the bodice of her choli, waved it around Munni's head three times and gave it to the bhangi girl, Rano, who happened to be around, mopping up the latrine.

Khatri and Omi were leaving for Ambala Cantt to see 'Uncle B.K.'.

'Plum station. How did he pull it off.' Khatri said in a whisper. Omi didn't answer because he knew his father knew the answer – his father-in-law was no ordinary stationmaster. He had connections up and down the line, as far as Delhi where such decisions were made.

'When will the transfer take place?' Munni asked Mali. It was an academic question. She didn't care when the transfer took place as long as she knew it was taking place.

'Order came this morning. Barri bibi is writing to you, Munni bibi. Transfer after the handover. In two-three months.'

This posed the question of Mali's own future. It was obvious that he hadn't given it a thought.

'What about you, Mali?'

'What about me, bibi?'

'Chandigarh station hasn't got a single flower growing there,' Munni said. She had never seen the place.

'What would you like me to do, Munni bibi?'

'I never want to part with you, Mali.'

Those few words flew straight into Mali's heart and severed his association with the Indian Railways. 'I am too old to dig up a whole new station, Munni bibi.'

That morning the Khatris got a live-in gardener.

'I knew. I knew,' yelled Omi, embracing Mali. 'We will stop by at Dhulkote and hand in your resignation.'

'And bring back all the details,' Munni said.

'Yes, boss. Plus a camel-load of banknotes from Uncle B.K.,' Omi agreed, following his father to the door.

It was easily the happiest day of Munni's life. Feeling as she was, she gave Maaii a piece of lattha cloth – a yard and a half in length, enough for a child's shirt – and the day off. Then, her mother's face persistently before her eyes, she sat down by the window to write her a long letter. She had just finished when she heard someone shout on the stairs:

'Munnishka! Munnishka!'

Only one person in the world called her Munnishka, and by now he was where lived she who Munni had been talking to on the paper a moment ago – *Mummy, Ma, My jaan . . .*

'Munnishka!'

It was a girl's voice. Ah! Suddenly Munni knew. What a a lovely surprise! But then today was a day of surprises.

'I was passing by and thought I would drop in to say hello. Hope I am not interrupting something.'

The vivacious-looking girl of the CM's At Home, the girl who had said she had a confession to make. And had made it, too. But what was her name?

'Titli?. . .'

Titli had chosen the day carefully. Using a false voice, she had phoned and found out that the 'old man' and his son had gone 'out of station'. She had dropped everything and raced to Sector 23.

'Come in, come in. Maaii, make us some tea. Oh, no, silly me. I've sent her away, given her the day off.' What was Munni going to do? She'd have to make it herself. Ask Seva to bring some goodies from the restaurant for her guest – a trayful of cakes and pastries and dry fruits. Munni had such a glamorous guest – why, the girl should be in films. She would be a *real* box-office hit. Flustered, Munni cranked the upstairs-downstairs phone.

'Seva, bring some tea and cakes and . . .'

'No, honestly . . .' Titli snatched the phone from Munni. 'I just dropped by to say hello. I don't want tea.'

'Then have a Vimto or . . .'

'No, honestly. Listen, you come with me. Let's go out.'

'Where?'

'For a short drive in my car. Then I'll drop you back. In half an hour or less.'

Munni would love to go. But.

'I don't know, Titli. I don't know if he would like that.'

'What is this, yaar – the Middle Ages or something? You are not his slave. Or are you?' Titli took Munni's hands in hers and looked into her eyes, smiling and rocking her hands to and fro. They looked like two little girls playing ring-a-ring-a-roses . . .

'It's not that, it's just that he gets angry.'

'Where is he? Let me talk to the swine. Never heard of such a thing.'

'He's gone to Ambala with Father.'

'Then they won't be back for hours.'

'I know. But still. I'll have to ask Mother. I don't know if she'll give me permission to go.'

'Munnishka, I don't believe it. In this how they treat you? Do you have to apply for permission to go out with a friend for fifteen minutes. We all know it's India, but . . .'

'You don't understand, Titli. I simply have to ask.'

'Who is it, girl? Who are you talking to?' shouted Paro from the bathroom.

'It's Titli, Ma.'

'Who is Titli? Where did you meet her?'

'At the Chief Minister's, Ma.'

'What does she want?'

Munni coloured. She was embarrassed. Titli pressed her hand and drew her closer, whispering, 'Don't worry, I understand.' India was full of these illiterate types.

'She's dropped by in her car, Ma.'

'All right, girl, I'm coming out.'

Paro emerged from the bathroom, half dressed and half undressed. Her hair was wrapped up in a towel. She looked Titli up and down in one quick steely look: she did not like women who drove cars. But she let Munni go, though not before she had satisfied herself about Titli.

'What caste are you, girl?' Paro said, her voice coming straight from Jamshed Pur Tata Steel Plant – strong and heavy.

'We are Mehras, Ma-ji,' said Titli, Tata steel herself, smiling. She couldn't tolerate the 'old bag', as she called Omi's mother in her throat, but she had to humour her and please her.

'Ah, a Mehra girl?' That was all right. Mehras, along with the Malhotras and the Kapoors, were the highest of the Kashatriyas and, like the Khatris, a very old Aryan tribe. 'What does your father do?'

'My father is a retired general, Ma-ji.' *Does that satisfy you, you wife of a third-rate halwai? Now shut your ugly face and let us go. I haven't got all day.*

A general's daughter coming to call on her daughter-in-law? That

204

couldn't be bad. Paro gave Munni the permission to go. 'But don't be gone long, girls.'

'No, Ma-ji. I'll bring her back in half an hour,' Titli said said from the stairs. 'Such a lovely day. An awful shame to spend it cooped up at home.'

'Is that what you do all day every day, Munnishka?' she said in the car.

'I have so much to do at home,' Munni said.

'Such a beautiful girl. What a waste. An utter waste.'

Munni was used to being told she was beautiful, but to be told that by someone equally beautiful and, what was more, so sophisticated and star-like and driving a car, made her blush. Titli noticed, and was pleased with the effect she had on Omi's wife. She went on. 'I have been thinking about you. I wanted to see you again, so I dropped by. I hope you don't mind.'

Mind? Munni didn't mind. She was happy to be sitting in a car, going at speed. She had never been anywhere on her own or with a friend, not like this. She was glad Titli had come, and she told Titli so.

Titli took Munni's hand in hers and pressed it warmly. 'You look so utterly ravishing. You know that?'

Munni felt wonderful and ravishing. 'You too,' she said.

'You are so sweet to say that. But I feel old and ugly. You look so young and fresh – a flower one would like to smell, a fruit one would like to taste. Tell me, doesn't he let you go anywhere, then?'

'Go where? We go everywhere together.'

'That's all right. But still, don't you go anywhere by yourself?'

'I don't want to. Go where, anyway? And how?'

'Like now. With a friend.'

'I don't have any friends, only Asha. And she . . .' Munni told Titli all about Asha.

'Oh, dear, how awful. India's curse – such husbands and such mothers-in-law. But aren't you lucky? You have such a devoted husband and such a caring mum-in-law. The funny thing about Indian men is they don't like their women to have friends. It's not funny. It's pathetic.'

'He is not like that.'

'I hope not. But I bet he'll throw a fit when he hears you've been out with Titli in her car.'

'Why should he?'

'Exactly – why should he? Where shall we go? To the Savoy for a spot of tea? No, he won't like that.'

'No, he won't. Nor do I.'

'Then let's go to my place. We'll have tea there.'

Titli lived in the North End where *everybody* lived. Her house was as grand and as sumptuous as the CM's Residence, with a private swimming-pool and what not.

'What a nice place you have here,' said Miss Doolittle in the Hollywood drawing-room.

A liveried servant, like the waiters in Simla Ritz, brought tea on a silver tray. Munni noticed, with a tinge of pleasure, that the tea service was the same as the one which had come in her dowry – Royal Albert – though it was used only when Lakhpatni visited without her children.

'At least,' Munni said to herself. At least they had one thing in common – a few pieces of china.

Titli poured tea, then she went to what Munni thought was a longish piece of furniture along a wall – a highly polished cabinet. Titli opened a door and Muni saw a record-player inside it.

'What do you think of this radiogram?' Titli said, putting on a record.

'It's cute.'

'You can have it. I am sick of it. We've had it for ages, and I'm getting a new one. So you can have it.'

'Nonsense.'

'No, no, I am getting a new one. Shall I have it sent round?'

'Of course not!'

'Do you like Cliff Richard? I am crazy about him.'

'I adore him.' Munni had never heard of the man.

'My favourite song – "Living Doll".'

'Mine too.'

'You see we even like the same things.'

'Why shouldn't we?'

'Exactly. Fancy a swim?'

'I don't know how to swim. I'm terrified of water.' Munni had never seen a swimming-pool before, only in magazines.

'Piece of cake. I'll teach you.'

'No. Another day. Don't you think it's rather cold for a swim?'

'A bit chilly. But there is hardly any breeze and the sun is strong. I have a swim every day. Let's go upstairs. I want to change.'

Titli took Munni up a curved, palatial staircase. In her bedroom, she stood her before a wall made entirely of mirror – floor-to-ceiling cupboards with floor-to-ceiling mirrors. The two girls studied each other.

'Mirror mirror on the wall, who is the fairest of us all?' Titli said, and laughed and pulled a face at Munni in the mirror and said, 'Munnishka!' It was an invitation to Munni to pull a face. Shyly, she pulled a face, not as successfully as her exuberant friend.

'You are sweet, Munnishka. I am so very glad you are here,' Titli said. Then she disappeared through a door. A couple of minutes later she was back, wearing a green two-piece swimsuit. 'From Harrods in London. How do I look?'

'Stunning.'

'Liar. Do you want to see how you look in a bikini?' Titli threw her a set of swimwear. 'Try it on. Just to see how you look.'

'No, Titli.' Munni felt a flush creep into her cheeks – there was something about Titli which made her afraid. What was it?

'Why not, dammit? You'll look out of this world. What bust are you – 34? This is 34, like me.'

Munni didn't know what bust she was – all her bras were home-made, made by her mother. Nor did it matter to her – *he* was happy with whatever size she was, and therefore so was she.

'No, honestly,' Munni said.

'Come on, yaar. Don't you want to see how you look in an "itsy-bitsy . . ." Any girl would.'

Munni wanted to. But she was afraid.

'What are you afraid of?'

Munni didn't know. She had never undressed before anyone except her mother, and of course him.

'We are sisters, dammit, you and I. Just try it on, just to see. God gave you a body – let's see what it looks like. No one else will see. Come on! Be a devil.'

'No.' There was this something about Titli. It was with difficulty that Munni managed to say no to her.

'Suit yourself.' Titli looked disappointed. Munni was sorry about it and nearly changed her mind about trying on the bikini. After all, what harm was there in just trying the thing on?

Titli's mood changed. She became less chirpy. 'I think you are right, Munnishka. It is rather chilly. I won't have a swim today, after all.'

They had another cup of tea downstairs and Titli took Munni back home. They met Paro sitting on Mali's Japanese grass, basking in the sun.

'Message just come from your father, girl,' Paro said.

'How, Ma?' Munni said.

'Dhulkote station phoned Chandigarh station. Chadigarh station phoned Pall Mall. The meeting in the Cantt is now tomorrow, so our men will now come back tomorrow evening.'

Titli's mood changed again. Her face lit up a little. 'Does this mean we can meet again tomorrow?' she said.

'Why not?' Munni said.

'I'll come at the same time.'

'We'll have tea here tomorrow.'

Paro sat on a charpoy in Munni's Mogul Gardens in the sun, making savian vermicelli. The machine was gripped to the side of the charpoy, and Paro fed lumps of dough into the hole at the top, turning the handle around slowly and ryhthmically. Thin tubes of vermicelli oozed out of tiny holes in the mouth of the machine like ever enlarging earthworms. When they were about eighteen inches long, Paro stopped rotating the handle and with a knife she expertly chopped the strands from the machine. She gathered them in both her hands and laid them down gently, spreading them a little so that they wouldn't stick to each other, on a white sheet covering another charpoy on the Japanese grass.

'You have magic hands, Ma-ji,' Titli said, coming in from the open back door – doors in the Punjabi homes are always open.

'Hah! You gave me a fright, girl,' Paro said. She had neither heard Titli's car nor her coming in.

'I parked the car right outside the door, Ma-ji.'

'I must be losing my mind.'

'Where is Munni?'

Munni had both heard and seen Titli's car from an upstairs window. She came racing down. The two girls took each other's hands and rocked them to and fro, like children. Paro saw from the corners of her eyes and went on turning the handle. What does this fashionable daughter of a retired general want from a retired sweet-vendor's daughter-in-law? What brings her here? Must be the girl's English – everyone had been enthralled by it at the CM's tea party.

Titli was holding the famous Sari Palace brown paper bag with a picture of a sexy-looking Goddess Lakshmi. It had two brand-new saris in it. Titli showed them to Munni.

'You just bought them?' Munni asked.

'No, I'm taking them back. I don't like them. Come with me?'

'But?' But what about their tea?

'Ma, can Munni come with me to the Sari Palace to return these saris?' Titli said to Paro.

208

Paro wasn't quite able to make out this girl. She was a little flattered, though, to be called 'Ma' by her.

'All right. Don't be long.'

'Tell you what, Ma, why don't you come with us? The Sari Palace has the world's most dazzling saris. You would love to see them.'

'Who wouldn't? But my hands are full. You go. And, beta, if you see one you like, buy it.'

In the Sari Palace in Sector 22 Titli returned her two Saris. She was shown a hundred more by the more-than-anxious-to-please Owner Properietor, Saudagar, who would have readily shown her another hundred – 'no problem' – had she not chosen two others. Munni bought one for herself and one for her mother-in-law. Hugging their bags, the two girls walked back to Titli's car.

'Your place or mine?' Titli said in the car.

'For what?' Munni said.

'To try these on. Let's go to my place. Lots of mirrors there.'

'But we were going to have tea at my place, Titli.'

'Let's compromise. We'll try these on at my place and go back to yours for tea – how about that?'

Munni didn't want to go to Titli's, but Titli simply whisked her away, smiling and pulling faces at her. 'You look gorgeous. If I were a man I would fall in love with you. Or, if you were a man I would be madly in love with you,' Titli said.

'I don't want to be a man.'

'I am so glad you aren't. Men are horrible, really. I don't mean your – you know who I mean. I mean men in general. They are all the same – selfish, self-centred, conceited . . . Urrgh. Women are sacrificing, loving, caring. Much nicer. You, for instance.'

'What do you mean?'

'I mean you are the sweetest and the most wonderful person I've ever known. Have you noticed I said "person", not "girl"?'

'But I am a girl.'

'And we are greatful for that. We adore you for that.'

'Who is we?'

'In this case me, and I suppose him too. Listen, don't let me talk too much, because then I will begin to cry.'

'Cry? Why?' Strange girl, this Titli.

'Because when I am in love I always want to cry.'

'But why?'

'Because I am happy. I am happy to be with you.' Titli changed gear and took Munni's hand in hers and pressed it.

They arrived at Titli's house. On their way up to her room, Titli

209

told a servant to bring tea. Once in her room she threw herself on her bed and declared she was exhausted – shopping tired her. She rose almost immediately, stood beside Munni in front of the great mirror, she opened a chest of drawers and pulled out a number of cholis. The tea came. Again she poured it herself and came and stood behind Munni, a choli in her hands. She put her arms around Munni and placed the blouse on her bosom.

'You look smashing,' Titli said. 'Try this blouse with the new sari. I'll try the other.' Titli wore salvar kamiz, the Punjabi pyjama-type leggings and shirt. So did Munni. Titli undid the cord of her salvar and let it drop at her feet and then took off her shirt and looked from Munni to herself in the mirror, unaware that she had caused Munni to blush at her behaviour.

'I don't like myself,' Titli said.

'What's wrong?' Munni said.

'I don't like my breasts. Come, try the blouse. Don't be shy. We are sisters, aren't we?' Titli lifted off Munni's shirt. Gently, she undid the cord of her salvar and let it fall in a circle around her feet.

'No, Titli.'

'Why no?'

The two girls stood in their slips and bras in front of the tall mirror. 'My God, how ravishing you look,' Titli said, turning towards Munni. As she did so, their breasts brushed each other's and Munni went red. She hated herself for being there. She was terrified, transfixed, ashamed. Yet . . .

'Close your eyes.'

'Why?'

'Just close them for a sec.'

There was something chilling and compelling about Titli. Munni closed her eyes for a second. Titli put her arms around her and held her almost-naked body against her own almost-naked body. Munni quickly opened her eyes and, dead, dead, of shame, stepped back.

'I am sorry, I shouldn't have done that. But I couldn't help it. There was this deep, urgent need to feel you close to me. I am sorry. Sorry, sorry, sorry. Please forgive me. Will you forgive me?'

Munni didn't know what to say. A storm raged inside her ribcage. Her cheeks burned.

'Will you forgive me? Do you forgive me?'

'Yes, I do.'

Titli put her arms around Munni again and crushed her breasts into her own. Then she placed her cheeks next to hers and began to cry.

'I do love you, you know. So very much. I know it is wrong, but what the hell, dammit? We like each other. We are good for each other. We love each other. What's wrong with it? Do you love me a little? A teeny-weeny bit, even?'

'I don't know.'

Titli took Munni's face in her hands and kissed her mouth lustily, just as her husband did morning, noon and night. Something happened to Munni, the simple girl from the dusty Dhulkote railway station. The energy of a locomotive suddenly filled her frail body and she pushed Titli away with such forece that Titli went reeling back, falling on the marble floor with a thud. Munni quickly slipped into her clothes, picked up her Sari Palace bag with the picture of Goddess Lakshmi, and ran out of the room and down the palatial staircase.

'Munnishka!'

Munni ran on.

'Memsahib going?' asked the liveried servant in English.

'What does it look like?' Munni said, running past the porch.

'Achaa! OK, then,' the silly man said, shaking his head.

'Munnishka . . .!'

At the street corner Munni was nearly struck down by a quaint-looking car, a certain Morris Minor.

'Well, well, well, have you robbed a bank or something? I thought the bank to be robbed was in Ambala Cantt . . .'

Munni had left home in a red car. She returned in one which was blue.

'Did the jernail's daughter dye her car on the way?' Paro said.

Munni had had some time to recompose herself. She hid the remainder of her confusion behind a smile and showed Paro the saris she had bought. She said she had met her Kurukshetra cousins in the shops in Sector 22, and they had dropped her home. Anticipating her mother-in-law's question – why hadn't they come up? – she explained that they had just arrived from the holy city and had other things to do, some business. They would call on their way back tomorrow morning. Like that they would be able to meet Omi as well.

Munni didn't mention a word about Titli. When her husband came back, she would tell him all about his rich and fashionable friend. She longed to. She couldn't wait for him to get back. She was burning for him. When would the evening come?

The evening was long a-coming. Omi came with it. But he didn't give her a chance to open her mouth.

*

Chilly, misty sunset. The tall mango, jumun and tahli trees whispered faintly against a murky golden sky, and the Munni birds sang: '*Munni, Munni, Munni.*' '*Love you. Love you. Love you.*'

Munni, wrapped up in a Kashmiri shawl – only her face showed, her big eyes twinkling – stood next to Paro on the balcony. They were sipping tea. They were waiting. A few minutes after six a rickshaw came to a halt outside their back door and Dabbu attacked it – their men had arrived. Khatri went straight to the Pall Mall to put some important papers in the safe and to make a couple of urgent phone calls. Omi embraced Dabbu and sprinted up the stairs. He was exploding with news.

'Tickety-boo, Ma. Tickety-boo,' Omi shouted on the stairs.

Everything had gone 'tickety-boo' with 'Uncle B.K.'. Money was on its way to Chandigarh. So were the Kandharis. Now the Khatris, too, could be on theirs – up, up, up. What had been happening here? He had been away for only thirty hours, but it seemed like thirty days. His hands itched to be inside that shawl for a good long body search, just to touch and feel and make sure everything was there.

'So what's been happening here?'

'Nothing much. Only Munni's got a new friend.'

'Oh! Who?'

'The fashionable car-driving jernails's daughter,' Paro said as Munni handed Omi a cup of tea.

Omi threw a fit when he heard of his wife's two outings with Titli. He went a step further, he jumped a step further – he went mad. The transformation was frightening. Paro, realizing a fight or something was on its way, left them and went downstairs to see her husband.

'You must never see her again. *Never!*'

Munni, confused and terrified, managed to say, 'All right, I won't.' But why should he say it and say it like that? She made a mistake: she asked. 'But why do you say it?'

'I do and that's that. Understood?'

'No.' Munni hadn't understood. Here she was, about to open her heart and soul to him – and there he was, shooting off his mouth like that. It didn't make sense. And it hurt.

Omi rested his tea on the balcony wall and glared at Munni for daring to question him. Away in the trees the Munni birds went on: '*Munni. Munni. Munni.*' '*Love you. Love you . . .*'

But this evening Omi didn't hear them. He glared. 'Tough shit. Understand this – you are never to see her again. I order you never to see her again.'

'You order me? I am not your servant.'

212

'You are my wife, damn you. Behave like a wife. Do what I tell you.'

'I can't believe my ears.'

'To hell with your ears.' Omi picked up the cup of tea he hadn't touched and smashed it against the wall. He stormed out of the balcony and made his way down the stairs, kicking everything in the way – chairs, tables . . .

Munni cried all evening. She didn't eat a thing.

'Mother says you haven't eaten anything all evening,' Omi said, coming up at midnight.

Munni didn't answer. She was still crying.

'Why don't you answer? Why haven't you eaten?'

'Don't shout. I am not deaf.'

'You are deaf and stupid. You can starve yourself to death if you want to, but you are not to see that bitch again. My orders.'

'Your orders. Who do you think you are? When did I say I was going to see her again?'

'Who do I think I am? Let me remind you, madam – your husband.'

'Then behave like a husband, not like the owner of a chattel, of a goat or a dog. I am not a goat or a dog.'

'A woman who doesn't listen to her husband is a bitch. A *bloody bitch*.'

'I am very disappointed in you.'

'Balls to your disappointment. To hell with your disappointment. I say you are not to see her again and that is it.'

'Not that I want to, but what would you do if I did want to? Beat me up?'

'Yes.'

'Then try. Now. Raise your hand. Let's see how really brave you are.'

Omi raised his hand. But he couldn't bring it down on her.

'Go on – I am a chattel, a dog, a goat. I am not a chattel, neither a goat nor a dog. I am me – the daughter of the stationmaster of Dhulkote! That piddle of a place where even your dogs won't cock their legs for a pee.'

'Don't talk to me like that, woman.'

'How should I talk to you?'

'Like a wife to her husband. We are Hindus.'

'Husbands, Hindus or not, are not owners of wives. Wives are not property.'

'Stop screaming, woman. Everybody in Sector 23 can hear you. You will wake up the whole city.'

'Good.'

'Good?'

The way Munni had said 'good' did it. Omi had restrained himself so far. No longer. He went berserk. He slapped and kicked. Munni fell. He kicked her more.

'The tragedy of the Indian women – husbands like you.'

'Husbands like me who put their wives on pedestal and treat them like a goddess, as I did? Why you are no goddess, only a disobedient, spoilt . . .' Gripped with madness, Omi hit out again. Once, twice . . . once, twice . . . and again.

'Hit me again. And again, if it satisfies your little ego.'

'I don't just want to hit you. I simply want to kill you.'

'Why don't you?'

Paro heard everything, but she didn't interfere. She would consult her husband. But Khatri didn't come upstairs till much later. By then an eerie silence prevailed in the house. By then the fight was over. Paro was sure by tomorrow it would be forgotten. She said nothing to Khatri when he finally did turn up.

Next morning, while father and son were in Bajwara for the day's shopping, Paro had a word with Munni.

'Beta, we are Hindus not mallachaas. Wives must obey. A little slap now and then never harmed one. Even your own mother would agree.'

Munni didn't reply. She just stared – at her feet. She didn't know how she felt. She didn't know anything any more. She just wanted to be with her mother.

'Ma, I want to go home.'

'Why?'

'Not because of what he did to me, but because of what he said. And the way he said it, Ma.'

'Only a molehill. Don't make a Himalaya of it.'

'No, Ma. I want to go.'

Paro tried to make the girl see sense – 'husbands' right to beat up wives if they want to'. But the girl wouldn't see sense.

'She wants to go home, you hear?' Paro said when Omi got back, alone – Khatri had gone on in the same rickshaw to see Bassi in Sector 16.

'Let her go and cool off. Let Seva Singh take her.'

214

'Don't invite your father's wrath. His brain is going to burst with anger, his mouth is going to explode when he hears about it. He might even go further, take his Peshawari chappal in hand and . . . in spite of the fact you are a married man now.'

Omi, too, feared all that. But the thing had become too big, a battle of wills. If he stopped Munni, even if he appeared to want to stop her, he was defeated. He would bear his father's wrath and take all that came, but he could not give in to his wife. Not now. He didn't answer his mother and trundled downstairs to speak to Seva Singh.

'In my opinion you should drink your anger and swallow your pride, Omi bau, and don't let her go,' Seva Singh said.

Omi didn't like that – he had expected understanding and support from his trusted and loyal old servant.

'In my opinion you should do what you are told, Seva Singh. Take Munni bibi to Dhulkote as soon as she is ready.'

'You are going to be sorry for yourself, Omi bau. Don't say afterwards that Seva didn't warn you.'

'Do as you are told.'

His head already less than upright, Omi trotted back upstairs. Munni was packing her suitcase quietly. Yet he heard her, and his heart started to travel against gravity, upwards, towards his throat. *Omi son, it's people like you who are the real shit of India. They never think. Reason why the country has become a dungheap. For once Seva is right – you are going to be sorry.*

Omi heard himself talk to himself. But he didn't listen to himself. Munni's suitcase was packed. As Bawa was sent to fetch two rickshaws – one for her and the other for Seva – the Morris Minor from the God's city turned up at their back door. It was a godsend. *Your last chance. Use it to your advantage. Humour her; bullshit your way around and make up and don't let her go.*

'Maharishi Kukoo-ji maharaj . . .' Embraces and more embraces. And laughter. Breakfast? No, no, no, only a cup of tea. Kurukshetra could stay in Chandigarh for 'ten minutes maximum' – he had a lecture at one-thirty, and couldn't afford to be late for it.

'One thing I never am – late for my lectures. Only when I haven't prepared them.'

In spite of that, the 'ten minutes maximum' slid into an hour. The one cup of tea multiplied into mouth-watering parathas and other goodies from the Pall Mall. Omi had all the time in the world, but blinded by anger and paralysed by pride, the fool did nothing to stop Munni going. In fact he encouraged her to do so in as many words.

215

'Your cousin is packed up to go home for a few days. Why doesn't she go with you?' Omi said to Kukoo.

So Munni went. An air of mourning, thick, black and evil-smelling, set in in the Khatri household. Even Dabbu, who had licked Munni's hands and feet all the way to the car and had made every effort to climb in through the window, was drained of life. He didn't bother to rise to greet Khatri when Khatri came home with some drawings from Bassi, he merely wagged his tail half-heartedly, which said, *O yes. So you are back, Lala-ji.*

Something was amiss and Khatri knew it. He looked around for a clue as he took off his turban and handed it to his son.

'Why is your face yellow like haldi, oi?' Khatri said, scratching his head with both his hands.

Omi didn't reply. Hastily, he moved away to his parents' room to hang the turban on its peg on the wall.

'What's the matter with your boy, Paro?'

Paro didn't answer either.

'What's the matter, boy? Your father dead? What is it, Parvati – your housewallah bunked off with a randi (whore)?'

There was still no answer – people in mourning are known to lose the faculty of speech. Annoyed, Khatri raised his voice. 'Where is the girl?'

'Don't ask me. Ask him whose wife she is, or was,' Paro said.

'What the hell do you mean, woman?'

'I mean she's gone.'

'Gone where? Speak.'

'Ask your rakshas son. The demon beat her and beat her last night and sent her away this morning.'

Khatri's frontier temper needed no more encouragement to flare. Neither did his nostrils.

'True, oi?'

'Father, we had a row last night . . .'

'What about? She's not the rowing type.'

'She's become disobedient. She answers back.'

'You lie. Dog!'

Khatri kicked the chappal off his left foot and picked it up. Paro held her breath. Omi trembled. But instead of hitting his son with it, Khatri hurled it angrily at the white-washed Le Corbusier wall.

'Dog! Son of a dog . . .' was all Khatri could say. Or do. He couldn't beat his son – Omi was not a boy of fifteen any more, he was grown man with a wife, leading a grown man's life. Scalded inside, Khatri took it out on his wife.

'Silly bitch, why did you let her go? Why didn't you stop her?'

'What could I do? She is a Kandhari, a girl of spirit. Well-read and well-written, too. She won't be treated like an ordinary Punjabi peasant by an ordinary jatt dhoosh (Punjabi peasant) which your son is.'

'This jatt dhoosh is a third-rate damn-fool. Like you.' Khatri took off his right chappal and sent it flying after the first one. 'Now she's gone, what is this son of a bitch going to do? I'll tell you – he is going to burn and boil in his own belly broth. Let him.'

Omi boiled in his own belly broth. Paro let him. Khatri let him. Omi kept away from lunch and didn't eat dinner. Paro didn't notice. Next morning, Omi overslept. Khatri didn't wake him up to go to Bajwara. When finally Omi did rise, ravenous, Khatri was already back with the day's shopping. Omi bathed, and for the first time in his life he did not shave. Eyebrows would have been raised on another day – Omi going unshaven! They were not today. Maaii produced breakfast. Omi nearly succumbed – the smell of the piping-hot butter parathas! But he shook both his hands – not hungry.

'Omi bau, you should take the bus,' Maaii said in a little whisper.

'Bus? Which bus? What for?' Omi said.

'Which bus? What for? O Omi bau!' Maaii said and left it as that.

That day, also, Omi went hungry. But at about four o'clock, when no one was looking, he quickly spread some mango chutney on a naan and gobbled it up – just to keep going – *after all hunger strikes are meant only for appearances, no?*

Who is the real shit of India, then? Omi asked himself the next morning, the morning of Day Number Three.

As usual, Maaii presented him with his breakfast. Omi moved away, otherwise that smell would have killed him. Or shattered his defences.

'Bau-ji, take the bus,' Maaii said again.

Take the bus, you real shit of India. Take the bus . . . Omi heard himself talking in his throat all day. Come Day Number Four Without Her, a Monday, still unshaven and empty of stomach, Omi sat down by the window and wrote a letter: '*Sorry . . . Can't live without you . . .*'

He knew there would be a letter for him on Day Number Six: '*I can't either. All is forgotten and forgiven. Come and fetch me . . .*'

On Day Number Six Without her Omi rose early to wait for the dakia. He waited and waited – the dakia didn't seem to be coming today. Yet he arrived dead on time. Omi ran downstairs to take his letter – he had read it several times even without seeing it.

'No letter for Mr O. P. Khatri Esq,' the boy postman said, walking on.

'What do you mean, no letter?'

'I mean nobody wrote you a letter.'

'You sure?' Omi didn't like the chutia sala (cunt). Never had.

'Sure as day is day and night night.' The postman didn't like Omi either, the 'Brylcreem-Parker-pen-type' show-off.

'Son of a bitch,' Omi said out of earshot and raced back upstairs. He shaved and bathed in five minutes flat. Maaii was not in today – she had to take one of her boys to the eye hospital because he had pus in his eyes. So Paro was cooking breakfast for Khatri.

'Ma, I am hungry,' Omi announced. He swaggered his way in to the kitchen and sat down in a peeri with a thud.

'Oh? How come?' Paro said.

'Hurry up, Ma. I have a bus to catch.'

Omi ate for a whole hockey team – eleven parathas.

'Enough?' Paro said.

'One more. For the referee.'

Omi dressed to kill. He told Seva Singh to make a parcel of all the Pall Mall goodies Munni bibi liked.

'Munni bibi is not fussy – you should know, Omi bau. But she likes tandoori chicken, naan and ras malai.'

Omi packed pyjamas and a toothbrush with his shaving kit. 'Ma, we'll be back by the first bus tomorrow morning,' he said from the stairs when everything was ready.

'All that hunger strike, for what? My men! They love martyring themselves,' Paro said.

'I wonder what would you do if you had two like him?' Khatri said.

'We would have to search the world to get him a wife like her.'

'The son of a dog doesn't appreciate her, does he?'

'Did you, when you got married to me?'

'Times were different then, woman.'

'Times are always different, it's only the people who are ever the same. Look at the father. Look at the son.'

The son couldn't be looked at. He was racing in a crowded Punjab Roadways bus towards where his troubled heart had already arrived. *Dhulkote.*

*

218

A year later, the Roadways bus arrived.

'Well, well, well, Om Parkash. Mother father well? Business well? You've become so thin. What, in less than a week? Evidently you have not been eating . . .'

Omi hated fathers-in-law, Indian fathers-in-law. He wished he had been born in a decent country like England or America. Half-heartedly, he bent down to touch the pair of railway feet and walked alongside the stationmaster to his house behind the flowers.

'We'll do something about that. Anyway, we were expecting you earlier. Perhaps you meant to come earlier, no?' What was it about his father-in-law which made Omi feel so small and ashamed of himself?

'Look, wife, look who is here,' Kandhari said at his doorstep.

Munni heard. She knew. She was done up, expecting him – she had been done up daily, expecting him daily. But she took her time. Then she appeared. One look at his silly face – and it looked really silly, pale, thin and long – one look at it and all was forgiven. Messages were delivered by eyes. Messages were received by eyes and spread to the rest of their bodies. Now all they wanted to do was that which they liked most in the world. But they had to wait . . . God knew when they would be left alone.

'The next train isn't due for another three hours. Isn't that nice? Gives us a bit of time to talk,' Kandhari said.

Omi said what was on his mind. 'I wish there was a mountain or a valley here.' He would take her up the mountain or down the valley with the naan and ras malai, and . . .

'What?' Kandhari said. He used to think he had married his daughter to a bright young man.

It snowed heavily in the Simla Hills. It snowed as far low as Kalka, which was hilly but was hardly in the Hills. Snow in Kalka? It had happened only once before in living memory – back in the year of the Jallianwala Bagh Massacre when the English General Dyer put bullets into the bodies of 1500 Indians 'to teach the darkies a lesson in civil obedience'. Not a very civil thing to do.

Everybody who was around remembered Dyer's shooting spree, just as they remembered Kalka's last snowfall. Even those who weren't around remembered.

For four days and nights a muddy white cloud clung to the Kasauli range, breathing a teeth-grinding cold varpour down on Chandigarh. On the fifth morning Chandigarhias woke up to find the muddy white cloud gone and the Kasauli mountain glowing in the sun like a towering ice-cream cone. Paro woke up to find she had caught a chill: her body burned, and she had a pain in her left leg and arm. Bawa was sent next door to borrow the thermometer.

'A hundred and one! Hum. Boy, go telephone,' Khatri said.

'I don't want to see Doctoress Phitt-phitti here. We are a Punjabi house, a rough-tough house. We don't need doctor-shoctors,' Paro said.

'Go, go, go, boy, go,' Khatri said.

'If the Doctoress comes here I'll lock myself in the room and it will not open till I am gone "upstairs" or she downstairs. So there.'

'Boy, your mother – top-class mule, the wah-wah type. When they selected her for me, what did they not say about her face? But not a word about her head – my mistake I didn't ask.'

'Just let the wah-wah type mule alone. A little massage and she'll be kicking again. If you do want to do something for her, send word to Vidya to come. She hasn't been here for four days.' Paro wanted to talk to Vidya about going to Goddess Durga's temple.

'I'll go and fetch Aunt Vidya myself, Ma. You lie down and let Munnishka massage your leg,' Omi said. Four days. He missed his aunt.

Father and son left the house – Khatri was meeting someone at the plot. Paro sprawled out on a charpoy on the balcony in the sun. While Munni massaged her legs, she fell asleep with one eye half open, one eye half on the world, as it were. She heard things. She saw things – great mountains heaped up with rocks and boulders of mammoth dimensions. They had words written on them, words she couldn't read. 'All words have a meaning, even those you can't read,' she heard herself say to herself. *If the boy was here I would ask him to read them and tell me what they mean. But who wrote them in the first place? Words on rocks? Paro, you are a mule going mad, seeing things and talking to yourself. Just go to sleep. We'll see how you feel when you get up. And what is this other rolla-bolla?*

Bawa came running upstairs, red in the face, panting and simply unable to speak.

'Ma-ji, Ma-ji . . .' was all he could say.

'What's stuck in your throat? frog?' said Paro without opening any more of that half-open eye.

'Ma-ji . . .'

'Speak properly like a man's son.'

'Ma-ji, there is a car downstairs.'

'You unread fool, it can't come upstairs. Or can it?'

220

'No, Ma-ji, you don't understand. Open both your eyes and look.'
Paro opened both her eyes and looked.

What Paro saw made her panic. In the back street was a long blue car with two police jeeps, two motor-cycles and eight policemen. A knot of people watched them from a little distance, as did people from the balconies and windows of their houses.

'They have come to arrest my man or my son, Munni.' This was what had been written on those rocks which she could not read, illiterate wretch.

'All this fuss. It's only me,' shouted someone from the stairs of Paro's house.

A woman's voice.

Paro panicked more – she had recognized the voice. Her temperature shot up to one hundred and seven. 'Munni. The bottle of oil,' she yelled, standing up.

'Oil? What oil, Ma?' Munni didn't understand the Khatris. The things they said and did! If she hadn't become a Khatri herself she would recommended treatment for them.

'Mustard oil, from the bathroom. Go fetch the bottle, girl. Run!'

Munni ran and fetched the bottle of the mustard oil the family used for their hair. In the mean time the visitor had laboured her way up the stairs with asthmatic breaths, holding up her biscuit-coloured woollen salvar to stop its ends sweeping the floor.

The Chief Minister's wife.

'Great is my karma that you have graced my threshold,' Paro said and poured oil on both sides of her threshold in welcome. 'But why didn't you send word you were coming? I would have laid a carpet of flowers for your feet.'

'Ever since the "attempt" Security won't let me advertise my aan-jaan (movements). Time was I could go anywhere just with a driver. Now they send a battalion of men to guard me. Listen, Paro, I love your garden. I want your gardener. Give me your gardener,' the Sardarni said, laying a hand on Munni's shoulder to steady herself. 'Jeeti raho, beta – continue to live,' she said to Munni.

'Take my gardener. Take what you want. It's all yours. But why didn't you send word? I would have strewn the street with roses for you.'

'Because you don't have a phone in the house.'

'Only in the shop.' For Paro, the posh Pall Mall restaurant was always the *shop*. 'They won't give us one upstairs. Applied ten times.'

221

'We'll do something about that.'

'Sit down. Sit, sit, sit.'

The Sardarni hitched up her salvar and sat down on Munni's sofa.

'You said come to drink tea in my house and here I am – in your house.'

'In my little house.'

'But it is nice and clean.'

'But very little.'

'You should have a big house, and you shall. Now, where is the tea?'

The Sardarni spent one whole hour with Paro. She drank three cups of tea and, with two fingers, picked at everything presented – from the famous Pall Mall cake to Paro's own humbler savian vermicelli. They talked like old schoolfriends, the natter of two young village girls. After every sentence the Sardarni put a hand on her mouth and looked at Munni's Mogul Garden and said: 'Haa hai!' She couldn't believe how beautiful it was. 'Haa hai.'

As Munni poured her the fourth cup, she shook a finger and stood up.

'Achaa. I'm going, but I'm not leaving here without your gardener, Paro. What's his name?'

'Mali.'

'Mali, come up here, fatta fatt,' the Sardarni yelled from the balcony.

Down in the garden Mali trembled. He laid his tools aside, wiped his hands on the front of his shirt and made his way up to the ladies.

'You are coming with me.'

Mali trembled more. He looked at the Punjab's most powerful woman, then at Paro, and finally at Munni bibi. He was not going anywhere, not to the Chief Minister's house nor even the Prime Minister's.

'Mali, your garden is heaven. More so than that of the President's Palace in Delhi. And you are coming with me to make mine as beautiful as Munni's. Go pack.'

'But?' Mali, trembling, managed to say. This woman frightened him. He looked at Munni – *save me, Munni bibi*.

The Sardarni saw that pleading look. 'All right, all right. Let's do what Indians always do when in a fix – let's compromise. We'll share you, fifty-fifty. Theek hai? Right? Now go and get your things.'

Mali had no choice. Paro had no choice. Munni had no choice.

'Sector 23 is going to be electrocuted with the *bijli* of envy. It is going to get the chilli of jealousy in the arse,' Paro said as the Chief Minister's wife left her street, raising a cloud of dust.

The same cloud of dust opened up to disgorge a sluggish rickshaw accompanied by a bored bicycle. In the rickshaw sat Vidya, on the bicycle Omi.

A ministerial cavalcade in his back street! It didn't make sense. Then it did.

'Aunt Vidya, we are made. We are made,' Omi screamed.

Close by, the leafy mango, jamun and tahli trees on the left side of the street also screamed: *Aho aho, Khatri boy, you are made.*

The Khatri boy outpaced the sleepy rickshaw-wallah by four to one and raced home.

'Ma, you are a genius,' he howled as he flung himself on Paro and showered her with kisses – on her cheeks and forehead and arms – and began dancing the bhangra with her.

Dabbu, watching, wanted a piece of the action. It was too good an opportunity to miss. He went wild and jumped on mother and son. Paro went wilder – if there was anything in this world she detested, it was dogs. She would be touched by a bhangi any day, but by a dog – not on your life!

'Out! Out!' She pushed her son away. 'Take this impure creature out of my sight. Shoot him with a bullet. Munni, go buy me a gun . . .'

'Ma, you are a genius Number One. Pukka genius. Oi, Dabbu, behave yourself, your hear?' Omi said and tied Dabbu to his chain. 'So she came, eh? What did I tell you, Ma?'

Omi wanted to know what the two women had talked about. So did Vidya. And so did Khatri – he arrived a minute after his son and Vidya.

As Paro talked, she remembered her temperature and her arm and leg. She spread herself on the charpoy in the sun, surrounded by her excited family.

Khatri sat down in an easy chair in the shade – the sun got into his eyes and he didn't like wearing sunglasses. *Time is passing. Time is.* Khatri didn't want it to pass, not this moment. He was looking and hearing. But he was not listening.

'Ma, the thing to do now is make use of her. Exploit her and I'll tell you how . . .'

'Shut up, you. She's my friend. One doesn't exploit friends.'

'One does, Ma. This is life . . .'

223

'Shut your mercenary mouth. Vidya is here and I want to talk to her, not you. Vidya, I'll take you and Munni to Goddess Durga Devi to beg,' Paro said, shutting an eye and a half.

'But who is going to take you, madam?' Khatri, quiet so far, said.

'You are,' Paro said, opening wide both her eyes.

Khatri had never given it a thought. Now he did. *Shadi Lal, the dhandha (business) of life never stops. So take a few days off and go and wash the Devi's fair feet with cow's milk. A dip in Her pool will cleanse your outside, a prayer said to Her in person will rinse your inside. So take them all with you and go. Time is passing. Time is. Catch a slice of it.*

'All right, woman, let's go. *All* of us,' Khatri said, meaning Vidya's husband too.

'What about the shops?' Paro and Vidya said.

'What about them? The dhandha of life never stops,' Khatri said, his voice carefree – 'the servants will look after the shops or we'll shut the damn shops for four days.' The Goddess's temple was far away in mountains high and mighty near Jammu.

The already excited family grew more excited.

'I have a list of things I want to ask Goddess Durga personally,' Omi said. He didn't believe in 'this Hindu shit, the *real* shit of India' – this business of trekking to temples on mountain peaks and flooring oneself before gods and goddesses. But at the same time he saw no harm doing a bit of begging – just in case it worked. *Who knows?*

'Don't make your list too long. Goddesses don't like it. Keep it to one or two things,' Paro said.

'Any sensible Goddess would know somebody like Mr O. P. Khatri Esq will ask for a little more than that, Ma. What the hell.'

'Ma, can Asha come too? She also wants to beg,' Munni said.

'What about her sass, that churrail (witch) Damyanti? She won't let her go.'

'Her mother-in-law now lets her do whatever she wants. She isn't risking another elopement,' Munni said.

'All right. Go tell her then. Tell the others as well. The more the better.'

The word went around. People came, Satya first. 'We are also coming.'

Next came the Doctorani, now friends again with Satya. 'Us too.'

'And me,' Chatkarni said.

'Anyone else?' Khatri said.

The pilgrims party, or 'paalty' as it came to be called, was growing.

224

Munni had a word in Omi's ear, and the two went to the office downstairs and booked a call to Kurukshetra. They got through straight away, but their cousins weren't at home. Omi left a 'deeply urgent' message – *we are going to Goddess Durga a-begging for you know what. You are invited to join us. Accept invitation heartily.*

Back came the reply within the hour: 'We accept invitation heartily.'

Lakhpatni heard, and came and said, 'What about us?' There should be a genuine millionaire in every pilgrims' 'paalty' – it makes the whole thing more prestigious. The pilgrims were delighted.

'And us?' said Pandit Ram Narayan of the Krishna temple. The presence of a proper priest in the begging expedition couldn't do it any harm at all. On the contrary, it could only influence the Goddess's decision about their requests in their favour.

'And us?' said the Sikh postmaster, K. P. Singh and his brother, P.P. For begging purposes, the Hindus and Sikhs shared their gods and gurus.

Word of the pilgrimage reached as far as Manimajra, five miles away. So Khatri's old friends Gulati and his uncle, driver Bhola Ram, also joined the 'paalty' – it was a thing not to be missed if your pocket could take it. Not to be missed even if it couldn't – 'the Devi will re-imburse' (she always did).

The head count grew with astonishing speed. With kid-kiddies and all, it quickly grew to fifty. They hired a Roadways 52-seater. Two servants – Maaii and Bawa – filled it to capacity. On the morning of the departure, Professor Bhatnagar turned up with a suitcase and a young lady who wore a scarlet silk sari embroidered with gold and silver threat. She was heavily made up – lipstick, talc, rouge, kohl and all. Quantities of gold dripped from her ears, nose and throat, and encased her wrists.

'Professor Bhatnagar!' Omi said.

Professor smiled like a starving man who has been put in charge of the king's kitchen.

'You didn't invite us to your wedding. You didn't even tell us!' Omi complained.

Professor and Mrs Bhatnagar's presence posed a serious problem – there simply wasn't any room for them in the bus.

'Aré yaar, this is India, so we'll manage. That's the beauty of it – we can always manage,' Professor Bhatnagar said. He was determined to go. Just married, he wanted to get on to the Goddess straight away and put in his request for a couple of early 'he-issues'.

'But how?' Omi said.

225

Not for the first time, a problem posed by one professor was instantly solved by another. 'We will squeeze-squeeze,' said Professor Kukoo.

The 'paalty' realized it needed a leader. All eyes turned to Lakhpati, the millionaire. He even looked the part – every inch a Congress leader in Gandhi cap, Nehru achkan and chooridars. But Lakhpati shook his head. He lacked officer-like qualities – he couldn't give orders, nor tell people off. The second choice was Khatri, the small but dignified restaurateur. He didn't like giving orders, but people listened to him when he opened his mouth. Besides, the whole thing was his idea – wasn't it? Though strictly speaking it was not, it being his wife's. As it turned out, all decision-making fell to the second-in-command, Omi. Omi loved giving orders.

They loaded the bus with 1001 parathas for the long ride and trek in the mountains. They took a hundred kilos of various kinds of dhals and bhajis – everything had to be vegetarian because it was a holy journey – and approximately a ton of fruit. The bus reeked of stale bread and overripe bananas and orange peel and vomit even before it set off. Then the leader waved a finger at the driver and the bus, bedecked with flowers like a marriage bus, slid out of Sector 23 with much dhoom dhaam (pomp and show), the Roadways man blowing his horn wildly and everybody singing and clapping and rolling their heads from side to side and clanging godly little cymbals and ringing godly little bells and pounding on dholuks (drums) held against the stomach.

Omi's first act of leadership was to tell everybody to shut up and get out of the 52-seater when it got a puncture seven miles out of town, right in front of the Guest-cum-court-house in Kharar.

'Quiet and out! Quiet and out!'

'Only building up the tempo, yaar.'

The tempo kept building up all the way. The bus stopped every thirty miles or so for fresh water or for a cup of tea. Or because someone wanted to pee (Omi discovered that, as the pilgrims progressed, their peeing pattern became sympathetic to each others'). If the bus stopped in a town or village, crowds gathered around it and helped to take the tempo to a higher pitch.

At last, just before nightfall, they arrived at the base camp, a place called Phool Bazaar at the foot of the Goddess's great mountain. Phool Bazaar – or Flower Bazaar – was a small township of daily changing itinerants, devotees on their way to or from the 'Mother of All'. The sole purpose of its existence was to serve pilgrims' needs. It

226

had a long bazaar which sold only flowers for the devotees. It had a few inns where the cooks were Brahmin 'by guarantee', and where sleeping room was free – you hired a charpoy for the night and the space for it came with it.

Night descended swiftly on the valley, as if the 'Mother of All' wanted all her followers to have a good long sleep – the trek to Her temple on top of the mountain was a day's climb and descent each way. It must begin early in the morning, usually at first light, and usually as a convoy of several bus loads, often a thousand or two thousand strong.

The Chandigarh 'paalty' slept well and long, being very tired. As a result it missed the convoy.

'Never mind. Who wants to be with nameless nobodys from nowhere?' said Chandigarh, the world's newest city. It wouldn't be seen mixing with rustic riff-raff from here, there and everywhere.

The climb was steep and the path carved in the mountainside by generations of human feet was narrow.

'Keep you eyes in your head,' Omi said as the procession got going. 'You know what I mean – tigers, leopards, bears and snakes etc . . .'

This dampened his party's enthusiasm a bit. But only a bit – which tiger, leopard, bear or snake would dare approach a body of men, women and children that made so much noise?

'Anyway, we are under protection, Her protection. So don't worry. Let the Devi come into us.'

The Devi came into them. Cymbals, bells and drums echoed in the valley as the Chandigarh 'paalty' trudged its way up. Breathing became a problem.

'Why gods and goddesses live in difficult terrains?' Ujjagar asked Dr Devan Chand.

'Good question,' replied Dr Devan Chand, asthmatically.

Ujjagar, not satisfied by the answer, turned to Pandit Ram Narayan. 'Pandit-ji, why do gods and goddesses make it a habit of living in high high mountains?'

'Because,' Pandit-ji said.

Half-way up, the party stopped for lunch and some rest. The flora here was different: every bush was a flower bush, and the path itself was strewn with flowers. Just as they started out again, Chatkarni broke out into song with such a loud and fine voice that everybody stopped in their tracks. What had happened to the usually quiet widow? Everybody knew what – the Devi had come into her more than them. The alms-taking widow in white suddenly acquired a halo behind her head, as vivid as, and only marginally less luminous than, the sun in the sky. Now another thing happened to confirm the fact that the Devi had come into her – each time she opened her mouth to sing, flower petals flew out of her mouth like musical notes in cartoon films.

'Are you witnessing what I am witnessing?' Professor Bhatnagar said to Professor Kukoo.

'Anything can happen on a pilgrimage. Anything,' Kukoo said. He came from *the* city of pilgrimages – Kurukshetra, where the God had spoken the Gita. He knew all about these things.

Chatkarni sang and sang. Everybody sang after her. Bells rang. Cymbals clanged. Dholuks pounded. The valley echoed. And flowers rained from the widow's mouth. The funny thing was nobody thought it odd.

'Things happen when you go to meet a god or goddess. We are Hindus, don't forget. The chosen people.'

'The Jews are a chosen people. The Muslims are a chosen people. Some Christians, too. But the Hindus are tops – the chosen chosen.'

The Devi came into everybody more and more.

'Look!'

The millionaire Lakhpati opened the cloth bag he carried over his shoulder – people noticed only just that very instant that he carried a bag at all. It contained one lakh in hundred-rupee notes. Lakhpati mounted a boulder twice the height of the Roadways bus and began feeding them to the valley. A wind whipped up. Chatkarni's singing became louder and louder. Cymbals clanged louder and louder. Bells rang louder and louder. Flowers flew helter-skelter, like leaves in a whirlwind – red, yellow and white. Now with them flew the blue hundred-rupee notes – first like a gentle snowfall, then, as the wind asserted itself, like a blizzard.

'Aré!' The leader was not sure what to make of it. He turned to look at his mother walking three paces behind his father. She, too, wasn't sure what to make of it. He wanted to say something to her, but did not know what.

'Ma, I love you. And your daughter-in-law. Now isn't that something?'

'Something *is* happening to us,' Paro said. Her cheeks had become rosy, her eyes were sparkling, and Omi saw that she, too, had a halo around her head like Chatkarni. It turned with her head. '*What* is happening to us?' Paro said again.

'Ma, you look beautiful. Honest.'

'Fool boy, what are you talking?'

'Father, don't you think Mother looks beautiful?'

228

Khatri turned to look at his wife. His heart missed a beat, for Paro was naked to the waist, her full breasts heaving up and down with the exercise of climbing the mountain. On the night of their wedding all that time ago she wouldn't let him undo her choli. First she wouldn't let him hold her hand in his. Then she wouldn't let him touch her arm and shoulders. And later in the night . . . (she had allowed herself to be kissed on the cheek) . . . she refused, categorically refused, to let him undo her choli even though he had touched her under it by then. Now here she was – bare to the waist – full, supple, desirable and . . . and his.

Khatri smiled to himself and scratched the middle of his sutthan, feeling a certain resurrection there. *Well, well, well.* He didn't understand. All he knew was that he wasn't looking at reality, only at a vision. But then visions had their own reality, didn't they? And a good thing too, that they did. *Things happen when you go to meet a god or goddess, Shadi Lal.* But why see his wife half naked, and why in a throng? Why did she look just like she had on their wedding night when, eventually, she had permitted first his hands, subsequently his eyes, and later his mouth, to devour her breasts? *Things happen. So let them happen. And, madam, kindly cover yourself up quickly, do you hear? There are others around. It was 52-seater bus we came on, you know.*

'Hai, my mother. How *they* stare at me – as if I were I don't know what. See how *they* ogle me, Vidya?' Paro said.

Vidya tiptoed on a bed of flowers. She no longer wore her shoes, she carried them in her hands – she didn't need them any more. Her step felt light, her heart even lighter. *Only, if my husband was a little more of a man – took my chin in one hand, steadied me with the other and . . . and lifted me in his arms, and laid me down on flowers a little way deeper in the valley, and unravelled this cumbersome sari – I never wanted to wear it, I wanted to wear a salvar kamiz, but Paro wouldn't let me – and filled me with a child . . .*

'Aunt Vidya, look!'

Aunt Vidya looked. She saw Munni running after a little boy approximately thirty and a half inches in height. No, it was a girl – a girl who looked just like Vidya herself, though Vidya no longer knew what she looked like. It made her wish it was a boy. Why? *'Because we are silly Hindus. We always want boys. But let me pick up the child and hold it – boy or girl, doesn't matter one bit.'* The child ran straight into Vidya. Vidya picked it up and discovered her cheeks were wet. *Fool girl, me. I am crying.*

'Why, Aunt Vidya?' Munni said.

'Why what, Munni?'

'Oh, nothing. I thought I saw tears in your eyes.'

'These things happen when you go to meet a goddess. You don't know, Munni.'

Munni didn't know these things. She hadn't a clue what happened or didn't when you were on your way to meet a goddess. She had never met one before. But this journey was quite extraordinary. *Just look at that aeroplane, flying as if it has all the time in the world. Aeroplanes should go fast. That's the whole idea – to get there quicker than by any other mode of travel. And what's it dropping?* The aeroplane was dropping leaflets. Suddenly the air was thick with small chits of white paper, thousands of them, floating down and flying away.

'Catch me one,' Munni cried.

'Catch you what?' Omi said.

'One of these. Oh, don't bother, I've got one.'

Munni had got one. It was five inches long and three inches wide, just as large as the Red Cross raffle ticket she had bought from little Kaka's brother the other day.

'What's written on it?' Omi said.

'Why should I tell you?'

'If you don't tell me I'll put you in the bottle-neck. Or worse, make you spread-eagle.'

'What, right here?'

'Right here. Do you think I am joking?'

'Try.'

Omi did. First bottle-neck, then spread-eagle.

'Behave yourself, fool boy. You are a BA Pass,' Paro yelled.

'Mother!' *Why is Mother always telling me off as if I were ten or nine or eight? Can't a man have a little wrestling match with his wife now and then?*

'The temple. The temple,' chorused the pilgrims.

The Khatris looked up. There, crowning a peak made entirely of rock, glinted the golden cones of the Devi's abode. And out of it, in the air, the Devi herself, seated milady-style – knees crossed – rode on a huge tiger. She had eight arms, each arm carrying a different weapon of war. But they were all medieval, some even dating back to the times of the world's very first Great War, the Mahabharata. There was a sword dripping with blood, a bow and a quiver of arrows, a trident, a spear, a frisbee-type decapitate-and-return flying disc with a razor-sharp edge and things like that. Ferocious in appearance, but outdated.

'Very outdated,' thought the leader. He took the liberty of re-arranging Her arsenal as she advanced to his 'paalty'. He placed a bunch of hand-grenades in one hand, a Russian-made automatic rifle in hand number two, a Smith and Wesson in the third, a rocket-launcher in the fourth, an ICBM in the fifth . . . *Even a goddess must keep up with the times.* He did as good a job as any arms dealer would do, and his efforts pleased the Goddess. Omi saw Her beam a smile. It was a smile only for him.

And She came, the Goddess. She came on through the air, Her tiger darting its pink tongue in and out of its fearsome mouth like a slice of honey roast ham.

'What do you want of me, Om Parkash? Ask. I'm here.'

The Roadways 52-seater came back on the fourth evening minus the flowers. It was market evening. The market came to a standstill and looked. It surrounded the bus.

The bus wore a thick coat of dust. Its fifty-two plus 'squeeze-squeeze' passengers also wore a thick coat of dust. But their faces glowed.

'With inner light,' the market said. The market wanted to know how *it* had gone.

'What did you beg, oi?' Seva Singh asked Bawa, slapping him on the head by way of greeting.

'Not telling you. Is between me and the Goddess,' Bawa said, ducking.

'I know what you begged – a wife, no? But who is going to give a wife to a nutmug like you?'

'The Goddess said to me person-to-person she's fixing it.'

'The day someone agrees to give you their sister daughter, I'll agree to shave off my beard.'

'You'll be doing yourself a favour. And to those who have to look at you every day.'

'Bawa, son of a dog, I am going to kill you.'

'Seva, you, too, should have come, and begged for a proper face in your next life. God didn't do you a favour giving you this one. Seems He ran short of time while making it.'

Seva Singh, the head waiter, went mad. He took off his shoe and killed Bawa there and then. The market looked. It raised not a little finger to save him.

Sector 23 had the chilli in the arse. It had got the chilli again a day after the Khatris left to meet the Goddess, when men came and installed a telephone in their house. It got it the third time when the

231

Sardarni came again after the pilgrims returned. Then it got the chilli in the arse every other week, when either she came to see Paro or her car came to pick Paro up. 'These Khatris. Soon they'll be moving out of here – to the North End where the paisa-wallah live the high high life,' Sector 23 said.

Sector 23 proved right. The Khatris soon moved to a big house with a big garden in Sector 9.

'That Paro. Did she have so much in the bank to be able to buy that house in Sector 9?' Satya asked.

'Fool question, number one. When you have the Chief Minister's wife in your pocket you don't need anything in the bank,' Ujjagar said.

'But what does she see in Paro? Paro is ordinary like you and me,' Satya said to the Doctorani.

'Paro is not like you and me. Paro is a daain (sorceress). Paro has power over people. You never felt that?' the Doctorani said.

'Come to think of it, yes. How she behaved in the Devi's temple! She had her eating out of her hand.' Satya said.

The Stationmaster's transfer was taking place on a Wednesday morning. The Kandharis were arriving at eight by the luxury *Queen of Hills* – the Punjabi *Orient Express*. It was essentially a summer train though it ran all the year round. Every night at 9.30 it set out from at the grisly Platform 4 of Delhi Junction, its destination Kalka, which was not in the Hills, only a footstool to them. There, its passengers de-trained next morning and boarded the mountain toy-train for the last leg of their journey to the *real* Queen of Hills – Simla. On its way back to Delhi later the same day, the *Q o H* changed names and became the Kalka Mail.

Eight in the morning! Omi was not amused. But he would take Munni to the station to receive her parents, no question about that.

They took the station bus. The station bus was a bore. The station itself was also a bore – it was full five miles out in the wilderness, past the Power House, past the dry river. It was so far away that going to it was 'like bloody going to another town'.

'I am feeling funny . . .' Munni said as soon as the bus came to a halt in the station yard. The bus was almost empty. The yard was completely empty.

'Don't joke, it's too early. Can't laugh on an empty stomach,' Omi said.

'Sorry. But I don't feel right. Just like the morning of the English

232

movie.' Munni had been feeling like that ever since she had woken up but she hadn't told anyone. Her parents were arriving: she simply had to go to receive them. Had she told Omi or Paro they wouldn't have let her go.

'Don't joke . . .' This was no place to be sick, miles out of nowhere with the little station on one side and jungle jungle jungle on the other three. 'Let's go inside and get you a drink. The train'll be here in fifteen minutes,' Omi said, and helped Munni out of the bus.

Munni wasn't sure she could last that long.

Omi and Munni had hardly gone a few paces when a car came and parked right in front of them. It had Titli, her mother and an ayah in it. Titli quickly got out and came over to them.

'I say, what a handsome couple you two make. But what are you doing here?' Titli said.

'Just came to look at the station. My wife is rather fond of railway architecture. But so are you,' Omi said.

'Am I? Who told you that?'

'That army chap, what's his name – Lt Balls or was it Captain Prick?'

'Oh, my God, what a crashing bore you are, Omi. Poor Munnishka. Munnishka, what's the matter?'

It was fast. Munni clutched Omi's sleeve and sank.

'Munnishka,' Omi groaned. He rested her head in his lap. Not knowing what to do, he slapped her gently on the cheek to revive her.

'Oh, my God,' Titli said.

Titli's mother and the ayah joined them, the ayah carrying a suitcase and a bag. 'Poor girl, what's happened to her? Why, she is unconcious,' said Titli's mother, every inch a retired general's wife – handsome, well-dressed and imperious.

Worried and confused, Omi thought he would run to the station, introduce himself to the outgoing stationmaster, get help, and get Munni taken to the new Kandhari home. It must be one of those houses over there by the side of the station. But what good would that be? The station was miles from anywhere. It would take ages to get a doctor here, and he simply had to get her to one straight away. But how?

Titli's mother solved the problem. She spoke to Titli. 'Darling, you'd better take your friend back to town. She needs a doctor. You needn't wait for the train. We'll be all right.'

'You sure, Mummy?'

The driver and the conductor of the station bus and a few people gathered around them. Someone ran to the station building and returned with a glass of water. But how could Munni drink? Deathly pale, Omi stared at Titli – *You bitch. Last time it was you: this time it is you again. And here, in bloody no-man's-land.*

Titli stared back. 'Let's take her. Quick,' she said.

Titli and the ayah helped Omi get Munni in the car. He sat in the back seat with her head in his lap. As Titli and her mother hugged each other in farewell, Omi held Munni's cheeks in his hands and bent down to hear if she was still breathing.

'She'll be all right,' Titli said as she started the car. People moved aside. Titli raced out of the station yard. 'I am sorry, Omi.'

'Faster.'

'I am doing fifty. Did she tell you we met while you were in Ambala?'

'She did. Go sixty.'

'Okay, sixty. What else did she say about me?'

'Nothing. Just that. We never talked about you. Can you go faster?'

'As fast as you want. Where to?'

'Sector 22. Doctoress Pritam Kaur's shop.'

At the Power House, Munni opened her eyes.

'Munnishka, my Bublashoo,' Omi said.

'How's she?'

'She's coming round. Maybe we should stop here and get her a drink?'

Titli stopped the car. There was a huddle of a few dhabas (wayside eatshops) on either side of the road at the Power House gate. Omi ran to them to get a glass of water.

'Munnishka, darling,' Titli said from the front seat. She turned and caressed Munni on the cheek. 'I am sorry – for today and for *that* day. How do you feel? What did he call you – Bublashoo? What does it mean?. . .'

Munni didn't know where she was. She saw Titli stare at her, but she didn't know who Titli was – all she saw was a naked girl in a mirror. 'He used to say such things to me once.'

Omi came back. 'Drink this.'

Munni drank the water. 'I am afraid I am going to be sick. Open the door. Quick.'

Omi just about managed to get Munni out of the car. By now a crowd of onlookers had gathered around it – men and boys who, till a moment ago, had been sitting on their haunches outside the dhabas. They wore tattered clothes; some had mufflers wrapped around their dusty faces, others were shrouded in shawls or khes cloth which could have been dipped in mustard oil. They had come to see a rich man's daughter or wife being sick by the roadside. Omi waved them away, but they only moved a few feet back and stared.

'Get lost,' Omi shouted. 'Never seen anyone vomiting?'

Obviously they hadn't seen anyone so rich and beautiful vomiting like one of them – depositing on the earth that which had come from the earth, albeit less gracefully than it had been consumed. They didn't get lost: they hung on, with a tinge of satisfaction on their faces. They dispersed only when the car drove off.

In spite of the early hour, Doctoress Pritam Kaur's shop was full of patients. She left them waiting to attend to the rich restaurateur's daughter-in-law. They didn't mind. Quietly, they waited. Glum-faced, Omi waited. This annoyed Titli, who hissed, 'Don't look like a broken-hearted pisspot – she isn't going to die.' She turned on her high heels and stormed out of the shop.

Fourteen minutes later the door of the shop's back room, the examining room, opened and Dr Pritam Kaur emerged.

'Well, Mr Om. It is *that*.'

'What's *that*, Doctoress sahiba?'

'Aré bhai, can't you guess? Your trip to Goddess Durga has been a resounding success . . .'

'Resounding what?'

'I still don't know why she passed out like that, but the rest is normal. Perfectly. No need for chinta (worry). No medicine required. Let her eat and drink normal and be sick normal. All normal normal.'

'How much?'

'Aré bhai, forget it. Happy news. Sweet news. We want our mouth sweetened. We'll wait for the laddus – fifty-one of them.'

Many permits were needed for construction materials.

'Worry not, Paro. My presents to you – permits. I do you a favour today, you'll do me one tomorrow, won't you? We owe it to each other. Sisters,' the Sardarni said.

'Of course. We owe it to each other – sisters,' Paro said. But what favour could she, an ex-sweet-vendor's wife, do for the Chief Minister's?

The permits came.

'Now finger by finger the hotel will rise,' the Sardarni said.

First they dug trenches, criss-crossing straight lines. Hindi-speaking, song-singing Rajasthani women labourers carried metal woks heaped with bajri (gravel) and cement on their heads to them. These women wore skin-tight colourful blouses which showed six inches of their belly and waist, doing no harm to their bustline at all. They laid the mixture in the trenches under the lustful eye of the master bricklayer, ustad Gainda Singh. The ustad was a sturdy Sikh made mainly of muscles. He had a keen eye for what the women wore and one ever keener to see what lay underneath what they wore.

The contractor was another Sikh, thekedar Lamba sahib. Lamba sahib carried the holy gutka in his pocket and a rosary in his hands. He was known to be 'a real saint' because he had 'no love for money', though he had seven lakhs in 'white money' and at least twice that in 'black'. His overseer was the solar-hatted Bhandari sahib. At five foot two he was low of stature but high of voice. When he shouted, the heavy metal woks fell off the Rajasthani women's heads and the foundation of the yet-to-be-built hotel shook.

Under these two men worked about twenty-five labourers. They were all Rajasthani men and their women (because they happily took two rupees per day instead of the regulation two and a half which the Punjabi worker demanded). Everybody knew who was boss – Paro.

Paro came daily and supervised from dawn to dusk. With her came the 'dipty boss' – Vidya. Omi and Khatri shuttled between the restaurant downtown in Sector 23, the rising hotel up north by the lake and the house in Sector 9. Munni came, but rarely, because she was not allowed to be in the sun. Now and then the Sardarni also came, accompanied by her bodyguard. The weather had changed – from very cold to cold to lukewarm to very warm. The Sardarni drank a bottle of Vimto or Coca Cola and talked of the good old pre-Partition days.

One day – it was blazing hot and the blue Kasauli mountain trembled in the glassy mirage waves that bounced off a scalding earth – the Sardarni came with another woman. This woman was a couple of years younger than Vidya and nearly as good-looking. She wore white, like the Brahmin widow, Chatkarni. Paro didn't like her. Something about her face – or was it the eyes?

The Sardarni had brought mangoes in a bucket of ice-cold water. 'Dusheri mango. Best mango. And cold,' the Sardarni said. 'Eat quickly, Paro. Eat eat eat.' Bottles of Vimto came out from the Pall Mall ice-box and the Dusheri mangoes from the Sardarni's bucket. As the ladies drank one and sucked the other, the Sardarni introduced her companion.

'Lehna's wife, Sukhni. I should call her Dukhni,' the Sardarni said with the slim elegant mango half in her mouth. Sukh means comfort and plenty; Dukh means its opposite – plenty of misery. This explained why the woman wore white.

236

At the mention of her husband's name, Lehna's wife burst out into a funny choking sob. It came straight from her chest, and it puzzled Paro. Who was this Lehna or whatever his name was, Paro asked her friend with her eyes.

'Lehna was . . .' and the Sardarni told her.

Paro, the diplomat, felt it appropriate to shed a tear to show her sympathy. Amazingly, the tear came. It came to Vidya, too. This had a chain reaction, for the Sardarni also became tearful while Sukhni sobbed and choked and laid aside the Vimto and the mango.

'Now, now, now . . .' the Punjab's most powerful woman said. 'Don't drown my good mangoes in tears.'

It took a while for the Vimtos to be drunk and for the mangoes to be finished. Then the Sardarni opened a huge umbrella with red and white stripes. 'Made in England,' she said and put an arm around Paro's shoulder and took her for a little walk in the green jungle.

'Paro, this Sukhni Dukhni is living in minus zero misery. Has three small children, small-small like this. Plus his doddering old parents, doddering like this . . .' The Sardarni showed Paro how small Dukhni's children were and how doddering her dead husband's parents. 'And the pension is also equal to minus zero . . .'

Paro was truly sorry and quite willing to shed another tear if it would help. But what did Dukhni's plight have to do with her?

'Paro, I have a request to make.'

'Make it, sister.'

If the Chief Minister's wife wanted a job for Dukhni, Paro would have to invent one for her. But what kind of job? There was only one kind going here – that of a labourer. *Surely the Sardarni doesn't mean that?* What then.

'I did you a favour,' the Sardarni said, taking her hand off Paro's shoulder and embracing the visible Khatri assets with it. 'Now you do me one. You said you would.'

'I said I would and I will.' Paro was a woman of her word.

'Make Lehna's wife a partner. Quarter three-quarters. Give the poor woman a quarter, Paro.'

Paro owned the earth she walked on. It slipped from underneath her feet.

'How can I, Sardarni-ji? My housewallah will not agree.'

'He will. He is a dunyadar (man of the world). He will understand.'

'He will tear the roof.'

'He will not. Sad Sukhni has no one else in the world except us. Tell your man. Tell him from me.'

*

237

Khatri tore the roof.

'No, no, no,' he yelled.

Suddenly, a host of hitches developed at work.

'The suppliers, Lala-ji,' Saint Lamba sahib came and said.

'The suppliers what?' Khatri said.

'They say the permits are bogus.'

'Bogus? But they are stamped and signed.'

'The suppliers say they are forgeries.'

'But you know it's not true, Saint Lamba sahib.'

'It doesn't matter what you and I know, what matters is what they say. They say they are forgeries, and you and I know what that means.'

'What does it mean?'

'That I go to jail if I press on for materials. So I have no choice but to quit. Man has to eat . . .'

Khatri had expected things to happen, but not so fast.

The solar-hatted overseer, Bhandari, came. He was employed by the Saint but his salary was paid to him by Khatri.

'Nothing personal, Lala-ji. Fact is I am made an offer I cannot refuse. Simply cannot.'

'Don't refuse it then.'

'Don't be like that, Lala-ji. I did say nothing personal. Would you refuse an offer of a job at Bhakra Dam, *the* Bhakra Dam?'

'No, I wouldn't.'

The work came to a standstill. Then came a call from the Residence.

'Paro, what did your man say?'

'He said yes.'

'What did I tell you, sister?'

'But he is working out the percentage.'

'So is Sukhni. Or shall I call her Dukhni? Lamba will report back tomorrow.'

'Kutti (bitch)! Why did you say yes when I had said no? Kutti!' Khatri tore the roof again.

'Unlike you, I used my head for once. What use is an unbuilt hotel in the jungle?' Paro said.

'I will pull it down with my bare hands. I will let the land lie waste waste waste. But I will not have a partner wrapped around my neck like this. This is blackmail. How can Raisingh do it to me? A great leader, eh? Why the man is a fraud. A great fart.'

'But, Father, he doesn't know a thing about it.'

'Then he should. If he is what he is, he'll put things right.'

'And she'll put them wrong again. She'll destroy you. She got us the land, the loans, the permits, everything. Even this house. She'll have everything taken away.'

'Let her! But I won't be blackmailed. Go tell her.'

Paro stuffed a handkerchief to her nose and started sobbing. Munni came and put an arm around her. 'Ma!' she said.

'What difference does it make – giving the woman twenty-five per cent? He's giving us enough, isn't He?' Paro sobbed, looking at the ceiling of the darkened drawing-room. It was a tandoori afternoon – 'hot hot'. Every outside door and window was covered with khas khas blinds to keep light out.

'No,' Khatri said.

'Father, let me handle this,' Omi said.

'No.'

'Father, please. I know what I'm doing. Okay, Ma, go tell the Sardarni bitch that we are thinking. That we might give Dukhni ten per cent.'

Paro blew her nose in the handkerchief, stood up and went to the phone.

'Ah, my dearer-than-life sister Paro, I knew you would phone soon soon. But there is a slight change in the air here . . .'

'What change, my dearer-than-life sister Sardarni?' Paro perked up – *Perhaps she has given up the idea of partnership after all? Maybe she was only testing my friendship? These leader types, always testing testing.*

'Change is this Sukhni. Doesn't agree to a quarter three-quarters. Wants fifty-fifty. And I have agreed.'

'Have you? Why?'

'Because I know my dearer-than-life sister Paro. I know she wants that hotel built.'

That did it. Paro was also, like the Sardarni, a Punjabi jatni – a full-blooded peasant woman of the land of five rivers, famous for, among other things, its people's short temper. The Bhakra Dam holding back the Sea of Gobind Sagar of anger broke. The Jawala-mukhi volcano erupted, belching red-hot molten lava.

'No, Sardarni, you don't know her. She doesn't want that hotel built,' the Punjabi jatni growled and hung up.

Her men were proud of her. Munni was proud of her. But this feeling vanished as quickly as it had made itself felt. An air of death replaced it. As they sat, vacant-eyed, the telephone rang. They knew who it was. They let it ring. But the caller was persistent: he or she knew what was going on in the collective Khatri mind. At the eleventh ring, Omi signed to Munni to take it.

'Three eight zero zero,' said Miss Doolittle.

'Who is it?' said the other Punjabi jatni in Punjabi.

'Munni, Auntie Sardarni,' Munni said.

'Jeeti raho, beta – continue to live. Call Paro to the phone.'

Munni handed the phone to Paro.

'Ungrateful woman, who got you the house. Who got you the loans? Who got you the permits? Who got you . . .?'

'Who is ungrateful? Who saved your housewallah's life by risking his own?'

'My housewallah belongs to the nation. It is the duty of every Indian to protect his life with their own.'

'And it is your duty to ruin theirs by blackmail?'

'Ungrateful bitch. Now you will sit on that unbuilt hotel for the rest of your life.'

'Yes, we will!'

Paro hung up on the Punjab's most powerful woman for the second time in five minutes. The Khatris looked at each other. Instead of each other, they saw a brick wall like a Cinemascope screen. There was luminous writing on it in all the four languages they knew jointly – Urdu, Punjabi, Hindi and English: *Khallas Khattam Shudh Samapat The End.*

The Khatris sat on the unbuilt hotel. A three-headed sheshnag (king cobra) stared them in the eye, each head spitting a stream of venom. There were repayments on the loan for the hotel land. There were repayments on the loans for the house. There were the 'arrears' to the suppliers and a hundred other unpaid bills. The Pall Mall 'bucket', in to which money once poured 'like rainwater', was sucked dry.

'What to do? What to do?' Khatri went to see everybody who was somebody. He talked to everyone who was anyone. They all shook their heads from left to right.

'Give in and get out of this damn-fool mess, Lala-ji,' they said. Then they became unavailable for further advice.

'In a storm it is the weak tree which survives. Why. Because it bends to the will of the wind. So bend, Lala-ji,' Lakhpati said.

Khatri's already small face had shrunk further. It had acquired a

240

permanent pale hue which bordered on green when he didn't shave. He could not eat. He could not sleep.

'Not to worry too much, Lala-ji. Everything turns out right in the end, as our elders said,' said Kandhari, turning up every second day to register his concern. He, too, had tried everybody who was anybody.

Omi had also lost his appetite. It was all his fault: he should have kept clear of that ganda (dirty) Nanda. But he kept his chin up. 'Pointless worrying too much, Father. Everything will be all right,' he said.

'How?' Khatri asked.

For once Paro said nothing. She stuffed an end of her sari to her nose and cried all day – it was all her fault, hobnobbing with the Bitch. Munni and Vidya, and Mrs Kandhari when she came, often cried with her. Maaii, too. When the Khatris were on their own, the four of them sat in silence. There was no one to turn to. They knew one thing though – Khatri had to act swiftly.

If not? Ruin. Bankruptcy. The house would go. The restaurant would have to be sold off. And they would become destitute, 'refugees' all over again, just as they had been that year of the holocaust, when they had fled from Peshawar with their lives and little else.

But if Khatri acted decisively, as he had done then, and sold off the hotel – *Arsehole Hotel* – and this house – *this beautiful house* – he could save at least his restaurant, his 'bucket' . . .

Khatri was paralysed. He did not have the heart to sell this lovely house, his first real home after being kicked out of Peshawar by the tide of politics and Indian madness – communalism and religionism. It had taken him all these years to get into it: he was not going to give it up, not without a fight. He would show the world yet what he was made of.

I will. I will!

And what about that unbuilt arsehole? Who would buy it? Selling or 'bending with the wind' was admitting he was beaten, beaten without a fight. This Khatri could not accept, would not accept – he was a Kashatriya, a twice-born. A warrior like his ancestors.

Khatri looked towards the Kasauli mountain. It was hardly visible because of the blinding haze, only as a ghostly shadow. He let his eye move to its right where he knew Dhalli was, and felt a gust of cool breeze caress his burning cheek momentarily. This was very strange, for only the oven-hot loo blew in Chandigarh – a heatwave was on its way.

*

241

Then one morning father and son took a matchbox-sized mountain bus. The Father's destination was the bottom of a valley, the son's the top of a mountain.

'Not very wise, this, Shadi Lal, taking on the Chief Minister,' Baba Gokul Swami said.

'But he doesn't know a thing about it, Your Grace.'

'Which is worse. Wives make greater enemies than their husbands – well-known fact, Shadi Lal.'

'Then what to do, gurudev?'

'Let us pray and the answer will come to us.'

They prayed all day. At sunset the guru stood up. Khatri stood up with him. Baba Gokul put an arm around his shoulder and led him to the river. He whispered something in his ear. The two men had a dip in the deliciously cold water and came back to the Baba's hut, dripping. 'Time for you to go, no?' the guru said.

'Achaa, then, gurudev,' Khatri said, bending down to touch his guru's bare feet in farewell.

'Achaa, then, Shadi Lal. Go do what you have to. And remember – everything happens for the best. Everything turns out right in the end.'

Khatri put the house on the market the next day.

Bunny hugged Omi again and again and thumped him right and left, calling him son of a bitch and fucker of a sister he never had. Punjabi men friends' friendship is expressed in terms of incest.

'But I am very angry with you. We both are.'

'Why?'

'Why didn't you bring my little sister, Munnishka?'

Omi would have told him in the first instance, had there not been so many people surrounding Bunny. 'She is . . . er . . .' Omi didn't know how to put it. 'Your little sister went to call on Goddess Durga near Jammu, and the moment she is not in a position to travel. Not in a mountain bus driven by a sardar-ji.'

'Did you hear that, Bunty? Did you hear that?' Bunny thumped Omi again – right and left, right and left. 'Well played, old chap. Well played! For when?'

Omi told him.

'You have to call him Bunny, okay? Or Bunty, if it is a girl. But it can't be a girl, it has to be a boy. I can write it down now on a piece of paper,' said oracle Bunny.

Omi also knew it was going to be a boy. He had never thought that it could be a girl.

'I say, it is dash good to see you. Dash good.'

'Dash good to see you too.

'You have thinned down, you know – is this how you fellows celebrate these things down in the plains? Up here we mountain men do them differently. We roll down a mountain . . .'

It was only then Omi noticed that Bunty also had a bulge.

'Well, well, well! You too been bribing Durga Devi?'

'Only from here. No, honest, you have thinned in the face, hasn't he, Bunts?'

'Yes and no,' Bunty said.

'What on earth do you mean? Has he or hasn't he? O never mind, let's go sit in the sun and have a tittle-tattle. I hear a big heatwave is blowing down there. When Mother India burns, naughty Simla blossoms. Ironic, that, but then life is full of ironies. Let's enoy the sun.'

They sat in the Ritz garden. Major and Mrs Mahesh joined them. Mr and Mrs So and So joined them. Shri and Shrimati Such and Such joined them. An old porter, Boy, brought the telephone on a silver tray, its flex trailing behind him all the way to a window in a wall. It was a 'long distance urgent' from Delhi or Bombay, Boy couldn't tell because the line was so faint. Bunny hello-hello'd loudly for a minute, then he shouted into the phone for a long time. After that he stood up, flushed in the face. Everybody around him stood up. Things didn't seem quite right – a crisis of some sort?

'Aimie, old boy, let's get away from it all. Let's go kill a beer at Tiger Tops. Does that grab you?'

It grabbed Omi. He had come all the way to Simla to talk with Bunny, and in the Ritz it was not possible.

'Now tell me, Aimie, what can I do for you?' Bunny said in Tiger Tops. He knew Omi had come for something.

Omi spread out the Lake View Hotel plans on the glass-topped, garden-green cane table. Bunny had a good look at them, then straightened his head and drained his glass in one go. Next he wiped his mouth with a snow-white napkin. Then he looked straight at Omi and smiled. Omi knew he had got him. Mission accomplished! In his head he telegraphed his father from the post office. *P.S. for Munnishka. Bublashoo, we are all right now. Relax, and wait for me. No bra nor anything else like that. Back by last bus. Then we . . .*

243

'Hum. On the face of it, I like it – going fifty-fifty. I would even say let's shake over it . . .'

Omi's right hand, resting in his lap, twitched as if an electric impulse had instructed it to behave in that manner, and nearly shot up to offer itself for a shake.

'You know we love you both, Aimie. So anything you propose I will accept with open arms if it is reasonable. And this proposition is reasonable. Very, by the look of it. Yet I have to ask you a dinky little question – why me, if everything is tickety-boo with you?'

'Everything is not tickety-boo at the moment.'

'I thought so. Let's sink another beer. Bearer, another bottle! Yes, what's the hitch? You were saying?'

'The hitch is . . .' and Omi explained.

'Aimie, you've been frank with me, I'll be frank with you. Had it been someone else, *anyone* else – this minister or that, even that N. K. P. D. Kesai himself – I would have told them to go tie their johnnies in knots. But the C.M. Punjab? Especially his madam? You don't know, but she's a famous make-break bitch. First she made you, now she's breaking you. She'll break me, too, even though Simla is in Himachal Pradesh, if she gets wind that I'm filling the blanks she wanted her party to fill. You follow me?'

'I follow you.'

'I hope this doesn't spoil our friendship.'

'No, it doesn't.'

'So let's leave it at that, and let me finally say – to hell with the bitch. To hell with her!'

'Bunny, I don't understand!' Omi no longer knew what to make of this strange man.

'I know you don't. But I am saying to hell with the bitch! I am saying I'll come partners with you at fifty-fifty. But not today, nor even tomorrow, for I have problems here, in case you didn't hear. That phone call from Bombay–Stock Exchange. Fourteen lakhs sucked up by an invisible arsehole 1200 miles away. You talk of your problems: listen to mine – bore your balls off. No, I won't do that to you, I love you too, too much for that. So there.'

'Bunny, I want your answer.'

Bunny had given his answer.

The heatwave showed no sign of relenting.

'Rivers will dry up. A drought will follow. Earth will crack,' the people said.

Rivers dried up. A drought set in. Every day newspapers carried 'prize-winning' photographs of Mother Earth as an endless vista of six-inch-wide cracks inhabited by skeletons of cows and buffaloes.

'Now man will die of heat and thirst.' There were daily reports of deaths from heat and thirst. India was used to such calamities, but this drought was the worst since records had been kept. Vegetables vanished from sight, then grain, and soon there was nothing to eat.

'Our government – third-rate. What is it doing?'

'That Nehru. Promised us Ram Raj milk and honey rule after Independence. Lo and behold Nehru's Ram Raj!'

The famine spread. It became clear that the government couldn't cope, and in desperation it turned to the West – 'our more fortunate brothers'. 'Our more fortunate brothers' wanted dollars for food grain, but India had dollars only for military hardware because the 'enemy', Pakistan, was massing troops on the Kashmir border. It was always doing that, especially when India had a catastrophe on its hands.

When all seemed lost, Russia set an example: it agreed to take rupees instead of dollars. America, shamed, then went a step further and decided to sell India wheat for half the market price, also in rupees. Shiploads of grain started arriving at Indian ports. But none of the grain was reaching the most badly afflicted areas in the north and the east – Bengal, Behar, U.P., Rajasthan . . . even parts of the Punjab, the traditional granary of India.

Still there wasn't a speck of cloud in the fearsomely blue sky. 'Emergency. Emergency,' clamoured the country. After several high-level cabinet meetings, Nehru agreed to declare a state of emergency. In a moving speech he called upon the nation to join him in a fast and prayer for rain. Usually he was loath to do these things – praying and such like. But he had made an exception 'for Mother India's sake'.

One morning in Delhi, the red-stone Lutyens-designed Parliament House resounded with ancient Hindu sounds. A hundred conch shells blared and two hundred saffron-robed Brahmins – the holiest in the land, flown in from all over India in IAF jets – chanted ancient mantras, invoking Indra, the god of rain, to shed a few drops on the holy land of Bharat. All opposition parties joined in: for once there was total unity in the Indian Parliament as it addressed itself to the Higher Parliament. Muslim MPs muttered mantras in a language they were congenitally allergic to – Sanskrit, the mother of all Hindu languages of the north. Chanting the same mantras were Christians from Manglore and Parsees from Bombay and Sikhs from the Punjab.

245

Nehru made India a secular state. Why is he now forcing this Hindu cowdung on us? The provinces copied the centre, and on the same morning as in Delhi, Le Corbusier's concrete-grey Assembly Hall in Chandigarh also echoed with the roar of conch shells.

'Please, God . . .' the 420 assembled begged.

'Please God . . .' two miles away Khatri begged. But he was not interested in rain, he was begging for a buyer for his house which had been on the market for two months. There had been a few inquiries – idle enquiries. This was strange, for Chandigarh was growing fast. People with money were flocking to it from all parts of the Punjab. Expatriate Punjabis from other parts of the country, even abroad, were also arriving with bulging pockets to retire or to set up new businesses. And Khatri had such a khoobsurat house to sell. He did not understand. He pressed his agent, the bald-headed Behari.

'What can agent do when God is against?' said Behari, shaking his bald head. He blamed the drought. 'Let's do the only thing we can do under the circumstances – lower the price a little and wait. For temperature to drop, too.'

Khatri lowered the price a little and waited. It was agonizing.

Still not a fleck of cloud in the sky.

The countryside was dying of thirst; cities were dying of thirst. But Chandigarh fared a little better. Being new, it had a modern water-supply system. At least it had enough drinking water, if only just, rationed by the Municipality to two ten-minute bursts daily – one very early in the morning, the other just before sunset.

Indians are a funny people. They love to bath at least once a day: they become miserable if they can't. In the summer they bath three times daily – morning, noon and sunset. But this summer there simply wasn't any water in the earth. Not even in Chandigarh, India's new prize city. Not for the luxury of bathing. As the city agonized, its Municipal Committee had a brainwave. It posted wooden notices in every street. The placard said: LOVE THY LAKE in English, Hindi and Punjabi in bold letters. Underneath it is said in small print: *By order, C.M.C.*

'What does it mean?' Paro asked her husband the question which was being asked all over town. They had just woken up, that very minute.

Khatri did not know. He said what was being said all over the city about the puzzling notice: 'It means our Municipality has struck its twelve o'clock and gone mad. Like our government.'

The Khatris slept on the roof in mosquito nets under the stars. As usual, the father had woken up first. The previous night Omi had, as he did every night, slipped into Munni's net under cover of darkness, but he had failed to return to his own which he usually did every morning before his parents rose. The two were asleep in each other's arms, naked. Khatri and Paro saw their intertwined pink bodies through the gauze of the net. Khatri picked up the slim-necked overnight pitcher of drinking water and the two made their way downstairs noiselessly and quickly – they didn't want to be around when the boy and his wife woke up.

Downstairs they saw Mali in the garden, sitting on his haunches and pulling at a beedi. He came rarely these days. The Bitch, as the Sardarni was called in the Khatri household, wouldn't let him.

Early morning was the best time of the day. The blue Kasauli mountain was at its bluest at this hour and brought God closer to the earth than at any other time. This was the moment for a stroll on His earth. Under that pretext, Mali had given the Residence the slip for a while and turned up at 'home'. He had with him some valuable information.

Khatri and Paro were glad to see old Mali, and Mali was glad to be there. He was longing for a glimpse of his little Munni bibi. He hadn't seen her for nearly a month now.

'Lala-ji, I know something you should know,' Mali said, throwing away the beedi and standing up as a sign of respect.

'Speak. I am listening.'

'She has a yaar lover,' Mali whispered, putting a hand to his mouth, afraid his voice might carry to the garden of the adjoining house where two Alsatian dogs chased each other.

'What!' Paro gasped.

This was a bombshell – the Chief Minister's wife had a lover? Now Paro could do to her what she had done to them – blackmail the bitch! Drag her name in mitti (dirt). Put a garland of shoes around her neck. Burn her hair. Get all the dogs of Chandigarh to pee on her. Make every street in the city ring out with the words: *randi, randi, randi* . . . All sorts of delicious ideas and sweet schemes of revenge passed through Paro's head. But she was disappointed.

'Not the Sardarni, bibi-ji. That Sukhni woman.'

This was no good. So what if Sukhni or Dukhni had a lover? Who cared? As far as Paro was concerned she could have ten, a whole battalion of them.

Paro heard the water taps in the house make a sporadic coughing noise – these days taps coughed loudly for several minutes like

247

bronchial old men before they let out any water – and she ran in to make sure the buckets were in place. By now Omi and Munni had come down and joined Khatri and Mali in the garden. Mali told them too that that woman Sukhni had a lover.

'So what if she has a lover?' Khatri said, irritated. This was his time to utter the God's name, to commune with Him before the business and worries of life took over.

'You don't understand, Lala-ji.'

'I don't, and I don't want her name mentioned in my house.'

'But guess who the lover is?'

'I don't give a damn whether it is a dog or a donkey,' Khatri said. He loathed gossip of this kind. He moved away to join Paro inside the house. Omi loved gossip of this kind. He edged closer to Mali.

'Who is the lover – a dog or a donkey?' Omi asked.

'Worse, Omi bau, much much worse . . .' Mali leaned over and whispered something in Omi's ear. Omi, leaning against a wall, slipped for no reason – or felt the wall slipping. He steadied himself. Mali went on. 'And one more thing – she is in the family way.'

Now this *was* a bombshell, if ever there was one – the most splendid ever to fall on Chandigarh. Too good to be true. Was Mali making it all up? *He likes telling stories.*

'How do you know, Mali?' Omi said.

'Because my eyes have seen. Because my ears have heard. Often he works late at night in his air-conditioned office with bodyguard Mahan Singh. This room is the last in the East Wing. Behind are servant quarters, but no servant lives in them, only old furniture and old files – and in one quarter that woman Sukhni. Month ago there is a dust-storm in the dead of night – remember? – and my only pyjama, this, flies away from the washing-line. Because I have to wear it to work in the morning I chase it to the servant quarters behind the East Wing and guess what I see? Her flying in the black black night like my white pyjama, and entering his open window. After that I see her entering it every sixth night. And last night I hear her cry and cry and cry say she *is*, and that she wants to die. Swallow pill of poison. Or jump in the lake.'

'Sure you're not making a mistake, Mali?'

'Omi Bau, I may have only half a body but I have a full mind.'

'Who else knows about it?'

'Not a soul.'

'Good. Don't breathe a word of it to either man, beast or bird. Understand? Very dangerous.'

248

'I am not breathing.'
'Now you'd better go back . . .'

Omi knew he had to think and plan carefully. He hardly opened his mouth in the Bajwara market. This was unusual.

'What's the matter, oi?' Khatri asked at one point.

Omi said it was nothing and Khatri did not press him further. He had much on his own mind – the bank, the house . . .

Back home, Omi 'dry-cleaned' himself because there wasn't enough water for a bath. 'Dry-cleaning' was wiping yourself all over with a wet towel. Then he dressed with care: a tie, white shirt and white trousers.

'Who are you going to devastate?' Munni asked.

Omi didn't answer and hopped on to his Raleigh. He went and borrowed Arun's Fiat. Fifteen minutes later he was at the CM's office in the Secretariat. Soldiers with bayoneted rifles guarded it. As Omi had arrived in a car and because he looked smart and important, they made way for him. He asked for the CM's PA, Mr S. S. Mann. After a wait of twenty-four minutes, a peon in khaki and red approached him.

'This way,' the peon said.

Omi pulled out a comb from his hip pocket, did his hair, and followed the man to the CM's PA's office.

'Good morning, Mr Mann. You recognize me, don't you?'

'Face is familiar, all right. If I didn't know it wasn't true, I would have thought it was a film actor from Bombay or somewhere. But what can I do for you?'

'I would like to see His Excellency.'

'O yes? You would like to see the CM, eh? You think he has time for you awara-type college loafers?'

'I am not an awara-type college loafer, and you know it. I saved the CM's life by risking mine. I want to see him about something important.'

'It is the duty of all of us to protect him. So what are you talking, may I ask?'

'I want to see him.'

'O yes? Seven ministers are waiting to see him. Seventeen business tycoons are wanting an audience with him. Twenty-seven journalists, foreign included, are seeking interview with him. Thirty-seven MLAs desperately need a moment with him. Now a college boy, too. What did you say your name was.'

'Written on the chit before your left eye,' Omi said. 'Please inform His Excellency I beg a brief audience.'

'Most urgent no doubt. I will tell. Come another day.'

Omi went the next morning. This time he combed his hair in the PA's office, a cigarette in his mouth.

'O yes? You want to see the CM? The CM doesn't want to see you. He is lacking time. Totally lacking.'

'Kindly tell him it is urgent. Matter of life and . . .'

'And death, no doubt. What is happening on the Pakistan border? What do you college types know?'

Omi knew that the man had never told the CM about his visits, but he began to turn up every day, pestering the PA, hoping the bastard would give up and go and tell the CM just to get rid of him. But he didn't know that Mr Mann had orders from the Sardarni not to let any member of the Khatri family anywhere near the CM.

Omi turned up early one evening when the Secretariat was closing down for the day and swarms of cyclists were pouring on to the road that led to other parts of the city. He hid in a corridor, hoping to catch the CM as he came out to go home. But he was spotted.

'Inspector Kapoor, take this young man somewhere and teach him how not to be public nuisance,' Mr Mann said.

'Done,' the police inspector said. Two of his men grabbed Omi by his arms and bundled him into a van. There was a tussle, but it was useless – Omi was overpowered. The van drove straight to the police station by the bus stand in Sector 17. Omi was thrown into a concrete cubicle measuring eight foot by eight.

'Inspector Kapoor, do me a favour. Tell your nephew and my bosom pal Anish where I am, so that he can tell my parents and my wife.'

'O, you are Anish's bosom pal? That's different, then. I was going to keep you here in 'father-in-law's house' for a whole week. But now I'll have to let you out tomorrow, otherwise Anish will kill me.'

LOVE THY LAKE. First, Chandigarhias were puzzled. Then they laughed – they had understood. 'Our Municipality – must hand it to it. Not as stupid as it seems,' people said and turned up in their thousands to bathe and to wash clothes. This posed civic problems: first the traffic and accidents, then a wave of crime in the city – when the people bathed in the lake, their unattended homes were burgled. Added to that was the question of hygiene – within a fortnight Chandigarh's small but lovely lake became ugly and milky grey as

250

tens of thousands of its inhabitants washed their dirty clothes in it with soap. Tens of thousands of fishes floated on its surface with their bellies turned to the sky, dead. The place stank. 'The Committee took on more than it could chew,' was the verdict of one and all.

The outraged Lake Comissioner, Grewal, posted his men all around the lake with orders to beat up anyone using soap for bathing or washing clothes. This did not go down well with the bathers. They, in turn, beat up his men. Things came to a head when the body of a bather was pulled out one fine morning – the morning after the night Omi spent in the 'father-in-law's house'. The matter would have gone unnoticed had it been an ordinary man. But it was not an ordinary bather, nor even a man. It was a woman, Sukhni.

The next day the press carried the story on its front pages. '*Congress Setback*,' ran the headline in the anti-Congress and anti-government paper, *Born Free*. '*Woman member of Raisingh household found floating in Capital's lake. Foul play not ruled out . . .*'

This on the eve of the election was bad news for Congress, whose leader in the Punjab was Chief Minister Raisingh. Telephone wires between Delhi and Chandigarh, the centre and the state, hummed furiously all that day and night. Before night fell, a police jeep parked quietly outside the Pall Mall in the back street, avoiding the front of the restaurant because of the evening market. Inspector Kapoor again, this time in mufti and looking all the more menacing for it. Father and son were not in the restaurant. Khatri was at the temple, 'begging' Lord Krishna for a buyer and thanking Him for removing 'at least one thorn' from his flesh – Sukhni. Omi was at home, getting ready for work.

'Where is Mr O. P. Khatri?'

'At home in Sector 9. Why?' said Seva Singh.

'Get back to work,' Inspector Kapoor said gruffly and returned to the jeep.

Even before he saw the police jeep, Seva knew Kapoor was a policeman. He shivered, and phoned Omi.

'Omi bau . . .'

Omi also shivered. But he kept a straight face – *I have done nothing so why should I worry?* – and said nothing when Paro asked what Seva wanted. A voice in him said, *Disappear*. But that would complicate matters. *Stay and meet the bull head on and catch him by the horns.* Nine minutes later, the bull was at his door.

Kapoor had orders to make a 'quiet arrest' that no one should see nor hear. His orders included a chilling warning – 'Your future depends on it.' The orders did not take account of the fact that arrests were seldom 'quiet'. Routine arrests were a thoka thaki job – a couple of back-handed slaps in the face and, if the men still resisted, the butt of the rifle in the chest, and handcuffs, and the van. But this was obviously no routine arrest. And Inspector Kapoor was troubled; he liked the boy. He couldn't understand what was going on.

'What's the charge?'

'Murder.'

'Whose?'

'The Lady of the Lake.'

'I always say to my bosom pal Anish he is barking mad. Didn't know it ran in the family.'

The Inspector's hands itched to lash out and make a chutney of the boy's face. But somehow he controlled himself – his future depended on it. He glared at Omi. Omi glared back, his cheeks bursting with rage. The whole thing was unbelievable.

'On whose orders are you arresting me?'

'My superiors'.'

'O yes – Mr S. S. Mann?'

'Anything you say will be taken in evidence against you.'

'Take, take, take. Write it down. Write down also that a certain great man was fucking a poor servant woman whose husband had lost his life while protecting his.'

'I am, and you are going to regret it. You are forgetting yourself. You don't know the gravity of the situation.'

Omi realized he was forgetting himself. *Omi, son, shut your big mouth. These people are mad, and dangerous. They can destroy your already fucked-up life.*

'Sorry, Inspector sahib, I didn't mean a word of what I said. It was shock and anger. Beg huge apology,' Omi said.

'That's better. Now are you coming quietly or . . .?'

'Just one thing, though. Please remember I was your house guest the night the poor lady drowned. On Mr Mann's orders.'

This Inspector Kapoor had not thought of. It ruled out the boy straight away. But the Inspector had his orders, and orders were orders.

'India – nation of fools! Don't worry, Ma. This fool will bring me right back first thing in the morning, you'll see,' Omi whispered to his stunned mother and wife while leaving.

During the night there was an autopsy and a post-mortem examination of the corpse pulled out of the lake. The cause of death was established to be – 'without the shadow of a doubt' – drowning. A statement signed by three doctors was issued to the press. There was not a mention of the three-month-old foetus inside the woman. Immediately afterwards, her body was taken to the shamshanghat (burial ground) behind the bhangi colony in Sector 27, and cremated then and there.

Chandigarh was free of suspicion. So was Omi – at the stroke of midnight, when the world slept with the exception of three violently troubled souls on the roof of house number 41 in Sector 9L.

Down in the front garden of the same house, there was another troubled soul – old Mali. Saying bugger-all to the consequences, he had run away from the Residence and come 'home' for good. Unable to sleep, he lay on a charpoy, counting the stars. He sprang to his feet as he heard Inspector Kapoor drop Omi at the gate and Dabbu go mad with his bark.

'Omi bau, I made a mistake, a heavy mistake. The lady in question was doing the carry-on job not with the great gentleman, but with his bodyguard. Fool man . . .'

'Mali, you and your bloody stories of poison pills . . .!' Omi nearly did to Mali in his twilight years what the tiger hadn't been able to do to him in his rose-garden days. He resisted the temptation and blew out a massive sigh of relief – Raisingh was in the clear. Omi loved Raisingh. *Omi son, how could you ever believe such trash about Napoleon Singh?* He wanted to kick himself. He embraced Dabbu and ran inside the house.

'It's 99° F inside.'

'Anybody's guess what it is outside, in the sun.'

The Government in Delhi sweated and prayed. The Government in Chandigarh sweated and prayed. People everywhere sweated and prayed. Omi only sweated. He couldn't pray. He was furious with God and government. He had a monstrous heat rash: spots the size of shirt buttons covered his back and, embarrassingly, his seat area. He scratched all the time which made matters worse. He couldn't sit nor lie on his back. Munni had applied all sorts of creams and powders, but they had been useless. There was only one cure – rainwater, a bath in the rain. But where was the rain?

'Monsoon has bypassed India this year,' said the lady of No 43 with the Alsatian dogs, Mrs Sikand.

'It is those atom-bomb tests. America and Russia,' said Mrs No 39, Shakuntala Duggal.

'God's taking revenge on man for becoming what he has become – greedy and heartless,' said Paro of No 41.

'Nothing to do with God, Ma. Nor with the Americans and the

253

Russians, Auntie Duggal. It's just that the monsoon is late this year,' Omi said.

'God's will. What can man do if He seals off the sky?' Mrs 45 said.

The same afternoon the sky began to unseal itself. A cloud, great and black as coal, spilled over the high Kasauli mountain, engulfing it completely. Soon it was rolling over the clay hills that lay between Kasauli and Chandigarh. People in the capital streamed out of their houses and gaped at it. There was a question mark in the air, though – five hundred feet in height, it dangled in the sky between Chandigarh and the clay hills like a giant kite. What if the cloud drifted away to the right or left? The thought made Chandigarhias tremble. Clouds were fickle like man. Often, like man, they didn't know which way to turn. If they did, India wouldn't have suffered as it had been doing for countless centuries.

'God can't do this to us. God can't.'

God didn't. With amazing consideration, He pushed the cloud forward. First, the distant grey High Court and the skyscraper of the Secretariat became greyer. Then a thick dark light enveloped them, gradually removing the two great buildings from sight. Soon the cloud became all-pervasive, and a thunderbolt lashed out, rattling a deafening announcement: rain, sweet rain! Birds flew helter-skelter in fright. Underlying that fright was a joy which filled every heart: man's, animals' and birds'.

Omi, now muttering his thanks to God with whom he was angry no more, walked about in their front garden, naked but for a langota (home-made jockstrap).

'Pelt, you bitch, pelt!' he ordered the rain.

Great fireworks erupted in the darkened heavens above, and roars of thunder shook the world as sheets of water began to pelt down on a parched earth, making a mother-father noise.

'I told you, Ma, I told you,' Omi yelled at the house, taking all credit for the arrival of rain. Khatri, Paro and Munni came out and sat in their clothes in the rain. People all over Chandigarh sat in the rain – men without clothes and women with them.

Five inches of rain fell in the first twenty-five minutes, making the capital a floating city. The Khatri garden became a garden of mud. Omi took his wife's hand and dragged her down and rolled in the mud with her.

'Silly boy, what are you doing to her?' Paro said.

'Only this,' Omi showed her. He took his mother's hand and pulled her down and rolled her in the mud too. Uninvited, Khatri joined them. He threw away his shirt and rolled with them in the

254

thick brown mud, as great sheets of water pelted down on their bodies. Then there was a diversion: a heavily hooded rickshaw pulled up inside their open gate, disgorging two important passengers – the Kandharis.

Paro was not amused to be caught frolicking in mud like an adolescent buffalo in the village pond. And what about Khatri? How did he feel on being seen behaving like a pig in a pool of mud? Khatri felt strangely light at heart in spite of all the worries of the world in his head. He neither felt nor looked embarrassed to be found in the state he was.

'The Khatris' problems are not financial, they are mental,' Kandhari hissed to his wife as he paid off the rickshaw driver. 'Do you think we made a mistake?'

'Too late. Matter of poor Munni's karma,' Mrs Kandhari hissed back.

'Ao-ji, ao-ji. Come, come, come,' Khatri said loudly to be heard through the mother-father noise of the rain.

'I can see you are celebrating the arrival of rains in style,' Kandhari said. Normally he would have embraced Khatri. Today he did not.

'We have a mud bath every time it rains. Like to join us?'

'Tempting. Tempting. But we'll resist, with your kind permission. We'll watch. You carry on,' Kandhari said.

'Mummy, come on!' Munni said.

'May snakes bite me dead and dogs pee on my corpse! Our girl, too?' Mrs Kandhari hissed without moving her lips.

'In England people pay pounds to have a mudbath. Here, mud comes free with rain,' Omi said. He loved to see that look on his in-laws' faces.

'Too true. Too true. God's gift. More people should take advantage. Things we Indians don't think about! Any news about the house?' Kandhari said, pushing his wife on to the veranda where they could be safe from rain.

'As you can see, it is still here,' Khatri said.

The house was still there, but only just. A day after the mudbath, a letter came from the bank. '*We have no choice but to take legal action . . .*'

'Legal action' meant bankruptcy. Bankruptcy meant neelami – a public auction of all they possessed conducted in the street. *This handsome dressing-table complete with full-length mirror and four drawers, original price 140 rupees. Bidding starts at rupees five. I'm bid five rupees . . . six . . . seven . . . eight . . . ten . . . twelve. To the sardar-ji there. Now this almost new georgette sari, shop price when brand new 50 rupees. Bidding begins at rupee one* . . . And the whole world looking!

The shame of it! The Khatris panicked. Omi kicked himself. He was sorry for himself, for Munni, and for his mother. He was sorry most of all for his father. *I'll make it, I promise I will. I'll yet beat this world, and every son of a dog in it.*

'We'll sell these, Ma,' Munni said, making a pile of her dowry jewellery. Paro added all hers to it. The royal jewels, too, went on the heap. Vidya only had a few trinkets but she placed them atop the others. This gave them a breather.

'Please, God,' the Khatris begged.

'A party. A party,' said Behari, the estate agent, coming early one morning. He rubbed his hands together and ran them over his oily hairless scalp and said, 'At last, Lala-ji, we have an interested party.'

While Khatri was receiving Behari, the dakia delivered a registered letter for him. Omi went and signed for it. He knew what was in it – a writ from the bank. But he opened it nonetheless.

'Father, come here a minute.'

Father and son conferred in private in another room. They saw the hand of God in it – a buyer turning up at the same time as the bank's writ. They were going to be all right.

'Let's sign and sell, then, boy,' Khatri said. He shouted at the kitchen, 'Paro, send us some cold lassi.'

Three glasses of lassi were already on the table when Khatri and Omi joined Behari in the drawing-room.

'But there is a little snag, Lala-ji,' Behari said, scratching the middle of his starched and ironed trousers.

'What kind of snag? And who is the interested party, Behari sahib?' Omi said. He had never liked Behari, even though the man had an impeccable reputation and was nicknamed Mr Clean Cut. Omi didn't like completely bald people, especially those with oily scalps. They reminded him of worms which oozed out of earth when it rained.

'The party is a company, and the snag is it will not pay the asking price. It will pay . . .' Behari whispered the sum – a third less.

It sounded too much like the last business deal. Father and son smelled a rat in it somewhere.

'What company, Behari sahib?'

'What difference does it make what company it is, Lala-ji? I have worked my balls flat on this deal, and now that I have got a party under my arms you are crucifying me on the dunghill of suspicion. I don't like that.'

256

'I want to know who I sell-buy to-from . . .'

'It is a Delhi-based company, wanting a house here for its rep. Here are all the papers. Look see and satisfy yourself.'

'And why will it pay a third less?'

'Because it can wait to buy but you can't wait to sell. Anyway, with the rise in property value you are only losing a little on what you paid. So or not so? So see sense and sign.'

'We have seen sense and we are not signing,' Omi said.

'That is entirely up to you. Entirely, Mr Om.'

Paro and Munni were listening at the door, the three men knew. 'Sip your lassi, Behari sahib, while we go and have a five-minute think with my wife,' Khatri said.

'Go have a ten-minute think. Have an hour's think. Our time is cheap. We are Indian, we know how to wait.'

'We are not selling,' Paro said.

'I have no choice. Either I sell, or it is neelami in the street or the jailhouse. Which do you want, woman?' Khatri said. He came back to Behari with an extinguished look.

Khatri signed. Then things moved with bewildering speed. Khatri was paid straight away. He paid off his debts straight away. He sent word to his old friend in Manimajra, driver Bhola Ram, to come with his lorry – 'empty'.

'It's going to break Mother's heart,' Omi said to Munni, putting his head to her tummy to hear his son kick. Not very long to go now.

Bhola Ram came late one afternoon as the sun went down, jerking his head from right to left, signalling the sadness in his heart. 'Man proposes and what does He up there do?. . .' Bhola Ram jerked his head again from right to left.

Seva, Bawa and Mali were already there. Everything inside the lovely Khatri house, no longer theirs now, was already packed. When Omi gave them the nod, they began piling up Bhola Ram's lorry with the Khatri belongings. Neighbours emerged from their houses and stood in little groups at their gates, watching. Omi was waiting for his mother to burst into sobs, but Paro surprised him. With a defiant look, she kept a close watch over what the men were doing: 'Be careful with the sofas, Seva Singh . . . Where are your eyes, Bawa, silly boy?'

Omi, also helping, was sore at heart. It was all his fault – his ambition to be a millionaire before he was twenty-five. And 'rubbing shoulders'. He had got what he deserved. *But why Mother and Father? And Munnishka – what has she done?*

Behari turned up. He carried a leather bag.

'All right. All right. We've seen worse days than this. Have you forgotten what we went through in the August of *that* year?' Paro said to Khatri, who was in a daze. His guru had said that everything happened for the best, that everything turned out right in the end. Did he know what he was talking about? *You must never question what the Baba says, Khatri, old cock.*

At this point Seva Singh broke down. 'Had never thought to see this day, Omi bau,' he said, tears rolling down his cheeks and disappearing into his beard starched and pressed down with Fixo. Omi put his arms around him and hugged him tight.

'Our life is God's playground. He plays games in it, with us.' Khatri spoke at last.

'All clear?' Behari said, agent-like, when the lorry was loaded up. He opened his bag and brought out a large Godrej padlock. Two keys and a paper tag dangled from it. He dropped the keys back in the bag and snapped the lock on the front door of House No 41, Sector 9L.

'Ughghgh . . .' Maaii choked and burst out into a hiccupping sob. 'Hai my mother, hai hai hai . . .'

'Had hoped never to see this sight,' Seva Singh said, wiping tears off his beard with a sleeve.

'All right, all right. Get in the lorry,' Paro said. She had seen days much worse in '47. Sixty of them in one truck of that Mountbatten's so-called Boundary Force. And sixteen days and sixteen nights of rain and mud and walking over headless corpses of Hindus and Sikhs and then of Muslims, amputated limbs dripping with blood and some still twitching. They had walked in hunger and thirst and dug roots with their bare hands and drunk from cholera ponds in malarial swamps. And they had survived. They would survive yet. 'Get in. Get in, Bhola Ram.'

'Man proposes, and what does He up there do?' Bhola Ram said.

The servants went with the luggage in the lorry. The Khatris went in a taxi, trailing the lorry fifty yards behind. The roads were bare except for the odd car, cyclist or rickshaw, as was usual at that time of the evening. But this evening there was something forbidding about it. This evening the roads looked like arteries carved in a barren landscape for no purpose. This was how Khatri felt about himself – a barren landscape. And the road he was on was not taking

258

him forward. It was not even going backwards – because the past was gone, only the scars it had left remained.

Khatri coughed and spat a teaspoon of phlegm through the taxi window in the direction of the Residence, hoping the wind would fly it there and land it smack on *her* face. 'Time is passing strangely. Let's see what awaits us.'

Khatri knew what awaited him immediately in Sector 23. Outside his Pall Mall, his son's name for the place, there would be a crowd of onlookers. Some would have pity in their eyes, others – and there would be more of them – joy. They would have a field day and say, 'These Khatris. Upstarts. Serve them right.' Some would merely say, 'Tut, tut, tut . . .' as one does on seeing a sad spectacle. But they would all be there – ex-neighbours, new neighbours and nameless tamashbeen (spectators) to witness his humiliating return.

And they were there, crowding the clearing in front of the shops. Hundreds of them.

'Hai, hai, hai.' A roar went up from the crowd when it saw the lorry and the taxi – a loud wail of pity that rent the sky. It rent every heart. 'Hai, hai, hai.'

It was then the Khatris saw – a cloud of smoke engulfed the Pall Mall, their beloved Pall Mall.

'Impossible!' Omi cried out.

'O God!' groaned Khatri, clutching his chest. His groan was that of an animal shot in the side.

'Hai, hai, hai,' screamed Paro, out of control. She began beating her breasts and pulling out her hair.

'Ma,' Munni wailed, and felt constrictions in her middle. She put her arms around her mother-in-law to stop her damaging herself.

'Boy, we are done for,' Khatri said. This was the end. The final curtain.

Doors of the taxi and the cab of the lorry were flung open. Father and son and their servants dashed out and raced towards the Pall Mall. The sea of humanity parted, making a narrow passage for them. Further on a long human chain was in operation, passing buckets of water from hand to hand. It was not clear where the buckets were coming from, but they were coming and it was quite an operation. Directing it, shouting orders and waving his arms about, Omi saw, was a young man with a luminous halo, like a messiah, a deliverer. The young man brisked about the place with authority,

259

everybody stepping aside to make room for him. People listened to him as if he were lord and master of the place.

'Bunny?'

'Sorry, dear boy. Awfully sorry for you. Had come to see if your hotel offer was still on, and what I saw! – My God! Sardar-ji, move out of the way. Oi you, friend, don't get too close . . .'

The water wasn't getting anywhere near what once was the elegant glass front of the capital's most famous restaurant. Yet it came, bucket after bucket, and men performed acts of surprising heroism to try to get some of it thrown inside.

'It's that Heeralal,' Omi shouted at his father. His voice was lost in the general din, which was now pierced by another, louder noise, that of ringing of bells.

'Move! Move! Move!' Bunny yelled as he waved people away to make way for the CMC Fire Brigade engine.

The Fire Brigade had some difficulty in locating the fire hydrant. Eventually, it was found under a heap of rubbish being sniffed at by three dogs near the paan-wallah's booth. More loud bell-ringing brought another fire engine to the scene. Long flat snakes of canvas were quickly rolled out on the ground, and, seconds later, came alive and swelled as water shot through them.

'What a fire! The capital's first.'

'Lucky everyone is accounted for.'

Under Bunny's command, and helped and hampered by hundreds of men and boys, three fire engines fought the fire bravely. It took an hour to extinguish it. Police arrived at the end of the hour, Inspector Kapoor again.

'It's that Heeralal,' the crowd said, unanimously. Everybody knew of Heeralal's public threat to 'smoke-burn' Khatri one day.

'Who is Heeralal?' Bunny said, his arms around Omi.

'Which Heeralal?' Inspector Kapoor said to the crowd.

'The one who farts from his mouth . . .' the crowd explained. Happily the crowd took the Inspector and his men to Heeralal's shop at the far end of the shopping centre. The shop was shut. They took the police to his house half a mile away. There was no one there, only the chawkidar.

'Where is Mr Heeralal?'

'Don't know.'

Inspector Kapoor gave the chawkidar a loud back-handed slap across his face.

'*Where is he?*'

'Gone to Durga Devi with wife and kid-kiddies,' blurted out the frightened man – a second's delay and he would get another one.

'Gone when?' The Inspector thumped the fool anyway.

'Since the day he signed the deal after making company in Delhi. Gone to thank the Goddess for his best fortune.'

'Which deal?'

'I can't tell, I'll get the sack. My lips are glued.'

Inspector Kapoor unglued the man's lips with two more back-handed slaps.

'Tell. Which deal?'

'The house he bought in Sector 9 in company's name.'

So! The mystery was solved.

The Pall Mall was completely burnt out. So was the flat upstairs. The Khatris were homeless.

'Refugees a second time. First it was Pakistan and Jinnah, now . . .' Paro no longer had the composure she displayed while leaving her home in Sector 9 earlier in the evening. She sobbed and beat her breasts.

'Man proposes . . .' Bhola Ram said.

'God's will. Bend to His will,' Satya said, hugging her old neighbour and weeping with her.

'At least you are all safe. All your luggage too. Thank God for that,' the Doctorani said, also hugging Paro and also crying with her.

'We'll be more than all right, Ma, with the insurance money and all. What more do we want?' Omi said. He alone looked happy that their restaurant had been burnt down. In fact he was jubilant – there was the insurance claim, and now Buny was coming in with them on the hotel. 'What more do we want, Father?'

'I want Heeralal. By his balls,' Khatri said.

'The police will do that. In the mean time be thankful to him – in a way he saved you. Did you best favour, if you ask me, Lala-ji,' Dr Devan Chand said.

'But how could have started the fire if he is near Jammu with Goddess Durga Devi?' Ujjagar said.

'Ujjagar-ji, sometimes you talk innocent like children – thing I like about you,' Dr Devan Chand said.

'But how could he have. Pray how? I am begging you to tell me.'

'The farting face hired an expert arsonist. This is India, you are forgetting, my dear friend. Here you can hire who you like – thief, robber, murderer . . . even an arsonist. You name it and we got it.

261

Part of our culture. I am pitying myself that my shop didn't get gutted,' Dr Devan Chand said.

'Maybe next time, Doctor sahib,' Omi said.

'Omi, that was stroke of master-genius – insuring Pall Mall four five times – must hand you that,' the homeopath said in English.

'My simple policy was, insure well if you are going to insure at all.'

'Best thing to happen to man in the shit – house gone, hotel sunk and future looking like a black hole – shop burning on insurance. Best gift Englishman gave India – the insurance idea.'

Bunny had gone to join his wife, saying they would meet again tomorrow to talk things over – they were staying for the night with friends in the North End. The neighbours offered to take the Khatris in, but Paro said no. She wanted to be with her sister. When the hullaballoo died down, Bhola Ram dropped them at their 'little shop' in Sector 15, two miles away. First the two sisters hugged each other and wept. Then they made sleeping arrangements for the night – they would all sleep in the shop, which was a single room measuring ten feet by fifteen.

Omi shook his head.

'We weren't exactly born in a palace,' Paro said.

'I was, and I am not sleeping here, Ma. Nor are you,' Omi said.

'Then where are we sleeping?'

'In the Blue Skies Hotel.' The Blue Skies was Chandigarh's Ritz, if there was such a thing. 'Now that we are going to be rich again I don't want us to sleep on the floor like pavement-dwellers of Calcutta.'

'I am,' Paro said.

'Me too,' Khatri said.

'*We* are not. Come on, Munnishka. Let's go,' Omi said.

'No, I am staying here. With Mother.'

In the end, Omi, too, stayed. Khatri was given Bhajjan's bed. The three ladies slept in Vidya's and Omi and Bhajjan roughed it on the floor. The room was crowded, but in a strange way it was comforting to be all together.

'Tomorrow morning Insurance, Police and Fire Brigade have a lot to do,' Khatri said by way of saying good-night.

Next morning Insurance, Police and Fire Brigade got together at the burned-out Pall Mall. They pinched their noses with thumb and finger and waded carefully through ash and coal. They turned the débris upside down. They inspected every nook and corner and kept coming back to the charred and mangled remains of the air-conditioning plant, nodding their heads.

'Yes,' Fire Brigade said.

'You sure?' Police asked.

'Cent per cent,' Fire Brigade said.

'You have to be two hundred per cent sure. Big claim, this,' Insurance said, looking sad.

'We are.' Fire Brigade knew what it was saying.

Khatri didn't like that. Omi liked it even less. For this meant that the rat Heeralal was not the 'perpetrator' of the great fire. Father and son wanted to catch the rat by the tail and . . .

'Why not get an expert's opinion?' Khatri said.

'We *are* the expert opinion, Lala-ji. What are you talking?' Fire Brigade said, annoyed that its opinion was challenged.

'I didn't mean it that way. I meant getting some qualified electricity expert like engineer Mehta of Power House. Can't do us any harm. The man knows electricity inside out.'

Police agreed it couldn't do any harm getting a second opinion. Insurance also. They sent for Mehta. Mehta came and inspected the plant.

'Hum,' Mehta said.

'Hum what, Mehta sahib?' Police said.

'The fault is electric, all right. But it could have been engineered by an interested party,' Mehta said.

This coming from the boss of the the Power House made everybody look at each other. Heeralal's fate was sealed.

'But where is this interested party?' Insurance asked.

'Leave that to us,' Police said.

'He tricked me out of my house and made me a refugee. Charge him. Arrest him,' Khatri said with tears of rage.

'Charge him. Arrest him,' Insurance said. It made their life easier to be able to name a culprit.

Heeralal was charged in his absence. He was arrested the day he returned to Chandigarh. He was released on his own bail the next day. It was decided that he would be tried, and a date was set for the trial. This took place, as it turned out, in the same court-room in Kharar seven miles away, and it was conducted by, as it happened, the same boy magistrate. Everything about the place was the same except a slight change in his name plate. It now said:

Mr B. K. Gangoli
PCS
Magistrate 1st Class

263

The court-room was fuller than the last time. It was so full that the crowd spilled out at the back and front of the court-cum-Guesthouse. All doors had to be left wide open so that those who could not get inside could hear, if not see, what they had come to hear and see. They had come to hear and see the legendary Gangadhar Joshi, MA Ll B Cantab, Chandigarh's top pleader whom Heeralal had hired.

Joshi rose to his name. In a resounding voice which made the court-room walls shake and the trees outside tremble, he spoke for one hour about his 'sadly maligned client, Shri Heeralal, Punjab's capital's most distinguished jeweller,' whose character was 'as blemishless as a diamond of the first water'. His speech made goose-pimples appear on the bare arms of most people inside and outside the court-room.

'The bastard speaks well,' Omi whispered to his companion, Professor Bhatnagar, whose brother, Dandeshwar, a mere BA Ll B, the Khatris had hired.

A pin-drop silence followed Joshi's speech. It was broken by the bird-like voice of Professor Bhatnagar's brother. He also spoke for one hour. Then the magistrate called upon the defendant to appear in the dock. Heeralal stood up with four voluminous books pressed to his bosom, two in each arm. The court was puzzled.

'Mr Heeralal, this is a court-room, not a library,' the boy magistrate said, calmly and coolly. He knew this nut. The last time he had been here he had made a thorough nuisance of himself. What was he up to this time?

'No need to tell me, Your Honour. I know it.'

'Then what are these books?'

'The Gita, the Granth, the Bible and the Koran . . .'

'What on earth for? Have you come here as a preacher or something? You stand here as the accused.'

But Heeralal was not listening. He went on. 'I swear by all of these books that I had nothing to do with the fire. I swear in any language on any holy book. I swear, I swear,' he said and burst out crying.

'Mr Heeralal, once again you are making a public fool of yourself and I warn you that unless . . .'

Heeralal cried loudly and bitterly. Indians' hearts are made of wax. They melt easily. Hearts in the court-room melted.

'I swear,' Heeralal wailed.

'Mr Heeralal,' the magistrate said.

'Mr Heeralal,' Pleader Joshi said.

'Mr Heeralal,' the Court Clerk said.

Heeralal listened to no one. He took over the court. 'True I said all those bad things to Khatri about smoke-burning him and what not – after all, the father and son had beaten me into the shape of a peacock's arse. True, I took my revenge and bought out his house, but I did it legal. What happened to him after – I had nothing to do with. I would not have wished it on my worst enemy even – him burning out like that. I had no hand in it. Not even my chichi little finger. I swear to God it is true. It is true. It is true.'

'It is true, Your Honour . . .' said Pleader Joshi and produced some electrical gadgetry, replicas of items from the air-conditioning machinery. Then he called two men and introduced them as supervisors in the firm that made that machinery (they had come all the way from Bombay at Heeralal's expense). They gave their 'professional opinion' and Joshi thundered it out. 'No man can, as these highly respected professionals confirm, tamper with this equipment while it is working without jeopardizing his life. And it has been established that the machinery had at no time been switched off that day. So no hired person could have . . .'

'Two sets of experts – here we have a distinguished engineer Mr Mehta on the one hand and the manufacturer's representatives on the other. The latter can't be without a vested interest. In giving evidence in favour of your client, they are defending their product at the same time. Besides, threats are not tolerated in a civilized society. Law cannot turn a blind eye to those that come true, however they come true. Mr Heeralal, you have not endeared yourself to this court. This country may be poor, but its citizenry is law-abiding, something Indians can be proud of, you included. One half of my heart says I should be very severe with you. The other half says I should be otherwise. What would you do if you were in my position?'

'I would listen to that other half of my heart. I would acquit me, Your Honour. Because I am one hundred and one per cent innocent.'

'You have been very foolish . . .'

'I have been, Your Honour. Just acquit me . . .'

While the jeweller was telling the judge what to do, a young man in great haste came tearing his way into the court-room. All eyes turned to him. Bawa! He was all smiles. He threaded his way through the crowd and whispered in Omi's ear: 'Daddy! Daddy!'

'What? Boy or girl?' Omi grabbed his arm.

'Not telling you,' Bawa said. It answered Omi.

'Constable, remove this intruder from my court, and lock him up for a day and night . . .' the boy judge roared.

Bawa tore his way out of the court in the same haste he had entered it, chased by the court policeman. The judge went on. 'And now I must turn to you, Mr Khatri junior. Mr Khatri junior, this is a court of law, not a college common room where idiots rush in and out at will. Firstly, I want to know what was so important that it had to be whispered to you in the middle of my judgement? What did that interloper say to you?'

'Your Honour, he said I've just been blessed with a son.'

'Haaa,' the court breathed.

'Well, well, well. A bit young for fatherhood, but you have our congratulations. Now secondly, what would *you* do if you were in my place – imprison him, hang him or acquit him? You can be generous in the light of your good news. Think hard.'

Omi thought hard. He decided to be generous. 'I would acquit him, Your Honour. But on one condition . . .' Omi wrote down his condition on a piece of paper. The paper was presented to the magistrate. The magistrate read it and smiled.

'To your condition I add one of mine,' the magistrate said.

'Name your condition, Your Honour. I accept with eyes shut,' Heeralal said.

'Condition number one is you shake hands with Mr Khatri senior and Mr Khatri junior and . . .'

'Agree, sir. Here's my hand. And what else?'

'And condition number two is you undo the wrong you've done them and let them have their house back for the price you paid for it.'

'Done, your honour. Done.'

'Arun, drive like a maniac,' Omi said in Arun's Fiat. Arun obliged.

Ten minutes after the handshakes in Mr Gangoli's court in Kharar, he brought Omi and his father to Chandigarh. Twenty-odd men in red and gold regimental uniforms crowded the back street of the Pall Mall. Cradling shiny brass musical instruments, they sat on their haunches in the shade of dusty mango, jamun and tahli trees that swayed leafily in the autumn breeze. At the sight of the Fiat, they sprang to attention and their brass came alive with Omi's favourite tune: 'Vive, vive l'amour . . .'

'But?' Arun was flabbergasted. 'How did they know it would be a boy and that you would win the case?'

'They didn't, I did. Behind the scene bandobast (arrangement) with the Fella with the blue umbrella,' Omi grinned as he surveyed the scene. At the door of Munni's Mogul Garden there stood a dozen men who looked like women – they wore saris and lipstick. A crowd spilled on to both sides of the door. 'This I hadn't arranged,' Omi said and hurried away to hold against his heart the cause of it all. But he was prevented – everybody wanted to embrace him.

'All-round Hero,' the embracers called Omi. Just then the band stopped and the men wearing saris and lipstick broke into a song welcoming the birth of his heir, clapping wildly.

It took Omi longer to get upstairs than it had taken his friend to drive him from the court to his house. Upstairs, however, the situation was unbelievable – half the female population of the capital packed the place, prominent among it Doctoress Pritam Kaur and Vidya.

'Not time for you yet, Om. Go catch the door,' snapped Vidya sweetly.

'But I want to be with my wife and son Bunny.'

'Only after the last of the 1001 mantras have been sung.'

'What number are you on, Aunt Vidya?'

'Never you mind that. Down and out. Out, out, out!'

'Aunt Vidya, you can't do this to me, your favourite and only nephew.'

'Yes, I can. Our customs. They come first.'

'Fuck our customs,' Omi hissed in English and pierced his way to where his smiling wife lay next to a little bundle, his son.

'Haa hai,' gasped the ladies collectively. No one had ever seen such a shameless brazen beast.